SNOW WHITE
AND OTHER TALES

THE tales gathered by the Grimm brothers are at once familiar, fantastic, homely, and frightening. Grand palaces, humble cottages, and the forest full of menace are their settings; and they are peopled by kings and princesses, witches and robbers, millers and golden birds, stepmothers, and talking frogs. Regarded from their inception both as uncosy nursery stories and as raw material for the folklorist, this translation fully represents the range of less well-known fables, morality tales, and comic stories as well as the classic tales, and includes variant stories that were deemed unsuitable for children.

JACOB and WILHELM GRIMM were born as the eldest of six children in 1785 and 1786 respectively, in Steinau on the Main, where their father was magistrate. On his sudden death in 1796 they moved to Kassel, in Hesse, the locality with which most of their tales are associated, where they were educated at the expense of an aunt with connections at the elector's court. They studies at Marburg, where Jacob came under the influence of the conservative jurist Friedrich von Savigny, and returned to Kassel as librarians in the employ of the elector, remaining there through the upheavals of the Napoleonic Wars. It was in these years that they began their collection of tales (first edition, 1812–15), much influenced by the collection of folk-songs, *Des Knaben Wunderhorn* (1805–8), made by their friends the poets Achim von Arnim and Clemens Brentano. While Wilhelm continued working on the successive editions of their *Kinder-und Hausmärchen*, Jacob turned to the study of historical grammar and lexicography and became the great founder of *Germanistik* as an academic discipline. The brothers had meanwhile been called to chairs at the University of Göttingen, but were dismissed in 1837 in the famous protest of the 'Göttingen Seven' against the abrogation by the new king of Hanover (Queen Victoria's uncle) of the constitution granted in 1830. Invited to Berlin, they resumed their collaboration, working together on the great *Dictionary of the German Language* (vol. I, 1852). Jacob never married, but lived with Wilhelm and his wife Dortchen. He died in 1863, four years after Wilhelm's death in 1859.

JOYCE CRICK taught German at University College London for many years. She has written on Kafka's first English translators, Willa and Edwin Muir, and on Günter Grass's modern fairy-tale *The Flounder*. She has edited Coleridge's translation of Schiller's *Wallenstein* for Princeton University Press's *Collected Coleridge* and translated Freud's *The Joke and Its Relation to the Unconscious* for Penguin Classics. For Oxford World's Classics she has translated Kafka's *The Metamorphosis and Other Stories* and *A Hunger Artist and Other Stories*, and Freud's *Interpretation of Dreams*, for which she received the Schlegel-Tieck Prize in 2000.

JACOB AND WILHELM GRIMM

SNOW WHITE

AND OTHER TALES

Translated with an Introduction and Notes by
JOYCE CRICK

OXFORD
UNIVERSITY PRESS

OXFORD
UNIVERSITY PRESS

Great Clarendon Street, Oxford, OX2 6DP,
United Kingdom

Oxford University Press is a department of the University of Oxford.
It furthers the University's objective of excellence in research, scholarship,
and education by publishing worldwide. Oxford is a registered trade mark of
Oxford University Press in the UK and in certain other countries

First published as an Oxford World's Classics paperback 2005
Reissued 2019

Impression: 1

Published in the United States of America by Oxford University Press
198 Madison Avenue, New York, NY 10016, United States of America

British Library Cataloguing in Publication Data
Data available

Library of Congress Cataloging in Publication Data
Data available

ISBN 978-0-19-883384-0

Printed and bound in Great Britain by
Clays Ltd, Elcograf S.p.A.

To Georgia,
Holly, Daisy, and Rose,
with love

ACKNOWLEDGEMENTS

As a latecomer to the well-ploughed field of Grimm studies, I have many debts: above all to the meticulous and extensive work on the textual history, sources, and language of the tales by Heinz Rölleke and his team. Rölleke has for the past thirty years been the dominant figure in Grimm studies. Without his scrupulous editing and diligent digging and delving, making so much new and reliable material available, the present translation and commentary would have sorely lacked scholarly underpinning. Gudrun Ginschel's account of Jacob Grimm's early intellectual development, *Der junge Jacob Grimm* (1965), was also indispensable. During much the same thirty years, fairy-tales entered mainstream literature and interpretive criticism; my debt here is more diffuse—and more to Angela Carter than to Tolkien—but I am grateful to a number of specific literary critics and scholars—Ruth Böttigheimer, Maria Tatar, Martin Sutton, Mererid Puw Davies, and Marina Warner, to name only a few—for hares to chase, new avenues to explore, and trees to bark up. Maria Tatar's recent, beautiful Norton edition of the *Tales* appeared too late for me to take advantage of it. Of the many, many translations from other pens, I would like to voice my admiration for David Luke's—and I have stolen one of his titles. If there is any doubt that these tales are still vividly alive, Eva Figes's *Tales of Innocence and Experience* (2003), her life-story of reading them, as child in Germany and grandmother in London, is a remarkable reminder that struck deep. Finally, my warmest thanks are due to my editor, Judith Luna, for her constant support and great patience towards a tardy translator with a receding deadline; and also to my friends and family for their tolerance of that tardy translator's refusal to be sociable until she had caught up with it.

CONTENTS

CONTENTS

CHILDREN'S LEGENDS

INTRODUCTION

A NEW translation of a text with a claim to be the most-translated of texts after the Bible needs some justification. Stories that have given pleasure, terror, and imaginative coping-space to generations of children may seem a curious choice for this series, whose main readership is among students and interested adults. But these tales have become classics, part of our literary hinterland, though of a more hybrid sort than just children's classics. The present edition has no pictures, though its conversations have certainly invited them, taking place as ever between a princess and a frog, or a wolf and a girl in a red bonnet, or two frightened children in the forest, but also between a disgruntled fiddler and a Jew, and between a boy-giant and an officious bailiff. So this selection finds itself aimed at readers who once read these tales in their childhood, or had them read to them, and are returning to them late, apple bitten, naivety lost, in history. It was Jacob Grimm who spoke of a 'lost Paradise of poesy'.

The present edition attempts, after so many predecessors, to give the tales back to the Grimms, as if that were possible. It aims to place their work in the literary and historical context of German Romanticism, where they had their beginnings—though their *Tales* acquired their greatest success in a later, staider era; to find a language that does not reappropriate theirs or retell their stories for them; and to be more representative than many selections of their collection as a whole. Finally, it takes the texts away from the Grimms and looks briefly at the long and varied afterlife of these tales, which have become such a familiar point of cultural reference.

Curiously, only a relatively small number of the tales are in fact widely known. A dozen or so come immediately to mind—instances where the main figures have a name—with perhaps a further twenty or so that can at least be recognized. But the final total of the collection was 201 plus ten: the familiar smaller 'core', mainly from the first volume of the first edition (1812), is highly selective, and does not give a picture of the whole. The ones we know best are the tales of supernatural wonder, the ones, following English usage, we call 'fairy-tales' (though there is not a single fairy in any of them). The Grimms called them by a double name: *Kinder- und Hausmärchen*,

Tales For Children and the Household. The generic label *Märchen*[1] can be broken down into many different sub-genres: animal fables, tall tales, moralities, comic peasant tales, religious tales known as *Legenden*, where the supernatural element has been Christianized, all of which are to be found in the brothers' collection. Their sources too are various: more from printed sources and good bourgeois contributors and fewer from authentic peasant voices than the myth of the Grimms has it. So the present selection has tried to be representative of this variety: the core of familiar stories of enchantment is certainly present—how could they be omitted?—but the unexpected and unfamiliar will, I hope, give as much pleasure and unease as those already known.

To English-speaking readers the brothers themselves seem to be as lost in the same sweet airs of distance, in Wilhelm Grimm's phrase, as the tales themselves, which are so fantastic and so homely, and seem to belong to no time, or to some distant feudal or absolutist time which was once upon a time; and to be set in no where, though they take place in humble cottages, grand palaces, and in the ever-present great forest, full of threat and opportunity; they are populated by figures with no names but strict characteristics: a princess and her father the king; a prince to take her away; a fox; a golden bird; a poor man and his wife who, like the queens and kings, long for a child; soldiers; robbers; millers; small elvish beings, malicious or grateful for kindness; a witch; a sorceress (not the same thing); a stepmother (perhaps the same thing); and so on—conventional functions in formulaic plots developed with variety and richness out of narrative bits and pieces recurring like echoes from one tale to the next. The plots themselves—of escape and rescue, resurrection and

[1] The word is a diminutive of the (now archaic) *Märe*: 'news', 'tidings'; which developed a pejorative use as 'rumour'; the diminutive suggests something not to be taken seriously or not necessarily true, and the word came to designate the most fictional of fictions, the short tale of wonder, with hints of myth and the supernatural. The term has different connotations from *Sage*: 'things said or told', which is also much used by the Grimms, and which, more narrowly construed, indicates things said of particular places or historical events which might once have been so, i.e. legend. The brothers' separate collection of *Deutsche Sagen* (*German Legends*: 2 vols., 1816–19) included such stories familiar to English-speaking readers as 'The Pied Piper of Hamelin' and 'Bishop Hatto's Mouse-Tower'. To complicate matters, the German term *Legende* refers to tales of the saints, exemplary or marvellous, and it is in this sense that the group of 'Children's Legends' at the end of the book is meant. For *Märchen* I shall generally use 'tale', but when it is a question of genre I shall revert to the German word. In any case, it is high time such a useful term was established in English.

retribution, of fears and dangers overcome—are mainly stories of
the journey to maturity and independence in the strange, familiar
world of the *Märchen*.

Brief Lives

Nevertheless, the brothers *are* attached to a place and a time: to the
German lands of the first half of the nineteenth century, particularly
to the Electorate of Hesse–Kassel, and to the scholarly fringes of
German Romanticism—indeed, these tales, existing in the triangle
of folklore, literary history, and what their compilers called 'Poesie',
turned into one of the most distinctive products of that movement,
and their rescuers, the brothers Jacob and Wilhelm Grimm, into two
of the most surprising of its authors.

The brothers were close companions all their lives, collaborators
and colleagues. With only a year between them (Jacob was born in
1785, Wilhelm in 1786), they enjoyed a happy childhood in Hanau—
'in the Main region', as their annotations put it—with their three
brothers and their sister Lotte; there were few tales from their
mother, but they had a maid who sang folk-songs[2] and there was a
Frau Gottschalk, Jacob recalled, who told them stories. After the
sudden death of their father, the magistrate of Steinau in 1796, they
made the traumatic move to school in Kassel, still sharing one study
and one bed. They both studied law at Marburg. Jointly they were
responsible for caring for their younger siblings after their mother
died in 1808. They were librarians together in the Royal Library in
Kassel, professors together in Göttingen, and in 1837 they were
dismissed from their posts together in the famous protest of the
'Göttingen Seven' against the new king of Hanover's abrogation of
the constitution. Together they moved to Berlin at the invitation of
the Prussian king Friedrich Wilhelm IV, and as academicians there
began work on their famous *Dictionary of the German Language*—
which after their deaths was continued by other scholars, and not
finished until 1961. When Wilhelm married in 1825 his bachelor
brother came to live with him and his wife Dorothea (Dortchen); and

---

[2] Jacob remembered 'Mrs Fox's Wedding' and 'Jorinda and Joringel' from his childhood; Wilhelm heard 'Playing Butchers' from his mother, and the strange prayer
'Urlicht' ('Primal Light')—the title is Brentano's—from their maid, which a century
later Mahler set in his Second Symphony.

when Wilhelm died in 1859 Jacob outlived him by only four years. But however close, their lives and interests were not identical. To simplify: Wilhelm's interests and talents were the more literary, while Jacob, the elder, was the more worldly, the more travelled of the two, more the political and public man. As secretary to the Hessian Legation, he was present in 1815 at the Congress of Vienna which, after the upheavals of the French Revolution and Napoleon's conquest of Europe, restored the power of the European princes; he was a delegate to the Frankfurt pre-parliament in 1848, which attempted—and failed—to introduce a new liberal constitution to the German lands. Disappointment at that failure was in large part Jacob's motivation in creating the Dictionary, as a monument at least, at most, to the unity of German culture. Of the two, Jacob was the initiator of their joint antiquarian and academic projects and the greater scholar. With his turn to the study of German historical grammar he made himself a major figure in the founding of *Germanistik* as a formal field of study. As the years went by, he left the editing of the *Tales*, one of their earliest projects, more and more to Wilhelm.

The Grand Project

When the brothers began collecting these tales some time between 1806 and 1808, they were young men in their early twenties, very poor, looking forward to lives of scholarly achievement, full of curiosity about the current new discoveries of ancient German and Norse poetry, trying out theories of its origins in ancient myth, and exploring how legend, history, and poetry related to one another. It was during these early years that Jacob conceived the grand project, possibly their life's work, of recovering from oral and ancient written sources old German legends, anonymous epics, chapbook stories, folk-songs and verses in older forms of the language, etymologies— all rather loosely called *Sagen*—with the aim, not yet fully theorized and still headily speculative, of revealing the deep similarities of ancient mythical content preserved in them through the changes of time and form and circumstance. The first step was to recover the material. Oral folk-tales were only one genre among many that they wanted to bring to light and print. Aware of the remarkable similarities existing between such tales and other genres widely separated in time and place, Jacob assembled a huge concordance of motifs[3] which was later useful in their annotations to the tales. The first small-scale materials the brothers gathered for the great enterprise they published in their journal, characteristically entitled *Altdeutsche Wälder* (*Ancient German Forests*), a miscellany of curious antiquarian lore. To the extent that Jacob had theorized the nature of these reliques of ancient poetry, they were 'natural poesy' (*Naturpoesie*) as opposed to 'made poetry' (*Kunstdichtung*), the poetry of the uneducated, not of the sophisticated, emerging pure and anonymous from the folk, not composed by a single author, existing both in history and outside it as myth, and so in some hypostatic union of both human and divine. And all were waiting to be recovered and synthesized into a history of ancient German poesy.

Arnim and Brentano's Des Knaben Wunderhorn *(1805–8)*

Part of the record was also to be found in folk-customs, and in laws which, unlike the Napoleonic system, were not codified but lived, embedded in long-standing local practices. This view of law was something Jacob had learned from his mentor and patron at Marburg, the conservative jurist Friedrich Karl von Savigny, whose assistant he had been on a nine-month research visit to Paris, capital of Napoleon's new empire, in 1805. Only months after Jacob's return home that autumn Napoleon defeated Austrian and Russian forces at Austerlitz and entered Vienna. The omnipresent threat of invasion by France and French culture coloured the attitudes and achievements of a generation of young German writers and poets with a new nationalism, which also embraced the brothers' interest in German antiquities. Aristocratic court culture had been French-influenced; the tales of the people would reinstate the authentic voice of the nation. There was, of course, no German nation in the political and constitutional sense, only a patchwork of smaller and larger states, more or less—often less—benevolently despotic, which Napoleon rationalized and reduced in number when he invaded;

---

[3] For examples, see Gunhild Ginschel, *Der junge Jacob Grimm, 1805–1819* (Berlin, 1965), 287–9. It was in the train of this concordance that the tremendous international index of folk-motifs was begun by the Finn Antti Aarne and continued by Stith Thompson: *Motif-Index of Folk Literature: A Classification of Narrative Elements in Folktale, etc* . . ., 6 vols. (Copenhagen, 1932–8; 2nd edn. 1955–8), an indispensable reference work for folklorists.

many of them constitutional relics of the Holy Roman Empire, which he abolished, electoral principalities, and episcopal fiefs as well as Free Cities and independent kingdoms. This came close to home when Napoleon made his brother Jérôme king of the newly formed Kingdom of Westphalia and installed him in the former elector's palace in Kassel (where, for the space of his brief reign, Jérôme also became Jacob's new employer). The poets of the second Romantic generation aimed to create a stronger sense of German cultural self-awareness as a precondition to forging a new nation as they rediscovered and rewrote the German past. This intention lay behind Savigny's jurisprudence, as it did Joseph Gorres's essay on popular sixteenth-century prose romances, *Die teutschen Volks-Bücher* (*German Folk Romances*, 1807), and above all, the collection of German folk-songs made by the poets and friends Achim von Arnim and Clemens Brentano, *Des Knaben Wunderhorn* (*The Boy's Magical Horn*, 2 vols., 1805–8). The discovery of folk-poetry was not new: Herder had already published his pioneering anthology of *Volkslieder* (*Folk-songs*) in 1778–9, but his scope had been worldwide, universal, not narrowly patriotic. Indeed, the discovery of the *Märchen* was not new: as a tale of marvels where the rules of the real world no longer applied, it made an ironical recreation for the sophisticated court culture of the Enlightenment.[4] But the nationalism was new, and so was the search for lost narrative naivety: both looked backwards and inwards for their cultural roots. In the eyes of the poets and their friends the young scholars, the reinvention of the nation would come with the rediscovery of its past.

The charismatic, erratic Brentano, in search of help with his own collecting, was introduced to the assiduous young Grimms by his brother-in-law Savigny. Brentano's entry into their quiet lives brought them into the literary mainstream; his interests in popular song and story acted as a stimulus to theirs, and as a model of how—and also how not—to treat such tales. He drew their attention to old printed sources from his library; in his enthusiasm for their painstaking copying and gathering he persuaded them to contribute a substantial number from their hoard of songs to the second *Wunderhorn*

---

[4] The eight volumes of J. K. A. Musäus's *Volksmärchen der Deutschen* (1782–6), rewritten from oral and written sources, are far more self-conscious and knowing in tone than the Grimms' cultivated naivety.

volume,[5] and encouraged them further in their collection of old tales. He was himself planning to publish such folk-tales, and here too the brothers were glad to help him, in September 1810 sending him their manuscript transcripts of some thirty tales they had already gathered. Mercifully, they were canny enough to take copies, for Brentano lost interest for the time being and never sent them back. Happily, they turned up in the early twentieth century in the monastery of Oelenberg in Alsace, which was just as well for posterity, as Wilhelm appears to have destroyed their own manuscript material after publication.[6] When Brentano returned to the genre it was to the *Märchen* as artwork, the tale of mystery and imagination which was the definitive genre—and more than genre, the air they breathed— for the Romantic poets. But these were the compositions of poets in their own name: Tieck, Novalis, Fouqué—Brentano one of the finest; they were not the redaction of some anonymous folk-tale. The brothers suspected as much at the time; their correspondence reveals their concerns about what Brentano might do to their humble stories.[7] They were not entirely at ease with the way he and Arnim had dealt with the *Wunderhorn* songs and ballads: two poets in their own right had taken possession of the verses, rewriting and re-creating them—characteristically and memorably, as their continued life witnesses; but the poets' procedure was too cavalier for the scholarly Grimms, who aimed to preserve the integrity of their sources. The brothers' sense of nation, too, was qualified by their awareness of how widespread internationally were their tales in all their variant versions. The purposes of folklorist and poet were at odds in these

---

[5] Among them Wilhelm contributed 'Urlicht' and the child's bedtime prayer about the fourteen angels which Humperdinck later set in his opera *Hänsel und Gretel* (1893). Wilhelm noted that he had heard it 'by word of mouth from our maid, who had learned it from her grandmother'.

[6] For Heinz Rölleke's important edition of them, *Die älteste Märchensammlung der Brüder Grimm*, see the Note on the Text.

[7] In a letter to Wilhelm in September 1810, Jacob wrote: 'Clemens can have the collection of children's tales with all my heart, even though his way of treating them is different from what we have in mind.' And Wilhelm to Jacob: '. . . we will really lose nothing, as he will make them longer and flashier.' The cycle of quasi-folk *Märchen* that Brentano did compose at this time, known as *Das Märchen von dem Rhein und dem Müller Radlauf* (*The Tale of the Rhine and the Miller Turn-Wheel*) was not published until 1846, after his death. *Die Mährchen vom Rhein*, ed. Brigitte Schilbach, in: Brentano, *Sämtliche Werke und Briefe*, XVII, *Prosa* II (Stuttgart, 1983). The editorial material includes an account of the relations between Brentano and the Grimms at the time of their shared—and differing—interests in collecting folk-songs and tales.

respects—which may have been behind the brothers' decision to publish their collection for themselves. But they were still one with their friends' patriotic cultural aims, and there is no doubt that their tales did contribute to an imagined Germany.

The First Contributors

So they went ahead with their own pioneering project. But if their collection of tales began as part of a grander philological-historical-mythological enterprise, it surely came to develop an unforeseeable separate life and afterlife of its own. The actual collecting was fun. It was sociable. For though they have left generations under the impression that these tales were gathered among the humble folk of specific German regions (the Main, the Münsterland, their own part of Hesse most of all), the brothers took down their very first stories from the young ladies next door, the Wild girls, daughters of the Kassel apothecary, who passed on lots of tales to them.[8] The circle was extended by the sisters Hassenpflug, their sister Lotte's friends, daughters of the future *Regierungspräsident* (Chief Administrator of the District). Their brother Ludwig, who later married Lotte, reported many cheerful hours at the Grimms'.[9] The family appears to have contributed a very large number of tales, including many alternative versions. Acquaintance with the aristocratic Westphalian families Haxthausen (whose son August was a collector too) and Droste-Hülshoff made the opportunity for visits and friendships and more stories.[10] These were not humble village people, but were

---

[8] Wilhelm later noted the provenance of a number of tales in his own copy of the first edition. For example, Elisabeth (Gretchen) Wild gave them 'Cat and Mouse As Partners', 'Our Lady's Child', and 'The Stolen Farthing'; Dorothea (Dortchen), who later became Wilhelm's wife, gave one version of Rumpelstiltskin, and told him 'The Singing Bone' ('19 January 1812 by the stove in the garden house in Nentershausen', he noted). For a full account of the contributors, see Rölleke, *Die älteste Märchensammlung*, 390–7, and, in schematic form, Heinz Rölleke's 1982 edition of the *Märchen*, III. 559–74. Henceforth cited as Rölleke, *KHM* (1982).

[9] Rölleke, *KHM* (1982), III. 600. From the Hassenpflug family came, among others, 'The Wolf and the Seven Little Kids' and 'Clever Hans'. Jeanette offered the first variant of 'Little Redcap' and Marie the second, as well as 'The Golden Key', which ends the collection, and many more besides.

[10] The Haxthausens provided, among others: 'The Good Bargain', 'The Three Children of Fortune', 'The Fox and the Geese', the first of the Children's Legends, 'St Joseph in the Forest', while Jenny von Droste-Hülshoff told them 'The Shoes That Were Danced to Tatters'.

from the minor aristocracy and the educated and well-connected middle class. The tales were oral, but the tellers literate. Moreover, Frau Hassenpflug came from a Huguenot family from the Dauphiné, and French was current in the household, so there is more than a possibility of a French—no longer Hessian peasant—input into their stories.[11] Indeed, Jeanette Hassenpflug gave the brothers a version of 'Puss-in-Boots' which they were happy to print in their first edition, but removed from the second because it too obviously derived from Perrault; that is, it was not German, when what Wilhelm wanted to listen for in these tales was 'traces of ancient German myth', as he put it in his first Preface. The brothers' wishful image of the authentic folk story-teller attached to the German soil coloured the way they gave their sources in their annotations: they blurred the nature of a tale's mediation, and named only the general region it came from, turning the local habitation and the name of their contributors into a German territory which supposedly generated their tale naturally, collectively, anonymously: the Wilds of the Markstrasse were turned into 'Kassel' or 'Hesse'; the Hassenpflugs, who came from Hanau, into 'the Main region'; the Haxthausens of Bökendorf into 'the Paderborn area' or 'the Münsterland'. There were many other contributors[12] besides these three families, especially after the first volume was published, but the notes obscured them with the same kind of broad geographical location—even their most authentic and gifted story-teller, the tailor's widow Frau Dorothea Viehmann, also from a Huguenot family, who came into the brothers' lives between their first and second volumes. She sold them her garden produce

---

[11] Much of this information has been available at least since Bolte and Polivka's *Anmerkungen* (1913–32), and it has been considerably filled out by Rölleke, whose impeccable philological researches may, it is hoped, have put to rest the accusations of bad faith made against the Grimms, particularly by John Ellis, *One Fairy Story Too Many* (Chicago, 1983). Even so, the brothers' wishful ideal of the story-telling peasant is very persistent, and in obscuring their immediate story-tellers, they were at the very least misleading.

[12] Among them the old soldier, Sergeant-Major Johann Friedrich Krause, who provided the tale of the old dog 'Old Sultan' as well as variants to others in exchange for cast-off clothes; Frederike Mannel, the pastor's daughter from Allendorf, a small town between Kassel and Göttingen, who provided variants to 'Our Lady's Child' and to 'Fitcher's Bird', but wrote protesting 'I really don't know any more; Clemens [Brentano] has drawn them all out of my memory'; the divinity student Ferdinand Siebert from Treysa, between Kassel and Marburg in the Schwalm valley, who provided a number, including variants of 'The Tale of the Boy Who Set Out To Learn Fear' and 'Mother Holle of the Snow'.

and they invited her in for coffee. Her arrival was a landmark in their collecting: they printed at least eighteen full stories of hers, and used the variants she gave them to at least another eighteen to improve or add to others.[13] Wilhelm honoured her by name in his second Preface, but in his pen-portrait stylized her into a woman of the people, while their notes to her tales simply give their source as her village: 'Zwehrn.' The theory of natural poesy got in the way of full and precise disclosure. Her figure as represented in brother Ludwig's etching, her sure peasant voice as described by Wilhelm, and her person, the caring grandmother of his footnote (dead by then, so that but for the brothers her stories would have been lost), went into constructing the invisible, defining story-teller of the collection. One of the earliest English translators, Edgar Taylor, brought an implicit peasant-grandmotherly story-teller of this kind into his title: *Gammer Grethel, or German Fairy Tales and Popular Stories* (London, 1839). And as a consequence of a myth-making late memory of Wilhelm's son Hermann, the eldest Hassenpflug daughter, Marie, was subsumed for generations into 'die alte Marie [Müller]', the Wild family's housekeeper, who filled the fictional role more aptly—until she was firmly demystified by Rölleke and restored to her true identity as the leading light of the family circle.[14] The question as to where Frau Viehmann or the *jeunes filles en fleur* got their stories from is not strictly answerable, and threatens infinite regress,[15] though, given the Huguenot associations, French sources such as Perrault, Mme d'Aulnoy, and Mme de la Force for many of their tales are more than likely, however indirect and however unwelcome this may have been to the brothers. But in general, written and oral became inextricably intertwined (see, for example, 'The Six Swans' and 'The Bearskin Man' and notes). The exceptions to such confusions are the cases of identifiable written sources, and these the Grimms of course did identify in their annotations, whether as originals or as possible variants.

---

[13] The present selection includes seven of her contributions, among them 'The Devil With the Three Golden Hairs', 'Sensible Elsie', and 'The Goose-Girl'.

[14] 'Die "stöckhessischen" Märchen der "alten Marie" . . .', *Germanisch-Romanische Monatsschrift*, NF 29 (1975), 74–86.

[15] 'The Table-Lay . . .' was supplied by Jeanette Hassenpflug ('Kassel'), who in her turn had heard it from 'old Mamsell Storch at Henschels' [Rölleke, *KMH* (1982), III. 457]'. And Mamsell Storch . . .?

They did in fact take a number of their tales from old printed texts,[16] as long as these indicated some oral or rustic source, for age guaranteed authenticity. And they did themselves, especially Wilhelm, go out into the country in search of such tellers of tales, but Wilhelm's forays were not as fruitful as his visits to friends. The only contributor the brothers actually named besides Frau Viehmann was the painter Philipp Otto Runge. Arnim sent on to them the two beautifully shaped tales in Low-German dialect which Runge had collected (and surely worked over?): 'The Tale of the Fisherman and His Wife' and 'The Tale of the Juniper Tree'. At first sight they seem to have little in common but their craftsmanship: the one is a comic, misogynistic morality, the other offers a profound glimpse of horror and beauty and redemption. But with their verses, repetitions, narrative build-up and finely paced crescendi, their talking creatures with magical powers, their strong single motifs and plot-line of transgression and final redress, and their utter acceptance of magic in the real world, Runge's two stories set a pattern for the brothers' treatment of many of their own tales. These are the true masterpieces of the collection.

Such questions of source are not unrelated to questions of meaning. The fact that so many of their contributors were women, and well-brought-up young women at that, had its effect on the nature of the collection. These are certainly not tales from the tavern. But it may account for more than the many lively heroines: brave Gretel who pushes the witch into the oven (13), the loyal sisters who rescue their twelve or six brothers (8, 36), the smart girls who outwit their murderous bridegrooms (30, 33), Redcap and her grandmother, who drown the wolf in the sausage-water (20, II). On the surface, many—

---

[16] Some from the seventeenth-century miscellanies and chapbooks Brentano had lent them: for example, Rollenhagen provided the 'Iron Henry' motif in 'The Frog King . . .'; Moscherosch 'The Tale of the Mouse, the Bird and the Sausage', which Brentano had already adapted, Hans Sachs 'The Unequal Children of Eve'. The brothers also mined more recent publications if they indicated antiquity or oral narration: Heinrich Jung-Stilling's autobiographical novel *Heinrich Stillings Jugend* (1777), for example, gave them the exceedingly literary 'Jorinda and Joringel', and its continuation *Heinrich Stillings Jünglings-jahre* (1778) 'Grandfather and Grandson'. 'Rapunzel' was rewritten from a story in vol. 5 of Friedrich Schulz's collection, *Kleine Romane*, who in turn had borrowed it from Mme de la Force (so it was French). The controversial item 'Playing Butchers' was an old anecdote reprinted in Kleist's journal *Berliner Abendblätter*, 39 (1810). In all these cases except 'Rapunzel', where the change of tone from worldly to naive is marked, the brothers' retelling in the first edition remains very close to their sources. For further details, see the notes.

(most?)—of the tales are remarkably asexual: the prince comes on the scene, whether as rescuer or as reward, to take a passive maiden away from her father's house—a good bourgeois marriage arrangement rather than a passionate attachment. (Only Snow-White appears to fall in love.) This buried ideological factor is one that helped to make the collection acceptable for parents to read to their young and perhaps helps to explain something of what Wilhelm meant when he described the book as one to bring up children on (see p. 4). It was innocent; it was safe. It insinuated an acceptable social model. But the surface, social, reading stops short. The undertow of myth the brothers sensed in these tales—and perhaps the bright girls and the hospitable mothers who told them did too—chimes in with the psychological meaning the modern reader finds, reading past the social norms to the imaginative articulation of a deep sexual fear in the representation of bridegrooms as murderous. 'The Frog King . . .', on the other hand, suggests a happier resolution to such fears.

Arguing with Arnim: Rewriting; Respecting the Sources; Tales for Children?

Arnim was a helpful friend. He found the book a publisher, and the first volume of the first edition appeared in time for Christmas 1812. The brothers dedicated it to his wife Bettina—Brentano's sister, and herself already a significant literary figure—for her very young son Johannes Freimund.

As he thanked the brothers for such a Christmas present, Arnim was also the first to raise questions which are still being asked of these texts: about the degree and nature of their adaptation of these oral tales for print, and, by extension, of the legitimacy in principle of reworking prior models—something that has come home to roost with the many late reworkings of the Grimms' tales themselves, now that they have become points of intertextual reference for later writers. He was also the first to raise the perennial doubts about the suitability of some of their tales for the young, in a collection which was for and of the household as well as for children, and intended—'primarily' by Jacob, 'also' by Wilhelm—as a contribution to the history of ancient oral poesy. Arnim's comments are useful because they provoked both brothers to clarify (and sometimes contradict) how they understood what they were doing, and draw to the surface some of the tensions arising from their dual devotion to folklore and poesy. Coming from a poet, they cast doubt on Jacob's arguments for the purity of their texts, as Arnim points out what the scholar, insisting on faithfulness to his sources, does not—or does not want to— see: that creative shaping and reshaping necessarily comes with writing:

I don't believe for a moment, even if you do, that you wrote the children's tales down just as you received them, the shaping, *onward*-creating impulse in humanity will conquer all we might intend and is quite simply ineradicable. God creates, and man, His image, works at continuing His creation; the thread is never cut, but another sort of flax is produced . . . and that is as it should be; all times and all humans exist in their own right.[17]

If the drafts of the Oelenberg manuscript are the nearest to the tales 'just as [the brothers] received them', then a comparison with the relatively modest narrative tidying-up they gave them for the first edition bears out Arnim's assertion. But his argument is not that of the modern folklorist: that the transition from oral to written changes the nature of the text; rather, that good transcription is creative transcription (as in his and Brentano's *Wunderhorn*). And he carries his argument further, to apply it to the larger transformations of texts and historical materials when they are adopted by later poets in later ages (as he did himself). Jacob, he declares, overestimates the new poet's newness and originality:

What you call *inventing* does not exist at all, not even in Christ. Nothing begins with the individual, and the most original work is after all only the furtherance of something which perhaps it had not been possible to see in quite that way . . . Whether there was a paradise of poesy [Jacob's phrase] I do not know, but I do know that if I possessed nothing but the oldest monuments of poesy, I would still write a lot more to fill out the gap that they do not understand or include. (Steig, 249)

That defence of modern poetry also sounds like a justification *avant la lettre* of the way Anne Sexton, say, or Günter Grass has more recently filled out certain gaps which the Grimms did not understand or include.

---

[17] Letter of 24 Dec. 1812, in Reinhold Steig, *Achim von Arnim und Jacob und Wilhelm Grimm* (Stuttgart and Berlin, 1904), 248–9. Henceforth cited in text as 'Steig'.

But Arnim's scepticism about the faithfulness of their transcriptions needed a reply. In the event, it caused Jacob to reaffirm his reverence for ancient poetry as the embodiment of ancient belief. Principles were involved: the Romantic scholar's truth to his source, and his lack of sympathy for new poetry, were underpinned by his faith in the mythical validity of ancient poesy: 'On the whole you are arguing more for the humanity, I for the divinity of poesy' (letter of 31 Dec. 1812; Steig, 254). All the same, by his insistence on closeness to source, which brought with it his disapproval of his friends' excessively free rewriting of their folk-songs, Jacob did not mean quite the untouched transcription the modern folklorist (with tape-machine) requires of the record. The words he uses to Arnim, as Wilhelm does in his Preface, are the moral words 'truth' and 'faithfulness', not the positivistic discourse of 'accuracy' and 'exactitude'—though accuracy is exactly what Jacob the scholar asks of his fellow-collectors of folklore when it comes to proposing a scholarly society of collectors (see Appendix C). But that is not contradicted, only qualified, by what he says to his poet-friend: absolute (Jacob calls it 'mathematical') precision is impossible and not to be expected; retelling entails using other words; another teller might do better or differently, but no less faithfully, for in substance the tale has not been added to or given a different turn (Steig, 255). The tales they took down were retold in that sense. By 'in substance' (*in der Sache*), Jacob appears to mean content: the basic situation and action, the main figures and motifs, underpinned by its validity as myth; not, as Arnim did, the stamp of an individual style or of a later period or just seizing the original tale and running with it.

Wilhelm too was happier with the idea of simply (but it wasn't so simple) entering the chain of retellers. 'That is why', he wrote to Arnim (28 Jan. 1813), 'I didn't make difficulties for myself in the words or the arrangement of metaphors and just spoke as it pleased me for the moment . . . However, *intentional* combining and altering is something else' (Steig, 267). This may have been his aim and his procedure for the pioneering and experimental first volume of the first edition, but with the hindsight brought by the successive revised editions, later readers are in a position to see that in the event Wilhelm's speaking as it pleased him for the moment very soon turned from tactful touching-up to make a rough tale readable—on the whole Jacob's procedure for the 1812 volume—into intentional combining and altering, something very close to artistic and ideological appropriation. Scholarly authenticity gave way to the aesthetic *appearance* of authenticity. But that was yet to come.

Finally, Arnim wrote not only as a poet, but as a protective young father. He saw difficulties in the combination of children's tales and household tales: of the two stories from Runge which he had passed on, he wondered if 'The Tale of the Fisherman and His Wife' was really a tale for children in the first place, and he had not been entirely happy about the violence in 'The Tale of the Juniper Tree', while one mother had told him that she could not put 'Playing Butchers' (see Appendix B) into her children's hands. Would a printed warning for parents to be selective be advisable? This objection to the cruelty contained in the stories is one still heard, particularly with regard to the notorious punishments for the wicked that bring the tales into just balance at the end; it has produced many subsequent versions more apt to sweeten the imagination, especially in English translations, where Snow-White's stepmother does not dance to her death in red-hot shoes, nor the huntsman fill the wolf's belly with stones. Story-telling grandmothers still pause to judge whether to read on, weighing children's vulnerability against their sense of reassurance that badness has been properly dealt with, recognizing their sense of fairness and justice—and their unholy glee. The psychiatrist Bruno Bettelheim's view of the cathartic effects of such resolutions seems wiser than Arnim's sense of propriety in this respect—but it is uncertain ground in the present over-anxious climate.

Arnim was also concerned that the archaic language or dialect of some of the pieces made them inaccessible, and that the comedy in others was too adult. The Grimms had taken the first of two versions of 'The Brave Little Tailor' from a sixteenth-century miscellany, Martinus Montanus' *Wegkürtzer*, and, true to written source, had reproduced it with all its crabbed and archaic turns of phrase. Wasn't this incomprehensible to a child schooled in modern German? And the tale of the fox with nine tails (29) was 'obviously a French frivolity' (letter of early Jan. 1813; Steig, 263)—'French' here being less an indication of source than a euphemism for 'obscene'.

The brothers have different answers to these doubts. Wilhelm is conciliatory. He recognizes 'Playing Butchers' to be a problem (but where exactly did he see the problem? In the representation of amoral childish violence, when the prevailing view of children was one of innocence?); it certainly influenced him, he tells his friend, when as a boy he heard his mother tell it: 'it did make me cautious and timid when I was playing' (28 Jan. 1813; Steig, 266). Or does that suggest some negative pedagogic value? Much is unclear, or unsaid. But he agrees with Arnim about 'Mrs Fox's Wedding': he hadn't wanted to include her, but then again, to the pure all things are pure. Jacob, on the other hand, is on the defensive: the story belongs to the larger complex of the ancient beast epic of Reynard the Fox—which he is working on; he swears the tale is innocent— but the French will give an obscene colouring to the holiest things; and, to clinch the matter, it is one of his favourite tales from his childhood. As for printing a warning to parents, that would be absurdly over-protective, and in any case would be a sheer invitation to the child to read on. ('See "Bluebeard" or "Our Lady's Child"', he might have added). With regard to the mixed readership envisaged in the book's title, he is against confining the children to the nursery of 'children's writing': children *belong* in the household. Similarly, on the question of language—and indeed of content— which might be beyond a child's grasp, he is brusque and sensible: the writer should not talk down, nor change his style for the benefit of a childish audience, but should write as best he can write, while for their part the children will take in what they are able to and leave what they are not. In any case, the concern about suitability is a diversion. He queries whether these tales are children's tales at all, rather than the last embodiments of ancient truths, to which the childlike are responsive. The book, he declares,

was not to my mind written for children at all—though they have welcomed it gladly and I'm very pleased at that. On the other hand, I would not have been happy working on it if I hadn't believed that it could become as important for poesy, mythology, and history in the eyes of the oldest and gravest as it does to me. The only reasons that these tales have their home among children and the aged are (1) because children are receptive only to stories (*Epos*), so it is thanks to their disposition that these records survive; (2) because the over-sophisticated scorn them. (28 Jan. 1813; Steig, 271)

In focusing on children as the main readership at this point, Arnim's remarks provoke Jacob to reassert the larger scholarly and speculative aims of the compilation: he still has the grand project in mind. In these exchanges the tensions latent in the collection's double nature, combining a visionary anthropology with literary-pedagogic pleasure, become clearer. In this respect, Wilhelm was right when he said in his 1819 preface that it was the only collection of its kind. There were other anthologies of children's tales, but without the underpinning of serious folklore. Their collection has two aspects, but they point in different directions.

This was all Brentano could see in it; the moving spirit of the *Wunderhorn* was deeply disappointed at the book's scholarly dullness, and made no bones about letting Arnim know.[18] The brothers' correspondence with Arnim, as generous as it was hard-hitting, from the very beginning of the book's changing history already broached the bigger questions these small texts still raise: of authorship, adaptation, and audience. By drawing out the brothers' replies—which at one moment put Jacob the scholar on the defensive, and at another sound like an improvised rehearsal for Wilhelm's preface to the second edition of 1819 (see pp. 3–10)—it opened the door to the major transformations that the tales underwent there.

The Second Edition (1819–1822) and After: 'Intentional *combining and altering is something else'*

Wilhelm was getting into his stride and had already taken over much of the editing of Volume II of the first edition,[19] for by 1815, as secretary to the Hessian Legation, Jacob was in attendance at the Congress of Vienna. But gathering material for the grand project was still on his mind, and with an introduction from Brentano to a group of like-minded literary amateurs there, he set about establishing a society for the collection of folklore materials, to correspond with and contribute to an organizational centre. Brentano and he had had a similar idea in the *Wunderhorn* years, but nothing had come of it. Now he formulated a circular inviting membership and suggesting a very wide range of material to be gathered, more than just the 'nursery and children's tales' at the head of his list: seasonal rites and

---

[18] See his letter to Arnim of Feb. 1813, in Arnim and Brentano, *Freundschaftsbriefe*, 2 vols. (Frankfurt a.M, 1998), ii. 674–5 and 927–8.

[19] Arnim spotted this at once. Thanking Wilhelm for a copy of vol. II, he wrote (10 Feb. 1815): 'you've been deft in your collecting, and deft at giving it a helping hand—which of course you won't tell Jacob—but you should have done it more often' (Steig, 319).

ceremonies, local legends, sayings, superstitions, and customary law (see Appendix C). His scholarly meticulousness can be seen in his insistence on accuracy of transcription, his cultural conservatism in the evocation of remote villages and time-hallowed trades. The society was conceived as a rescue operation. 'We were perhaps only just in time to record these tales', adds Wilhelm in his 1819 Preface. For a long time that has been the cry of the collectors of folk-song and story who followed: as the modernization of society proceeds faster and faster, the remote corners where they are still (are they still?) told and sung have been sought out, until the last singer of the last song will have been captured on tape. But industrialized society has developed its own, shorter-lived, rites and ceremonies, sayings and superstitions. Recording them does not have to share the Grimms' nostalgia for a lost paradise of poesy. There is still scope for the modern folklorist.

How far Jacob's society actually got off the ground is not clear—certainly the number and geographical scatter of their later contributors extended considerably. But in 1815 the grand project the society was to serve received a setback in the form of a harsh review of *Altdeutsche Wälder* in the *Heidelberger Jahrbücher* by the critic and literary historian A. W. Schlegel. He criticized their journal as amateurish and over-speculative, contesting that article of faith, anonymous collective composition, and ascribing the recurrence of tales and motifs in widely separated cultures to transmission, not to mythical archetype or single source. Crucially for Jacob, he argued that the essential prerequisite for a history of ancient poetry was that it should be grounded in an account of its ancient language, that is, what was first needed was a historical grammar of German. That was the direction Jacob took after 1815. He became the great grammarian and lexicographer, but never abandoned his belief in the organic unity of language, poetry, and national culture. However, though he continued to have a share in the notes to subsequent editions of the *Tales*, he left the editing mainly to Wilhelm. More tales and more variants came their way, and Wilhelm's way with them developed more freely.

He had listened to Arnim. The new edition underwent a radical revision and expansion under his hands. The alterations were ideological in part, in large part literary, and in part they were moving away from Jacob's anthropological interests and more towards a book for children, or their parents: 'a book to bring children up on', as Wilhelm's Preface claimed. Arnim's worries about the suitability of particular tales for children were heeded: 'Playing Butchers' was removed; the archaic language of 'The Brave Little Tailor' over-hauled; 'Mrs Fox's Wedding' remained, but there was some discreet bowdlerization elsewhere: in 'Rumpelstiltskin' the queen no longer 'lay in childbed', but 'brought a beautiful child into the world'. In the first edition Rapunzel, ignorant of her pregnancy, reveals the existence of the prince when she asks her sorceress–godmother why her clothes are so tight; in the second, she betrays him by merely asking why her godmother is so much heavier to pull up the tower than the prince. A foolish question and a weak substitute. This prac-tice contradicts Wilhelm's sturdy words in the Preface—but indi-cates the shift in interest. His revision of other tales reveals some religious finger-wagging: in 'Godfather Death', the poor man's bit-ter rejection of the good Lord as his son's godfather—'you give to the rich and let the poor go hungry'—is glossed in the second edi-tion by the editorial rebuke: 'The man asserted this because he was ignorant of how wisely God distributes riches and poverty.' The tales are being prepared for the bourgeois nursery. Further removals were motivated by the persistence of the brothers' cultural national-ism: tales from obviously non-Germanic sources were dropped: ver-sions of 'Puss-in-Boots' and 'Bluebeard' were too close to Perrault; 'The Hand with the Knife' was Scots. The language of the tales too was subjected to etymological cleansing: words of French origin were removed and replaced by German equivalents. This cannot be entirely visible in a translation, but it went much further than turn-ing a 'princess' into a 'king's daughter', or a 'fairy' into a 'wise-woman': 'march' even turned into 'trot' in 'The Golden Goose'. Still, it is not the least contradiction about the brothers' interest in folk-tales that, for all the German focus of their *Tales*, their notes recorded the widespread similarities with tales from other countries; they were in contact with collectors from other nations; Jacob cor-responded with Sir Walter Scott and the Serb nationalist collector and poet Vuk Karadžić; Wilhelm translated Crofton Croker's (not entirely reliable) *Fairy Legends and Traditions of the South of Ireland* (London 1825) as *Irische Elfenmärchen* (Leipzig 1826); they had intended a translation of one of the earliest compilations, Giam-battista Basile's Neapolitan *Il Pentamerone* (*Five Days' Tales*) of

1637, and used it as a comparative touchstone from their first edition on, as they had Francesco Straparola's earlier collection of stories, comic tales, and riddles *Le tredeci piacevoli Notti* (*Thirteen Delightful Nights*) of 1573. Both contained early versions (sources? variants?) of some of the most familiar folk-tales: Basile of the basic tales of 'Briar-Rose', 'Rapunzel', and 'Ashypet', for example; Straparola of 'Puss-in-Boots'.[20] The brothers' own first publication had by mid-century stimulated the study of folk-lore and the nationalisms it fed in other countries too, and Wilhelm's '[Survey of the] Literature' ranged by 1856 from Africa to India, besides European lands. As for the notes to the second edition, they were expanded, and took on the standard form of (a) provenance (merely geographical), (b) content of available variants, and (c) comparable motifs in ancient poetry and mythology from many, though still predominantly Germanic, cultures. These fuller annotations were hived off to a later (1822) third volume of their own; the scholarship was now separated from the composition. Confronted with several variants of the same basic story—far more of them by now—both brothers' solution to the problem of what to privilege for print was, as Wilhelm describes it in his Preface: to conflate the 'best' elements from several variants to produce the 'best' version, synthesizing them into a coherent and rich episodic narrative—a method deplored by modern folklorists. From the wealth of comparative material accumulated by the Grimms and still more by later collectors, it has become clear that the characteristic folk-tale is made up of a sequence of typical situations, rudimentary narrative elements which are put together and given local colour in countless different combinations and variations, echoing from one tale to another, but maintaining their separateness; they are houses of bricks, not of pancake mix; and parataxis rules the plot as well as the sentence. Wilhelm was aware of this: he uses the add-on method to good effect in the revised 'Brave Little Tailor', for example (see

[20] According to Wilhelm's judgement of Basile in his 1856 '[Survey of the] Literature': 'He tells his tales wholly in the spirit of a lively, witty, and humorous people, with constant references to customs and way of life, even to ancient history and mythology, which are in general quite widely known in Italy. This reveals their contrast to the quiet and simple style of the German tales.' His view of Straparola's mixed collection is less happy: 'a great deal is told agreeably, naturally, and not without delicacy; elsewhere, on the other hand, the style is not just indecent but obscene to the point of shamelessness . . . However, the *Märchen* are pretty free of such smut, just as in any case they form the best part of the work as a whole.'

note). Indeed, sometimes the joins still show.[21] And in arranging the order of the tales he allowed common themes to echo and mirror from one to another. On the other hand, with many of his variants he was blending, not joining, synthesizing into a through-composed whole, not just linking. By 'best' he appears to mean vividness of motif or episode and the potential for overall narrative coherence: aesthetic considerations rather than scholarly or even ideological. (The approach works beautifully with 'Rumpelstiltskin', where the components fused were in fact quite fragmentary, less so with 'Hansel and Gretel', where the revision incorporates another full and already moralized version—see the notes). For although the tales develop in a wholly illogical manner—arbitrary things happen, figures turn up unexpectedly—once that illogic is accepted as the essential characteristic of the genre, the unexpected *in* the tale becomes the expected *of* the tale and it develops its own peculiar logic: the episodes follow a clear line, the conventions of character and of plot fall into place,[22] and the marvellous is taken for granted. And where they did not fall into place, Wilhelm gave them a helping hand.

How the brothers proceeded from first transcription to first edition, and how Wilhelm continued into the revisions of the second, can be seen from the versions of 'Rumpelstiltskin'. The earliest transcription is 'Rumpenstünzchen', which Jacob sent to Savigny to tell to his children Bettine and Franz in April 1808 (see Appendix A and note). This is the merest scenario for oral performance. The high point of the tale, which anyone who has ever told it or read it aloud knows, is the guessing game, an invitation to wild improvisation, when more often than not the teller is outdone by her infant listeners. Here it is reduced to the merest indication: 'all sorts of names'—

[21] As in 'The Frog King, or Iron Henry', where the combination of two stories is signalled in the title. See also 'The Golden Bird' and 'The King of the Golden Mountain', for example.

[22] The quest, the test, the forbidden action, the bargain, the transformation, the ending in marriage or accession to the throne, the hero, the simpleton, the underdog, in constellations of three or two—three brothers, two sisters—the stepmother, the false bride, the helper—animal or elf—who has been helped, the punishments and rewards, and so on: these are conventions of plot and character which function as the structural elements of folk narrative. They were analysed in abstract terms on the basis of Russian folk-tales in Vladimir Propp's influential *Morphology of the Folktale* (English version, London and Austin, Tex., 1968). In their copious accumulation of comparative analogues to the Grimms' tales, Bolte and Polívka analyse a number of them into their shared narrative elements, though those elements are not necessarily the same as Propp's (see Bibliography).

for Jacob is relying on his friend to fill it out. When it comes to the first edition of 1812, this has been minimally and not very imaginatively expanded to 'Thomas' or 'Richard'. But by the revisions of 1819, no longer having any first transcription to restrain him, Wilhelm has seen the playful possibilities and, building up the tension, comes up first with the names of the three magi, a bit garbled, and then triumphantly invents three comic names: 'Skinnyribs perhaps, or Sheepshanks, or Pegleg.' This is much more colourful—but it marks the crossing-place from oral to written where these tales dwell. Bare outline is not enough for print. The story is turning into a tale to be read, not said.

This transition may also lie behind the great increase in dialogue in the 1819 edition and thereafter, not only in this tale but in most of them. The second edition introduces a consistent—and very deft—shift from indirect to direct speech throughout. Unlike a teller, a reader can no longer be relied upon to enact what the figures might say, so what the editor has made them say is *given* her to *re*-enact.

It is often said that the genre of the *Märchen* has no psychology: Powerful feelings are present—fear, joy, sorrow, wishing, pride, destructive malice—but they are external, incorporated into action and situation, rather than lying within the characters. It is certainly true that its schematic figures have no inner life, but some qualification is needed in the case of Wilhelm's revisions, which frequently introduce comprehensible motives and human feelings. The development of 'Rumpelstiltskin' will again provide an illustration. In the final version the girl's feelings are dramatized as she explains her fears to the manikin. As for motivation: the tears of the girl in the tale for Savigny are mysterious; we are left wondering 'why?' The miller's daughter, on the other hand, has good reason to be afraid—the king has demanded the impossible. But what has moved her father to lie to the king? Not even the extensive rewriting of 1819 does much to motivate this, though without it the story has no first cause. Here too we are left wondering 'why?' Not until the sixth edition of 1850 does Wilhelm provide a rationale: 'to make himself look big.' Bravado. Wilhelm understands the motivations of the powerless. Such strategies, simple though they are, belong to the novel more than to the *Märchen*, and continue the move towards literariness. The leaps and gaps which Herder noted as being characteristic of the folk ballad, and which are also to be seen in the earlier forms of this tale, are being filled in.

Further Developments

This tendency towards writtenness, already present in the second edition, was perpetuated in all the later 'revised and enlarged' editions. It brought with it greater freedom of invention as well as moralizing by the back-door. Where the true folk-tale is marked by strict conventions, Wilhelm, while still observing them, on occasion allows himself much greater flexibility in scene-setting and additional incident: the snow-white bird in 'Hansel and Gretel', for example, does not fly in until the fifth edition of 1843; 'Snow-White and Rose-Red', added to the third edition of 1837, appears in all but its basic plot to be almost entirely his own composition (see note). He introduces folksy phrases and metaphors he and Dortchen had found and noted down. Above all, what in the true folk-tale would be a bald indication of the expected situation he elaborates with colourful detail: the dwarves' household in 'Snow-White', the attitudes of court and kitchen frozen in a hundred-year sleep in 'Briar-Rose'; the sister's gift of the lilies to the brothers at table and the filling-out of the old woman's role in 'The Twelve Brothers'; the little man's busy whirr-whirring with wheel and bobbin and the piles of gold from straw in 'Rumpelstiltskin'. In this respect the successive changes undergone by 'The Frog King', as the first tale in the collection, make it a kind of manifesto for the genre as Wilhelm came to create it (see Appendix A). Structurally too, he will conflate variants, and even augment oral story-telling by material from a written source, as in 'Godfather Death' (see note), where the addition of the (literary) motif of the candles of life gives the tale a profundity that is greater than mere admonition. Many determinants went into these alterations. Wilhelm grew older; he became the father of a family himself; the editions accompanied him through his lifetime. As Jacob developed into a great grammarian and scholar, his influence on the text of the tales receded. The wider social and intellectual climate changed after the restoration of the princes' power, from adventurous Romanticism to the social conformity of tasteful, domesticated Biedermeier. Lacking political power, the middle classes withdrew to the orderly privacy of the family and to the consolations of culture.

In Wilhelm's hands the collection moved over time from pioneering anthropology to becoming the classic of the bourgeois nursery.

Snow-White's home-making is characteristic of the shift; so is the idyll of 'Snow-White and Rose-Red', the tale that was largely Wilhelm's invention (see note); so is the rustic, but less than idyllic 'Reviewing the Brides' (added in the second edition). Gender roles become more sharply differentiated: brave Gretel of the first edition becomes tearful and dependent upon brother Hansel in the fifth of 1843 (for a fuller discussion, see note). Fables of the established moral and social order are added, such as 'The Unequal Children of Eve' (added in 1843). As part of such conservative domestication, Wilhelm's adaptations also showed an increasing tendency to Christianize even pagan tales. In 'The Seven Ravens', for example, the opening religious cause of the parental curse upon the brothers is both strengthened and sentimentalized by Wilhelm's changes: from the mother's curse on her sons in 1812 for playing cards in church, to the father's curse on them in 1819 for endangering their frail newborn sister's immortal soul by failing to return with the christening water (see note). The cause for his curse is greater, and the curse accordingly more powerful. The growing girl's beauty, the village gossip, and her questions to her parents on hearing it are also added in, to produce their pious reply: 'it was a fate decreed by God.'

The general shift was confirmed in 1825, the year he married, when Wilhelm prepared a one-volume special selection of fifty tales for the young, known as the *Kleine Ausgabe* (Little Edition). He had been encouraged to make it partly by the success of the first English translation by Edgar Taylor, *German Popular Stories* (London, 1823). It was the Little Edition that really defined the work with the reading public and became a best-seller. Its fifty tales are in fact still the best-known.[23] It chiefly includes the tales of enchantment, especially the ones with a happy ending, though there are exceptions: cruel fathers are not excluded (the king in 'The Twelve Brothers'); even so, Snow-White's jealous mother is mitigated into a jealous stepmother, and there is further discreet bowdlerization of detail. Still, 'The Juniper Tree', with its unalterable cannibalism, keeps its place, as does the cruel comedy of 'The Jew in the Thorn Bush'. The

---

[23] In the present selection, the following thirty-four are to be found in the *Kleine Ausgabe*: 1, 3–5, 7–9, 12–14, 16, 18–21, 26, 28, 32–34, 37–8, 41, 44–5, 49–50, 53, 58–9, 63, 68.

punishments for the wicked remain painfully inventive and just—
and Briar-Rose's suitors continue to hang on the thorns. But the
worldly animal fables with a dark outcome have no place.

Wilhelm never really let the tales go. Without ever rewriting quite
as drastically as he did the tales for the second edition, he continued
to 'revise and enlarge' all the later editions, fine-tuning the language,
editing and adding and adjusting, particularly the third edition of
1837 and the fifth of 1843. It was out of such accretions that the
classic text of 1857 was finally made. The text as then established
was the product of many contradictions. There had been from the
first a tension between the aims of scholarship and the 'poesy' which
was its subject-matter and its fabric. The brothers' patriotic focus on
German regional tales went hand in hand with wide-ranging comparative study of the tales of other lands, increasingly so as they
themselves provided a model for collectors of other nations. They
were concerned with oral folk origins, but heard their tales mediated
by literate tellers. They thought in terms of an antithesis between
nature and artifice, but their own gentle practice dissolved the
sharpness of the distinction. They went in search of ancient myth,
but in the figure of Frau Viehmann and the imagined Germany of
her tales, they made their own. Wilhelm's great literary achievement
was to create a genre respectful of the oral tale, but in the end
composed with delicacy and skill for a reading audience. Beginning
as a pioneering rescue operation of peasant lore, the tales became the
mainstay and classic of the bourgeois nursery. But it is in the nature
of a classic that it is not frozen, and will give rise to many re-
readings. 'All true poesy is capable of the most diverse interpretations', wrote Wilhelm[24]—and passed what the brothers had rescued
from a receding past on to the future.

Brief Afterlives

For the English-speaking reader, the long afterlife of the *Tales* began
with the translations, first with the widely read and initially anonymous *German Popular Stories* translated by Edgar Taylor in 1823 and
1826. The grotesque illustrations by George Cruikshank, who later
did the pictures for Dickens's *Oliver Twist*, no doubt contributed to

---

[24] Introduction to vol. I of 2nd edn., 1819: 'Über das Wesen der Märchen' (On the
Nature of *Märchen*), *Kleinere Schriften*, I (Berlin, 1881), 335.

their popularity. 'Popular tales' were transformed into 'Fairy stories' with the selection *The Fairy Ring*, done into English in 1846 by Edward Taylor and prettily illustrated by Richard Doyle, and as such more attractive to a genteel readership. The fate of the tales in Victorian England seemed to replicate their fate in Biedermeier German lands: domesticated and cleaned up for the nursery of the well-brought-up young. Martin Sutton's study of them in translation, *The Sin Complex* . . ., shows that their bowdlerization went even further in English. But, given the confines of daintiness and duty, their figures wore their stays with charm. The youngest daughter in Wehnert's (anonymous) version of 'The Shoes That Were Danced To Tatters' (1853) is skilled in polite conversation. When her prince remarks that his boat seems much heavier than usual (it is also carrying the invisible soldier), her reply is fit for the very best drawing-room: 'It must be because of the warm weather . . . I'm feeling quite warm myself today.'

But the fate of the tales in Germany and English-speaking lands divided. Their afterlife in their own land is another story. The translations became invisible as translations and the tales once more anonymous, with 'Grimm' at best a mysterious name for an indispensable handful out of the two hundred and one. There was a surge of Europe-wide interest at the turn of the nineteenth to twentieth century. On the one hand the Symbolist cultivation of dark fantasy can be seen Walter Crane's decorative art nouveau illustrations to his wife Lucie's selected translations; and on the other, the development of folklore produced Andrew Lang's anthologies of tales from many traditions, *The Red/Blue/Green Fairy Books*, and Margaret Hunt's first complete translation. This was a time when there was also a great growth in literature written expressly for children, both realistic and fanciful. But the stories of J. M. Barrie and A. A. Milne are no longer tales for children *and* the household. The worlds of adult and child are represented as utterly separate. Maturity is problematic, childhood a sheltered idyll. The Edwardian nursery still could not quite accommodate the rites of passage, the dangers of the forest which, despite Wilhelm's efforts, compounded by his translators, were ineradicably present in the Grimms' tales.

However, harmless child literature had found a market and come to stay. Towards mid-century the great technological takeover arrived. Although out of the canonical handful of fairy-tales in general, far more derive from the English tradition and the—equally anonymous and invisible—tradition of Perrault's Mother Goose, the Grimms' 'Snow-White [and the Seven Dwarves]' (see note) was the first to receive the Disney makeover into film (1937), and by extension into marketing and on to Disneyland. Stories which were once popular and widespread have become popular and widespread once again. But the scale and the society have changed: the brothers' 'reverence for small things', and their worry that even Brentano's wit and grace would make their tales longer and flashier, have succumbed to the full-length, wide-screen treatment of the entertainment industry. The Grimms already perceived the way of life bound up with these tales as being in retreat; now their 'seats by the kitchen hearth' have been relocated to the Odeon dark, the new family group is part of a passive mass audience. Image has ousted imagination. The means of re-creating and disseminating a tale are technical, the version is fixed and endlessly reproducible, the rendering coarser to suit the magnified medium, and shallower to reach a global mass market. Oddly, the re-tellers are once again collaborative and—but for the rapidly rolling credits—anonymous, the audience once again worldwide. Disney's talent is for the grotesque: the comic and the scary—in this case shown in the dwarves (their names and personalities a Disney invention) and the wicked queen (a Disney masterstroke); the heroine and her prince are in comparison vapid—empty screens for fantasy-identification with mid-century gender roles, at least for little girls. In these respects, the monstrously transformed nature of the medium had little effect on the naivety of the narration or its reception. Disney did not question the tale. He took it seriously, and so did his audience.

After the Second World War the Grimms and their tales did not escape the deep suspicion felt in English-speaking lands for many aspects of German culture: had the brothers not been the pedagogues of national sadism? But the generation of refugees had brought their German culture with them. The psychoanalyst Bruno Bettelheim, who had fled from Vienna in 1939, published his influential recuperative study, *The Uses of Enchantment: The Meaning and Importance of Fairy Tales* in 1976—indeed, it has been so influential that subsequent critics have scarcely stopped arguing with it. His interpretations of certain tales are based on how he had used them (most of them from Grimm) in his Chicago clinic in the psychoanalytic treatment of troubled children. As the title indicates, his is a therapeutic, not a literary, reading; it starts from the child reader's identification with the hero or heroine of the tale. In line with Freud's aim of turning desperate neurosis into ordinary unhappiness, Bettelheim uses the stories as archetypal models, in whose perilous plots his young patients might come to recognize representations of their own distresses, enabling them to work through to a reassuring resolution and live a normal life in their society. His interpretations assume that the figures and situations in the tales are as absolute in their patterning as, in analytic theory, the anatomy of the human psyche. The figures in the tales are read as the archetypes of the nuclear family: king, queen, oedipal child, rival siblings; the plots variations on the family romance. The fundamental dispute with this psychoanalytic approach is that it has no sense of history or of historical change: in healing his patients, Bettelheim was adapting them to the silent norms of their society; but these are historical, not archetypes dwelling eternally in the human psyche, and so, argued his feminist critics in particular, are changeable and in need of change. Jack Zipes and Marina Warner in their several ways have further argued that treating the figures and their constellations as archetypal excludes any conception of the tales as expressions of external social realities. But since Bettelheim almost everyone writing on fairy-tales, including his critics, have adopted his way of reading them as symbolic externalizations—the debated question is 'of what?'; for our present purposes, it is not his least achievement that he helped to return the Grimms' tales to readability.

The Grimms' bicentenary of 1985–6 gave great impetus to studies of the tales, philological and critical. Not only Bettelheim, but the tales themselves, came in for interrogation in the 1970s and 1980s, both from imaginative writers and, interacting with them, from scholars and critics.[25] These decades saw a great upsurge in vividly

[25] See in particular the items in the Bibliography by Ruth Böttigheimer, Maria Tatar, Marina Warner, and Jack Zipes. Böttigheimer in particular documents how Wilhelm's emendations build up the masculine roles and reduce the feminine. Warner, though dealing primarily with French, and authored, material, delves deep into mythology with an erudition to match the Grimms', and far greater imaginative freedom, to tease out the possible construction of Mother Goose, the teller of fairy-tales, and to interpret the changing social and critical tendencies of the tales themselves. Zipes is largely concerned with locating the tales in their social and historical contexts. Tatar's book is a

imaginative fantasy literature, particularly from the new generation of feminist writers. Its main representative is, of course, Angela Carter, but she is by no means the only one. The canonical tales—more from Perrault than from Grimm—play a central part in her work. Her variants on them are authored fairy-stories for grown-ups, both playful and terrifying, on the one hand reclaiming the tales from their long infantilizing, on the other taking gleeful advantage of their rich symbolic potential, changing the tradition—with liberating and critical effect. She reverses the genre-bound functions of the figures, shuffles the motifs, and upsets the plots, all to transform the patriarchal norms embedded in them (see notes to 'Snow-White' and 'Little Redcap'). At the heart of her rewriting is a refusal to accept the fixed roles and predictable plots of the fairy-tale: the questing male hero, the devouring mother, the curse of Eve's curiosity, silencing and drudgery, the reward of living happily ever after with a rescuing prince—indeed, one of the characteristics of many of the neo-fairy-tales, not just of Carter's, is their will to ask what happened *after* they lived happily ever after. Anne Sexton's seventeen poems in her volume *Transformations* (1971), written in the witty voice of a middle-aged witch, do just that in a sceptical-comic spirit. Conscious reconfiguration of plot and role are characteristic of A. S. Byatt's neo-fairy-tales too, though her view of the potential of story-telling for change is less ambitious and more realistic than Carter's Utopian intent. The story-teller has the power to change the story, but as a means of changing the world, literature is unpredictable and indirect. 'We collect stories and spin stories and mend what we can and investigate what we can't', says—no, not one of the brothers, nor yet Frau Viehmann, though it could have been any of them, but one of Byatt's fictional fiction-spinners.[26] Still, who can measure what changes the brothers' tales have indirectly brought about in the shifting imaginations of countless children across almost two centuries? The figures in the tales have become permanent inhabitants of the adult's psyche, returning with the years and acting as a bridge between the old who remember them and the

major summing up of these positions which never loses sight of Wilhelm's narrative art. All refuse to regard the texts as established and stable, and reject reading the tales as universal psychical archetypes. They deserve a story to themselves.

[26] 'The Story of the Eldest Princess', in *The Djinn in the Nightingale's Eye: Five Fairy Stories* (London, 1994).

young who hear them fresh. Eva Figes,[27] for one, has found in the classic situation of grandmother telling these tales to her small granddaughter a means of recovering and memorializing her personal and historical past in the composition of her own dark versions; to her the tales from her German childhood are the occasion both for bleak subversion and for existential anchorage.

There has to be a postscript. These postmodern neo-fairy-tales are not naive and do not pretend to be. Authored *Märchen* rarely are, certainly not the Romantic *Märchen* of the brothers' contemporaries Tieck and Brentano, which were highly conscious and playful, and against which Wilhelm sought and found his ingenuous narrative tone. Naivety was already problematic under the pressures of modernity, even then. How much more so now, in the disenchanted modes we call postmodern? Where even Disney assumed the audience's naivety, *Shrek* exploits its knowingness, and the audience is complicit. What place can the tales have in this climate? It may be that only the very young can still accept them in good faith—but so can those whose minds are still populated by their figures. The knowing adult still recognizes their imaginative power. The neo-fairy-story does not devalue them, but it needs them as a template; it does not empty them of their significance, but at its best gives them new meaning—a less mysterious meaning perhaps, for their depths have been brought to the surface. But it sees their infantilizing for what it was, and brings them back into the adult world where they once belonged. The rewriting continues.

[27] *Tales of Innocence and Experience: An Exploration* (London, 2003).

NOTE ON THE TEXT

THE text of the tales selected and translated is that of the two volumes of 1857 which were the last published in the brothers' lifetime, that is, of the seventh edition of what, from the third, had become known as the *Grosse Ausgabe* (Large Edition). It was the end-result of a long process of re-editing and rewriting, rearranging, and renumbering, removing for the second edition and—more copiously—adding, through several editions, largely by Wilhelm. (For some account of the process of editorial revision, see the Introduction.) The second edition (1819–22) in particular, but also the third (1837) and the fifth (1843), are the ones that show such heavy revisions, but no edition is entirely untouched, neither in its text nor in its arrangement. To illustrate some of these changes, Appendix A includes the versions of three tales (1, 11, and 41) as they appeared in the first edition (I, 1812); four versions from earlier manuscripts (41 from 1808; 19, 37, and 41 from 1810), and three tales which were present in the first edition but removed from the second (I, 1812: [8, 22, 68]). The tales in the present translation are printed in the same sequence as that of the Grimms' final edition, but as it is a selection only, the numbering is not the same as theirs.

The *Kleine Ausgabe* (Little Edition) of 1825 was Wilhelm's selection of fifty tales, made with a readership of children (and their parents) in view. This edition has come with time to define the 'core' of best-known stories, but by omission and focus it altered the character of the collection as a whole. By including more of the lesser-known tales—short exampla, moralizing fables, comic stories, tall tales, gleanings from written sources—the present selection of eighty-two tales attempts to reflect more closely the overall pattern of the 201 plus ten of the final edition.

In view of the persistent editorial rewriting, an overview of the sequence of editions may be desirable, beginning with an important manuscript selection. As part of the brothers' collaboration with Brentano, on 17 October 1810 they sent him the transcripts of thirty tales they had gathered, most of them still in unworked form. Improbably, the manuscript survived (see Introduction), and, as

Wilhelm destroyed their own materials on publication, it is all the more valuable. It has been impeccably edited by Heinz Rölleke as *Die älteste Märchensammlung der Brüder Grimm: Synopse der handschriftlichen Urfassung von 1810 und der Erstdrucke von 1812*, (Cologny-Genève: Fondation Martin Bodmer, 1975).

1. *Kinder- und Haus-märchen. Gesammelt durch die Brüder Grimm*, 2 vols. (Berlin: in der Realschulbuchhandlung, 1812–15). Vol. I (1812), containing eighty-six tales, begins with the Dedication, 'To Baroness Elisabeth von Arnim for little Johannes Freimund', and a Preface by Wilhelm, followed by 'Some Notes on Children's Lore'; Vol. II (1815) has for its frontispiece the etching of Frau Dorothea Viehmann of Niederzwehrn, entitled *Märchenfrau* (Story-wife), by the Grimms' artist brother Ludwig, a Preface by Wilhelm introducing her, and a further seventy tales. Both volumes have endnotes. About 900 copies were printed; Vol. I sold well, Vol. II only slowly.

2. *Kinder- und Haus-märchen. Gesammelt durch die Brüder Grimm.* Zweite vermehrte und verbesserte Auflage (Second, enlarged and improved edition), 3 vols. (Berlin: G. Reimer, 1819–22). Vol. I (1819), containing tales numbered 1–86, has the Dedication, an extended Preface by Wilhelm, and an Introduction by him 'Über das Wesen der Märchen' (On the Nature of *Märchen*). Vol. II (1819), containing tales numbered 87–161 and with the addition of nine 'Children's Legends', is preceded by Wilhelm's Introduction, which is made up of two compilations from literary and folk sources: 'Kinderwesen und Kindersitten' (Children's Nature and Children's Customs) and 'Kinderlehre' (Children's Lore). Vol. III (1822) is made up of notes to each tale, fragments, a selection of 'Zeugnisse' (Statements) on the folk-tale by other hands, from Luther to Sir Walter Scott, and a survey of other collections and of the current literature on the topic. Fifteen hundred copies were printed, which sold slowly, especially Vol. III. The 1819 Preface, translated for the present volume, was reprinted in subsequent editions, while each has its own short Preface as well.

Kinder- und Hausmärchen. Gesammelt durch die Brüder Grimm. Kleine Ausgabe (Little Edition), (Berlin: G. Reimer, 1825). Fifty tales selected by Wilhelm from the 1819 edition, with further editorial emendations. This is the edition that made the work a public success: ten editions, incorporating the latest revisions, were published in the brothers' lifetime.

3. *Kinder- und Hausmärchen. Gesammelt durch die Brüder Grimm.* Dritte vermehrte und verbesserte Auflage (Third, enlarged and improved edition), Grosse Ausgabe (Large Edition), 2 vols. (Göttingen: Dieterich, 1837). Vol. I contains tales 1–86, Vol. II tales 87–168 and nine 'Children's Legends'.

4. *Kinder[-] und Hausmärchen. Gesammelt durch die Brüder Grimm.* Vierte vermehrte und verbesserte Auflage (Fourth, enlarged and improved edition), Grosse Ausgabe (Large Edition), 2 vols. (Göttingen: Dieterich, 1840). Vol. I contains tales 1–86, Vol. II tales 87–178 and nine 'Children's Legends'.

5. *Kinder[-] und Hausmärchen. Gesammelt durch die Brüder Grimm.* Fünfte, stark vermehrte und verbesserte Auflage (Fifth, much enlarged and improved edition), Grosse Ausgabe (Large Edition), 2 vols. (Göttingen: Dieterich, 1843). Vol. I opens with a new, memorializing, Dedication to 'Lady Bettina von Arnim', and contains tales 1–86; Vol. II contains tales 87–194 and nine 'Children's Legends'.

6. *Kinder[-] und Hausmärchen gesammelt durch die Brüder Grimm.* Sechste vermehrte und verbesserte Auflage (Sixth, enlarged and improved edition), Grosse Aufgabe (Large Edition), 2 vols. (Göttingen: Dieterich, 1850). Vol. I (1850) contains tales 1–86 and a 'Survey of the Literature Since 1822'; Vol. II contains tales 87–200 and ten 'Children's Legends'. There is a third volume (1856) which is more strictly the third edition of the brothers' notes: the first notes appeared as endnotes to the first edition, the second as a separate volume (1822) to the second. The third is made up of vastly expanded notes to each tale, fragments, 'Statements', and a much-enlarged review, headed 'Literature', of old and new collections available, national and international, and on the literature on the subject, ending with Wilhelm's last thoughts on the *Märchen*. An extract from these last pages is translated for the present volume (Appendix D).

7. *Kinder[-] und Hausmärchen gesammelt durch die Brüder Grimm.* Siebente Auflage (Seventh Edition), Grosse Ausgabe (Large Edition), 2 vols. (Göttingen: Dieterich, 1856 and 1857). Vol. I contains tales 1–86, Vol. II tales 87–200 and ten 'Children's Legends'. The text of this edition, as edited by Heinz Rölleke: *Kinder- und Hausmärchen. Ausgabe letzter Hand*, 3 vols. (Stuttgart: Reclam, 1982) (see Bibliography), is used as the basis for the present translation. Rölleke's third volume consists of a facsimile of Vol. III, *Anmerkungen* (Notes)

(1856), which included Wilhelm's '[Survey of the] Literature' (see above). This provides the basis of the translated extract in Appendix C.

Jacob Grimm's *Circular Letter Concerning the Collection of Folk Poesy* (Vienna, 1815), also in Appendix C, is translated from the facsimile edited by Ludwig Deneke (Kassel: Brüder Grimm-Museum, 1968).

NOTE ON THE TRANSLATION

THESE tales must be among the most-translated in the western world, certainly into English: from Edgar Taylor's (anonymous) contemporary *German Popular Stories* (1824–6) to more recent selections by David Luke (1982) and complete collections by Ralph Manheim (1977) and Jack Zipes (1987).[1] But the peculiar thing about the tales is that they have also invited a host of renderings which are scarcely to be called translations in the narrow sense, but versions, retellings, and rewritings, *Nacherzählungen*, as the Germans say, which extend to adaptations—from pantomime and puppets to Carol Ann Duffy's brilliant versions for the theatre—and on to picturing and illustrating—all the way from George Cruikshank, with his Rumpelstiltskin name, who illustrated Taylor's first translation, to Maurice Sendak, not omitting Disney. One reason for this extraordinarily pliable afterlife lies in the brothers' claim that these were oral tales, already told and *re*-told countless times by humble storytellers whose stories carried the last remnants of ancient myths. The tales were themselves already versions, retellings—and, when the brothers first came to write them down, they in their turn were also rewriting, though in their view remaining true to their sources. Indeed, they—or rather Wilhelm, mainly—went on rewriting from edition to edition until the appropriation was complete (see Introduction). One consequence is that the collection seems—though only *seems*—to lack an Authorized Version; for where, and who, is the author? And this gives its readers, including its translators, a quite peculiar freedom to adapt, elaborate, accommodate to prevailing norms of what is suitable for children's ears, modernize, and deconstruct.

Given this glut of retellings, it may be timely to return to the Grimms' own texts and present a translation with no greater claim than to show how they themselves treated the tales, that is, by the time they, or rather Wilhelm, had perfected their own way of

[1] For a full account of the influential early translations into English, see Martin Sutton, *The Sin Complex: A Critical Study of English Versions of the Grimms' Kinder- und Hausmärchen in the Nineteenth Century*, Schriften der Grimm-Gesellschaft, NF, 28 (Kassel, 1996).

presenting them—for indeed, there *is* an authorized version, based on the authority of discovery, recovery, and editorial adaptation. However, even a translation of this kind cannot be transparent, certainly not one coming so late, as I soon found: the tradition of the tales-in-translation imposing itself, for example, in the verse exchange between the queen and her mirror in 'Snow-White' or in the choice of names and titles. Sometimes an English name, such as Snow-White's, is too strong a presence to alter. Sometimes the German name, such as Rumpelstiltskin, is an essential element of the tale and so deeply embedded in our English literary preconscious that it has to be retained. So is Rapunzel's, but her name is more problematic because she is named after a plant—a pretty obscure one. Here its familiar strangeness overrides any temptation to punning ingenuity (though Sutton notes a Violet and even a Lettice!). But what of Cinderella? Proverbial as she is, she has a fairy godmother and a glass slipper; her story and her name belong to Basile and Perrault and pantomime, not to the rewriters of Aschenpüttel, who has a magic tree for mother, helpful birds, and a slipper of gold. The basic story is widely known in countless versions and in many countries, including Scotland, so I picked up a clue from the Grimms' notes and culled their reference to an old Scots dictionary: she has become Ashypet. And I used a current Scots oral model for Allerleirauh and called her Coat o' Skins. Little Redcap I have given back to the Grimms literally.

Rendering the fixed fairy-tale formulae for beginnings and endings required a more consistent strategy. I have not naturalized them to the haunting English conventions of 'Once upon a time . . .', and '. . . and they lived happily ever after', but retained the Grimms' own formula—to German readers equally haunting—of 'Es war einmal . . .' 'There was once . . .' In fact they frequently vary their formulae for both beginnings and endings, though of course the endings all (except the worldly wise animal stories) assure us of happiness.

Many of these tales have a child at the centre, so the old problem of gender arises: the grammatical gender of 'das Kind' in German is neuter, and often the shorter moralities offer no clue as to whether a little boy or a little girl or either is meant. Reluctant to call them 'it', I have just had to decide one way or the other. I have given the first story in 'Tales of Toads and Adders' to a little boy, but I cannot help feeling this is arbitrary. 'The Wilful Child' actually loses by having a gender ascribed to him (? her?). No matter which, this wilful child is any wilful child whose offence—the mother's too—carries on beyond the grave.

The apparent artlessness of these tales brings its own problems. The diction Wilhelm developed is plain, the range of vocabulary narrow, with sudden moments of vivid folksy colouring in little verses, metaphor, and proverb. There are echoes of Luther's biblical language, particularly in the syntax, and some archaisms, which go towards making an effect of long tradition. This homespun texture was not only an aesthetic choice: the tales were meant to be read as *German* tales, old folklore from Hesse and its villages, from the Rhineland, Westphalia, and so on, so the Grimms also, deliberately, came to banish words of foreign, that is, French, origin. Princesses in the first edition were turned into kings' daughters in the second. When Jacob translated 'The Hand with the Knife', the Scottish Highland tale collected by Mrs Anne Grant (see Appendix B), he rendered her 'fairy' by 'Elfe', not 'Fee'. True, he knew that Scottish fairies are stranger beings than the dainty name might suggest, but he was also Germanicizing. In the present translation it has not, on the whole, been too hard to stay with words of Germanic origin—it has actually helped in achieving plainness—except in one crucial literary field: magic! The words for 'fairy' and 'fairy-tale', 'ogre' and 'enchantress', for 'magic' itself, are French in origin and all-pervasive in most English renderings, perhaps witness to the older influence of Perrault's *Contes de ma Mère Oie* (1697) with English readers. But they are words which by now have become too pretti-fied. 'Enchanted', for example, will not do for 'verwünschen', which means 'under a spell', sometimes 'haunted' and even 'accursed'. But for 'Zauberer' and 'Zauberin' I had to break my self-denying ordinance and look to the French words 'sorcerer' and 'sorceress'—certainly not 'enchantress', not for one who could turn herself into night-owl by day! And because the *Märchen* is a wider category than the tale of enchantment we are accustomed to call 'fairy-tale', I have simply called all these stories 'tales', or, where genre is an issue, have adopted the German word (see Introduction, p. xiv, n.1).

Simplicity of treatment is even more marked in the paratactic sentence structure, appropriate to such single-stranded linear narra-tives as these. The reader is carried forward with 'und dann . . . und dann', varied by with 'da geschah es . . . und da kam . . .' with an occasional 'darauf'. But it is an artful simplicity, with fine rhythms and pauses, the outcome of Wilhelm's constant small-scale revisions. Not all the tales, of course, show equally subtle variations of tempo, but in general I found this the most taxing aspect of his prose to get even halfway right, because, slight as it may seem, it is an unobtrusive but crucial factor in every link in the chain of sentences. The tales should sound as if they were once told with the spoken voice, even if that was a long, long time ago; and so, now that they are printed in a book, they should still at least be readable aloud. This may at first look like an argument for a modern retelling, but on a second glance is much the same problem that the brothers themselves had to solve, at one remove. They had to manage the shift from speech to print, keeping the illusion of story-*telling*. I have understood it as one of performable tempo. In translating, this has entailed frequent small changes in sentence-breaks, lots of semi-colons for sentences within sentences—and the discovery that English appears to have fewer resources for natural-sounding parataxis than German. 'And then . . . and then . . .' can become monotonous; 'thereupon' is impossibly archaic. Wilhelm's word-of-all-work, the self-effacing and resourceful 'da', has no exact equivalent in English usage: it is more narrative filler than bearer of meaning. But it does small wonders for the rhythm (as well as being symptomatic of the adult-to-child attitude). Sometimes a 'there', sometimes another 'then', and often 'so' have to do service for it, though the first two carry rather too much weight; and 'so' tends to give speech and actions rather more logical causality than they have in the Grimms' German.

In finding a spoken voice, contractions are a help: I have used them in dialogue to distinguish informal and intimate speech from formal and authoritative: in 'Our Lady's Child', Our Lady commands: 'Do not open the twelfth door', while the girl says to herself: 'Now I'm by myself, I'll peep inside'. The Grimms themselves differentiate between authoritative and ordinary statement by using different verbs: 'Er sprach' and 'sie sagte'. It is a distinction difficult to maintain in English, where both tend to assimilate to 'he said'; I have sometimes (over-)translated the former with 'announced', 'declared', and the like, but sparingly. In the course of the actual narration I have also used contractions where it seemed appropriate to the story-telling moment. For this is story-*telling*, with the potential for performance.[2] Performance too has sometimes determined smaller choices: when in 'The Rose', one of the 'Children's Legends', the mysterious child is described as 'so klein', it is as possible for the spoken stress to fall on '*s-o-o* klein' as on 'so *klein*'— so I translated it as '*that* small' as a cue for a gesture of flat hand just a foot from the ground. Small words, small point.

One group of small words gave me pause: the diminutives Wilhelm is so fond of. True, they sound more exaggerated when spelt out into an additional English word—but there are far too many of them, even for infant pleasure in repetition. The frog wants to eat from his princess's little golden plate with her little spoon and sleep in her little silken bed, and the seven dwarves and the seven swans all have their tiny beds and tiny table-settings of tiny cutlery and crockery. This little tic crept in more and more as the editions became intended more and more for children, or for the nineteenth-century parent coming down to their tiny level. But I set a limit to such tweeness, and though I have kept a lot of 'littles', I have lost a lot too.

One important aspect of the collection is regrettably missing from this translation: a substantial number of the tales appear in dialect, mainly in Low German, but there are also a few from Austria and Switzerland. To do justice to these the translator should try to find an appropriate dialect voice—it will be literary, of course, but the trick is to make it seem natural—but unless he or she can do so successfully, the result will be not so much artificial as false. I know of two such successful versions: Gilbert McKay's Scots versions from Low German and Philip Schofield's Irish versions from Swiss and Austrian German, all to be found in David Luke's fine selection. These are colourful vernaculars where the traditional story-telling voice is still alive and well. I have included only two of the dialect tales, done simply into—I hope—speakable English, the two classics that could not possibly be left out: 'The Fisherman and His Wife', and 'The Tale of the Juniper Tree'. But the salt is lacking.

Appendices A and B include translations of some versions of the tales as they appeared in the early Oelenberg manuscript and in the first edition. I have matched these against the template of the

[2] Brian Alderson has caught this beautifully in his selection *Popular Folk-Tales from Grimm* (London, 1978).

versions in the Grimms' seventh edition, the text I used as the basis
for the main selection, so that—as far as it is possible to do so in
a translation—small verbal alterations, as well as larger ones of
substance, might be visible.

Finally there is the language of the brothers when they are writing
as themselves. Here are the complex syntax and organic metaphors
of scholars who are also Romantics. The prose of Jacob's *Circular
Letter* is crabbed, but businesslike. Wilhelm's Preface of 1819 is
neither. It is couched in the metaphorical language of antiquarian
romanticism; its syntax is complex, but scarcely clear; its abstrac-
tions sonorous and poetically evocative rather than precise. He *has*
an argument, but it is clouded by the 'sweet airs of distance' he
conjures up. In the effort to understand, this translator has been
tempted to clarify and explicate, but often the difficulty lies in knowing exactly what he means in the first place. Both brothers' very open
use of the term *Sage*, which strictly refers to 'things spoken'—tales,
legends, even rumours and gossip; that is, what 'they say'—is usually
rendered by 'legends', but in some cases I have explicated with the
qualifier 'oral'. The German compound noun, too, which leaves the
relations between its elements unspecified, itself demands decisions
that are interpretations. What does Wilhelm mean when he calls the
Tales 'ein Erziehungsbuch'? An educational book in what sense? A
book for parents to bring up children on? A child's primer of reward
and punishment? A stimulus to the imagination? I have opted for
the first. And as for the overall compound title, *Kinder- und
Hausmärchen*: are these tales *for* children or *about* children or *owned
by* children? And what is the relation in meaning and in grammar of
'children' to 'household'? The translating possibilities are either
clumsy or coloured in some way: the present offering, *Grimms' Tales*,
avoids the issue. But at least they are not *fairy*-tales.

SELECT BIBLIOGRAPHY

Primary Sources

THERE is as yet no 'historical-critical' edition of the *Kinder- und Hausmärchen*, though one is planned in the long term by the Brüder Grimm-Gesellschaft as part of the new 'Kasseler Ausgabe' of the brothers' collected works and letters, and a tremendous amount of preparatory work has already been done over the years on a variorum edition by Heinz Rölleke and his seminar at Wuppertal (see below).

Grimm, Jacob, *Circular wegen Aufsammlung der Volkspoesie* (Vienna, 1815); facsimile edn. by Ludwig Deneke (Kassel: Brüder Grimm-Museum, 1968).

—— *Kleinere Schriften* I, ed. K. Müllenhoff (Berlin: Dümmler, 1864). Includes 'Gedanken, wie sich die Sagen zur Poesie und Geschichte verhalten' (Reflections on the relation of legend and epic to poesy and history) (1808), in which he considers the distinction between natural poetry and made poetry.

Grimm, Jacob and Wilhelm, *Die älteste Märchensammlung der Brüder Grimm: Synopse der handschriftlichen Urfassung von 1810 und der Erstdrucke von 1812*, ed. Heinz Rölleke (Cologny-Genève: Fondation Martin Bodmer, 1975). The Oelenberg manuscript versions of the tales.

—— *Kinder- und Hausmärchen. Gesammelt durch die Brüder Grimm*, 2 vols. (Berlin, 1812–15); facsimile edn. by Ursula Marquart and Heinz Rölleke, 2 vols. (Göttingen: Vandenhoek & Ruprecht, 1986). Facsimile of Wilhelm's annotated and revised copy.

—— *Kinder- und Hausmärchen*, 2nd edn., 2 vols. (Berlin, 1819); ed. Heinz Rölleke, 2 vols. (Cologne: Diederichs, 1982).

—— *Kinder und Hausmärchen gesammelt durch die Brüder Grimm*, 3rd edn., 2 vols. (Göttingen, 1837); ed. Heinz Rölleke (Frankfurt a.M: Deutsche Klassiker, 1985). Also includes the Grimms' *Notes* (1822).

—— *Kinder- und Hausmärchen. Ausgabe letzter Hand*, 7th edn., 3 vols. (Göttingen, 1856 and 1857); ed Heinz Rölleke, 3 vols. (Stuttgart: Reclam, 1982). Vol. III contains a facsimile of the Grimms' *Notes*, including Wilhelm's '[Survey of the] Literature' (1856).

—— *Märchen aus dem Nachlass der Brüder Grimm*, ed. Heinz Rölleke (Bonn: Bouvier, 1977).

—— *Die Entwicklung der Kinder- und Hausmärchen der Brüder Grimm seit der Urhandschrift. Nebst einem kritischen Texte der in die Drucke übergangenen Stücke*, ed. Kurt Schmidt (Halle: 1932) (*Hermaea* 11).

Pioneering variorum edition of editorial adaptations made to the tales from the Oelenberg manuscript through the subsequent seven editions.

Grimm, Wilhelm, *Kleinere Schriften* I, ed. G. Hinrichs (Berlin: Dümmler, 1881). Includes the Prefaces to the first and second volumes of the 1st edn. (1812 and 1815), the Preface to the 2nd edn. (1819), translated below, and the Introductions to the first and second volumes of the 2nd edn., respectively: 'Über das Wesen der Märchen' (On the Nature of *Märchen*) and 'Kinderwesen und Kindersitten' (Children's Nature and Children's Customs).

Letters

Grimm, Jacob and Wilhelm, *Briefe der Brüder Grimm an Savigny*, ed. Wilhelm Schoof and Ingeborg Schnack (Berlin, 1953).
—— *Briefwechsel zwischen Jacob und Wilhelm Grimm aus der Jugendzeit,* ed. Wilhelm Schoof, 2nd edn. (Weimar, 1963).

Biographies

Michaelis-Jena, Ruth, *The Brothers Grimm* (London, 1970).
Zipes, Jack, *The Brothers Grimm: From Enchanted Forest to the Modern World* (New York and London, 1988).

General Reference Works

Aarne, Antti and Thompson, Stith, *The Types of the Folktale: A Classification and Bibliography* (Helsinki, 1928).
Bolte, Johannes and Georg Polívka, *Anmerkungen zu den Kinder- und Hausmärchen der Brüder Grimm*, 5 vols. (Leipzig, 1913–32).
Deneke, Ludwig, *Jacob Grimm und sein Bruder Wilhelm* (Stuttgart, 1971) (Sammlung Metzler 100).
Enzyklopädie des Märchens. Handwörterbuch zur historischen und vergleichenden Erzählforschung, ed. Kurt Ranke and others (Berlin and New York, 1971–).
Lüthi, Max, *Märchen*, revised Heinz Rölleke, 8th edn. (Stuttgart, 1991) (Sammlung Metzler 16).
Propp, Vladimir, *Morphology of the Folktale* (London and Austin, Tex., 1968).
Thompson, Stith, *Motif-Index of Folk Literature: A Classification of Narrative Elements in Folktale, Ballads, Myths, Fables, Mediaeval Romances, Exempla, Fabliaux, Jest Books and Local Legends*, 6 vols., 2nd edn. (Copenhagen, 1955–8).
Zipes, Jack, *The Oxford Companion to Fairy Tales* (Oxford, 2000).

Selected Secondary Works

Arnim, Achim von and Clemens Brentano, *Des Knaben Wunderhorn* (1805–8); ed. Heinz Rölleke, 3 vols. (Stuttgart, 1987).

Bettelheim, Bruno, *The Uses of Enchantment: The Meaning and Importance of Fairy Tales* (1976; New York, 1989).

Böttigheimer, Ruth, *Grimms' Bad Girls and Bold Boys: The Moral and Social View of the Tales* (New Haven and London, 1987).

Bruford, A. J. and D. A. MacDonald, *Scottish Traditional Tales* (Edinburgh, 1994).

Byatt, A. S., *The Djinn in the Nightingale's Eye: Five Fairy Stories* (London, 1994).

Carter, Angela, *The Bloody Chamber* (London, 1995).

—— (ed.), *The Virago Book of Fairy Tales* (London, 1991).

Davies, Mererid Puw, *The Tale of Bluebeard in German Literature* (Oxford, 2001).

Dundas, Alan (ed.), *Little Red Riding Hood. A Casebook* (Madison, Wisc., 1989).

Ellis, John, *One Fairy Story Too Many: The Brothers Grimm and Their Tales* (Chicago, 1983).

Figes, Eva, *Tales of Innocence and Experience: An Exploration* (London, 2003).

Gilbert, Sandra M. and Susan Gubar, *The Madwoman in the Attic* (New Haven and London, 1979).

Haase, Donald (ed.), *The Reception of Grimms' Fairy-Tales* (Detroit, 1993).

Jacobs, Joseph (ed.), *English Fairy Tales* (London, 1993). Selection from the original two volumes of 1890 and 1893.

Kamenetsky, Christa, *The Brothers Grimm and Their Critics: Folktales and the Quest for Meaning* (Athens, Ohio, 1992).

Lang, Andrew (ed.), *The Blue Fairy Book* (1889). Further anthologies, *Red*, *Green*, and *Pink*, in 1890, 1892, and 1897.

Murphy, G. Ronald, *The Owl, the Raven, and the Dove: The Religious Meaning of Grimms' Fairy Tales* (Oxford, 2002).

Philip, Neil, *The Cinderella Story* (Harmondsworth, 1989).

Sexton, Anne, 'Transformations' (1971), in *Selected Poems* (London, 1988).

Sutton, Martin, *The Sin Complex: A Critical Study of English Versions of the Grimms' Kinder- und Hausmärchen in the Nineteenth Century*, Schriften der Grimm-Gesellschaft, NF 28 (Kassel, 1996).

Tatar, Maria, *The Hard Facts About the Grimms' Fairy-Tales*, 2nd edn. (Princeton, 2003).

Warner, Marina, *From the Beast to the Blonde: On Fairy Tales and Their Tellers* (London, 1995).

Zipes, Jack, *The Trials and Tribulations of Little Red Riding Hood* (London, 1983).
—— (ed.), *Don't Bet on the Prince* (Aldershot, 1986).

Selected Translations

Most of these are selections: Hunt, Manheim, and Zipes are complete, and the Wehnert edition almost so. For full critical discussion, see Sutton above.

Alderson, Brian (tr.), *Popular Folk-Tales from Grimm* (London, 1978).

Hunt, Margaret (tr. and ed.), *Grimms' Household Tales. With the Author's Notes*, with an Introduction by Andrew Lang, 2 vols. (London, 1884). The first complete translation. It was revised by James Stern (London, 1948) and is still published in this form.

Luke, David (tr.), *Jacob and Wilhelm Grimm: Selected Tales* (Harmondsworth, 1982). Includes dialect versions by Gilbert McKay and Philip Schofield.

Manheim, Ralph (tr.), *Grimms' Tales for Young and Old: The Complete Stories* (London, 1978).

—— *Dear Mili* (Harmondsworth, 1988). Illustrated by Maurice Sendak.

[Taylor, Edgar] (tr.), *German Popular Stories*, 2 vols. (London, 1823–6). Translated in conjunction with 'my friend, Mr. Jardine.' A bestseller, illustrated by George Cruikshank.

—— *Gammer Grethel, or German Fairy Tales and Popular Stories* (London, 1839).

Taylor, John Edward (tr.), *The Fairy Ring, a New Collection of Popular Tales* (London, 1846). Illustrated by Richard Doyle.

[E. H. Wehnert and others] (tr.), *Household Stories*, 2 vols. (London, 1853). Very long-lived, through many editions and publishers.

Zipes, Jack (tr.), *The Complete Fairy Tales of the Brothers Grimm*, 2 vols. (Toronto etc., 1988).

Further Reading in Oxford World's Classics

Aesop, *Aesop's Fables*, trans. Laura Gibbs.

Andersen, Hans Christian, *Fairy Tales*, trans. L. W. Kingsland, ed. Naomi Lewis.

Goethe, J. W. von, *Faust Part One* and *Faust Part Two*, trans. David Luke.

Hoffmann, E. T. A., *The Golden Pot and Other Tales*, trans. Ritchie Robertson.

Pañcatantra, trans. Patrick Olivelle.

A CHRONOLOGY OF THE GRIMM BROTHERS

1785   4 Jan.: Jacob Ludwig Carl Grimm born in Hanau.

1786   24 Feb.: Wilhelm Carl Grimm born in Hanau.

1789   French Revolution.

1792   French occupation of Mainz.

1796   10 Jan.: father dies.

1798   Brothers sent to school in Kassel.

1802   Jacob begins studies of law under Savigny at Marburg.

1803   Wilhelm joins Jacob at Marburg. Acquaintance and beginning of collaboration with Brentano.

1805   Jacob in Paris as Savigny's assistant. Publication of Vol. I of Arnim and Brentano's folk-song collection *Des Knaben Wunderhorn* (*The Boy's Magical Horn*) (Vols. II and III, to which the Grimms contribute, 1808).

1806   Jan.: Jacob employed as secretary to the War Cabinet in Kassel. The brothers begin collecting folk-songs, legends, and tales; Prussia defeated by Napoleon at Jena; Nov.: French occupation of Kassel.

1807   Brothers' first scholarly publications on early German poetry. First two dated tales collected from Gretchen Wild. Publication of Görres's essay *Die teutschen Volks-Bücher* (*German Folk Romances*) and of 2nd edn. of Herder's *Volkslieder* (*Folksongs*) (1st edn. 1778–9), now retitled *Stimmen der Völker* (*Voices of the Peoples*); Aug.: Kingdom of Westphalia set up by Napoleon, with his brother Jérôme as king.

1808   April/May: Jacob writes to Savigny enclosing six tales for Savigny's children. Jacob employed as Jérôme's librarian.

1809   Beginnings of the brothers' systematic project of a history of early 'Poesy', including the collecting of legends and the setting up of an index of motifs.

1810   17 Oct.: The brothers send their manuscript collection of tales to Brentano.

1811   Fire in the palace at Kassel; Jacob saves the library. Publication of Jacob's *Über den altdeutschen Meistergesang* (*On the Old German Mastersong*) and of Wilhelm's translation of *Altdänische Helden-*

lieder, Balladen und Märchen (*Ancient Danish Heroic Songs, Ballads, and Tales*).

1812 Publication of Vol. I of 1st edition of *Tales*. Napoleon in retreat from Moscow.

1813 Napoleon defeated at battle of Leipzig. Russian occupation of Kassel. King of Hanover returns; Feb.: Wilhelm appointed librarian in Kassel; 7 Apr. 1813–4 Sept. 1814: Frau Dorothea Viehmann tells her stories to the brothers; Dec.: Jacob appointed secretary to Hessian Legation; in attendance at allied headquarters in Paris (until June 1814). Publication of periodical *Altdeutsche Wälder* I (*Ancient German Forests*), containing early essays (II, 1815; III, 1816).

1815 Defeat of Napoleon by the allies. Jacob, as secretary to the Hessian Legation, in attendance at Congress of Vienna; circulates his *Letter Concerning the Collection of Folk Poesy*; official duties in Paris. Publication of edition, with Wilhelm's translations, of extracts from Old Icelandic *Eddas*. A.W. Schlegel attacks uncritical antiquarianism of *Altdeutsche Wälder* I. Publication of Vol. II of 1st edition of *Tales*. 17 Nov.: Death of Frau Viehmann (not 1816, as Wilhelm puts it in his footnote to p. 6).

1816 Jacob appointed librarian in Kassel; beginning of 'the thirteen happiest years of my life'. Publication of Vol. I of *Deutsche Sagen* (*German Legends*) (Vol. II 1819).

1819 Constitution established by king of Hanover. Publication of 2nd, much revised edition of Vols. I and II of *Tales*, and of Vol. I of Jacob's *Deutsche Grammatik* (*German Grammar*) (Vol. II, 1825; Vol. III, 1831; Vol. IV, 1837).

1822 Feb.: Wilhelm seriously ill. Publication of *Tales*, Vol. III, as a separate volume of notes.

1825 Wilhelm marries Dorothea Wild. Publication of *Kleine Ausgabe* (Little Edition) of *Tales*.

1830 July: Revolution in France; sporadic uprisings in several German states. Jacob appointed librarian and professor, Wilhelm underlibrarian and later (1835) professor, at Göttingen.

1834 Jacob's edition of the Middle High German beast epic *Reinhart Fuchs* (*Reynard the Fox*) published.

1835 Publication of *Deutsche Mythologie* (*German Mythology*).

1837 Ernst August, duke of Cumberland, becomes king of Hanover, revokes constitution. Protest of the 'Göttingen Seven'. Jacob and Wilhelm dismissed their posts, return to Kassel. Publication of 3rd edition of *Tales* (2 vols.).

1840 Brothers appointed to Prussian Academy of Sciences in Berlin. Publication of 4th edition of *Tales* (2 vols.).

1841 Move to Berlin; beginning of work on the *German Dictionary*.

1843 Publication of 5th edition of *Tales* (2 vols.).

1846 First meeting of Germanists in Frankfurt a.M.

1848 Revolutions in several European countries, including (briefly) the German states and Austria. Establishment of National Preparliament in Frankfurt a.M. with Jacob a delegate. Publication of Jacob's *Geschichte der deutschen Sprache* (*History of the German Language*) (2 vols.).

1850 Wilhelm ill. Publication of 6th edition of *Tales* (2 vols.).

1854 Publication of Vol. I of *Deutsches Wörterbuch* [*German Dictionary*].

1856 Publication of revised Vol. III of notes to the *Tales*.

1857 Publication of 7th, last authorized edition of *Tales* (2 vols.).

1859 16 Dec.: Wilhelm dies.

1863 20 Sept.: Jacob dies.

THE TALES

PREFACE TO THE
SECOND EDITION (1819)

IT is good, we find, when an entire harvest has been beaten down by storm or some other heaven-sent disaster, that beneath lowly hedges and wayside bushes some small corner has still managed to preserve a shelter, and single heads of corn have remained standing. Then, if the sun shines kindly again, they go on growing solitary and unnoticed: the sickle does not cut them down early for storage in great barns, but in late summer, when they have ripened and grown full, the hands of the poor come in search of them, and, laid head to head, carefully bound and more highly prized than are entire sheaves elsewhere, they are borne home, providing nourishment all through the winter and also, it may be, the only seed corn for the future.

That is how it seemed to us when we saw how, of so much that once flourished in times now past, nothing has survived—even the memory of it has been almost entirely lost—except, among the common folk, their songs, a few books, legends, and these innocent household tales. The seats beside the stove, the kitchen hearth, the attic stair, holidays when they were still holy days, pastures and hushed forests—these are the hedges that have sheltered them and handed them on from one age to another.

We were perhaps only just in time to record these tales, for those who should be their keepers are becoming ever fewer. True, those who still do know them commonly know a great deal, for though their listeners may be deserting them, these stories still live on. But the custom itself is declining more and more, as all the secret, homely places in house and garden, which used to endure from grandfather to grandson, give way to the fickleness of an empty ostentation, which is like the smile people give when they refer to these household tales: it looks superior—but costs little. Where they *are* still present, their life is such that no one thinks of asking whether they are good or bad, poetical or too slight for clever persons' taste; folk know them and love them because they take them just as they were given, and take pleasure in them without any reason to. This living custom is so fine and strong—indeed, this too is something poesy has in common with all things imperishable—that one cannot but love it, even against one's other inclinations. Besides, it is easy to see that in the main the custom has persisted only where a livelier openness to poesy or an imagination not yet stifled by the perversities of life was present. In like spirit, we have no wish to glorify these tales, or even to defend them against contrary opinion: their mere existence is sufficient to protect them. What has delighted, moved and instructed us over and over again in so many ways bears its own necessity within itself, and has surely come to us from that eternal spring which bedews all living things; and, even if it be but one single drop caught in the fold of one small leaf, it still shimmers in the first light of dawn.

That is why these works of poetry are suffused within by that purity which makes children seem so marvellous to us, so blessed: they have, so to speak, the same flawless, shining blue eyes[1] which cannot grow any bigger, while their other limbs are still tender, weak, and not yet ready for earthly service. That is why in making our collection we not only wanted to render a service to the history of poesy and mythology, but at the same time it was our aim that the poesy which is alive in them to make its own effect and give delight to whomsoever it may; that is, for it to serve also as a book to bring up children on. For such a book we do not look for that purity which is attained by anxiously filtering out anything that refers to certain conditions and situations that occur every day and are quite impossible to keep hidden—under the illusion that what is possible to do to a printed book can also be done in real life. We look for purity in the truth of an honest story that hides nothing wrong behind its back. At the same time we have carefully removed all expressions not suitable for those of childish years. Nevertheless, if it is still objected that this or that might embarrass parents or strike them as offensive, making them reluctant to put the book directly into their children's hands, their concern may have good cause in individual cases, and then, if so, they can easily make a selection: but by and large—that is, for children of a sound constitution—it is certainly unnecessary. We have no better defence than Nature herself, who made the blossoms and leaves grow in these particular colours and forms; anyone whose individual disposition makes them difficult to stomach cannot

---

[1] Which children grab at so readily (Fischart, *Gargantua* 129b, 131b) and would like to have for themselves. [Footnotes are Wilhelm's own.]

demand that they should therefore be dyed and pruned differently. Or then again: rain and dew fall as a benefit to everything on earth, but anyone who dare not plant his seedlings outside because they are too tender and might be damaged, preferring to sprinkle them with warm water indoors, surely cannot expect the rain and the dew to stay away. But all things natural have the potential to encourage healthy growth, and that should be our aim. Besides, there is not a robust and vigorous book of popular edification that we know of—the Bible first and foremost—which has not roused such scruples to a far greater extent; right and proper use will discover nothing bad in it, but rather, as an apt saying puts it, a testimony of our heart. Children will point at the stars without fear, whereas others, according to popular belief, insult the angels by it.

We have been collecting these tales for some thirteen years. The first volume, which appeared in 1812, contains mostly what we had gathered little by little from oral traditions in Hesse, in the regions around the River Main and Kinzig in the County of Hanau, where we come from. The second volume was finished in 1814 and was put together more quickly, partly because the book itself had made friends who helped it along once they saw what its spirit and intent were, and partly because we were favoured by that luck which may look like accident, but is the familiar friend of persistent and diligent collectors. As soon as one is used to noticing such things they are really to be met with more frequently than is usually thought, and with folk customs and characteristics, sayings and sallies, that is generally the case. We owe the fine Low German tales from the principality of Münster and Paderborn to especial kindness and friendship: the natural intimacy of the dialect as well as the internal coherence of the story are shown here to particular advantage. There, in the regions famed of old for German freedom, are many localities where these legends and tales have been preserved as an almost customary recreation on festival days, and the countryside is still rich in inherited folkways and songs. In places where on the one hand the written word has not yet intruded by importing what is foreign, nor deadened by overloading, and where on the other it has been a safeguard, ensuring that memory does not yet become remiss—altogether among peoples without a significant literature, tradition habitually appears more strongly and clearly as a substitute for it. Accordingly, Lower Saxony too seems to have preserved more than any of the other regions. How much more complete and internally rich a collection would have been possible in Germany in the fifteenth century, or even in the sixteenth in the time of Hans Sachs and Fischart.[1]

However, it was by one of those happy accidents that we made the acquaintance of a peasant woman from the village of Niederzwehrn near Kassel, who told us the most and the best of the tales in the second volume. Frau Viehmann was not much over fifty years old, and still spry. Her features had something steady, sensible, and agreeable about them, and the gaze from her large eyes was clear and sharp.[2] She preserved the old legends firmly in her memory, and said herself that this was a talent not given to everyone, and there were many who were unable to retain anything connectedly. At the same time she told her stories with deliberation, securely, and with a rare liveliness, taking pleasure in them herself, relating them first quite freely, and then, if we wanted, once again slowly, so that with some practice we were able to transcribe what she said. A great deal has been retained word for word in this way and its authenticity is unmistakable. Anyone convinced that tradition is easily corrupted and carelessly preserved, consequently believing it to be the rule that it cannot be long-lived, should have heard how exact she always remained in her story-telling and how zealous she was to be accurate. In repeating a tale she never altered anything in the substance, and would correct a mistake herself at once in mid-flow the moment she noticed it. The attachment to tradition in persons who continue unchanging in the same manner of life is stronger than we, with our fondness for change, are able to understand. That is the very reason why it has within it, preserved in so many forms and usages, a certain affecting intimacy and vigour that other ways of life, which may

---

[1] It is remarkable that among the Gauls it was forbidden to write down their traditional lays, although writing was used for all other affairs. Caesar, who noted this (*De bello Gallico*, VI, 4) believed that they wanted to prevent a reliance upon script from making them become careless about learning and remembering the songs. Thamus too reproves Theuth (in Plato's *Phaedrus*) with the harm that the invention of letters would do to training the memory.

[2] Our brother Ludwig Grimm has etched a very good natural likeness of her which can be had in the collection of his prints (Weigel, Leipzig). The good woman was driven by the war into poverty and misfortune, which charitable folk were able to relieve but not remove. The father of her numerous grandchildren died of a nervous fever, the orphans brought sickness and the greatest distress to her cottage, poor as it already was. She fell ill and died on the 17th of November, 1816.

appear more brilliant on the outside, do not attain so easily. The epic foundation of folk poetry resembles the green that extends in a variety of hues throughout all nature: it satisfies and soothes, without ever wearying.

As well as the tales for the second volume, we received numerous supplements to the first, and better narratives for many that we had been given there, from the same source or from other similar ones. As a land of mountains, lying remote from the great military roads and primarily occupied with agriculture, Hesse has the advantage of being better able to preserve old customs and traditions. A certain gravity, a sound, vigorous, and steadfast cast of mind, which will not go unnoticed by history; even the tall and handsome frame of the men from these regions which were once the true seat of the Chatti tribe, have been preserved in this way, and make their lack of ease and nicety, which one easily notices in contrast to other lands such as Saxony, seem rather an advantage. Then one also feels that these regions—harsher, it is true, but often outstandingly beautiful, just like a certain austerity and frugality in their way of life—belong to the whole nation. Altogether, the folk of Hesse should be counted among the peoples of our fatherland who have more than any held on firmly to their distinctive character through the changes of time, just as they have to their ancient dwelling-places.

We wanted to incorporate what we had so far acquired for our collection in the second edition of the book. That is why the first volume has been almost completely revised, incomplete material supplemented, several tales told more simply and purely; and there will not be many items which do not appear in an improved form. Anything that seemed doubtful—that is, which might have been foreign in origin, or corrupted by additions—was scrutinized once again and then rejected. Instead, their place has been taken by new items, among which we also number some contributions from Austria and German Bohemia, so readers will find many which until now have been quite unknown. Previously we were allotted only a small space for our notes, but with the expanded scope of the book we are now able to give them a third volume to themselves. This has made it possible not only for us to impart what we had reluctantly withheld before, but also for us to provide new material belonging to this section as well, which, we hope, will make the value of these traditional materials to scholarship even clearer.

As to the way in which we have collected these tales, our primary concern has been with faithfulness and truth. For we have added nothing from our own resources; we have not embellished any detail or feature of the story told itself, but rather rendered its content just as we received it. That the expression and the execution of detail should in large part have originated with ourselves goes without saying, but we have tried to keep all the curious and distinctive features we noticed so that in this respect too the collection should preserve the variety of nature. Besides, anyone engaged in similar work will understand that this cannot be called an idle or careless approach; on the contrary, it requires attentiveness and a tact which is only acquired with time to distinguish the simpler, purer, and nevertheless, deep down, the more perfect version from the corrupt one. In cases where narratives varied, if they complemented one another and if there were no inconsistencies to remove in combining them, we have related them as a single story; but if they diverged— and usually in such cases each one had its own peculiar features—we gave preference to the best and reserved the others for the notes. For to us these variations appeared to be more remarkable than they do to those who see in them mere modifications and deformations of an original which once actually existed, when perhaps on the contrary they are only attempts along diverse paths at approaching an archetype which is available, inexhaustible, merely in the mind. Repetitions of single sentences, certain features, and introductory phrases are to be regarded like lines in the epic which recur again and again once the keynote they sound is touched, and are not really to be understood in any other sense.

A distinctive dialect is something we have been happy to keep. If this had been possible everywhere, the story-telling would have gained from it. This is a case where the accomplishments of education, artifice, and eloquence come to nought, and one has the feeling that a refined literary language, however adept it may be at everything else, has become more lucid, more transparent, but also more insipid, and no longer firmly attached to the heart of the matter. It is a pity that the Low Hessian dialect from the neighbourhood of Kassel, being on the borders of the old Saxon and Frankish regions of Hesse, is a loose mixture of Low Saxon and High German, and not to be captured in any purity.

As far as we know there are no other collections of tales along these lines in Germany. Either just a few preserved by chance have been related or they have simply been regarded as raw material for the composition of larger narratives. We declare ourselves outright to be against such adaptations. Certainly there is no doubt that all living feeling for poetry embraces poetic shaping and reshaping, without which a tradition too would be a dead and barren thing— indeed, this is the very reason why every region tells its stories in its own distinctive way, and every teller tells them differently. But there is still a great disparity between this half-unconscious weaving together, which resembles the continuous, quiet growth of plants and is watered by the immediate source of life, and intentional alter- ation, which joins everything together according to caprice—and with glue, at that: this, however, is what we cannot approve. The only line to guide the poet then would be the view, depending on his education, he happened to be taking at the moment; whereas in that natural reshaping, the spirit of the folk prevails in the individual and does not permit any chasing after a particular desire. If one grants that these traditions have a scholarly value—that is, if one concedes that certain structures and attitudes of ancient times are preserved in them—then it goes without saying that this value is almost always destroyed by such adaptations. But poesy does not gain from it either, for where is it really alive but in the place where it touches the soul, where it truly cools and refreshes, or brings warmth and new vigour? But any adaptation of these legends which removes their simplicity, innocence, and unadorned purity wrenches them out of the sphere where they belong and where no one tires of demanding them over and over again. It can happen—and this is the best case— that in exchange the poet may offer a delicacy, an ingenuity, and especially a wittiness which will also draw on the absurdity of the times, and a sensitive depiction of feeling such as would not be too difficult for a cultivated mind nourished by the poesy of all nations; even so, this gift is more for dazzle than for use; it expects to be read or heard just once, for that has become the habit of our time, and so it piles up its attractions and makes them more piquant to serve it. But wit wearies us with repetition, and what has permanence is something tranquil, quiet, and pure. The hand practised in such adaptations is like the girl with the unhappy gift of transforming everything she touched, including food, into gold; in the midst of riches it is powerless to make us eat and drink our fill. Especially where mere imagination is meant to summon up mythology and its images, how bare, inwardly empty, and formless it all looks, despite the finest and strongest of words! By the way, this is only said in opposition to so-called adaptations which are minded to dress up the tales and trick them out more poetically, not against the poet's free interpretation of them for his own poetic compositions which belong entirely to his own times—for who would wish to set boundaries to poesy?

We commend this book to well-disposed hands, thinking as we do so of the power to bless that lies in them, and with the wish that to those who grudge the poor and frugal these crumbs of poesy it may remain entirely hidden.

Kassel, 3 July 1819

1. *The Frog King, or Iron Henry*

In the old days, when wishing still helped, there lived a king whose daughters were all beautiful, but the youngest was so beautiful that the sun itself, which after all has seen so many things, marvelled whenever it shone upon her face. Not far from the king's palace there lay a big, dark forest, and in the forest, beneath an ancient linden tree, there was a well. Now if it was a very hot day, the king's daughter would go out into the forest and sit at the edge of the cool well; and if she was bored, she would take a golden ball, throw it up high, and catch it again; and that was her favourite toy.

Now it happened one day that her golden ball did not fall back into her little hand, raised high to catch it, but bounced past her onto the ground and rolled straight into the water. The king's daughter followed it with her eyes, but the ball disappeared and the well was deep, so deep that you could not see down to the bottom. Then she began to cry, and she cried louder and louder, and was quite inconsolable. And as she was lamenting like this, someone called to her: 'What's the matter, king's daughter? Your wailing is enough to make a stone take pity on you.' She looked round to see where the voice was coming from, when she saw a frog reaching his fat, ugly head out of the water. 'Oh, it's you, old paddle-puddle,' she said. 'I'm crying because my golden ball has fallen into the water.' 'Be quiet and don't cry,' answered the frog. 'I know what to do, but what will you give me if I fetch your toy back up for you again?' 'Whatever you want, frog dear,' she said, 'my clothes, my pearls and jewels, even the golden crown I'm wearing.' The frog replied: 'I don't want your clothes, nor your pearls and jewels, nor your golden crown, but if you will love me and have me for your companion and playfellow, if you will let me sit next to you at your little table, and eat from your little golden plate, and drink from your little goblet, and sleep in your little bed, if you promise me this, I will go down and fetch your golden ball back up for you again.' 'Oh yes,' she said, 'I promise you everything you want, if only you will bring me back my ball.' But she thought: 'What nonsense that silly frog is chattering, sitting in the water with his own kind and croaking; he can't be a companion for any human.'

The frog, once he had her assent, plunged his head beneath the water, sank down, and in a little while came swimming up again; he had the ball in his mouth and threw it onto the grass. The king's daughter was full of joy when she saw her beautiful toy again, picked it up, and leapt away with it. 'Wait, wait,' called the frog, 'take me with you; I can't run like you.' But what good did it do him to croak his 'quawk, quawk' after her as loud as he could? She didn't listen, sped home, and she had soon forgotten the poor frog, who had to clamber back down into his well again.

Next day, just as she had sat down to table with the king and all the courtiers and was eating from her little golden plate, something came crawling splish, splash, splish, splash, up the marble stairs, and when it had reached the top it knocked on the door and called: 'King's daughter, youngest daughter, let me in.' She ran to see who it was outside, but when she opened the door there sat the frog. She slammed the door shut quickly, sat down at the table again, and felt very frightened. The king could see how wildly her heart was beating and said: 'My child, what are you afraid of? Is there a giant perhaps outside the door, wanting to carry you off?' 'No,' she replied, 'it's not a giant, but a nasty frog.' 'What does the frog want of you?' 'Oh father dear, when I was sitting by the well in the forest yesterday my golden ball fell into the water. And because I was crying so much the frog fetched it back up again, and because he kept demanding it, I promised him that he should be my companion. But I never thought that he'd be able to get out of the water. Now he's outside and wants to come in to me.' Meanwhile there came a second knock at the door, and a voice:

> 'King's daughter, youngest daughter,
> Let me in.
> Have you forgotten
> What yesterday you said to me
> By the cool water?
> King's daughter, youngest daughter,
> Let me in.'

Then the king said: 'If you made a promise, then you must keep it; so go and let him in.' She went and opened the door. The frog hopped in, all the time following in her footsteps, right up to her chair. There he sat and called: 'Lift me up to you.' She took her time, until at last the king commanded her to do so. Once the frog was on the chair he wanted to be put on the table, and once he was sitting there he said: 'Now push your little gold plate closer to me so that we can eat together.' She did so, it's true, but it was clear to everyone that she did it very charily. The frog ate with gusto, but as for her, almost every little mouthful stuck in her throat. At last he said: 'I've eaten my fill, and I'm tired. Now carry me up to your bedroom and make your little silken bed, for we shall lie down and sleep.' The king's daughter began to cry and was scared of the clammy frog, for she didn't dare touch him and he was now supposed to sleep in her beautiful clean little bed. But the king grew angry and said: 'If someone helped you when you were in distress, you should not disdain him afterwards.' So she picked him up between finger and thumb, carried him upstairs and put him in a corner. But when she was lying in bed he came crawling to her, saying: 'I'm tired: I want to sleep in comfort, like you. Lift me up, or I'll tell your father.' Then she became really angry, picked him up, and hurled him with all her strength against the wall. 'Now take your rest, you nasty frog.'

But as he fell he was not a frog, but a king's son with beautiful, kind eyes. Now, at her father's command, he was to be her dear companion and husband. Then he told her how he had been put under a spell by a wicked witch, and she alone had the power to deliver him from the well, and tomorrow they would journey together to his kingdom. Then they went to sleep, and next day, when the sun woke them, a carriage drove up drawn by eight white horses. They had white ostrich plumes on their heads, and their harness was chains of gold; at the rear stood the young king's serving-man, Faithful Henry. Faithful Henry had been so grieved when his master had been transformed into a frog that he had three iron bands fastened around his heart, so it should not break in pieces for sorrow and woe. Now, the carriage was to fetch the young king away to his kingdom; Faithful Henry lifted them both inside, took his place at the rear again, and was full of joy at his master's deliverance. And after they had travelled a part of the way the king's son heard a cracking behind him, as if something had snapped. He turned round and called:

'Henry, the carriage is breaking.'
'No, lord, not the carriage.

It is a band from my heart,
Which suffered grief and smart
When you were imprisoned in the well,
When you were a frog beneath the spell.'

Again and yet again a cracking was heard on the way, and each time
the king's son imagined the carriage was breaking, but it was only the
bands bursting from Faithful Henry's heart because his lord had
been delivered and was happy.

2. *Cat and Mouse As Partners*

A CAT once made the acquaintance of a mouse, and spun her such a
tale of the love and friendship she bore her that at last the mouse
agreed to live together with her in one house and share the housekeeping. 'But we must provide for the winter, or else we'll go
hungry,' said the cat. 'You can't risk going out and about, mousie;
you'll fall into a trap, and I don't want that.' So this good advice was
followed, and a pot of lard was purchased. But they didn't know
where to put it. At last, after long reflection, the cat said: 'I don't
know of a single place where it would be better kept than in the
church; no one dares to steal anything from there: let's put it under
the altar, and we won't touch it until we really need it.' So the pot
was safely stowed away. But it wasn't long before the cat began to
hanker after it, so she said to the mouse: 'I wanted to tell you,
mousie: I've been invited by my cousin to be godmother. She has
brought a little son into the world, white with patches of brown, and
I'm to hold him over the font at his christening. Let me go away for
today, and you look after the house by yourself.' 'Yes, of course,'
answered the mouse. 'Do go, for goodness' sake, and if you have
something good to eat, think of me; I'd enjoy a drop of sweet red
christening wine too.' But none of it was true: the cat didn't have a
cousin, and she hadn't been invited to be godmother. She went
straight to the church, stole to the pot of lard, and licked off the skin
of the fat. Then she took a stroll on the town roofs, viewed the lie of
the land, stretched out in the sun, and cleaned her whiskers as she
thought of the pot of lard. It was evening before she came home.
'There you are,' said the mouse. 'I'm sure you've had an enjoyable

day.' 'It went off well,' answered the cat. 'What name did they give the child?' asked the mouse. '*Skinoff*,' said the cat dryly. 'Skinoff!' cried the mouse. 'That's a very strange, peculiar name; is it a family name?' 'What's there to say?' said the cat. 'It's no worse than "Crumb-thief", as your godchildren are called.'

Not long afterwards a craving came over the cat once more. She said to the mouse: 'Do me a kindness and look after the house on your own again; I've been asked to be godmother for a second time, and as the child has a white bib, I can't refuse.' The good mouse agreed; but again the cat stole behind the town wall to the church and ate up half the pot of lard. 'Nothing tastes better', she said, 'than what you eat yourself,' and she was very pleased with her day's work. When she came back the mouse asked: 'Well, what name did they give this child, then?' '*Halfgone*,' answered the cat. 'Halfgone! You don't say! I've never heard that name in all my life. I bet it's not in the calendar.'

Very soon the cat's mouth was watering again for the delicious titbit. 'All good things come in threes,' she said to the mouse. 'I'm to be godmother again; the child is all black, and just has white paws, otherwise not a white hair on its body; that happens only once every few years. You will let me go out, won't you?' 'Skinoff! Halfgone!' answered the mouse. 'They're such curious names, they make me suspicious.' 'You sit there at home in your dark-grey dressing-gown and long pigtail,' said the cat, 'and you get odd ideas. That's what happens when you don't go out in the daytime.' While the cat was away the mouse cleared up and tidied the house, and the greedy cat ate up all the pot of lard. 'You only stop worrying when it's all eaten,' she said to herself. It was night-time before she came back, fat and full up. Straight away the mouse asked what name the child had been given. 'I doubt if you'll like it,' said the cat. 'He's called "*Allgone*".' 'Allgone!' cried the mouse. 'That's the most suspicious name of all. I've never seen it in print before, ever. Allgone! What's that supposed to mean?' She shook her head, curled up, and went to sleep.

From now on no one asked the cat to be godmother any longer, but when winter came and there was nothing more to be foraged for, the mouse thought of their supplies and said: 'Come on, cat, let's go along to our pot of lard, the one we set aside; we'll enjoy that.' 'Right,' said the cat, 'you'll enjoy it as much as if you were to stick your dainty tongue out of the window.' They set off, and when they arrived the lard pot was still in its place all right, but it was empty. 'Oh,' said the mouse, 'now I see what's happened; now it's coming to light; you're a real true friend. You ate it all up while you were being godmother; first the skin off, then half gone, then . . .' 'You'd better be quiet,' cried the cat. 'One word more and I'll eat you up.' 'All gone' was already on the tip of the poor mouse's tongue. It was scarcely out of her mouth when the cat leapt at her, seized her, and gobbled her up. There, you see, that's the way of the world.

3. *Our Lady's Child*

ON the edge of a great forest there lived a woodcutter and his wife. They had only one child, a little girl of three years old. But they were so poor that they no longer had their daily bread and didn't know how they could feed her. One morning the woodcutter went out into the forest to his work, full of cares, and as he was cutting wood, all at once there stood before him a beautiful tall lady, who had a crown of shining stars on her head. She spoke to him: 'I am the Virgin Mary, mother of the Christ-child. You are poor and needy; bring me your child and I will take her with me, be a mother to her, and care for her.' The woodcutter obeyed, fetched his child, and delivered her over to the Virgin Mary, who took her with her up to heaven. All was well for her there. She had cake to eat and sweet milk to drink, and clothes made of gold, and the little angels to play with. Now once, when she was fourteen years old, the Virgin Mary summoned her and said: 'Dear child, I am going on a long journey; take the keys to the thirteen doors of heaven into your keeping; you may open twelve of them and gaze on the splendours within, but the thirteenth, which has this little key, is forbidden to you. Take care that you do not open it, or else misfortune will befall you.' The girl promised to be obedient, and when the Virgin Mary was away she began to view the heavenly dwellings; each day she opened one of the doors until she had gone through all the twelve. In each there was seated an apostle surrounded by a great radiance, and she rejoiced in all the glory and magnificence, and the little angels, who always accompanied her, rejoiced too. Now the forbidden door was the only one left, and she felt a great longing to know what was hidden behind it, and she said to the little angels: 'I won't open it all the way, and I won't go in, but I will unlock it, so that we can see through the crack just a little.' 'Oh no', said the little angels, 'that would be a sin; the Virgin Mary has forbidden it, and it could well become your misfortune.' Then she was silent, but the desire in her heart wasn't silent; rather, it gnawed and pecked at it with a will, and gave her no peace. Once, when the angels had all gone out, she thought: 'Now I'm by myself, and I could peep inside; no one will know if I do.' She picked out the key, and the moment she held it in her hand she put it in the lock too, and the moment she put it in the lock she turned it too. Then the door fell open, and she saw the Trinity seated there, radiant and fiery. She stood for a while and gazed at it all in wonder, then she touched the radiance with her finger just a little, and her finger turned all golden. Straight away she felt a mighty fear, and she slammed the door shut and ran away. Her fear would not leave her, whatever she tried to do, and her heart went on pounding and would not grow still. The gold stayed on her finger too, and wouldn't go away, however much she washed it and wiped it.

Not long afterwards the Virgin Mary returned from her journey. She called the girl to her and asked to have the keys of heaven back. When she handed over the bunch of keys, the Virgin looked her in the eyes and said: 'Haven't you opened the thirteenth door?' 'No,' she answered. Then the Virgin laid her hand on the girl's heart and felt how it pounded and pounded, and she clearly saw that the girl had broken her commandment and had opened the door. Then she said once again: 'Are you sure you haven't opened it?' 'No,' said the girl for the second time. Then the Virgin caught sight of the finger that had turned golden from touching the heavenly fire, and clearly saw that the girl had sinned. She said for the third time: 'Did you not open it?' 'No,' said the girl for the third time. Then the Virgin Mary said: 'You have not obeyed me, and what is more, you have lied. You are no longer worthy to be in heaven.'

Then the girl fell into a deep sleep, and when she woke she was lying on the earth below, in the midst of a wilderness. She wanted to call out, but she was not able to utter a single sound. She leapt up and tried to run away, but wherever she turned she was always stopped short by thick hedges of thorn which she couldn't break through. In the desert where she was confined there stood an old, hollow tree which she had to make her dwelling. So she crawled inside when night came and slept there, and when storms rose and rain fell she found shelter there; but it was a wretched life, and when she thought of how beautiful it had been in heaven and how the angels had played with her, she wept bitterly. Roots and wild woodland berries were her only food, which she gathered from as far around as she could go. In autumn she harvested fallen nuts and leaves and carried them into the hollow. The nuts were her food in winter, and when snow and ice came she crawled like some poor little animal into the leaves so as not to freeze. It wasn't long before her clothes were ragged, and one garment after another fell away from her body. As soon as the sun shone warm again she went outside and sat in front of the tree, and her long hair covered her on all sides like a cloak. Year after year she sat like this, and felt the grief and misery of the world.

Once, when the trees had put on their fresh green again, the king of that land was hunting in the forest and went in pursuit of a deer; and because it had fled into the bushes that enclosed the forest clearing, he got down from his horse, tore the tangled brush apart, and hacked himself a path with his sword. When at last he had pushed his way through, he saw a marvellously beautiful girl sitting under a tree, who sat there covered by her golden hair right down to the tips of her toes. He stood still and gazed at her, full of amazement. Then he spoke to her and said: 'Who are you? Why are you sitting here in this desolate place?' But she gave no answer, for she couldn't open her mouth. Then the king went on to say: 'Will you come with me to my palace?' Then she nodded with her head just a little. The king lifted her up, carried her to his horse, and rode home with her. And when he arrived at the royal palace he had beautiful clothes made for her and gave her everything in abundance. And although she couldn't speak, even so she was fair and gracious, so that he loved her with all his heart, and before long he married her.

After about a year had passed the queen brought a son into the world. Afterwards, at night, when she was lying alone in her bed, the Virgin Mary appeared to her and said: 'If you tell the truth and confess that you unlocked the forbidden door, I will open your mouth and give you back your speech: but if you persist in your sin and stubbornly deny it, I shall take your newborn child away with me.' It was granted to the queen to reply, but she remained obstinate and said: 'No, I did not open the forbidden door,' so the Virgin Mary took the newborn child from her arms and disappeared with him. Next day, when the child was not to be found, it was murmured amongst the people that the queen ate human flesh, and that she had killed her own child. She heard it all, and was not able to utter a word of denial. But the king would not believe it, for he loved her so much.

A year later the queen bore a son once more. And the Virgin Mary came in once more to her at night and said: 'If you confess that you opened the forbidden door, I will give you back your child and loose your tongue. But if you persist in your sin and deny it, I shall take this newborn child away with me as well.' Then the queen again said: 'No, I did not open the forbidden door.' And the Virgin took her child from her arms and went off with him up to heaven. Next morning, when the child had disappeared again, the people said out loud that the queen had devoured him, and the king's counsellors demanded that she should be brought to judgement. But the king loved her so much that he would not believe what was being said, and commanded his counsellors on pain of death not to speak of it again.

The following year the queen bore a beautiful little daughter. The Virgin Mary appeared to her at night for the third time and said: 'Follow me.' She took her by the hand and led her up to heaven and showed her her two elder children, who smiled at her and played with the world orb. As the queen was filled with joy at the sight, the Virgin Mary said: 'Has your heart not softened yet? If you admit that you opened the forbidden door, I will give you back your two little sons.' But the queen answered for the third time: 'No, I did not open the forbidden door.' Then the Virgin let her sink back down to earth, and took her third child from her too.

Next day, when the rumour spread, all the people shouted aloud: 'The queen eats human flesh. She must be condemned.' And the king could no longer refuse his counsellors. She was brought to trial, and because she was unable to answer and defend herself, she was condemned to be burnt alive. Wood was piled together; and as she was tied to a stake and the fire began to burn around her, the hard ice of her pride melted and her heart was moved by remorse, and she thought: 'If I could only confess before I die that I opened the door,' and at that moment she found her voice again and she called out loud: 'Yes, Mary, I did open the door!' At once the heavens began to rain and put out the flames of fire, and a light shone out above her, and the Virgin Mary descended with the two little sons at her side and the newborn daughter in her arms. She spoke kindly to her: 'Whosoever repents of their sin and confesses it is forgiven,' and she gave her the three children, loosed her tongue, and granted her happiness for all her days.

4. *The Tale of the Boy Who Set Out To Learn Fear*

THERE was once a father who had two sons. The elder was clever and sensible and knew the right thing to do in all circumstances, but the younger boy was stupid, and couldn't understand anything nor learn anything. And when folk looked at him, they would say: 'He's going to be a burden to his father!' If there was something that needed doing, it was the elder boy who always had to see to it. But if his father told him to fetch something late in the evening or even at night-time, and his way went past the churchyard or some other shuddery place, he would reply: 'Oh no, father, I won't go that way; it makes my flesh creep!' For he was scared. Or if stories were being told round the fire at evening—the sort that make your hair stand on end—the listeners would sometimes say: 'Oh, it makes my flesh creep!' The youngest son would sit in the corner and listen to what they were saying, but he couldn't grasp what it was supposed to mean: 'They keep on saying: "It makes my flesh creep! It makes my flesh creep!" My flesh doesn't creep: likely it's another of those skills I don't understand.'

Now it so happened that his father once said to him: 'Listen to me, you in the corner, you're getting to be a big, strong boy; you must learn some trade, so that you can earn your keep. Look at the pains your brother takes, but you're just a waste of beef and bread.' 'Oh, father,' he answered, 'I'd be glad to learn something; if I could, I'd like to learn flesh-creeping; I don't understand it at all so far.' The elder boy laughed when he heard that, and thought to himself: 'Heavens above, what an idiot my brother is; he'll be useless all his life long. As the twig is bent, so the tree grows.' His father sighed and answered: 'You'll learn flesh-creeping soon enough, but you won't earn a living by it.'

Not long afterwards the sexton came visiting their house, and the father complained to him about his troubles, telling him how his younger son did so badly at everything, knew nothing, and learnt nothing. 'Think of it: when I asked him how he was going to earn a living, he actually wanted to learn flesh-creeping.' 'If that's all he wants,' answered the sexton, 'he can learn that from me. Just send him to me, and I'll soon knock the corners off him.' The father was content with this, for he thought: 'After all, this will make the boy shape up a bit.' So the sexton took him into his house, and it was his job to ring the bell. After a few days the sexton woke the boy around midnight, told him to get up, and climb the church tower and ring the bell. 'You shall learn what flesh-creeping is all right,' he thought, and went stealthily ahead of the boy. When the boy had reached the top and turned round to grasp the bell-rope, on the stairs opposite the window he saw a figure in white. 'Who's there?' he called, but the figure gave no answer, and didn't move or stir. 'Answer me,' called the boy, 'or be off with you. You've no business to be here at night.' But the sexton remained motionless, so that the boy would believe it was a ghost. The boy called for a second time: 'What do you want here? Say something, if you're an honest fellow, else I'll throw you downstairs.' The sexton thought: 'He doesn't really mean it,' uttered not a sound, and stood there as if he were made of stone. Then the boy shouted at him for a third time, and as that too was in vain, he took a run and kicked the ghost down the stairs, who fell ten steps down and ended up lying in a corner. Then the boy rang the bell, went home, and without saying a word, went to bed and fell fast asleep. The sexton's wife waited a long time for her husband, but there was no sign of his return. In the end she grew fearful, and she woke the boy and asked: 'Do you know where my husband is? He went up the tower ahead of you.' 'No,' answered the boy, 'but there was someone standing on the stairs opposite the window. He wouldn't answer and he wouldn't go away either, so I took him to be a villain and kicked him downstairs. If you go over, you'll see whether it was him. If so, I'm very sorry.' The sexton's wife ran off and found her husband lying in a corner and moaning, with a broken leg.

She carried him down and rushed off screaming to the boy's father. 'Your boy', she cried, 'has brought calamity upon us; he threw my husband downstairs so that he's broken his leg. Get that good-for-nothing out of our house.' The father was horrified, came running up, and gave the boy a good dressing-down: 'What kind of godless tricks are these? The devil must have put the idea into your head.' 'Father,' he answered, 'just listen, I'm innocent. He was standing there in the night like someone who was up to no good. I didn't know who it was, and I told him three times that he should say something or be off.' 'Oh,' said his father, 'you bring me nothing but calamity; out of my sight; I don't want to see you again.' 'Yes, father, I'll be glad to. Just wait until it's day, and then I'll go out and learn flesh-creeping. And then I will have a skill that will keep me fed.' 'Learn what you want,' said his father, 'it's all the same to me. Here are fifty talers. Take them with you out into the wide world and don't tell anyone where you come from or who your father is, for I can only be ashamed of you.' 'Yes, father, as you wish; if you don't expect anything more than that, I can keep that in mind easily.'

Now when day broke, the boy put his fifty talers in his pocket and went out onto the great highway, saying to himself all the time: 'If only my flesh would creep! If only my flesh would creep!' Just then a man came by who overheard the conversation the boy was having with himself, and when they had gone a bit further, so that they could see the gallows, the man said to him: 'Look, that's the tree where seven men have just married the hangman's daughter, and now they're learning to fly. Sit yourself beneath it and wait until night comes. Then you'll learn flesh-creeping all right.' 'If that's all it takes,' answered the boy, 'it's easily done; but if I can learn flesh-creeping so quickly, you shall have my fifty talers. Just come back tomorrow morning and see.' Then the boy went up to the gallows, sat down beneath it, and waited until evening. And because he was cold, he lit a fire. But around midnight the wind was so chill that, in spite of his fire, he couldn't get warm. And when the wind jostled the hanged men against one another, so that they swayed to and fro, he thought: 'You're freezing down here with a fire; how they must be freezing and shivering up there!' And because he was a kind-hearted boy, he leaned the ladder against the gallows, climbed up, unhooked them one by one, and fetched them down, all seven. Then he stoked the fire, blew on it, and sat them around it to warm themselves. But they just sat there without stirring, and the fire caught their clothes. Then he said: 'Take care, else I'll hang you back up again.' But the dead men didn't hear him; they sat there in silence and let their rags go on burning. Then he grew cross and said: 'If you don't look out, I can't do anything for you; I don't want to burn with you,' and he hung them back up in a row. Then he sat down by his fire and went to sleep. Next morning the man came up to him and wanted to have the fifty talers, saying: 'Well, now do you know what flesh-creeping is?' 'No,' he replied, 'where am I supposed to have learnt it? That crew up there haven't opened their mouths, and they were so stupid that they let the few old rags they were wearing catch fire.' The man saw that he wasn't going to win his fifty talers that day, so off he went, saying: 'I've never seen anyone like that before.'

The boy went his way too, and began to talk to himself once again: 'Oh, if only my flesh would creep! Oh, if only my flesh would creep!' A carter who was striding along behind overheard him and asked: 'Who are you?' 'I don't know,' answered the boy. 'Where do you come from?' 'I don't know.' 'Who is your father?' 'I mustn't say.' 'What are you muttering to yourself all the time?' 'Oh,' answered the boy, 'I wanted my flesh to creep, but nobody can teach me.' 'Give over your stupid chatter,' said the carter. 'Come with me, and I'll see about finding a place for you.' The boy went with the carter, and that evening they reached an inn where they meant to stay the night. Then as they were entering the parlour he said once again, out loud: 'If only my flesh would creep! If only my flesh would creep!' The innkeeper, who heard him, laughed and said: 'If that's what you're after, there should be plenty of opportunity here.' 'Hush,' said his wife, 'so many have paid for their curiosity with their lives already. It would be a shame and a pity for his pretty eyes if they weren't to see the light of day again.' But the boy said: 'Even if it is very hard, I really do want to learn it really; after all, that's why I set out.' He gave the innkeeper no peace until he told him that not far away there was a haunted castle where a body could certainly learn what flesh-creeping was. All he had to do was keep watch there for just three nights. The king had promised that whoever dared to risk it might take his daughter for his wife, and the daughter was the most beautiful maiden that the sun had ever shone upon. There were great treasures hidden in the castle too, guarded by evil spirits. The treasures would then be opened, and could make a poor man rich enough. Many had gone in, for sure, but nobody yet had come out again. Next day the boy went before the king and said: 'With your permission, I would like to keep watch for three nights in the haunted castle.' The king gazed at him, and because the boy was to his liking, he said: 'You may ask for three things—but they must be things without life—and you may take them with you into the castle.' So he answered: 'Then I would ask for fire, a turner's bench, and a woodcarver's bench with a knife.'

The king had these things taken to the castle for him by day. When night began to fall the boy went up and lit a bright fire for himself in one room, placed the carver's bench with the knife next to it, and sat on the turner's bench. 'Oh, if only my flesh would creep!' he said. 'But I won't learn it here either.' Towards midnight he was about to stoke up his fire; as he was blowing on the embers, there came a sudden wail from one corner. 'Miau, miau! We're freezing!' 'You fools,' he called, 'what are you wailing for? If you're freezing, come and sit by the fire and warm yourselves.' And just as he'd said this, two huge black cats came with a mighty leap and sat down on either side of him, and looked at him fiercely with their blazing eyes. After a while, when they had warmed themselves, they said: 'Friend, shall we play a game of cards?' 'Why not?' he answered. 'But show me your paws first.' Then they stretched out their claws. 'Aha,' he said, 'what long nails you have! Wait, I must cut them first.' Then he grabbed them by the collars, lifted them onto the carver's bench, and clamped their paws down tight. 'I've been keeping an eye on you,' he said, 'I've lost my appetite for card-playing', then he killed them dead and threw them out into the moat. But when he had sent the two to their rest and was about to sit down by his fire once more, black cats and black dogs on red-hot chains came out from every corner, more and more of them, so that he couldn't get away from them any longer. They roared and screamed horribly, stamped on his fire and pulled it apart, wanting to put it out. He watched calmly for a while, but when it seemed to him to be going too far, he seized his carving-knife and cried: 'Away with you, you riff-raff', and struck out at them in all directions. Some of them leapt away, others he killed dead and threw out into the moat. When he came back he blew on the sparks to stoke up his fire afresh, and warmed himself. As he was sitting there like that, he could no longer keep his eyes open, but the wish for sleep came over him. He looked round and saw a huge bed in the corner. 'That suits me fine,' he said, and lay down on it. But just as he was about to close his eyes the bed began to move of its own accord, and carried him all round the castle. 'That's fine,' he said, 'only do it faster.' So the bed went rolling as if it were being pulled by six horses, in and out of doorways and up and down stairs; all of a sudden, flop, flip, it turned upside down, topsy-turvy, so that it lay on top of him like a mountain. But he threw the covers and pillows into the air, clambered out, and said: 'Climb aboard, anyone else who wants a ride is welcome to it,' lay down by his fire, and slept until day. In the morning the king arrived, and when he saw him lying there on the ground, he thought the ghosts had killed him and that he was dead. 'It's a pity; he was such a handsome boy.' The boy heard him, sat up, and said: 'It hasn't come to that yet.' The king was amazed, but he was very glad, and asked how he had fared. 'Pretty well,' he replied. 'One night has gone by, and the other two will go by as well.' When he returned to the inn, the innkeeper opened his eyes wide. 'I didn't think', he said, 'that I'd set eyes on you alive again; have you learnt what flesh-creeping is now?' 'No,' said the boy, 'it's all been in vain. If only somebody could tell me!'

The second night he went up into the old castle again, and began his same refrain once more: 'Oh, if only my flesh would creep!' As midnight approached a thudding and a banging could be heard, softly at first, but then louder and louder, then it went quiet for a moment, till at last half a man came tumbling down the chimney with a loud shout, falling right in front of him: 'Hey,' he cried, 'you need another half still; one is not enough.' Then the din started up again, roaring and howling, and the other half fell down too. 'Wait a moment,' said the boy, 'I'll just blow the fire up for you.' Once he'd done that and looked round again, the two halves had joined together and a fearsome-looking man was sitting on his seat. 'That wasn't the bargain,' said the boy, 'that's my bench.' The man made to push him off, but the boy wasn't going to put up with that, shoved him heartily away, and sat down on his own seat again. Then still more men fell down the chimney, one after another. They fetched nine dead men's shinbones and two dead men's skulls, set them up, and played a game of skittles. The boy wanted a game too, and asked: 'Listen, can I join in?' 'Yes, if you've got any money.' 'Enough,' he answered, 'but your bowls aren't quite round.' So he took the skulls, put them on the turner's lathe, and turned them until they were round. 'There, now they'll skim more sweetly,' he said. 'Hey, now we'll have fun!' He joined in the game and lost some of his money, but when twelve o'clock struck everything vanished before his eyes. He lay down and went peacefully to sleep. Next morning the king arrived and wanted to find out what had happened. 'How did you fare this time?' he asked. 'I played skittles,' the boy replied, 'and I lost a few farthings.' 'Didn't your flesh creep, then?' 'What's the use?' he said, 'I just had fun. If I only knew what flesh-creeping was!'

On the third night he sat down on his bench once again and said, quite out of humour: 'If only my flesh would creep!' As it was growing late there came six tall men bearing a coffin on a bier. Then he said: 'Oh, that's my close cousin, for sure, who died only a few days ago.' He beckoned with his finger, calling: 'Come here, cousin, come.' They placed the coffin on the ground, but he went up to it and took off the lid: a dead man was lying in it. He felt his face, but it was as cold as ice. 'Just a moment,' he said, 'I'll warm you up a bit,' went to the fire, warmed his hand, and laid it against his face. But the dead man still remained cold. Then he lifted him out of the coffin, sat down by the fire, and took him on his lap, rubbing his arms to set his blood in motion again. When even that was no help, it occurred to him that when two lie together in bed they warm each other, so he took him to bed, covered him up, and lay down at his side. After a while the dead man warmed up too and began to stir. Then the boy said: 'You see, cousin, haven't I warmed you up!' But the dead man rose and cried: 'Now I shall throttle you!' 'What!' he said, 'is that all the thanks I get? Back in your coffin with you this moment', lifted him up, threw him inside, and shut the lid. Then the six men came and bore him away again. 'My flesh just won't creep,' he said. 'I'm not going to learn how to do it here if I stay all my life.'

Then a man entered who was taller than all the others, and who looked terrifying; but he was old and had a long white beard. 'Oh, you miserable rogue,' he cried, 'you shall learn very soon what flesh-creeping is, for you are to die.' 'Not so fast,' replied the boy, 'for if I'm to die, then I must be in at the death too.' 'I'll come and get you,' said the fiend. 'Gently, gently, don't talk so big; I'm as strong as you are, stronger, I expect.' 'We'll see about that,' said the old man. 'If you are stronger than I am, I will let you go; come, let's see.' Then he led him down dark passages to a smithy, took an axe, and with a single blow struck one anvil into the ground. 'I can do better,' said the boy, and went up to the other anvil; the old man stood close by him, wanting to watch, and his white beard hung down. Then the boy seized the axe, split the anvil with one stroke, and trapped the old man's beard in the cleft as he did so. 'Now I've got you,' said the boy, 'now you're the one to die.' Then he seized an iron rod and went for the old man, beating him until he whimpered and begged him to stop, saying he would give him great riches. The boy drew out the axe and let him go. The old man led him back into the castle, and in a cellar showed him three chests full of gold. 'Of these,' he said, 'one is for the poor, the other is for the king, and the third is yours.' Meanwhile it struck twelve, and the spirit vanished, so that the boy was standing in the dark. 'I'll be able to find my way out, though,' he said. He groped about, found his way into the room, and there he fell asleep by his fire. Next morning the king arrived and said: 'Now have you learnt what flesh–creeping is?' 'No,' he answered, 'but what is it? My dead cousin was here, and a man in a beard turned up, who showed me a lot of money down below, but as for flesh–creeping, nobody told me what it is.' Then the king said: 'You have released the castle, and you shall marry my daughter.' 'That's all fine and good,' he replied, 'but I still don't know what flesh–creeping is.'

Then the gold was brought up from the cellar and the wedding was celebrated, but the young king, dearly as he loved his wife, and happy as he was, still kept on saying: 'If only my flesh would creep! If only my flesh would creep!' At last she was vexed at this. Her chambermaid said: 'I'll come to the rescue; he shall learn flesh–creeping all right.' She went out to the brook that flowed through the garden and fetched a whole bucketful of little fishes. At night, when the young king was asleep, his wife was to pull off the coverlet and pour the bucket of cold water with the gudgeons over him, so that the little fish all wriggled on top of him. Then he woke up and cried: 'Oh, my flesh is creeping! My flesh is creeping, wife dear! Yes, now I do know what flesh–creeping is.'

5. *The Wolf and the Seven Little Goats*

THERE was once an old nanny-goat who had seven little goats, and she loved them as a mother loves her children. One day she wanted to go into the forest to forage for food, so she called all seven to her and told them: 'Children, I want to go out into the forest, so be on your guard against the wolf, for if he comes in he'll gobble you up, every last morsel. The villain often pretends to be someone else, but you'll recognize him at once by his hoarse voice and his black feet.' The little goats said: 'Mother dear, we'll take care. You can go away without worrying.' At that the old nanny–goat bleated and set off, reassured.

It wasn't long before someone knocked at the house door and called: 'Open up, children dear, your mother's here and she's brought something back for each of you.' But the little goats could tell from the hoarse voice that it was the wolf. 'We shan't open the door,' they called, 'you're not our mother. She has a sweet high voice, but your voice is hoarse; you're the wolf.' So the wolf went off to the grocer's and bought himself a big piece of chalk: this he ate, and it sweetened his voice. Then he went back, knocked at the house door, and called: 'Open up, children dear, your mother's here and she's brought back something for each of you.' But the wolf had put his black paw in at the window. The children saw it, and called: 'We shan't open the door. Our mother hasn't a black foot like yours: you're the wolf.' So the wolf ran to a baker and said: 'I've hurt my foot. Cover it with dough for me.' And when the baker had wrapped his foot, the wolf ran to the miller and said: 'Sprinkle my paw with white flour.' The miller thought: 'The wolf wants to hoodwink somebody,' and he refused, but the wolf told him: 'If you don't do what I want, I'll eat you up.' Then the miller was afraid, and whitened his paw for him. Oh yes, that's people for you.

Then the villain went up to the house door for the third time, knocked on it, and said: 'Open up children, your dear mother has come home and she's brought something back from the forest for each of you.' The little goats called: 'First show us your paw, so that we can tell if you're our dear mother.' So he put his paw in at the window, and when they saw it was white they believed that everything he said was true, and opened the door. But the creature that came in was the wolf. They were terrified and tried to hide. One of them dived underneath the table, the second into the bed, the third into the stove, the fourth into the kitchen, the fifth into the cupboard, the sixth under the washbasin, the seventh into the case of the grandfather clock. But the wolf found them and made short work of them; he gulped them down his throat, one after the other; he missed only the youngest in the clock-case. When the wolf had gratified his desires he took himself off, lay down beneath a tree out in the green meadow, and fell asleep.

Not long afterwards the old nanny-goat returned home from the forest. Alas, what must she see! The house door stood wide open; table, chairs, and benches were overthrown; the washbasin lay in pieces; coverlet and pillows were pulled off the bed. She hunted for her children, but they were nowhere to be found. Then she called their names one after another, but no one answered. At last, when she reached the youngest, a little voice called: 'Mother dear, I'm hiding in the clock-case.' She brought him out, and he told her that the wolf had come and eaten up all the others. You can just imagine how she wept over her poor children.

At length, in her grief, she went outside, and the little goat ran with her. When she reached the meadow there was the wolf lying by the tree, snoring so much that the boughs trembled. She looked at him hard from all sides, and noticed that in his full belly there was something squirming and wriggling. 'Oh Heavens!' she thought, 'what if my poor children, swallowed for his supper, should still be alive?' So the little goat had to run home and fetch scissors, needle, and thread. Then the mother goat cut the monster's fat belly open, and she had hardly made the first cut before one little goat popped his head out, and as she went on cutting all six bounded out, one after the other, and they were all still alive and hadn't even been harmed, because in his greed the monster had swallowed them whole. What joy there was! They hugged their mother and they all hopped about like a tailor at his wedding. But the old mother goat said: 'Now go and look for big stones; we'll fill this godless beast's belly with them while he's still asleep.' So the seven little goats made haste to drag the stones up to the wolf, and they filled his belly with as many as they could get inside. Then the old nanny-goat sewed him up again as fast as she could, so that he noticed nothing and didn't even stir.

When the wolf had finished sleeping at last he got up on his feet, and because the stones in his stomach had made him so thirsty, he wanted to go down to a well to drink. But as he began to walk there, and moved this way and that, the stones in his belly bumped and rattled against one another. He called out:

> 'What's bumping and jumping
> Around in my belly?
> I thought it was six goats I ate,
> I must be full of stones instead.'

And when he reached the well and leaned over the water, the heavy stones dragged him in and he had to drown miserably. When the seven little goats saw this they came running up, crying: 'The wolf is dead! The wolf is dead!' and danced for joy with their mother all around the well.

6. *Faithful John*

THERE was once an old king who was sick. He thought: 'This will surely be my deathbed where I lie,' and he said: 'Send for Faithful John to come to me.' Faithful John was his dearest servant, and was called by that name because he had served his king so faithfully all his life. When he came up to the bed now, the king said to him: 'John, my most loyal servant, I feel my end is drawing near, and my one concern is for my son: he is still young in years, of an age lacking wisdom, and if you do not promise to instruct him in everything he needs to know, and be a guardian to him, I shall not be able to close my eyes in peace.' To this Faithful John answered: 'I will not desert him and I will serve him faithfully, even if it costs my life.' The old king spoke: 'Then I shall die comforted and at peace.' And he spoke further: 'After my death you are to show him all round the whole palace, all the chambers, halls, and vaults and all the treasures in them; but you are not to show him the last room in the long corridor where the portrait of the Princess of the Golden Roof is hidden. If he catches sight of that picture he will be filled with an ardent love for her, he will fall in a faint, and for her sake he will come into great danger; you must protect him from that.' And when Faithful John had given the old king his hand upon it once more, he fell still, laid his head upon the pillow, and died.

When the old king had been borne to his grave Faithful John told the young king what he had promised his father on his deathbed, saying: 'I will most surely keep my promise and be faithful to you, as I was to him, even if it costs my life.' The period of mourning passed, then Faithful John said to him: 'It is now time for you to view your inheritance: I will show you your father's palace.' So he led him around everywhere, upstairs and down, and showed him all the treasure and the magnificent rooms; only the one room, where the dangerous picture stood, he did not open. But the picture was placed in such a way that when the door was opened you looked straight at it, and it was so splendidly painted that you imagined it lived and breathed and that there was nothing lovelier or more beautiful in the whole world. But the young king noticed that Faithful John always walked past one door, and asked: 'Why do you never unlock this one for me?' 'There is something inside it', he answered, 'which will fill you with terror.' 'I have seen the whole palace so now I also want to know what is in there,' and he went and tried to force the door open. But Faithful John held him back, saying: 'I promised your father before his death that you should not see what is in that room; it could bring great misfortune on you and on me.' 'No,' answered the young king, 'if I don't go in there it will be my certain ruin; I would have no rest, day or night, until I had seen it with my own eyes. Now I shall not move from this spot until you have unlocked the door.'

At this, Faithful John saw that nothing could be done, and with a heavy heart and much sighing he chose the key out of the great bunch he carried. When he had opened the door he stepped in first, thinking he would cover the portrait so that the king wouldn't see it before him; but what was the use? The king stood on tiptoe and looked over his shoulder. And when he saw the maiden's portrait, which was so splendid and shone with gold and precious stones, he fell to the ground in a faint. Faithful John lifted him up and carried him to his bed, thinking anxiously: 'The calamity has happened! Lord, what will come of this!' Then he refreshed the king with wine until he came to himself again. The first words he spoke were: 'Ah, who is in that beautiful picture?' 'That is the Princess of the Golden Roof,' answered Faithful John. The king continued: 'My love for her is so great that if all the leaves on the trees were tongues, they could not express it. I will hazard my life to gain her. You are my most loyal John: you must help me.'

The faithful servant thought hard and long how to set about it, for it was difficult to come into the princess's presence. At last he thought of a way, and he said to the king: 'Everything she has about her is made of gold: tables, chairs, dishes, goblets, bowls, and all the household utensils; in your treasury there are five tons of gold; have one of the goldsmiths in your kingdom fashion it into all manner of vessels and articles, into all manner of birds and small deer and marvellous beasts. That will please her. Let us journey there and try our luck.' The king summoned all his goldsmiths, who had to work day and night until finally the most splendid things were finished. When they were all loaded onto a ship Faithful John put on merchant's clothes, and the king had to do likewise to make himself quite unrecognizable. Then they sailed over the sea, and they sailed until they came to the town where the Princess of the Golden Roof dwelt.

Faithful John bade the king remain behind on the ship and wait for him. 'Perhaps', he said, 'I shall bring the princess back with me, so see to it that everything is in order; put the gold vessels on display and have the whole ship adorned.' Then he put an assortment of the golden articles into his merchant's apron and headed straight for the royal palace. As he entered the palace courtyard there was a beautiful girl standing by the well, who was holding two golden pails and drawing water. And as she was about to carry the shimmering water away, she turned round and saw the strange man and asked who he was. 'I am a merchant,' he answered, opening his apron and letting her see inside. Then she cried: 'Oh, what beautiful golden things!' putting down her pails and gazing at one after another. The girl said: 'The princess must see these—she takes such pleasure in anything made of gold that she'll buy them all from you.' She took him by the hand and led him inside, for she was the chambermaid. When the princess saw his wares, she was delighted, and said: 'They are so beautifully worked that I'll buy them all from you.' But Faithful John said: 'I am only the servant of a rich merchant; what I have here is nothing in comparison with what my master has on his ship—and they are the most cunning and exquisite things that have ever been worked in gold.' She wanted to have them all brought to her, but he said: 'The quantity is so great that it would take several days to display it, and take up so many rooms that your house is not big enough for it all.' At this her curiosity and desire were roused even more, so that at last she said: 'Take me to the ship. I shall go myself and view your master's treasures.'

So Faithful John led her to the ship, and the king, when he set eyes on her, saw that her beauty was even greater than in her picture, and his only thought was that his heart would burst. Now she came aboard the ship and the king led her inside, but Faithful John remained behind with the helmsman and ordered him to cast off. 'Spread all sails, so that the ship flies like a bird in the air.' The king, within, for his part showed her the golden objects one by one, the dishes, goblets, bowls, the birds, the small deer and the marvellous beasts. Many hours passed while she inspected everything, and in her joy she did not notice that the ship was sailing away. After she had viewed the last one, she thanked the merchant and made to go home, but when she came to the side of the ship she saw that it was riding full sail on the high seas, far from land. 'Oh,' she cried in terror, 'I have been deceived. I have been carried off and fallen into a merchant's clutches. I would sooner die!' But the king grasped her by the hand, declaring: 'I am no merchant; I am a king, and no less in birth than you; but it was my uncontrollable love for you that made me carry you off by a ruse. The first time I saw your portrait I fell to the ground in a faint.' When the Princess of the Golden Roof heard that she was reassured, and her heart inclined towards him so that she gladly agreed to be his consort.

But it so happened, while they were sailing on the high seas, that Faithful John, who was sitting forward on the ship and making music, caught sight of three ravens flying along. He stopped playing and listened to what they were saying among themselves, for he could understand their talk very well. One of them called: 'Oh, he is leading the Princess of the Golden Roof home.' 'Yes,' answered the second, 'she is not yet his own.' Said the third: 'She *is* his own, though: she is sitting beside him in the ship.' Then the first began again, calling: 'What good is that to him! When they reach land, a chestnut horse will ride towards him; he will try to leap onto it, and if he does it will gallop away with him up into the air and he will never see his maiden again.' Said the second: 'Is there no way of saving him?' 'Oh yes: if someone else mounts it quickly and takes out the pistol there in the holster and shoots the horse dead, the young king will be saved. But who is there who knows this? And the one who does know, and who tells the king, will turn into stone from his toe to his knee.' Then the second said: 'I know more than that: even if the horse is killed the young king will not keep his bride; when they enter his palace together a ready-stitched wedding shirt will be lying there in a dish, looking as if it were made of gold and silver, but the whole thing is nothing but brimstone and pitch: if he puts it on it will burn him down to the marrow and bone.' Said the third: 'Is there no way of saving him?' 'Oh yes,' answered the second, 'if someone seizes the shirt with gloves on and throws it onto the fire so that it is burnt, the young king will be saved. But what good is that! The one who knows this, and who tells the king, half his body will turn into stone from his knee to his heart.' Then the third said: 'I know more than that: even if the wedding shirt is burnt the young king will still not have his bride for his own: after the wedding, when the dancing begins and the young queen dances, she will suddenly turn pale and fall as if she were dead; and if someone does not lift her up and suck three drops of blood from her right breast and spit them out again, she will die. But if the one who knows this reveals it, his whole body will turn into stone from his crown to his toe.' When the ravens had spoken among themselves they flew on, and Faithful John had understood all they said very well, but from that time onwards he was still and sad. For if he remained silent about what he had heard, misfortune would strike his master; if he revealed it to him, he would have to sacrifice his own life. At last he said to himself: 'I will save my master, even if I should myself be destroyed doing so.'

Now when they landed it happened as the raven had foretold, and a splendid chestnut horse galloped up. 'Fine,' said the king, 'he shall carry me to my castle,' and was about to mount when Faithful John moved in front of him, quickly swung himself into the saddle, drew the gun out of the holster, and shot the horse down. At that the king's other servants, who were not at all well disposed towards Faithful John, cried: 'How shameful, to kill the fine steed that was to carry the king to his castle!' But the king said: 'Silence! Let him be. He is my most loyal John—who knows what good that did?' Then they entered the palace, and there in the hall stood a vessel with the ready-stitched wedding shirt lying in it, looking exactly as if it were made of gold and silver. The young king went up and was about to take hold of it, but Faithful John pushed him away, seized it with gloves on, carried it swiftly to the fire and burned it. The other servants began to grumble again, saying: 'Look, now he's even burning the king's wedding-shirt.' But the young king said: 'Who knows what good that did? Let him be, he is my most loyal John.' Now the wedding was being celebrated. The dancing began, and the bride joined in too. Faithful John was alert, watching her countenance; all at once she turned pale and fell to the ground as if she were dead. Then he leapt towards her hastily, lifted her up, and carried her into a chamber. There he laid her down, knelt, and sucked the three drops of blood from her right breast and spat them out again. At once she breathed again and was restored, but the young king had seen it all and could not understand why Faithful John had done this. He became angry and cried: 'Throw him into prison!' Next morning Faithful John was condemned and led to the gallows. As he was standing aloft, about to be executed, he declared: 'Every man who is to die is permitted to speak one last time before his end. Shall I too have that right?' 'Yes,' answered the king, 'it shall be granted you.' Then Faithful John spoke: 'I have been unjustly condemned and I have always been faithful to you,' and he told how, while at sea, he had heard the ravens' conversation, and how he was compelled to do everything to save his master. Then the king called out: 'Oh, my most faithful John! Mercy! Mercy! Bring him down.' But with the last word he had spoken Faithful John had fallen lifeless, and was a stone.

At this the king and queen were filled with great sorrow, and the king exclaimed: 'Oh, how ill I have rewarded such great loyalty!' And he had the stony image lifted up and placed in his bedchamber, beside his bed. Whenever he looked at it he wept, saying: 'Oh, if only I could bring you back to life, my most loyal John.' Some time passed, and the queen bore twins, two little sons, who flourished and were her great joy. Once, when the queen was in church and the two children were sitting with their father and playing, he looked sorrowfully at the stony figure once again, sighed, and cried: 'Oh, if only I could bring you back to life, my most loyal John.' Then the stone began to speak, saying: 'Yes, you can bring me back to life, if you expend the dearest thing you have to do so.' Then the king cried: 'Everything I have in the world I will sacrifice for you.' The stone spoke on: 'If you chop off the heads of your two children with your own hand, and anoint me with their blood, I shall regain my life.' The king was horrified when he heard that he was supposed to kill his dearest children himself, but thinking of his servant's great loyalty, and that Faithful John had died for him, he drew his sword and with his own hand struck off the children's heads. And when he had anointed the stone with their blood, life returned and Faithful John stood before him once again, hale and strong. He said to the king: 'Your faithfulness shall not go unrewarded,' and he took the heads and put them on the children, anointing the wounds with their blood. At once this made them whole again, and they skipped about and went on playing as if nothing had happened. Now the king was overjoyed, and when he saw the queen coming he hid Faithful John and the children in a big cupboard. When she came in he asked her: 'Did you pray in church?' 'Yes,' she answered, 'but all the time I was thinking of Faithful John and how we brought such misfortune upon him.' Then he said: 'Dear wife, we can restore his life, but it will cost us our two little sons; we have to sacrifice them.' The queen grew pale and her heart was seized with sudden fear, but she said: 'We owe it to him on account of his great loyalty.' He was filled with joy that she thought as he had thought. He went and unlocked the cupboard, and brought out the children and Faithful John, saying: 'God be praised, he is released and we have our little sons back again,' and told her how everything had come about. Then they lived together in happiness until the end of their days.

7. *The Good Bargain*

A COUNTRYMAN once drove his cow to market and sold it for seven talers. On the way home he had to go past a pond, and from far off he could already hear the frogs croaking 'eex, eex, eex, eex'. 'Of course,' he said to himself, 'they don't know what they're croaking about. I sold her for seven, not for six.' As he drew near the water he called out to them: 'Silly creatures, don't you know any better? It was seven talers, not six.' But the frogs persisted with their 'eex, eex, eex'. 'Well, if you don't believe me, I'll count them for you.' And he took the money out of his pocket and counted out the seven talers: twenty-four groschen for every taler. But his reckoning didn't make the frogs change their tune, and once again they called 'eex, eex, eex'. 'Oh well then,' cried the countryman grumpily, 'if you think you know better than I do, count it yourself,' and he threw all the money at them, down into the water. He stood there waiting until they finished counting and brought him back his money, but the frogs persisted in their opinion, went on crying 'eex, eex, eex, eex', and they didn't throw his money back either. He waited for a good while longer, until it was evening and he had to go home. Then he swore at the frogs, crying: 'You paddle-paws, you goggle-eyed fatheads, you've got a big mouth and you can croak till my ears hurt, but you can't count seven talers. Do you think I'm going to stand here until you've finished?'

And off he went. But the frogs still called 'eex, eex, eex' after him, so that he arrived home in a very bad temper.

Some time later he did a deal for another cow. He slaughtered her and worked out that if he sold the meat for a good price, he would make as much money as the two cows were worth—and he'd have the hide into the bargain. Now as he was approaching the town with his meat, there was a whole pack of dogs gathered outside the gate, and at their head a big greyhound. He leapt around the meat, sniffing and barking 'Bow-wow, what now? Bow-wow, what now?' As the dog just wouldn't stop, the countryman said to him: 'Yes, I get the point: you're barking "What now?" because you want some of the meat. I'd get a fine reception if I gave it to you, though.' All the dog replied was 'Bow-wow, what now?' 'Will you promise not to eat it all up and be answerable for your companions there?' 'What now?' said the dog. 'Well, if you persist, I'll leave it with you. I know you quite well, and I know who your master is. But I tell you, in three days I have to have my money, else you'll be in trouble: you can just bring it out to me.' With that he unloaded the meat and turned back for home. The dogs fell on it, barking loudly: 'Bow-wow, what now?' The countryman, hearing it from far off, said to himself: 'Listen to that, now they all want some, but the big dog will be my surety.'

When the three days had gone by the countryman thought cheerfully: 'This evening you'll have your money in your pocket.' But no one turned up to pay him. 'You can't rely on anybody,' he said, and in the end he lost patience and went into town to the butcher and demanded his money. The butcher thought he was joking, but the countryman said: 'I want my money. Didn't the big dog bring you all the meat three days ago from the cow I slaughtered?' At that the butcher turned angry. He reached for a broomstick and drove the countryman out. 'Wait,' said the countryman, 'there is still justice in the world!' and he went to the royal palace and begged for an audience. He was led before the king, who sat there with his daughter and asked what injury had been done him. 'Oh,' he said, 'the frogs and the dogs have robbed me of my own, and the butcher has paid me with a stick,' and he told them at great length what had happened. The king's daughter began to laugh aloud at his story, and the king said to him: 'I cannot give you justice here, but instead you shall have my daughter for your wife: all her life long she has never laughed, except just now at you, and I have promised her to the one who would make her laugh. You may thank God for your good fortune.' 'Oh,' answered the countryman, 'I certainly don't want her. I have my one and only wife at home, and she is too many for me: when I go home, it's as if I had one standing in every corner.' Then the king grew angry and said: 'You're a lout.' 'Oh, my Lord King,' replied the countryman, 'what do you expect from an ass but hee-haw!' 'Wait,' said the king, 'you shall have another reward. Be off with you now, but come back in three days and you shall be paid five hundred in full.'

When the countryman came outside the door, the sentry said to him: 'You made the king's daughter laugh. You'll have got something pretty good for that.' 'Yes, that's what I think,' answered the countryman, 'I'm going to get five hundred.' 'Listen,' said the soldier, 'give me some. You won't know what to do with all that money.' 'Because it's you,' said the countryman, 'you shall have two hundred. Come before the king in three days' time and have them pay it to you.' A Jew, who was standing nearby and had overheard the conversation, ran after the countryman and caught him by the coat, saying: 'God's miracle, are you a lucky man! I'll exchange it for you; I'll change it into small coin for you; what do you want with those talers in hard cash?' 'Jew,' said the countryman, 'there are still three hundred you can have. Give them to me right now in small change, and in three days' time you'll have them paid by the king.' The Jew was delighted with his profitable little deal and brought the countryman the sum in bad currency: three groschen in this coin were worth the same as two good ones. When three days had passed, the countryman, as commanded, went before the king. 'Take off his coat,' the king ordered, 'he shall have his five hundred.' 'Oh,' said the countryman, 'they don't belong to me any longer; I gave two hundred away to the sentry; and the Jew has exchanged three hundred for me, so by rights nothing is due to me at all.' Meanwhile the soldier and the Jew came in, demanding the share they had got out of the countryman. And they received the blows in the right quantities. The soldier bore them patiently, for he had already had a taste of them. But the Jew moaned and groaned: 'Oy weh, is this the hard cash?' But the king couldn't help laughing at the countryman. All his anger had vanished, and he said: 'Because you lost your reward even before it was handed out to you, I'll give you something in its place. Go into my treasury and take as much money as you want.' The countryman didn't need to be told twice, and he filled his vast pockets with as much as they could take. After that he went to the tavern and counted over his money. The Jew had stolen after him and heard how he growled to himself: 'Now that rogue of a king has still played a trick on me. If he'd given me the money himself, I'd know what I had, but how can I know if it's right when I just filled my pockets regardless!' 'God forbid', said the Jew to himself, 'he's speaking disrespectfully of our lord. I'll run and inform on him; then I'll get a reward and he'll be punished into the bargain.' When the king heard what the countryman had been saying, he fell into a rage and ordered the Jew to go and bring the sinner before him. The Jew ran to the countryman: 'You must come to our lord the king this minute, just as you are.' 'I know what's proper better than that,' answered the countryman. 'First I'll have a new coat made; do you think a man with so much money in his pocket should present himself in this ragged old coat?' When the Jew saw that without another coat the countryman was not to be moved, and because he was afraid that if the king's rage evaporated he would be without his reward and the countryman without his punishment, he said: 'For sheer friendship I will lend you a fine coat just for that short time. What doesn't a man do for love!' The countryman was content, put on the coat the Jew had offered, and went along with him. The king charged the countryman with the wicked remarks the Jew had reported. 'Oh,' said the countryman, 'what a Jew says is always a lie; he never lets a word of truth leave his mouth. That fellow there is capable of saying that I'm wearing his coat.' 'What do you mean?' cried the Jew. 'Isn't the coat mine? Didn't I lend it to you out of sheer friendship so that you could come before our lord the king?' When the king heard this he said: 'The Jew has certainly deceived one of us: either me or the countryman,' and he had the Jew paid a little more in hard cash. But the countryman went home with the good coat and the good money in his pocket and said: 'This time I made it!'

8. *The Twelve Brothers*

THERE was once a king and a queen who lived at peace with each other. They had twelve children—but they were all boys. The king then told his wife: 'If the thirteenth child you bring into the world is a girl, the twelve boys shall die, so that her wealth shall be great and the kingdom be hers alone.' And indeed he had twelve coffins made, already filled with wood-shavings, and in each there lay a pillow for the dead. He had them taken to a locked chamber, then he gave the queen the key and commanded her never to speak of it to anyone.

But the mother sat the whole day grieving, so that her smallest son, who was always with her and whom she had called Benjamin, according to the Bible, said to her: 'Mother dear, why are you so sad?' 'Dearest child,' she answered, 'I may not tell you.' But he gave her no peace until she went and unlocked the chamber and showed him the twelve caskets already filled with wood-shavings. Then she said: 'Benjamin, my dearest, your father has had these coffins made for you and your eleven brothers, for if I bring a girl into the world you are all of you to be killed and buried in them.' And as she was weeping while she was saying this, her son comforted her, saying: 'Don't cry, mother dear, we'll take care of ourselves and we'll go away.' But she said: 'Go with your eleven brothers out into the forest. Always have one of you sit in the tallest tree to be found. Keep watch and look out towards the tower here in the castle. If I bear a little son I will raise a white flag; if I bear a little daughter I will raise a red flag, and then you must flee away as fast as you can—and the good Lord protect you. I will rise every night and pray for you: in winter that you have a fire to warm you, in summer that you do not pine away in the heat.'

So, after she had blessed her sons, they went out into the forest. One after another they kept watch, sitting up in the tallest oak and looking out towards the tower. After eleven days had gone by and it was Benjamin's turn, he saw that a flag was being raised. But it wasn't the white flag—it was the red flag of blood, which signalled that they were all meant to die. When the brothers heard this they grew angry, and said: 'Are we supposed to suffer death on account of a girl! We swear that we shall take our revenge: wherever we find a girl, her red blood shall flow.'

At that they went deeper into the forest, and in its midst, where it was darkest, they found a little cottage lying empty, which had been put under a spell. So they said: 'Let us live here, and you, Benjamin, you are the youngest and weakest, you shall stay at home and keep house. The rest of us will go out and look for food.' Then they took off into the forest and shot hare and wild deer, birds and doves, and whatever there was to eat; they brought these to Benjamin, who had to prepare them so that they could stay their hunger. For ten years they lived together in the little house, and time passed swiftly for them.

The little daughter their mother, the queen, had borne was a grown girl by now, kind of heart and fair of face, and she had a golden star upon her brow. Once, on a big washday, she saw twelve boys' shirts among the washing and asked her mother: 'Who do these twelve shirts belong to? They're much too small for father, surely?' Then her mother answered with heavy heart: 'My dear, they belong to your twelve brothers.' Said the girl: 'Where are my twelve brothers? This is the first time I've heard of them.' Her mother answered: 'Heaven knows where they are; they are wandering about the world.' Then she took the girl and unlocked the chamber for her and showed her the twelve coffins with the wood-shavings and the pillows for the dead. 'These coffins', she said, 'were meant for your brothers, but they went away secretly before you were born.' And she told her everything that had happened. Then the girl said: 'Mother dear, do not weep. I will go and look for my brothers.'

So she took the twelve shirts and went straight away out into the great forest. She walked the whole day, and in the evening she came to the little house bound by the spell. She walked inside and discovered a young boy, who asked: 'Where have you come from, and where are you going?' and was amazed that she was so beautiful, with royal garments and a star upon her brow. So she answered: 'I am a king's daughter, and I am looking for my twelve brothers, and I will go as far as the sky is blue until I find them.' And she also showed him the twelve shirts that belonged to them. Then Benjamin saw that she was his sister, and said: 'I am Benjamin, your youngest brother.' And she began to weep for joy, and Benjamin too, and they kissed and hugged each other most lovingly. Afterwards he said: 'Sister dear, there is still one difficulty. We have agreed that any girl we encounter is to die, because it was on account of a girl that we were forced to leave our kingdom.' Then she said: 'I will gladly die, if that is how I can save my twelve brothers.' 'No,' he said, 'you shan't die. Hide under this tub until my eleven brothers come back. I will sort things out with them.' That is what she did, and as night fell the others came in from hunting, and their meal was ready for them. As they were sitting at table and eating, they asked: 'What's the news?' Said Benjamin: 'Don't you have any?' 'No,' they answered.

He went on: 'You have been out in the forest and I have stayed at home, but I still know more than you.' 'Then tell us,' they cried. He answered: 'Then promise me in return that the first girl we encounter shall not be killed.' 'Yes,' they all cried, 'she shall have mercy. Just tell us.' So he told them: 'Our sister is here.' And he lifted the tub and the king's daughter came out in her royal garments with the golden star upon her brow, and she was so beautiful, and so tender, and so delicate. They all rejoiced, flung their arms around her neck, and loved her with all their hearts.

Now she stayed at home with Benjamin and helped him with the chores. The eleven took off into the forest, caught game, deer, birds, and doves to eat, and Benjamin and their sister got them ready for the table. She gathered wood for cooking and herbs for vegetables, and put the pans on the fire so that the meal was always ready when the eleven came home. She kept the little house in order in other ways too, and made the beds neat and clean with white sheets, and all the time the brothers were content and lived with her in great harmony.

On one occasion the two at home had prepared a fine meal, and when they were all together they sat down and ate and drank and were full of happiness. But there was a little garden belonging to the cottage bound by the spell with twelve lily-flowers (that some call student-lilies) growing in it. The sister wanted to give her brothers a treat, so she picked the twelve flowers, meaning to give one to each of them at their meal as a present. But as she was picking the flowers, at that very same moment the twelve brothers turned into twelve ravens and flew away over the forest, and the house together with the garden vanished as well. Now the poor girl was alone in the wild forest, and as she looked around there stood an old woman next to her, who said: 'My child, what have you done? Why didn't you leave the twelve white flowers growing where they were? They were your brothers, and now they have been turned into ravens for ever.' In tears, the girl said: 'Is there no way of saving them?' 'No,' said the old woman, 'there is no remedy in the whole world but one, but that is so hard that you will not be able to save them with it, for you must be silent for seven years. You may not speak, nor laugh, and if you utter a single word, and there is only one hour of the seven years left to run, it will all be in vain, and your brothers will be killed by that one word.'

So the girl vowed within her heart: 'I know for sure that I shall save my brothers.' So she went and sought out a tall tree, sat high up in it with her spinning, and neither spoke nor laughed. Now it happened that a king was hunting in the forest. He had a big greyhound, who ran up to the tree where the girl was sitting, bounded around it, and barked and bayed up at her. Then the king came along and saw the fair king's daughter with the star upon her brow, and he was so enraptured by her beauty that he called up to her, asking if she would be his consort. She made no reply, but gave a little nod with her head. So he climbed the tree himself and carried her down, set her on his horse, and led her home. Then their wedding was celebrated with great splendour and rejoicing; but the bride neither spoke nor laughed. When they had been living together happily for a few years, the king's mother, who was a wicked woman, began to slander the young queen, saying to the king: 'That's a common beggar-girl you've brought home; who knows what godless tricks she's up to in secret! Even if she is dumb and can't speak, she could laugh once in a while, but those who do not laugh have a bad conscience.' At first the king didn't want to believe her, but the old woman carried on for so long, and accused her of so many wicked things, that at last the king allowed himself to be persuaded and condemned her to death.

Now a great fire was lit in the courtyard, where she was to be burned. The king stood at the window above and watched with eyes full of tears, because he still loved her so much. And just as she was already bound to the stake, and the fire was licking at her clothes with its red tongues, the very last moment of the seven years was up. Then a whirring was heard in the air and twelve ravens came flying and sank to the ground; and as they touched the earth they were her twelve brothers, whom she had saved. They scattered the fire, put out the flames, set their dear sister free, and kissed her and hugged her. But now that she could open her mouth and speak, she told the king why she had been silent and had never laughed. The king rejoiced when he heard that she was innocent, and now they all lived together in harmony until the day they died. The wicked stepmother was brought to judgement, put in a barrel filled with boiling oil and poisonous snakes, and died a terrible death.

9. *The Pack of No-good, Low-life Ruffians*

COCK said to Hen: 'Now is the time when the nuts are growing ripe. Let's go up the mountain together and eat our fill before the squirrel carries them all off.' 'Yes,' answered Hen, 'let's go and have a good time together.' So off they went, the two of them, to the mountain, and as it was a bright day they stayed on until evening. Now I don't know whether it was because they'd got fat with eating so much, or whether they were getting above themselves, but, to put it in a nut- shell, they didn't want to walk home on foot, and Cock had to build a little cart out of nutshells. When he'd finished, Hen sat inside and said to Cock: 'Now you can get between the shafts.' 'You're a fine one,' said Cock. 'I'd rather walk home than be put between the shafts. No, that wasn't the bargain. I'll be coachman all right, and sit on the box, but pull it myself? Not me.'

While they were arguing like this, a duck came quacking by: 'You thieves, who told you to go to my nut-mountain? Just wait, you'll catch it!' And she went for the cockerel with open beak. But Cock was just as quick off the mark and laid into the duck good and proper; at last he hacked her about with his spurs so fiercely that she begged for mercy, and was glad to be put between the shafts before the cart as a punishment. Cock sat on the box as coachman and then they went galloping away. 'Duck, race as fast as you can!' When they had gone part of the way they met a pin and a needle going on foot. These called 'Stop! Stop!', saying it would soon be as dark as stitch, and they couldn't go a step further, and the road was so muddy, mightn't they ride in the cart for a little. They'd been staying at the tailor's hostel outside the town gate and had lingered over a beer. As they were very thin and didn't take up much room, Cock let them both get in, but they had to promise not to tread on his toes, nor on Hen's neither. Late that evening they came to an inn, and because they didn't want to drive any further at night, and the duck wasn't too steady on her feet, waddling from one side to the other, they went in to ask for a bed. At first the host raised all sorts of objections: the house was full already, or at least was expected to be; probably he thought they weren't grand enough to be his guests. But at last they persuaded him with sweet talk, promised him he could have the egg Hen had laid on the way, and that he could keep the duck, so at last he agreed that they could stay the night. Then they ordered a fine meal and really lived it up. Early next morning, as dawn was breaking and everyone was still asleep, Cock woke Hen, fetched the egg, pecked it open, and they polished it off together, throwing the shell onto the fire. Then they went up to the needle, who was still asleep, grabbed her by the head, and stuck her in the cushion on the innkeeper's chair; as for the pin, they stuck her in his hand towel. Finally, without more ado they flew up and off, over the heath and far away. The duck, who preferred sleeping in the open air and had stayed out in the yard, heard them whirring off, and cheered up. She found a brook and swam away down the stream, which was much faster than pulling the cart. It wasn't until a few hours later that the innkeeper got up from his bed. He washed and went to dry himself on his towel, but the pin scratched him on the face and made a red mark from one ear to the other. After that he went into the kitchen and was about to light his pipe, but as he drew near the hearth the eggshells spat up into his eye. 'Everything's aiming for my head this morning,' he said, and lowered himself in vexation into his easy chair. But he promptly leapt up again, crying 'Ouch!'—for the needle had pricked him even harder, and not in his head. Now he was really very angry, and suspected the guests who had arrived so late yesterday evening; but when he went to look for them, they were gone. Then he made an oath that he would never again take a pack of low-life ruffians into his inn, who would eat his pantry empty, pay not a penny, and on top of that, by way of thanks, get up to all sorts of no good.

10. *Little Brother and Little Sister*

LITTLE BROTHER took his Little Sister by the hand and said: 'Ever since our mother died, we have not had one good hour; our step-mother beats us every day, and when we go to her she kicks us away. The hard leftover crusts of bread are our food, and the little dog under the table is better off than we are: at least she sometimes throws him a tasty bite to eat. God have mercy, if only our mother

knew! Come, let us go out into the wide world together.' They
walked for the whole day over meadows, fields, and stones, and when
it rained Little Sister said: 'God and our hearts are weeping
together.' In the evening they came to a great forest, and they were so
weary from grief, hunger, and the long way they had come that they
sat down in a hollow tree and fell asleep.

Next morning, when they woke up, the sun was already standing
high in the sky, hot and shining into the tree. Then Little Brother
said: 'Little Sister, I'm thirsty. If I knew where there was a little
brook, I'd go and drink from it. I think I heard one murmuring.'
Little Brother stood up, took Little Sister by the hand, and they went
in search of the brook. But their wicked stepmother was a witch, and
of course she had seen how the two children had run away. She had
stolen after them secretly, as witches steal, and had put a spell on all
the brooks in the forest. Now, when they found a little brook leaping
and twinkling over the pebbles, Little Brother wanted to drink from
it. But Little Sister heard what it was murmuring: 'Whoever drinks
from me will turn into a tiger; whoever drinks from me will turn into
a tiger.' So Little Sister cried: 'Please, Little Brother, don't drink. If
you do, you'll turn into a wild beast and tear me to pieces.' Little
Brother didn't drink, although he was so thirsty. He said: 'I'll wait
until the next stream.' When they came to the second little brook,
Little Sister heard what this was saying too: 'Whoever drinks from
me will turn into a wolf; whoever drinks from me will turn into a
wolf.' So Little Sister cried: 'Little Brother, please don't drink; if
you do, you'll turn into a wolf and you'll eat me.' Little Brother
didn't drink, and said: 'I'll wait until we come to the next stream, but
then I must drink, whatever you say—I'm much too thirsty.' And
when they came to the third little brook, Little Sister heard what it
was murmuring: 'Whoever drinks from me will turn into a deer;
whoever drinks from me will turn into a deer.' 'Oh, Little Brother,
please don't drink. If you do, you'll turn into a deer and you'll run
away from me.' But straight away Little Brother had knelt down by
the stream, bent over, and drunk the water, and as the first drops
touched his lips, there he lay in the shape of a roe deer fawn.

Now Little Sister wept over her poor spellbound brother, and the
little roe deer wept too, and sat so sadly by her side. Then at last the
girl said: 'Don't cry, fawn dear, I'll never leave you.' Then she undid
her golden garter and tied it round the roe-deer's neck, and picked

some rushes and plaited them into a soft rope. She tied it to the little animal and led it further, going deeper and deeper into the forest. And after they had been walking for a long, long time, at last they came to a little house. The girl looked inside, and as it was empty she thought: 'We'll be able to stay and live here.' Then she went in search of leaves and moss to make a soft bed for the fawn, and every morning she went out and gathered roots and berries and nuts. And for the little roe she brought tender grass, which he ate from her hand, gambolling happily before her. In the evenings, when Little Sister was tired and had said her prayers, she would lay her head on the young fawn's back, which was her pillow, where she would fall gently asleep. And if Little Brother had only had his human form, it would have been a wonderful life for them.

For some time they were alone like this in the wilderness. But it came about that the king of the land held a great hunt in the forest. Then the blowing of the horns, the baying of the dogs, and the cheerful shouts of the huntsmen sounded through the trees, and the little roe-deer heard them and would so much have loved to join in. 'Oh,' he said to Little Sister, 'let me out for the hunt, I can't stand it any longer,' and he begged for so long that she gave in. 'But', she said to him, 'mind you come back to me in the evening. I shall lock my door against the wild huntsmen, and so that I'll know it's you, knock and say: "Sister mine, let me in." And if you don't say that, I shan't open my door.' Then the roe leapt out, and he felt so happy and joyful in the open air. The king and his huntsmen saw the fine creature and set off after him, but they couldn't catch up with him, and when they thought they had caught him for sure, away he leapt over the bushes and vanished. When it was dark he ran to the little house, knocked, and said: 'Sister mine, let me in.' Then the little door was opened to him, in he bounded, and took his rest on his soft bed the whole night through. Next morning the hunt began afresh, and when the little roe-deer heard the bugle-horn and the huntsmen's 'Halloo' again, he grew restless and said: 'Little Sister, open the door for me, I must go out.' His sister opened the door for him and said: 'But you must be back here by evening and say your little verse.' When the king and his huntsmen saw the roe-deer with the golden collar again, they all chased after him, but he was too fast and nimble for them. That went on for the whole day, but that evening the huntsmen surrounded him at last and one of them wounded him lightly in the foot, so that he couldn't help limping and ran away slowly. Then a huntsman stole after him as far as the little house and heard him calling: 'Sister mine, let me in,' and saw that the door was opened for him and then promptly closed. The huntsman kept all this firmly in mind, and went to the king and told him what he had seen and heard. Then the king declared: 'Tomorrow we shall hunt once more.'

But Little Sister was terribly alarmed when she saw that her fawn was wounded. She washed the blood from his wound, laid herbs upon it, and said: 'Go and lie on your bed, little roe, so that your wound will heal.' But the wound was so slight that next morning the fawn no longer felt it. And when he heard the sport of the hunt outside again, he said: 'I can't help myself; I must be there too; and they won't catch me so quickly this time.' Little Sister wept and said: 'Now they will kill you, and I shall be alone here in the forest, deserted by all the world. I shan't let you out.' 'Then I shall die here of misery,' answered the roe-deer. 'When I hear the bugle-horn, I feel I might leap out of my shoes!' There was nothing else Little Sister could do, so with a heavy heart she opened the door for him and the little roe bounded away, hale and hearty, into the forest. When the king caught sight of him he said to his huntsmen: 'Now chase after him all day until nightfall, but see that no one does him any harm.' As soon as the sun had gone down the king said to the huntsman: 'Now come and show me the little house.' And when he stood before the door, he knocked and called: 'Dear sister mine, let me in.' Then the door opened and the king stepped inside, and there stood a girl who was so beautiful that he had never seen her like. The girl was frightened when she saw that it was not her little roe-deer, but a man who came in, wearing a golden crown on his head. But the king looked at her kindly, stretched out his hand to her, and said: 'Will you come with me to my palace and be my dear wife?' 'Oh yes,' answered the girl, 'but the little roe must come too, I shan't leave him.' Said the king: 'He shall stay with you for as long as you live, and he shall lack for nothing.' Meantime the roe came bounding in, so Little Sister fastened the rope of rushes to him once again, took it in her own hand, and went with him out of the little house in the forest.

The king took the beautiful girl onto his horse and led her into his palace, where their wedding was celebrated with great splendour.

And now she was the lady queen, and for a long time they lived happily together; the little roe-deer was cared for and cosseted, and he gambolled about in the palace garden. But the wicked stepmother, who had caused the children to go out into the world, thought for sure that Little Sister had been torn to pieces by the wild beasts in the forest and that Little Brother had been shot dead by the huntsmen as a deer. Now when she heard that they were so happy, and that all went so well for them, envy and malice stirred in her heart and gave her no rest, and her sole thought was how, in spite of all, she could still bring misfortune upon the two. Her own daughter, who was as ugly as night and had only one eye, nagged at her and said: 'To become queen—that should have been my good fortune.' 'Just be patient,' said the old woman. 'When the time is ripe, I'll be at hand all right.' Now when the time had come and the queen had brought a bonny little boy into the world, just when the king was away hunting, the old witch took on the shape of the waiting-woman, went into the room where the queen was lying, and said to the sick woman: 'Come, your bath is ready. It will do you good and give you fresh strength. Quickly, before it gets cold.' Her daughter was also at hand. They carried the frail queen into the bath-room and laid her in the bath. Then they locked the door and ran off. But in the bath-room they had built such a hellfire that the lovely young queen was soon bound to suffocate.

With that seen to, the old woman took her daughter, put a cap on her head, and laid her in the bed in place of the queen. She also gave her the figure and appearance of the queen, only she couldn't restore the missing eye. So that the king shouldn't notice it, she had to lie on the side where she had no eye. In the evening, when the king came home and heard that a little son had been born to him, he rejoiced with all his heart and wanted to go to his dear wife's bed to see how she was. Quickly the old woman cried: 'No! No! On your life! Keep the curtains drawn. The queen may not look at the light yet, and she must have her rest.' The king went away, and didn't know that a false queen was lying in the bed.

But when midnight came and everyone was asleep, the nurse who was sitting by the cradle in the child's room, the only one still awake, saw how the door opened and the rightful queen came in. She picked up the child, cradled him in her arms, and let him drink. Then she shook out his little pillow for him, laid him in the cradle again, and covered him up with his little blanket. She didn't forget the little roe-deer either, but went to the corner where he was lying and stroked his back. Then, without a sound, she went out through the door again. Next morning the nurse asked the watchmen whether anyone had entered the palace during the night, but they answered: 'No, we've seen nobody.' The queen came for many nights in this way, and all the while said not a word; the nurse saw her each time, but dared not tell anyone.

After some time had passed, the queen began to speak at night, saying:

> 'How fares my child? How fares my roe?
> I'll come but twice, and then no more.'

The nurse didn't answer, but when the queen had vanished again she went to the king and told him everything. Said the king: 'Heavens, what can it mean? Tomorrow night I shall keep watch by the child.' He went into the child's room at evening, and around midnight the queen appeared once again, and this time she said:

> 'How fares my child? How fares my roe?
> I'll come but once, and then no more.'

Then she tended the child as she usually did before vanishing. The king did not dare to speak to her, but he kept watch the following night as well. Again she said:

> 'How fares my child? How fares my roe?
> I come but this once, and then no more.'

Then the king could not hold back, but sprang towards her and said: 'You cannot be anyone but my dear wife.' Then she answered: 'Yes, I am your dear wife.' And at that moment, by God's grace, she received her life again; she was rosy, fresh, and well. Then she told the king of the mischief the wicked witch and her daughter had done her. The king had them both taken before the court, and judgement on them was pronounced. The daughter was taken out into the forest, where the wild beasts tore her to pieces, but the witch was cast into the fire, where she burned woefully to death. And as she was burnt to ashes, the roe-deer was transformed and recovered his human shape. And Little Brother and Little Sister lived happily together until the end of their lives.

11. *Rapunzel*

THERE once lived a husband and a wife who had long wished for a child, but in vain. At last the wife had hopes that the good Lord would fulfil her wish. In the parlour at the back of their house they had a little window, and from it they were able to look out onto a splendid garden full of the most beautiful flowers and herbs. But it was surrounded by a high wall, and no one dared enter it because it belonged to a sorceress who had great power and was feared by all the world. One day the woman was standing by this window and looking down at the garden, when she noticed a bed planted with the most beautiful rampions, or rapunzels; and they looked so fresh and green that she began to hanker after them, and felt a great craving to eat some of the rapunzels. Each day her craving grew, and as she knew that she couldn't have any of them, she grew thin and looked pale and wretched. Her husband was alarmed, and asked: 'What's the matter, dear wife?' 'Oh,' she answered, 'if I don't get any of the rapunzels to eat from the garden behind our house, I shall die.' Her husband, who loved her, thought: 'Sooner than let your wife die, you'll get some of the rapunzels for her, cost what it may.' So in the evening twilight he climbed over the wall into the sorceress's garden, hastily dug up a handful of rapunzels, and took them to his wife. Straight away she made herself a salad of them and ate them greedily. But she enjoyed them so much, so very, very much, that next day her craving was three times as great. If she was to be at peace, her husband had to climb into the garden once again. So at evening twilight he climbed over again, but when he had clambered down the wall he was mightily frightened, for he saw the sorceress standing before him. 'How do you dare', she said with an angry look, 'to climb into my garden and steal my rapunzels like a thief? It will cost you dear.' 'Oh please,' he answered, 'let mercy rule, not justice. I only decided to steal because I had to: my wife saw your rapunzels from the window, and she has such a great craving for them that she would die if she did not eat some.' Then the sorceress's anger abated, and she said to him: 'If it is as you say, I will permit you to take as many rapunzels as you wish. But I shall make one condition: you must give me the child your wife will bring into the world. All shall go well with her, and I will care for her like a mother.' In his fear the man agreed to everything, and when his wife's time came the sorceress appeared straight away, named the child 'Rapunzel', and took her away with her.

Rapunzel was the most beautiful child under the sun. When she was twelve years old the sorceress locked her in a tower in a forest which had neither stair nor door, only one little window right at the top. When the sorceress wanted to get in, she would stand below and call:

> 'Rapunzel, Rapunzel,
> Let down your hair to me.'

Rapunzel had beautiful long hair, as fine as spun gold. When she heard the sorceress's voice, she would undo her braids, wrap them round the window-catch above, and then her hair would fall twenty ells far below and the sorceress would climb up it.

After a few years it happened that the king's son was riding through the forest and came past the tower. Then he heard singing that was so lovely that he stopped and listened. It was Rapunzel, who passed the time in her loneliness by letting her sweet voice ring out. The king's son wanted to climb up to her and looked for a door in the tower, but there was none to be found. He rode home, but the singing touched his heart so deeply that he went out into the forest every day and listened to it. Once, when he was standing behind a tree and listening, he saw a sorceress approach and heard how she called up:

> 'Rapunzel, Rapunzel,
> Let down your hair.'

Then Rapunzel let down her tresses, and the sorceress climbed up to her. 'If that's the ladder to climb, I'll try my luck too.' And next day, as it was beginning to grow dark, he went up to the tower and called:

> 'Rapunzel, Rapunzel,
> Let down your hair.'

At once her hair fell down, and the king's son climbed up.

At first Rapunzel was terribly frightened when a man came in to her, for she had never set eyes on one before. But the king's son began speaking very kindly to her, and told her that his heart had been so deeply moved by her singing that it gave him no peace, and he had to see her for himself. Then Rapunzel lost her fear, and when he asked her if she would take him as her husband, and she saw that he was young and handsome, she thought: 'He'll love me more than old Dame Godmother,' and said yes, and put her hand in his. She said: 'I'd gladly go with you, but I don't know how I would be able to get down. Each time you come, bring a thread of silk with you; I'll weave a ladder with it, and when it's finished I'll climb down and you shall take me away on your horse.' They arranged that until then he should come to her every evening, for the old woman came during the day. And the sorceress didn't notice anything until one day Rapunzel started to say to her: 'Tell me, Dame Godmother, how is it that you are much heavier to draw up than the young king's son, who only takes a moment to reach me?' 'Oh, you godless child,' cried the sorceress, 'what's this I hear? I thought I had kept you apart from all the world, but even so you have deceived me!' In her rage she grabbed Rapunzel's beautiful hair, wound it a few times round her left hand, seized a pair of scissors with her right, and snip, snap, cut it off, and the beautiful tresses lay on the ground. And she was so pitiless that she brought poor Rapunzel to a desert place, where she had to live in great wretchedness and misery.

But on the same day that she had cast Rapunzel out, that evening the sorceress fastened the tresses she had cut off high up onto the window-catch, and when the king's son came and called:

'Rapunzel, Rapunzel,
Let down your hair',

she let Rapunzel's hair down. The king's son climbed up, but at the top he did not find his dearest Rapunzel but the sorceress, who looked at him with a wicked and venomous eye. 'Aha!' she cried scornfully. 'You want to fetch your lady love, but the pretty bird is no longer sitting and singing in her nest. The cat has got her, and will scratch your eyes out too. Your Rapunzel is lost to you and you will never see her again.' The king's son was beside himself with grief, and in his despair he leapt down from the tower. He managed to escape with his life, but he fell into thorns and they pierced his eyes. And so he strayed blindly in the forest: all he ate was roots and berries, all he did was weep and grieve over the loss of his dearest wife. And so he wandered about in misery for several years, and at last he came upon the desert place where Rapunzel was living, wretched and exiled, with the twins she had borne, a boy and a girl. He heard a voice, and it seemed so familiar to him, so he made his way towards it, and as he approached Rapunzel recognized him, and flung her arms about his neck, and wept. But two of her tears fell upon his eyes and then they grew clear again and he could see with them as he had always done. He led them to his realm, where he was welcomed with joy, and they lived long and happily together.

12. *The Three Little Men in the Forest*

THERE was once a man whose wife had died, and there was a woman whose husband had died. Now the man had a daughter, and so did the woman. The girls knew each other, and one day they went for a walk together and afterwards went to the woman's house. Then the woman said to the man's daughter: 'Listen, tell your father I would like to marry him, and when I do you shall wash yourself every morning in milk, and have wine to drink, but my own daughter shall have water to wash in and water to drink.' The girl went home and told her father what the woman had said. The man said: 'What shall I do? Marriage is a pleasure, but it's also a torment.' At last, because he couldn't come to a decision, he took off his boot and said: 'Take this boot. It has a hole in the sole. Take it up to the attic, hang it on the big nail there, and pour water into it. If it holds the water, I'll take a wife again, but if the water runs out, I won't.' The girl did as she was told; but the water shrank the hole, and the boot was full to the brim. She told her father what had happened. Then he went upstairs himself, and when he saw that it was so he went to the widow and wooed her, and the wedding took place.

Next day, when the two girls got up, there in front of the husband's daughter stood milk for her to wash in and wine for her to drink, but in front of the wife's daughter there stood water for her to wash in and water for her to drink. On the second day there stood water to wash in and water to drink before the husband's daughter as well as before the wife's. And on the third morning there stood water to wash in and water to drink in front of the husband's daughter, and milk to wash in and wine to drink in front of the wife's daughter—and that's how it stayed. The wife began to hate her stepdaughter like poison, and did all she could to make things worse for her from one day to the next. She was envious too, because her stepdaughter was beautiful and sweet, while her own daughter was ugly and spiteful.

One day in winter, when the ground had frozen hard as stone and hill and valley lay covered in snow, the wife made a dress of paper, called the girl, and said: 'There, put on this dress, go out into the forest, and fetch me a basket of strawberries. I've a hankering for them.' 'Heavens,' said the girl, 'strawberries don't grow in the winter; the ground is frozen, and the snow has covered everything too. And why am I to go out in this paper dress? It's so cold outside that your breath will freeze. The wind will blow through it, and the thorns will tear it from my body.' 'Defy me still, would you?' said the stepmother. 'Be off with you, and don't let me see you again until you've filled the basket with strawberries.' Then she gave her a piece of hard bread as well, and said: 'You can have this to eat for the day', and she thought: 'Out there she'll freeze and die of hunger, and be out of my sight for ever.'

Now the girl did as she was told, put on the paper dress, and went out with the basket. There was nothing but snow far and wide, and not a green blade of grass to be seen. When she came into the forest she saw a little house, with three little elf-men peering out of it. She wished them good-day and knocked humbly at the door. They called 'Come in,' and she walked into the parlour and sat down on the bench by the stove, for she wanted to get warm and eat her breakfast. The little elf-men said: 'Give us some too.' 'You're welcome,' she said, broke her piece of bread in two, and gave them half. They asked: 'What are you doing in your thin little dress in winter here in the forest?' 'Oh,' she answered, 'I'm supposed to gather a basketful of strawberries and I mustn't go home until I can take them back with me.' When she had eaten her bread they gave her a broom and said: 'Clear away the snow at the back door with this.' But while she was outside the three little men consulted among themselves: 'What gift shall we make her, for she is so sweet and good and shared her bread with us?' Then the first one said: 'The gift I shall bestow shall be for her to grow more beautiful every day.' The second said: 'The gift I shall bestow shall be for gold pieces to fall from her mouth whenever she utters a word.' The third said: 'The gift I shall bestow shall be for a king to come and take her to be his wife.'

The girl for her part did what the little elf-men had bidden: she brushed the snow behind the little house with the broom, and what do you think she found? Ripe strawberries, no less, growing dark and red out of the snow. Then in her joy she hastily filled her basket, thanked the little men, gave each of them her hand, and ran home, intending to give her stepmother what she had demanded. As she entered and said: 'Good evening', straight away a gold piece fell from her mouth. Then she told them what had happened to her in the forest, but with every word she uttered gold pieces fell from her mouth, so that very soon the entire room was covered with them. 'Look at the grand lady,' cried her stepsister, 'throwing her money around like that,' but secretly she was full of envy, and wanted to go out into the forest and look for strawberries too. Her mother said: 'No, daughter dearest, it's too cold. I don't want you to get frozen.' But as she gave her no peace, she finally gave in, sewed a splendid coat of fur for her, which she insisted she should wear, and gave her buttered bread and cake to eat on the way.

The stepsister went into the forest and headed straight for the little house. The three little elf-men peered out again, but she gave them no greeting, and without glancing round at them or bidding them good-day, she stumped into the room, sat down by the stove, and began to eat her buttered bread and cake. 'Give us some,' the little men cried, but she answered: 'There's not enough for me; how can I give any to someone else?' When she had finished eating they said: 'Here's a broom. Brush the yard outside the back door clear for us.' 'Brush it yourself,' she answered, 'I'm not your servant-girl.' When she saw that they were not going to make her a present of anything, she went out by the door. Then the little men consulted among themselves: 'What gift shall we make her, for she's so bad, with a wicked, envious, grudging heart?' The first said: 'The gift I shall bestow shall be for her to grow uglier every day.' The second said: 'The gift I shall bestow shall be for a toad to jump out of her mouth with every word she utters.' The third said: 'The gift I shall bestow shall be for her to die a miserable death.' The stepsister searched for strawberries outside, but when she found none she went home in a bad temper. And as she opened her mouth to tell her mother what had happened to her in the forest, with every word a toad jumped out of her mouth, so that everyone shrank from her in disgust.

Now the stepmother was even more vexed, and her only thought was how she might cause the man's daughter, whose beauty grew with every day, great harm and sorrow. At last she took a cauldron, set it on the fire, and put yarn to boil in it. When it was boiled she hung it over the poor girl's shoulder and gave her an axe. She was to go onto the frozen river, hack a hole in the ice, and swill out the yarn. She did as she was told, went down to the river, and hacked a hole in the ice. When she was in the middle of hacking a splendid carriage came driving by, in which the king was sitting. The carriage stopped and the king asked: 'My child, who are you, and what are you doing there?' 'I'm a poor girl and I'm swilling out yarn.' Then the king felt great compassion, and as he saw how very beautiful she was he said: 'Will you come away with me in my carriage?' 'Oh yes, with all my heart,' she answered, for she was glad to get away from her stepmother and stepsister.

So she got into the carriage and drove off with the king, and when they arrived at his palace their wedding was celebrated with great splendour, just as the little men had granted. A year later the young queen bore a son, and when the stepmother heard of her great happiness she came to the palace with her daughter and pretended she wanted to pay a visit. But when the king had gone out and no one else was present, the wicked woman seized the queen by the head and her daughter seized her by the feet, and they lifted her from the bed and threw her out of the window into the stream that was flowing past. Then the ugly daughter lay down in the bed, and the old woman covered her up right over her head. When the king returned and wanted to speak with his wife, the old woman cried: 'Gently, gently, now is not the time; she is lying in a great sweat. You must let her rest today.' The king had no suspicions and didn't come back until next morning; when he spoke with his wife and she replied, with every word she uttered a toad jumped out, even though a gold piece had fallen out before. Then he asked what was the matter, but the old woman said it came from the great sweating, but it would soon pass.

But that night the kitchen-boy saw a duck come swimming up the gutter, who spoke and said:

'What are you doing, king?
Are you sleeping or waking, king?'

And when he gave no reply, she said:

    'And are my guests asleep?'

Then the kitchen-boy replied:

    'They're sleeping deep.'

She went on to ask:

    'And my baby in his cradle?'

He replied:

    'Asleep as fast as he is able.'

Then she went upstairs in the shape of the queen, let the baby drink, shook out his little bed, covered him up, and swam off along the gutter as a duck again. She came like this for two nights, and on the third she said to the kitchen-boy: 'Go and tell the king that he should take his sword and on the threshold swing it over me three times.' The kitchen-boy ran and told the king, who came with his sword and swung it three times over the spirit; and at the third swing his wife stood before him, alive and fresh and well, just as she had been before.

    The king was overjoyed. But he kept the queen hidden in a chamber until the Sunday when the baby was to be christened. And when he was christened, the king said: 'What is right and just for someone who lifts another from their bed and throws them in the water?' 'Nothing better', answered the old woman, 'than for the villain to be put in a barrel studded with nails and rolled down the hill into the water.' Then the king said: 'You have pronounced your own sentence.' He sent for just such a barrel and had the old woman and her daughter put in, then the bottom was hammered shut and the barrel was rolled downhill until it fell into the river.

13. *Hansel and Gretel*

ON the edge of a great forest there lived a poor woodcutter with his wife and his two children; the little boy was called Hansel and the girl Gretel. He had little enough to put in his belly, and once, when a great famine came upon the land, he could not even provide their daily bread. As he lay in bed one evening, brooding over this and tossing and turning with worry, he sighed and said to his wife: 'What's to become of us? How can we feed our poor children when we've nothing left for ourselves?' 'Do you know what, husband?' answered his wife. 'Tomorrow morning, very early, let us take the two children out into the forest where it is thickest. There we'll light them a fire and give each of them an extra piece of bread, then we'll go off to our work and leave them on their own. They won't find their way back home, and we'll be rid of them.' 'No, wife,' said the man, 'that I won't do; how could I have the heart to leave my children alone in the forest; it wouldn't be long before the wild beasts came and tore them to shreds.' 'Oh, you fool,' she said, 'then we're bound to die of hunger, all four of us; you can just plane the boards for the coffins.' And she gave him no peace until he complied. 'But I'm sorry for the children, all the same,' the husband said.

The two children had not been able to sleep for hunger either, and they had heard what their stepmother had said to their father. Gretel wept bitterly and said to Hansel: 'Now it's all up with us.' 'Hush, Gretel,' said Hansel, 'don't fret, I'll get us out of this.' And when the grown-ups had fallen asleep, he got up, put on his jacket, opened the door downstairs, and slipped out. The moon was shining clear, and the white pebbles in front of the house were glistening as bright as pennies. Hansel stooped down and crammed his little pocket with as many as could fill them. Then he went back and said to Gretel: 'Don't worry, sister dear, go to sleep peacefully. God won't forsake us,' and lay down on his bed.

At daybreak, even before the sun had risen, the woman came and woke the two children. 'Get up, you pair of lazybones, we want to go into the forest to fetch wood.' Then she gave them each a little piece of bread, saying: 'Here's something for midday. But mind you don't eat it before then, because you're not getting any more.' Gretel took the bread beneath her apron, because Hansel had the stones in his pocket. Then they all made their way together towards the forest. After they had been walking for a little while Hansel stopped and looked back towards the house, and he did so over and over again. His father said: 'Hansel, what are you looking back at? Why are you dawdling all the time? Watch out, my boy, and mind where you're going.' 'Oh, father,' said Hansel, 'I'm looking back at my little white cat; she's sitting up on the roof and wants to say goodbye.' The woman said: 'Little fool, that's not your cat; that's the morning sun shining on the chimney.' But Hansel hadn't been looking back at the cat; instead, each time he had dropped one of the bright pebbles from his pocket.

When they had come to the middle of the forest their father said: 'Now, go and gather some wood, children. I'll light a fire so that you don't get frozen.' Hansel and Gretel gathered up brushwood, a little mountain of it. The brushwood was lit, and when the flames rose high the woman said: 'Now lie down by the fire, children, and have a rest. We're going into the forest to cut wood. When we're finished we'll come back and fetch you.'

Hansel and Gretel sat by the fire, and when midday came they each ate their piece of bread. And because they heard the blows from the woodman's axe, they thought their father was nearby. But it wasn't the woodman's axe; it was a bough he had tied to a dead tree, blowing to and fro in the wind. And as they had been sitting for such a long time, their eyes closed with weariness and they fell fast asleep. At last, when they woke, darkest night had fallen. Gretel began to cry, and said: 'How are we to get out of the forest now?' But Hansel comforted her: 'Just wait a little while until the moon has risen, and then we'll find our way, that's for sure.' And when the full moon had risen Hansel took his little sister by the hand and followed the pebbles, which were shining like new-minted pennies and showed them the way. They walked all through the night, and as day was dawning they arrived at their father's house. They knocked at the door, and when the wife opened it and saw that it was Hansel and Gretel, she said: 'You bad children, falling asleep for so long in the forest like that. We thought you would never come back.' But their father was glad, for it had cut him to the quick that he had left them so dreadfully alone.

Not long afterwards there came another time of hardship everywhere and the children heard what their mother was saying to their father in bed at night: 'The cupboard is empty again; all we have left is half a loaf of bread. After that, it's all finished. We have to get rid of the children. We'll take them deeper into the forest, so that they won't be able to find their way out; there's no saving us otherwise.' At this the man's heart grew heavy, and he thought: 'It would be better if you shared your last bite with the children.' But the woman would not listen to anything he said, and scolded and berated him. If you take the first step, you must take the next, and because he had given in the first time he was bound to do so the second time as well.

But the children were still awake, and they had listened in to this conversation. When the grown-ups were asleep Hansel got up again and tried to go out and gather pebbles. But the woman had locked the door and Hansel could not get out. But he comforted his little sister, saying: 'Don't cry, Gretel, go to sleep quietly, the good Lord will help us.'

Early next morning the woman came and fetched the children from bed. They were given their bit of bread, but it was even smaller than the last time. On the way to the forest Hansel crumbled it up in his pocket, and kept stopping to drop a crumb onto the ground. 'Hansel, why are you standing and looking round?' his father said. 'Get on your way.' 'I'm looking back at my little dove. She's sitting on the roof and wants to say goodbye,' answered Hansel. 'Little fool,' said the woman, 'that's not your dove; that's the morning sun shining on the chimney.' But bit by bit Hansel dropped all the crumbs along their path.

The woman led the children still deeper into the forest, where they had never been before in their lives. Once again a big fire was lit, and their mother said: 'You children, just stay and sit there, and if you're tired you can sleep a while. We're going into the forest to cut wood, and in the evening, when we're finished, we'll come and fetch you.' When it was midday Gretel shared her bread with Hansel, for he had scattered his piece along the way. Then they fell asleep. Evening came and went, but no one came to fetch the poor children. They did not wake until it was dark night, and Hansel comforted his little sister and said: 'Just wait, Gretel, until the moon rises, and then we'll see the crumbs of bread I scattered. They'll show us the way home.' When the moon rose they got up, but they didn't find any crumbs, for the thousands and thousands of birds who fly about in forest and field had pecked them all up. Hansel said to Gretel: 'We'll surely find our way.' But they didn't. They walked the whole night long and the next day from morning to evening, but they couldn't get out of the forest, and they were so hungry, for they had eaten nothing but the few berries they had found lying on the ground. And because they were so weary that their legs could no longer carry them, they lay down beneath a tree and fell asleep.

And now three days had passed since they had left their father's house. They began walking again, but only went deeper and deeper into the forest, and if help didn't come soon they were bound to die of hunger. When midday came they saw a lovely snow-white bird sitting on a bough and singing so beautifully that they stopped to listen. And when it had finished it spread its wings and flew ahead of them, and they followed it until they came to a little house, where it perched on the roof, and when they came quite close they saw that the house was made of bread and the roof was made of cake; as for the windows, they were made of pure sugar. 'Let's fall to,' said Hansel, 'and say grace for such a meal. I'll eat a bit from the roof, and Gretel, you can eat some of the window, that'll taste sweet.' Hansel reached up and broke off a little of the roof to eat, to see what it tasted like, and Gretel stood by the window-panes and nibbled at them. Then a little voice called out from the parlour:

> 'Nibbledydee, nibbledyday,
> Who's nibbling at my house today?'

The children answered:

> 'The wind, the wind,
> The heavenly friend',

and they went on eating unconcernedly. Hansel, who was really enjoying the roof, tore down a big piece, and Gretel pushed out a whole round window-pane, sat down, and ate it up with pleasure. Then all at once the door opened and an ancient woman, leaning on a crutch, came creeping out. Hansel and Gretel were so dreadfully frightened that they dropped what they were holding in their hands. But the old woman shook her head and said: 'Well, well, children dear, who's brought you here? Come right in and stay with me. You won't come to any harm.' She took them both by the hand and led them into her little house. There was good food on the table, milk and pancakes with sugar, and apples and nuts. Afterwards there were two lovely little beds with white sheets, and Hansel and Gretel lay down in them and thought they were in heaven.

The old woman had only pretended to be so kind; she was really a wicked witch who lay in wait for children, and she had only built the little bread house to lure them to her. If one of them fell into her clutches she would kill him, cook him, and eat him, and to her that was a proper feast day. Witches have bloodshot eyes and they can't see very far, but they have a very fine sense of smell, like the animals, and they can tell when human children come their way. When Hansel and Gretel drew near her, she laughed spitefully and said, gloating: 'I've got them. They shan't escape me again.' Early next morning, before the children had woken, she was already up, and when she saw the two of them resting there so sweetly, she muttered to herself: 'That'll make a good mouthful.' Then she grabbed Hansel with her skinny hand and carried him off into a little pen and locked him up behind the bars; shout as he might, it was no good. Then she went up to Gretel, shook her awake, and cried: 'Get up, you lazybones, fetch water and cook something tasty for your brother. He's locked in the pen outside and has to be fattened up. When he's nice and fat, I'll eat him.' Gretel began to cry bitterly, but it was no use; she had to do what the wicked witch commanded.

Now poor Hansel had the very best meals cooked for him, but Gretel got nothing but the shells from the crayfish. Every morning the old woman stole to the little stable and called: 'Hansel, stick out your finger, so that I can feel how soon you'll be fattened.' But Hansel stuck a little bone out for her, and the old woman, whose eyes were dim, could not see it and thought it was Hansel's finger, and she was puzzled that he wasn't fattening up at all. When four weeks had gone by and Hansel still remained bony, she was overcome by impatience and wouldn't wait any longer. 'Hey, Gretel,' she called to the girl, 'look sharp and bring water: fat or lean, tomorrow I'll slaughter Hansel and stew him.' Oh, how his poor little sister wailed as she had to fetch the water, and how the tears poured down her cheeks! 'Dear Lord, please help us,' she cried. 'If only the wild beasts had eaten us, we would at least have died together.' 'Save your moaning,' said the old woman, 'it won't do you any good.'

Early next morning Gretel had to go out, hang up the cauldron full of water, and light the fire. 'We'll do the baking first,' said the old woman. 'I've already fired the oven and kneaded the dough.' She shoved poor Gretel out to the baking-oven, from which the flames were already blazing. 'Crawl inside,' said the witch, 'and see whether it is the right heat, so that we can push in the bread.' Once she had Gretel inside she was going to shut the oven door, and Gretel would roast in there and she would eat her up as well. But Gretel saw what she had in mind and said: 'I don't know how to do it. How do I get inside?' 'Stupid goose,' said the old woman, 'the opening is big enough. As you can see, I can get in myself.' And she hopped towards Gretel and stuck her head in the oven. Then Gretel gave her a shove so that she was pushed far inside, shut the iron door fast, and fastened the bolt. Oh, then she began to howl, enough to make your flesh creep; but Gretel ran off, and the godless witch burned miserably to death.

Gretel, though, ran straight off to Hansel, opened his little pen, and called: 'Hansel, we're saved; the old witch is dead.' Then Hansel leapt out like a bird from a cage when its door is opened. How glad they were, they hugged each other, and skipped about and kissed! And because they need be afraid no longer they went into the witch's house, and in every corner there stood chests full of pearls and precious stones. 'These are even better than pebbles,' said Hansel, and stuffed his pockets with as much as they could hold; and Gretel said: 'I'll take something home with me too,' and filled her apron full. 'But let's go away now,' said Hansel, 'so that we get out of the witch's forest.' After they had been walking for a few hours they came to a great stretch of water. 'We can't get across,' said Hansel, 'I can't see a footway, nor a bridge.' 'There isn't a boat here, either,' said Gretel, 'but there's a white duck swimming. If I ask her, she'll help us to get over.' Then she called:

> 'Little duck, little duck,
> Here are Gretel and Hansel.
> No bridge and no track,
> Let us ride on your white back.'

And the little duck really did swim up to them. Hansel sat on her back and told his sister to sit by him. 'No,' answered Gretel, 'it will be too heavy for the little duck. She can carry us over one by one.' The good little creature did so, and when they were over without mishap and had been walking for a little while, the forest seemed to them to become more and more familiar, and at last from afar they could see their father's house. Then they began to run, burst into the parlour, and flung their arms about their father's neck. The man had not had a glad hour since he had abandoned the children in the forest; as for his wife, she had died. Gretel shook out her little apron so that the pearls and precious stones leapt about in the parlour, and Hansel threw one handful after another from his pockets as well.

Then all their cares were at an end and they lived in sheer joy together. My story's done. See a mouse run. And whoever catches it can make a great big furry hood from it.

14. *The Tale of the Fisherman and His Wife*

THERE was once a fisherman and his wife who lived together in a piss-pot right next to the sea, and the fisherman went every day and fished: and he fished and he fished. One day he went and sat with his rod and gazed all the time at the clear water: and he sat and he sat.

Then his line was pulled to the bottom of the sea, deep down, and when he hauled it up he brought up a huge flounder. Then the flounder spoke to him. 'Listen to me, fisherman. Spare my life, I beg you. I'm not a real flounder. I am a prince under a spell. What good will it do you if you kill me? You wouldn't enjoy eating me. Put me back in the water and let me go.' 'Well,' said the man, 'you don't need to make such a fuss about it. I'd have let a talking flounder go anyway.' With this he threw him back into the clear water. The flounder swam to the bottom, letting out a long trail of blood behind him. Then the fisherman stood up and went back to his wife in their piss-pot.

'Husband,' said his wife, 'haven't you caught anything today?' 'No,' said her husband. 'I did catch a flounder who said he was a prince under a spell, so I let him go.' 'Didn't you make a wish for anything?' said his wife. 'No,' said her husband, 'what should I wish for?' 'Oh,' said his wife. 'It's so nasty, living here all the time in a piss-pot that stinks and is so foul. You could have wished for a little cottage for us. Go back and call him. Tell him we want to have a little cottage. He'll do that for sure.' 'Oh,' said the man, 'why should I do that?' 'For heaven's sake,' said his wife, 'you did catch him after all, and you did let him go. He's sure to do it. Go down right now.' The man didn't really want to, but he didn't want to cross his wife either. So he went down to the sea.

When he got there, the sea was all green and yellow, no longer clear. So he went and he stood and he said:

'Flounder, flounder, in the sea,
Come up again and speak to me,
For my wife, my Ilsebill,
Will not as I'd have her will.'

Then the flounder came swimming up and said: 'Well, what does she want then?' 'Oh,' said the man, 'I did catch you, after all, so my wife said I should have wished for something. She doesn't want to live in the piss-pot any longer. She'd like to have a cottage.' 'Go back,' said the flounder. 'She has it already.'

So the man went away, and his wife wasn't sitting in the piss-pot any longer. Instead there stood a little cottage, and his wife was sitting on a bench outside the door. Then his wife took him by the hand and said to him: 'Come on in, look, that's much better, isn't it?' Then they went in, and in the cottage was a little hallway, and a lovely little parlour, and a bedroom where their bed was, and a kitchen and a pantry, and all fitted out with the best of household wares, pewter and brass, just right for it. And outside was a little yard with hens and ducks, and a little garden with vegetables and fruit. 'Look,' said his wife, 'isn't that nice?' 'Yes,' said the man, 'and that's how it shall stay. And now we'll live content.' 'We'll think about that,' said his wife. At that they had something to eat and went to bed.

Everything went well for one or two weeks, when the wife said: 'Listen to me, husband. The cottage is much too pokey and the yard and the garden are much too small. The flounder could easily have given us a bigger house. I'd like to live in a great stone palace. Go down to the flounder and tell him he should give us a palace.' 'Oh wife,' said the man, 'the cottage is good enough. Why should we want to live in a palace?' 'What!' said the wife. 'Just go right down. The flounder can do it every time.' 'No wife,' said the man, 'the flounder has only just given us the cottage. It might make him angry.' 'Off with you,' said the wife. 'The flounder can do it all right and be glad to. Off you go.' The man's heart grew heavy and he didn't want to go. He said to himself: 'It's not right.' But he went all the same.

When he came to the sea the water was all violet and dark blue and grey and thick, and no longer green and yellow, but it was still calm. Then he went and he stood and he said:

'Flounder, flounder, in the sea,
Come up again and speak to me,

For my wife, my Ilsebill,
Will not as I'd have her will.'

'Well, what does she want now?' said the flounder. 'Oh,' said the man, half afraid, 'she wants to live in a great stone palace.' 'Go back. She's already standing before the door,' said the flounder.

So the man went away, thinking he was going home, but when he got back there stood a great stone palace, and his wife was standing on the flight of steps and was just about to enter. Then she took him by the hand and said: 'Come on in.' At that he went in with her, and in the palace was a great hall with marble paving, and there were so many servants, who flung the great doors open wide, and the walls were all shining and hung with beautiful tapestries, and the rooms were filled with chairs and tables of gold, and crystal chandeliers hung from the ceiling, and all the bedrooms and chambers had carpets underfoot, and the tables were loaded to breaking-point with food and the very best wine. And outside was a great courtyard with stables and stalls for horses and cows, and coaches of the finest. There was a splendid great garden too, with the most beautiful flowers and fine fruit trees, and a park fully half a mile long; it had stags and deer and hares in it and everything that you could ever wish for. 'There,' said the wife: 'isn't that beautiful!' 'Oh yes,' said the man, 'and that's how it shall stay. Now we'll live in this beautiful palace and be content.' 'We'll think about that,' said the wife, 'and we'll sleep on it.' At that, they went to bed.

Next morning the wife woke up first; day was just breaking, and from her bed she saw the splendid country lying before her. The man was still stretching himself when she gave him a dig in the side with her elbow and said: 'Husband, look out of the window. Couldn't we be king over all that land?' 'Oh wife,' said the man, 'what do you want to be king for? I don't want to be king.' 'Well,' said his wife, 'if you don't want to be king, I do. Go down to the flounder and tell him I want to be king.' 'Oh wife,' said the man, 'why do you want to be king? I can't say that to him.' 'Why not?' said the wife. 'Go down right now. I must be king.' 'It's not right, it's not right,' he thought. He didn't want to go down, but he went all the same.

And when he came to the sea the sea was all grey-black, and the water rose up from the deep, and stank foully too. Then he went and he stood and he said:

'Flounder, flounder, in the sea,
Come up again and speak to me,
For my wife, my Ilsebill,
Will not as I'd have her will.'

'Now what does she want?' said the flounder. 'Oh,' said the man, 'she wants to become king.' 'Go home,' said the flounder. 'She's king already.'

So the man went away, and as he came to the great stone mansion their palace had become much bigger, with a great tower and magnificent ornaments on it, and the sentries were standing before the door, and there were so many soldiers and drums and trumpets. And when he entered the house everything was made of pure marble and gold, with velvet covers and great golden tassels. Then the doors were flung open to the hall where the court in its splendour was waiting, and his wife was sitting on a high throne of gold and diamonds, and she had on a great golden crown, and a sceptre in her hand of pure gold and precious stones, and on both sides stood her maids-in-waiting in a row, each one a head smaller than the next. Then he went and he stood and he said: 'Oh wife, you're king now?' 'Yes,' said the wife, 'now I'm king.' So he stood up and looked at her, and when he had gazed at her like this for a while, he said: 'Oh wife, let be, now that you're king. Now we won't wish for anything more.' 'No, husband,' said the wife, becoming very cross, 'time hangs so heavily for me: I can't stand it any longer. Go down to the flounder and tell him that as I'm king now, I must become emperor as well.' 'Oh wife,' said the man, 'what do you want to become emperor for?' 'Husband,' she said, 'go to the flounder and tell him I want to be emperor.' 'Oh wife,' said the man, 'he can't make you emperor. I can't say that to the flounder; there's only one emperor in all the realm; the flounder really can't make you emperor; he cannot and cannot.' 'What!' said the wife. 'I am the king and you are my husband. Will you go this instant? Go right now. If he can make a king, he can make an emperor. I will and I will be emperor. Go right now.' So he had to go. But as he was going he was really afraid, and going along like that, he thought to himself: 'This will not and will not come to good. To want to be emperor is just too brazen. The flounder will grow tired of it in the end.'

At that he came to the sea; and the sea was all black and thick, and it began to heave and swell from below so much that it bubbled and foamed, and a wind so keen blew over it that it curdled. And the man shuddered with fear. Then he went and he stood and he said:

> 'Flounder, flounder, in the sea,
> Come up again and speak to me,
> For my wife, my Ilsebill,
> Will not as I'd have her will.'

'Well, what does she want now?' said the flounder. 'Oh flounder,' said the man, 'my wife wants to become emperor.' 'Go home,' said the flounder. 'She's emperor already.'

So the man went away, and when he got back he found the whole palace was made of polished marble, with alabaster figures and golden ornaments. Before the door there were soldiers marching and blowing trumpets and beating all kinds of drums. In the house, though, there were barons and earls and dukes going about like servants. Then they flung open the doors, which were made of pure gold, and when he entered there was his wife sitting on a throne made of a single piece of gold and two miles high, and she had on a great golden crown that was three ells tall and set with brilliants and carbuncles; in one hand she held the sceptre and in the other the imperial orb, and by the door on both sides there stood her gentlemen-at-arms, each one smaller that the other, from the biggest giant, who was two miles tall, down to the smallest dwarf, who was as big as my little finger. And in front of her there stood so many princes and dukes. Then the man went and stood among them and said: 'Wife, are you emperor now?' 'Yes,' she said, 'I am emperor.' Then he went and stood and looked about him, and when he had gazed like that for a while, he said: 'Oh wife, now that you're emperor, let be.' 'Husband,' she said, 'why are you standing there like that? Now that I'm emperor, I want to become pope as well. Go down to the flounder.' 'Oh wife,' said the man, 'what is there that you don't want? You can't become pope. There's only one pope in all Christendom. He can't make you pope.' 'Husband,' she said, 'I want to become pope. Go straight down to the flounder. I must become pope this very day.' 'No wife,' said the man, 'I can't say that to him. It's no good. It's too much. The flounder can't make you pope.' 'Husband, what non-sense!' said the wife. 'If he can make me emperor, he can make me pope too. Be off to him. I am the emperor and you are my husband. Are you refusing to go?' Then he was frightened and he went down, but he was faint and trembling, and shaking and weak at the knees. And such a wind blew over the land, and the clouds flew as it grew gloomy towards evening; the leaves fell from the trees and the water rose and foamed as if it were boiling, and it crashed upon the shore; and in the distance he could see ships in danger firing off their guns and pitching and tossing on the waves. Still, there was just a little bit of blue in the middle of the sky, but on all sides it was as red as in a heavy storm. Then, very fearfully, he went and stood in terror and said:

> 'Flounder, flounder, in the sea,
> Come up again and speak to me,
> For my wife, my Ilsebill,
> Will not as I'd have her will.'

'Well, what does she want now?' said the flounder. 'Oh,' said the man, 'she wants to be pope.' 'Go home. She's pope already,' said the flounder.

So he went away, and when he got back there was a great church all surrounded by palaces. He pushed his way through the crowd of people. Inside, though, it was all lit by thousands and thousands of candles, and his wife was clad in pure gold, and she was sitting on a much higher throne, and she had on three great golden crowns, and around her was so much priestly pomp, and by the door on both sides there stood two rows of candles, the tallest as wide and as tall as the tallest tower, down to the smallest kitchen taper. And all the emperors and the kings were on their knees before her and kissing her slipper. 'Wife,' said the man, looking at her hard, 'are you the pope now?' 'Yes,' she said, 'I'm the pope.' Then he went and he stood and he looked at her hard, and it was as if he was looking into the bright sun. When he had gazed at her for a while he said: 'Oh wife, let be, now that you're pope.' But at first she went as stiff as a post, and didn't move or stir. Then he said: 'Wife, now be content; now that you're pope, after all, there's nothing more that you can become.' 'I'll think about that,' said the wife. At that, they both went to bed, but she wasn't content, and her desires would not let her sleep: she was thinking all the time of what she still wanted to become.

The man slept soundly and well, for he'd run around a great deal that day, but his wife couldn't get to sleep and tossed so much from one side to the other the whole night long, thinking all the time of what she could still become. But even so, she couldn't think of anything more. Meantime the sun was about to rise, and when she saw the red of dawn she sat up at the end of the bed and looked out of the window and she saw the sun rising. 'Hah!' she thought. 'Can't I make the sun and moon rise too?' 'Husband,' she said, giving him a dig in the ribs with her elbow, 'wake up. Go down to the flounder and tell him I want to become like God.' The man was still half asleep, but he was so frightened that he fell out of bed. He thought he hadn't heard aright, and he rubbed his eyes and said: 'Oh wife, what did you say?' 'Husband,' she said, 'if I'm not able to make the sun and the moon rise and if I just have to watch the sun and the moon rising, I shan't stand it, and I shan't have a quiet moment ever again if I can't make them rise myself.' She looked at him so balefully that a shudder ran through him. 'Oh wife,' said the man, and fell on his knees before her, 'the flounder can't do that. He can make you emperor and pope; think again, I beg you, and stay pope.' Then she flew into a rage; her hair flew wildly round her head, she tore her stays and gave him a kick with her foot and screamed: 'I won't stand it and I won't stand it any longer. Won't you be off!' So he slid into his breeches and leapt away like a madman.

But outside a storm was raging, and it was blowing so hard that he could hardly stand on his feet. The houses and trees toppled over, the mountains shook, and the boulders rolled into the sea. The heavens were all black as pitch, and it thundered and lightened, and the sea rose in black waves as tall as church towers and as high as mountains, all crowned with a white crest of foam. Then he shouted, and he could hardly hear his own words:

> 'Flounder, flounder, in the sea,
> Come up again and speak to me,
> For my wife, my Ilsebill,
> Will not as I'd have her will.'

'Well, what does she want now?' said the flounder. 'Oh,' he said, 'she wants to be like God.' 'Go home. She's back sitting in the piss-pot.'

And there they are sitting to this day.

15. *The Brave Little Tailor*

ONE summer morning a little tailor was sitting on his table by the window. He was in a good humour, and he was sewing with all his might. Just then a farmer's wife came down the street crying: 'Good jam cheap! Good jam cheap!' This sounded sweet to the little tailor's ears, so he stuck his neat little head out of the window and called: 'Up here, good woman, you'll get rid of your wares up here.' The woman climbed the three flights of stairs with her heavy basket up to the tailor, and he made her unpack all her pots in front of him. He inspected them all, lifted them up, sniffed them, and said at last: 'The jam looks good to me; weigh me out four ounces, good woman, and if it comes to a quarter of a pound, that's all right by me.' The woman, who had hoped to make a good sale, gave him what he wanted, but went away grumbling and very cross. 'Now God shall bless this jam,' cried the little tailor, 'and it shall give me health and strength.' He fetched a loaf of bread from the cupboard, cut a slice across the whole loaf, and spread on the jam. 'That's not going to taste bitter,' he said, 'but first I'll finish this jerkin before I take a bite of it.' He put the slice of bread down at his side, went on sewing, and in his pleasure made his stitches bigger and bigger. Meanwhile the smell of the sweet jam rose up the wall where a lot of flies were sitting, so that they were attracted to the jam and settled on it in swarms. 'Hey, who invited you?' said the little tailor, and drove the unwelcome guests away. But the flies, who didn't understand English, were not put off, but turned up in bigger and bigger parties. At last the tailor lost his rag, as they say now; he reached for a cloth from his glory-hole, and—'Wait, I'll give it to you!'—he brought it down mercilessly. When he lifted it and counted, he had before him no less than seven: dead and with outstretched legs. 'Is that the sort of fellow you are?' he said, and couldn't help admiring his own bravery. 'The whole town shall learn of this.' And quickly the little tailor cut out a belt for himself, sewed it, and in big letters embroidered on it the words: 'Seven at one blow!' 'Town, indeed,' he said, 'the whole world shall learn of it!' And his heart quivered with joy like a lamb's tail.

The tailor slung the belt around his waist and decided to go out into the world, for to his mind his workshop was too small for his valour. Before he set out he looked around in the house to see if there was anything he could take with him, but he found nothing but an old cheese, which he put in his pocket. Outside the town gate he noticed a bird caught in a thicket; that had to go into his pocket with the cheese. Then he marched bravely on his way, and because he was light and nimble he didn't feel weary. The road took him up a mountain, and when he reached the highest peak there was a mighty giant sitting there, gazing around and taking his ease. The little tailor went up to him boldly and addressed him, saying: 'Good morning, friend, so you're sitting there, viewing the great wide world? I'm just on my way there to try my luck. Would you like to come too?' The giant looked at the tailor with scorn, and said: 'You beggar! You miserable fellow!' 'We'll see!' answered the little tailor, unbuttoning his coat and showing the giant his belt. 'You can read the kind of man I am there.' The giant read: 'Seven at one blow,' and thought it meant people that the tailor had struck dead. So he became more respectful towards the little fellow. Even so, he wanted to test him first, so he took a stone in his hand and squeezed it so that water dripped out of it. 'Copy that,' said the giant, 'if you've any strength.' 'Is that all?' said the little tailor. 'That's a game in our trade.' He put his hand in his pocket, took out the soft cheese, and squeezed it so that the whey ran out. 'So,' he said, 'that was a bit better, wasn't it?' The giant didn't know what to say, and couldn't believe it of the little man. So the giant lifted up a stone and threw it so high that human eyes could scarcely see it any longer. 'Well, little manikin, copy that.' 'That's a good throw,' said the tailor, 'but the stone still had to fall back down to earth again. I'll throw you one that won't come back down at all.' He put his hand in his pocket, took out the bird, and threw it into the air. Happy to be free, the bird rose up, flew off, and never came back. 'How do you like that trick, friend?' asked the tailor. 'You certainly can throw,' said the giant, 'but now let's see if you are fit to carry a tidy load.' He led the little tailor to a huge oak tree which had been cut down and was lying on the ground. He said: 'If you're strong enough, help me carry this tree out of the forest.' 'With pleasure,' answered the little man. 'You take the trunk on your shoulder, I'll lift the branches with the twigs and carry them—they're the heaviest, after all.' The giant took the trunk on his shoulder, but the tailor seated himself on a branch, so the giant, who couldn't look round, had to carry the entire tree and the little tailor into the bargain. He was very cheerful and in high good humour at the back, and whistled the song: 'Three tailors rode out of the town, the town,' as if carrying trees were child's play. After the giant had dragged the heavy load part of the way, he couldn't go any further and called out: 'Listen, I have to drop the tree.' The tailor sprang nimbly down, took hold of the tree with both arms as if he had been carrying it, and said to the giant: 'You're such a big fellow and you can't even carry the tree.'

They went on together, and as they were passing a cherry-tree the giant took hold of the top of the tree, where the ripest fruits were hanging, bent it down, put it in the tailor's hand, and told him to eat. But the little tailor was much too weak to hold the tree, and when the giant let go it shot back and the tailor was thrown up into the air with it. When he fell back down again, unharmed, the giant said: 'Aren't you strong enough to hold that weak little reed?' 'I'm strong enough all right,' answered the little tailor, 'do you think that's anything for someone who has killed seven with one blow? I jumped over the tree because the huntsmen down in the bushes were shooting. Copy that, if you can.' The giant made the attempt, but he couldn't jump over the tree; instead, he remained hanging in the branches, so here too the little tailor kept the upper hand.

The giant said: 'If you're such a brave fellow, come with me to our cave and spend the night with us.' The little tailor was ready to, and followed him. When they reached the cave there were more giants there sitting round the fire; each of them had a roast sheep in his hand, and was eating it. The little tailor looked round and thought: 'It's a lot roomier here than in my workshop.' The giant showed him a bed and told him to lie down and have a good sleep. But the bed was too big for the little tailor, so he didn't lie down in it but crept into a corner. When it was midnight and the giant thought that the tailor was fast asleep, he got up, took a great iron rod, and struck the bed through with one blow, and he reckoned he had finished off that grasshopper for good. Very early next morning the giants went out into the forest. They had quite forgotten the little tailor, when all at once he came striding along as cheerful and daring as you like. The giants were terrified, for they were afraid he would strike them all dead, and they ran off in haste.

The tailor went on his way, always following his sharp nose. After he had travelled a long way he came to the courtyard of a royal palace, and as he was tired, he lay down in the grass and went to sleep. While he was lying there the people came and gazed at him from all sides, and they read on his belt: 'Seven at one blow.' 'Oh,' they said, 'what does a great warrior want here in the middle of peacetime? He must be a mighty lord.' They went and informed the king, and they reckoned that if war were to break out he would be an important and useful man whom they should at all costs try to keep with them. This advice pleased the king, so he dispatched one of his courtiers to the little tailor to invite him, when he woke, to enter the king's armed service. The envoy remained standing at the sleeper's side. He waited until he had stretched his limbs and opened his eyes, and then announced his embassy. 'That's just why I've come here. I am ready to enter the king's service.' So he was received with honour, and a special dwelling was assigned to him.

But the soldiers took against the little tailor, and wished him a thousand miles away. 'What will come of it?' they said amongst themselves. 'If we have a quarrel with him, and he hits out, seven will fall at every blow. None of us can survive that.' So they came to a decision, took themselves off to the king, all of them, and requested their discharge. 'We are not made of the stuff', they said, 'to hold out against a man who strikes seven with one blow.' The king was sad that he should lose all his faithful servants just for the sake of one; he wished that he had never set eyes on the tailor, and would gladly have been rid of him. But he dared not discharge him, because he was afraid the tailor might strike him dead, together with all his people, and sit on the royal throne himself. For a long time he pondered this way and that, and at last he had an idea. He sent to the little tailor with the message that, because he was such a great warrior, he wanted to make him an offer. Two giants, he said, were living in a forest in his lands, causing great harm robbing, murdering, burning, and laying waste: no one could approach them without endangering his life. If he was able to overcome these two giants and kill them, then he would give him his only daughter for wife and half the kingdom for a dowry; in addition, a hundred horsemen were to ride with him for support. 'That would be something for a man like you,' thought the little tailor. 'You're not offered a beautiful king's daughter and half a kingdom every day of the week.' 'Oh yes,' he replied, 'I'll tame the giants all right, and I shan't need the hundred horsemen to do it. Someone who has hit seven at one blow doesn't need to be afraid of two.'

The little tailor set out, and the hundred horsemen followed him. When he reached the edge of the forest he said to his companions: 'Halt and remain here. I'll finish off the giants by myself.' Then he leapt into the forest and looked around him to right and left. After a little time he caught sight of the two giants: they were lying under a tree asleep, and snoring the while, so that the boughs rose and fell with their snores. The little tailor, sharp as ever, filled both pockets with pebbles and climbed up the tree. When he was halfway up he slid onto a branch until he was right above the sleepers, and he dropped one pebble after another onto one giant's chest. For a long time the giant felt nothing, but in the end he woke up, nudged his companion, and said: 'What are you hitting me for?' 'You're dreaming,' said the other, 'I'm not hitting you.' They lay down to sleep again. Then the tailor dropped a pebble onto the second giant. 'What's this about?' the other one cried. 'Why are you throwing things at me?' 'I'm not throwing anything at you,' answered the first with a growl. They argued for a while, but because they were tired they let things rest and closed their eyes once more. The little tailor began his game all over again, picked out the biggest pebble, and threw it with all his might onto the first giant's chest. 'This is too bad!' shouted the giant, jumping up like a madman and shoving his companion against the tree so hard that it shook. The other paid him back in the same coin, and they became so enraged that they tore up trees and struck out at each other until in the end they both fell to the ground at the same time—dead. Then the little tailor jumped down. 'A piece of luck', he said, 'that they didn't tear up the tree I was sitting on, else I'd have had to leap onto another like a squirrel. But in my trade we're agile.' He drew his sword and gave each of them a couple of sturdy strokes in the chest, then he went back to the horsemen and said: 'The work is done. I've finished them both off. But it was a hard fight. They tore up trees and defended themselves when they were hard-pressed, but none of that is any good when someone like me comes along, who strikes seven at one blow.' 'Aren't you wounded, then?' asked the horsemen. 'That's right,' answered the tailor, 'they haven't touched a hair of my head.' The horsemen wouldn't believe him and rode into the forest. There they found the giants swimming in their own blood, and round about lay the trees, torn up.

The little tailor asked the king for his promised reward, but the king regretted his promise and pondered afresh how he could be rid of the hero. 'Before you receive my daughter and half my kingdom,' he said to him, 'there is one more heroic deed you must accomplish. There is a unicorn abroad in the forest, causing great harm. You must capture it first.' 'A unicorn frightens me even less that two giants. Seven at one blow, that's my business.' He took a rope and an axe with him, went out into the forest, and again instructed the attendants appointed to him to wait on the edge of the wood. He did not need to look for long. The unicorn soon came by, and leapt straight at the tailor, as if it intended to spear him without more ado. 'Gently, gently,' he said, 'it can't be done as quickly as that.' He stood still and waited until the beast was quite close, then he leapt nimbly behind the tree. The unicorn ran with all its strength against the tree and speared its horn so firmly in the trunk that it didn't have the strength to draw it out again, and in this way it was caught. 'Now the bird is taken,' said the tailor. He came out from behind his tree and first put the rope around the unicorn's neck. Then with his axe he struck the horn out of the tree and, as all was now in order, he led the beast away and took it to the king.

The king still didn't want to grant him his promised reward, and made a third demand. Before the wedding the tailor was first to capture a wild boar that was causing great harm in the forest. The huntsmen were to help him. 'With pleasure,' said the tailor, 'it will be child's play.' He didn't take the huntsmen with him into the forest, and they were quite content with that, for the wild boar had given them such a reception so often already that they had no wish to waylay it. When the boar set eyes on the tailor it ran at him with mouth foaming and teeth gnashing, and made to hurl him to the ground, but the agile hero skipped into a nearby chapel and with one bound leapt out of the window again. The boar ran in after him, but the tailor hopped around outside and slammed the door shut behind him: the enraged beast was caught, for it was much too heavy and clumsy to jump out of the window. The little tailor called the huntsmen over, for they had to see the prisoner with their own eyes. But the hero took himself off to the king, who now, whether he would or not, had to keep his promise and surrender his daughter and half his kingdom up to him. If he had known that it was not a heroic warrior but a little tailor who was standing before him, it would have cut him to the quick even more sharply. So the wedding was held with great splendour and little joy, and it turned a tailor into a king.

After some time the young queen heard her husband talking in his dreams at night. ' 'Prentice, make me that jerkin and patch me those breeches, or I'll beat you round the ears with my yardstick!' Then she realized what street the young lord had been born in, complained to her father the next morning, and begged his help to rid her of a husband who was nothing but a tailor. The king consoled her, saying: 'Leave your bedroom door open tonight. My servants shall wait outside, and when he has fallen asleep they shall go in, tie him up, and carry him on board a ship that will take him out into the wide world.' The wife was content with this, but the king's esquire, who had overheard it all, was well disposed towards his young lord and secretly told him of the whole plot. 'I'll bolt the door on that plan,' said the little tailor. That evening he went to bed with his wife at the usual time. When she thought he had fallen asleep she got up, opened the door, and lay down again. The little tailor, who was only pretending to sleep, began to call out in a clear voice: ' 'Prentice, make me that jerkin and patch me those breeches, or I'll beat you round the ears with my yardstick! I have struck seven with one blow, killed two giants, led away one unicorn, and captured a wild boar—and I'm supposed to be afraid of the fellows standing outside my door!' When they heard the tailor talking like this they were filled with terror and ran away as if they were being pursued by the wild hunt, and not one of them would venture against him ever again. So the little tailor was and remained a king all his life long.

16. *Ashypet*

A RICH man had a wife who fell gravely ill, and when she felt that her end was drawing near she called her only little daughter to her bedside and said: 'Dear child, stay godly and good, and the good Lord will always be your strength, and I will look down on you from heaven and be with you.' Then she closed her eyes and departed. Every day the girl went out to her mother's grave and wept, and stayed godly and good. When winter came the snow covered the grave with a white kerchief, and when the sun melted it in spring the husband took another wife.

The wife brought two daughters into the house with her, who were beautiful and fair of face, but mean and black of heart. That was the start of a hard time for the poor stepchild. 'Is the silly goose supposed to sit with us in the parlour!' they said. 'If you want to eat, you must earn your keep: away with the kitchen-maid.' They took her beautiful clothes from her, dressed her in an old grey pinafore, and gave her wooden clogs. 'Look at the proud princess now, all dressed up!' they cried, laughing, and took her into the kitchen. There she had to do the heavy work from morning to evening, get up early before day-break, carry water, light the fire, do the cooking and the washing. On top of that the sisters bullied her in every way you could imagine, jeered at her, and dropped peas and lentils in the ashes so that she had to sit and pick them out again. In the evenings, when she had worked herself weary, she had no bed to go to but had to lie by the hearth in the ashes. And because this always made her look dusty and dirty, they called her Ashypet.

It happened one day that the father intended to go to the great fair, and he asked his two stepdaughters what he might bring back for them. 'Fine clothes,' said the one; 'pearls and jewels,' the second. 'But what about you, Ashypet?' he said, 'What would you like?' 'Father, the first sprig that brushes against your hat on your way home, pick that for me.' So he bought fine clothes, pearls and jewels for the two stepsisters, and on his way back, as he was riding through a green thicket, a sprig of hazel brushed against him and knocked off his hat. So he broke off the sprig and took it with him. When he came home he gave his stepdaughters what they had asked for, and to Ashypet he gave the sprig from the hazel-bush. Ashypet thanked him, went to her mother's grave, and planted the sprig there, and wept so much that her tears fell upon it and watered it. But it grew and became a handsome tree. Three times each day Ashypet went down to it and wept and prayed, and each time a little white bird came and settled on the tree, and if ever she said she wished for something, the little bird would drop down to her what she had wished for.

But it came about that the king arranged a great celebration which was due to last three days, and to which all the beautiful maidens in the land were invited so that his son could choose a bride. When the

two stepsisters heard that they too were to make an appearance, they
were in high good humour. They called Ashypet and said: 'Comb
our hair, brush our shoes, and fasten our buckles. We're going to the
festivities at the king's palace.' Ashypet obeyed, but she cried,
because she too would have liked to go to the ball, and she begged
her stepmother to allow her to go. 'You're always so dusty and dirty,
Ashypet,' she said, 'and you want to go to the festivities? You haven't
any clothes or shoes, and you want to dance!' But as she persisted in
her pleading, at last her stepmother said: 'I've just spilt a bowl of
lentils in your ashes. If you can pick out the lentils in two hours, you
shall go too.' The girl went out of the back door into the garden and
called: 'You tame doves, you turtle-doves, all you little birds beneath
the sky, come and help me pick them out,

> the good ones in the pot,
> the bad ones in your crop.'

Then in at the kitchen window flew two white doves, and after them
the turtle-doves, and in the end all the birds beneath the sky flitted
and flocked inside and settled around the ashes. And the doves nodded
with their little heads and began peck, peck, peck, peck, and then all
the rest began peck, peck, peck, peck as well, and sorted out all the
good grains into the bowl. An hour had scarcely gone by before they
had finished, and they all flew out again. Then the girl took the bowl
to her stepmother, full of joy, believing that now she would be
allowed to go to the festivities too. But she said: 'No, Ashypet, you've
no clothes, and you don't know how to dance. You'll be laughed at.'
But as the girl cried, she said: 'If you can pick two bowlfuls of lentils
from the ashes for me in one hour, you shall go too'; but to herself
she thought: 'She'll never be able to do it.' After her stepmother had
spilt the two bowls of lentils into the ashes, the girl went out of the
back door into the garden and called: 'You tame doves, you turtle-
doves, all you little birds beneath the sky, come and help me pick
them out,

> the good ones in the pot,
> the bad ones in your crop.'

Then in at the kitchen window flew two white doves, and after them
the turtle-doves, and in the end all the birds beneath the sky flitted
and flocked inside and settled around the ashes. And the doves

nodded with their little heads and began peck, peck, peck, peck, and then all the rest began peck, peck, peck, peck as well, and sorted out all the good grains into the bowls. Then the girl took the bowls to her stepmother, full of joy, believing that now she would be allowed to go to the festivities too. But she said: 'None of that is any use. You're not coming with us because you have no clothes and you don't know how to dance: we'd be ashamed of you.' Then she turned her back on her and hurried away with her two proud daughters.

Now that there was no one left at home, Ashypet went to her mother's grave beneath the hazel-tree and called:

> 'Shake and quake, good hazel-tree,
> Cast gold and silver over me.'

Then the bird threw down to her a gold and silver gown, with slippers embroidered in silk and silver. In haste she put on the gown and went to the festivities. But her sisters and her stepmother didn't recognize her; to them it seemed she must be a king's daughter from foreign lands, she looked so beautiful in her golden gown. They didn't give a thought to Ashypet, and supposed she was sitting at home in the dirt, picking the lentils out of the ashes. The king's son went up to her, took her by the hand, and danced with her. And he had no wish to dance with anyone besides her, so that he wouldn't let go of her hand, and if anyone else came and invited her to dance, he would say: 'This is my dancing-partner.'

She danced until evening, and then she made to go home. But the king's son said: 'I shall go with you and escort you,' for he wanted to see who it was that the beautiful girl belonged to. But she slipped away from him and skipped into the dovecote. Then the king's son waited until the girl's father arrived, and told him that the strange girl had skipped into the dovecote. The old man thought: 'I wonder if it could be Ashypet,' and sent for an axe and hooks so that he could smash the dovecote in two; but there was no one inside. And when they went into the house Ashypet was lying in the ashes in her dirty clothes, and a dim oil-lamp was burning in the chimney, for Ashypet had jumped down quickly behind the dovecote and had run to the little hazel-tree. There she had taken off her beautiful clothes and laid them on the grave, and the bird had taken them away again. Then she had gone to sit in the kitchen in the ashes, wearing her little grey pinafore.

The next day, when the festivities began afresh and the parents and stepsisters had left the house again, Ashypet went to the hazel-tree and said:

> 'Shake and quake, good hazel-tree,
> Cast gold and silver over me.'

Then the bird threw down a gown that was much finer than the day before's. And when she appeared at the festivities in this gown everyone was astonished at her beauty. For his part, the king's son had waited until she came. He took her by the hand straight away, and danced only with her. If the others came and invited her to dance, he would say: 'This is my dancing-partner.' Now when it was evening she made to leave, and the king's son followed her, for he wanted to see whose house she would enter; but she skipped away from him and into the garden behind the house. There stood a fine tall tree, with the most splendid pears hanging from it. She clambered up between the branches as nimbly as a squirrel, and the king's son had no idea where she had got to. But he waited until the girl's father arrived, and said to him: 'The strange girl slipped away from me, but I believe she climbed the tree.' The girl's father thought: 'I wonder if it could be Ashypet,' sent for the axe, and chopped the tree down, but there was no one in it. And when they went into the kitchen there was Ashypet lying in the ashes as usual, for she had jumped down from the other side of the tree, taken her beautiful clothes to the bird on the hazel-tree once again, and put on her little grey pinafore.

On the third day, when the parents and sisters were gone, Ashypet went again to her mother's grave and said to the little tree:

> 'Shake and quake, good hazel-tree,
> Cast gold and silver over me.'

Now the bird threw her down a gown that was so radiant and splendid that she had never had the like before, and her slippers were all golden. And when she arrived at the festivities in that gown no one knew what to say for sheer admiration. The king's son danced with no one but her, and if anyone invited her to dance he would say: 'This is my dancing-partner.'

Now when evening came Ashypet made to leave, and the king's son wanted to escort her, but she slipped away from him so quickly that he could not follow. But the king's son had employed a ruse and had the entire flight of stairs covered with pitch: as she leapt down them, the girl's left slipper remained stuck in it. The king's son picked it up: it was small and dainty and all golden. Next morning he went with it to the old man and said: 'No one shall be my wife except the one whose foot this shoe will fit.' The two sisters were delighted, for they had beautiful feet. The eldest took the shoe to her room to try it on, and her mother was standing beside her. But with such a big toe, she couldn't get her foot in. The shoe was too small for her. So her mother offered her a knife, saying: 'Cut off your toe: when you're queen you won't need to go on foot any more.' The girl chopped off her toe, forced her foot into the shoe, bit back her pain, and went out to the king's son. Then he took her on his horse as his bride and rode away with her. But they had to ride past the grave, where two doves were sitting on the little hazel-tree and calling:

'Proo-proo, proo-proo,
If you look you'll find there's blood in the shoe:
The shoe is too tight;
In the house still waits your rightful bride.'

Then he looked at her foot and saw how the blood was pouring out. He turned his horse around and brought the false bride back home, saying that she was not the right one and the other sister should put on the shoe. So she went to her room and managed to fit her toes nicely into the shoe, but her heel was too big. So her mother offered her a knife, saying: 'Cut off a bit of your heel: when you're queen you won't need to go on foot any more.' The girl chopped a bit off her heel, forced her foot into the shoe, bit back her pain, and went out to the king's son. Then he took her on his horse as his bride and rode away with her. As they rode past the little hazel-tree, the two doves were sitting on it and calling:

'Proo-proo, proo-proo,
If you look, you'll find there's blood in the shoe:
The shoe is too tight;
In the house still waits your rightful bride.'

He looked down at her foot and saw how the blood was pouring out of the shoe and had seeped all red up her white stockings. Then he turned his horse and brought the false bride back home. 'She's not the right one either,' he said. 'Haven't you another daughter?' 'No,' said the father, 'there's only a grubby little kitchen-girl left by my late wife: she can't possibly be your bride.' The king's son told him to send her up, but the mother answered: 'Oh no, she's much too dirty. She's not fit to be seen.' But he insisted, and Ashypet had to be summoned. First she washed her hands and face clean, then she went up and curtseyed before the king's son, who offered her the golden shoe. Then she sat on a stool, took the heavy wooden clog from her foot, and put her foot in the slipper, which fitted it like a mould. And when she stood up and the king looked her full in the face, he recognized her as the beautiful girl who had danced with him, and he cried: 'This is the rightful bride!' The stepmother and the two sisters gave a start and turned pale with fury. But he took Ashypet on his horse and rode away with her. As they rode past the little hazel-tree, the two white doves called:

> 'Proo–proo, proo–proo,
> If you look, you'll find there's no blood in the shoe:
> The shoe's not too tight,
> He's bringing home his rightful bride.'

And after they had called out their verse, they both came flying down and settled on Ashypet's shoulders, one on the right, the other on the left, and they remained sitting there.

When her wedding to the king's son was due to be celebrated the false sisters turned up, wanting to ingratiate themselves and have a share in her good fortune. As the bridal couple were going to the church the eldest was on their right hand and the youngest on their left; then from each of them the doves pecked out one eye. Afterwards, as they were leaving the church, the eldest was on the left hand and the youngest on the right; then from each of them the doves pecked out the other eye. And so, for their malice and deceit, they were punished with blindness for the rest of their lives.

17. *The Tale of the Mouse, the Bird, and the Sausage*

ONCE upon a time a mouse, a bird, and a sausage fell in with one another and kept house together, living long and well and delightfully, at peace with themselves and prospering in their goods. It was the bird's task to fly out into the forest every day and gather wood. The mouse was to carry water, light the fire, and lay the table. As for the sausage, she was to do the cooking.

'Too much prosperity—greedy for novelty!' Well, one day our bird met another bird and boasted to him, telling him of his excellent situation. The other bird mocked him for being a poor idiot who always had so much work to do while the other two had an easy time at home. For once the mouse had lighted her fire and carried the water, she would retire to her little room and rest until she was called to lay the table. The sausage would stay by the pot and see that the food was cooking nicely, she would swish herself a few times in the gravy or the vegetables, and there it was, fattened and flavoured and ready to eat. Then, when the bird came home and put his burden down, they would sit down at table, and after they had had their supper they would sleep their fill until next morning, and that was a splendid life.

Next day, stung by this, our bird didn't want to go out and gather wood any more, saying he'd been a servant for long enough, and they must have been making a fool of him, you might say. They should take turns and try a different arrangement. And although the mouse, and the sausage too, pleaded with him fervently, the bird had the upper hand: they had to try it and cast lots. It fell to the sausage to gather wood; the mouse became cook, and the bird was to fetch water.

What happened? The sausage set off to gather wood, the bird lighted the fire, the mouse put the pot on, and they waited alone for the sausage to come home, bringing the wood for the next day. But the sausage stayed out for so long that they both feared the worst, so the bird flew out a little way to meet her. But not far off he found a dog on the road, who had met the poor sausage and treated her as fair game: he had seized her and swallowed her up. The bird accused the dog loudly of highway robbery, but his words were of no use for, declared the dog, he had found forged papers on the sausage, on account of which her life was forfeit to him.

Sad at this, the bird picked up the wood, flew home, and told the mouse what he had seen and heard. They were very upset, but agreed to do their best and stay together. So the bird laid the table and the mouse saw to the food; she was about to serve it up and, like the sausage, she wanted to swish and swirl among the vegetables to butter them, but before she was halfway though, she was brought to a stop and lost everything, hide and hair, and life and limb.

When the bird came in and wanted to serve their dinner, there was no cook to be seen. In alarm, the bird scattered the wood all over the place, called and searched, but he couldn't find his cook at all. Owing to his carelessness the wood caught fire, so that a great blaze arose. The bird rushed to fetch water, but the bucket fell down the well and he fell with it, so that he couldn't stop himself from drowning.

18. *Mother Holle of the Snow*

THERE was once a widow who had two daughters. The one was beautiful and hard-working, the other was ugly and idle. But she loved the ugly, idle girl better, because she was her own daughter, while the other girl had to do all the work and be the Ashypet of the household. Every day the poor girl had to sit by a well on the highway, and she was forced to spin so much yarn that the blood ran from her fingers. Now it came about once that her spindle was covered in blood, so she leaned over the well, holding it to wash it clean; but it started out of her hand and fell to the bottom. She cried, and ran to her stepmother to tell her of the mishap. But her stepmother gave her such a scolding, and was cruel enough to tell her: 'You dropped the spindle, so you bring it back up.' So the girl went back to the well, at her wits' end. In her terror she jumped into the well to fetch the spindle. She lost consciousness, and when she woke and came to herself again, she was in a beautiful meadow where the sun was shining and thousands and thousands of flowers were growing. She walked along this meadow and came to a baker's oven which was full of bread. But the loaves were crying: 'Take us out, take us out, or else we'll burn! We were done long ago.' So she went up to the oven, and with the baker's shovel she drew out all the loaves one after another. After that she went on and came to a tree full of apples. It called out to her: 'Oh shake me, shake me! We apples are ripe, all of us.' So she shook the tree until the apples fell like rain, and she went on shaking until there were no more left on the tree; and when she had put them all together in a pile, she went on again. At last she came to a little house. An old woman was peering out of it, but because she had such great teeth the girl was frightened, and wanted to run away. But the old woman called after her: 'Why are you afraid, dear child? Stay with me, and if you're willing to do all the housework aright, all will be well for you. You must just take care to make my bed well, and shake it out properly so that the feathers fly: then it will snow in the world.[1] I am Mother Holle of the Snow.' Because the old woman spoke so kindly to her, the girl took heart, consented, and entered her service. And she looked after everything to her satisfaction, always shook the bed out vigorously so that the feathers flew about like snowflakes, and in return she had a good life with the old woman, not a cross word and every day stews and roasts. Now, after spending a while with Mother Holle she grew sad, and at first she did not know herself what was wrong, but at last she recognized it was homesickness. Although her life here was a thousand times better than at home, she still longed to return. At last she said to the old woman: 'I'm grieving for home, and even though my life down here is so good, all the same I can't stay here any longer; I must go back up to my own people again.' Mother Holle said: 'I'm pleased with you for wanting to go back home, and because you have served me so faithfully I will take you back up myself.' She took her by the hand and led her to a great gateway. The gate was opened, and just as the girl was standing underneath, it rained gold in great torrents, and all the gold clung to her so that she was completely covered with it. 'You shall have this because you have worked so hard,' Mother Holle told her, and she also gave her back the spindle she had lost when it fell into the well. Then the gate shut, and the girl found herself up in the world, not far from her mother's house. When she walked into the yard the cockerel was sitting on the well, and he cried:

> 'Cock-a-doodle-doo,
> Your golden maid's come back to you.'

So she went inside to her mother, and because she was all covered with gold she was well received by her mother and her sister.

The girl told them all that had happened to her, and when the mother heard how she had come into her great wealth, she wanted to help the other ugly, idle daughter to the same good fortune. She had

[1] That is why in Hesse they say, when it snows, that Mother Holle is making her bed [the Grimms' note].

to sit by the well and spin, and to make her spindle covered in blood she pricked her finger and thrust her hand into the thorn-hedge. Then she threw the spindle into the well and jumped in after it herself. She arrived, like her sister, on the beautiful meadow, and she walked along the same path. When she reached the baker's oven the loaves called out again: 'Oh, take us out, take us out, or else we'll burn! We were done long ago.' But the idle girl replied: 'Wouldn't I just like to get dirty!' and went on. She soon arrived at the apple-tree, which called: 'Oh, shake me, shake me! We apples are ripe, all of us.' But she replied: 'That's just what I thought: one of you could fall on my head'—and went on her way. When she arrived in front of Mother Holle's house she wasn't afraid, because she had already heard of her great teeth, and so she entered her service straight away. On her first day she forced herself to work hard and follow what Mother Holle told her, for she was thinking of all the gold that Mother Holle would give her. On her second day she already began to idle, on her third day still more, and then she wouldn't get up in the mornings. Nor did she make Mother Holle's bed as she should, for she didn't shake it so that the feathers flew. Mother Holle soon became tired of this and gave her notice. The idle girl was well content with that, for she thought that now it would rain gold. Mother Snow led her too to the gateway, but as she stood underneath it a great cauldron of tar was emptied over her. 'That's as a reward for your services,' said Mother Holle, and she closed the gate. So the idle girl went home, but she was all covered with tar, and when he saw her the cockerel on the well cried:

> 'Cock-a-doodle-doo,
> Your dirty maid's come back to you.'

But the tar stuck fast to her, and for as long as she lived it wouldn't go away.

19. *The Seven Ravens*

THERE was once a man who had seven sons, but he still didn't have a little daughter, however much he wished for one. At last his wife again gave him hope of another child, and when the baby came into the world it was indeed a little girl. Their joy was great, but the baby was small and frail, and because she was so weak she was to be baptized at once. Their father sent one of the boys to the well in haste to fetch christening water; the other six ran along with him, and because each of them wanted to be the first to draw the water, the pitcher fell into the well. There they stood, not knowing what to do, and none of them dared go home. When they still hadn't come back their father grew impatient, saying: 'They're sure to have forgotten it playing some game, the godless boys.' He was fearful that the little girl would be forced to quit this life unbaptized, and in his anger he cried out: 'I wish the boys would all turn into ravens.' The words were hardly out of his mouth when he heard a whirring in the air above his head. He looked up—and saw seven coal-black ravens flying off and away.

The boys' parents were unable to take back this curse, but although they were sad at losing their seven sons, they were in some measure consoled by their dear little daughter, who soon grew strong and became more beautiful with every day. For a long time she didn't even know that she had had any brothers, for her parents took care not to mention them, until one day by chance she heard folk talking about her: certainly the girl was beautiful, they said, but she was to blame really for the dreadful thing that had happened to her seven brothers. She was very troubled at this, and went to her father and mother and asked whether she had once had any brothers, and what had become of them. Now her parents could conceal the secret no longer, but they said it was a fate decreed by Heaven, and that her birth was only the innocent occasion for it. However, it troubled the girl's conscience every day, and she believed she had to save her brothers. She had neither rest nor repose until one day she set off and went out into the wide world to seek her brothers, wherever they might be, and set them free, cost what it may. She took nothing with her but a little ring from her parents to remind her of them, a loaf of bread for when she was hungry, a little pitcher of water for when she was thirsty, and a little seat for when she was weary.

Then she walked on and on, far, as far as the world's end. She went to the sun, but the sun was too hot and frightening, and he ate up little children. In haste she ran away and ran off to the moon, but the moon was far too cold and like the sun unkind and cruel, saying when he noticed the girl: 'I smell, I smell the flesh of a human child.' Quickly she made off and came to the stars, who were kind and friendly towards her, and each one was sitting on his own special little seat. As for the morning star, he stood up and gave her a chicken-bone, saying: 'Without this little bone you will be unable to unlock the glass mountain, and the glass mountain is where your brothers are.'

The girl took the little bone, wrapped it safely in a kerchief, and departed, walking all the way until she reached the glass mountain. The gate was locked and she was about to take out the little bone, but when she undid her kerchief it was empty, and she had lost the kind star's gift. Now what was she to do? The good little sister took a knife, cut off her little finger, put it into the lock, and opened the gate with ease. When she had gone inside a little dwarf came towards her, saying: 'Child, what are you looking for?' 'I'm looking for my brothers, the seven ravens,' she answered. The dwarf said: 'My masters, the ravens, are not at home, but if you wish to wait until they arrive, then enter.' Then the dwarf carried in the ravens' meal on seven little plates and in seven little goblets, and from each of the plates their sister ate a little morsel, and from each of the goblets she drank a little sip; and as for the last goblet, she dropped the little ring she had brought with her into it.

All at once she heard a fluttering and a flapping. At this the dwarf said: 'My masters, the ravens, are flying home now.' They arrived, and wanting to eat and drink they sought out their plates and goblets. Then one after another they said: 'Who's been eating from my plate? Who's been drinking from my goblet? It was a human mouth.' And as the seventh reached the bottom of his goblet, the little ring rolled towards him. He looked at it, and recognized that it was a ring belonging to their father and mother, and he said: 'God grant it was our sister here, for then we would be set free.' When the girl, who was standing behind the door listening, heard this wish she stepped out—and all the ravens regained their human form once more. And they hugged and kissed one another, and full of joy they made their way home.

20. *Little Redcap*

THERE was once a sweet little wench who was loved by everyone who simply cast eyes on her, but she was loved most of all by her grandmother, who gave the child all the presents she could think of. Once she gave her granddaughter a little cap made of red velvet, and because it looked so pretty on her and she wouldn't wear any other, she was always called Little Redcap. One day her mother said to her: 'Come, Little Redcap, here's a cake and a bottle of wine. Take them out to your grandmother; she's weak and ill, and she'll feel all the better for enjoying them. Be on your way before it gets hot, and once you're out in the country walk along nicely and don't stray from the path, or else you'll fall and break the glass and grand-mother will have nothing. And when you go into her parlour, don't forget to say "Good morning", and don't peek into every corner before you do.'

'I'll do just as you say,' Little Redcap told her mother, 'I promise.' But her grandmother lived out in the forest, half an hour from the village. Now, as Little Redcap was entering the forest she was met by the wolf. But she had no idea what a wicked beast he was, and wasn't afraid of him. 'Good morning, Little Redcap,' he said. 'Thank you, wolf.' 'Where are you off to so early, Little Redcap?' 'To grand-mother's.' 'What are you carrying under your apron?' 'Cake and wine. We did the baking yesterday; this is to do grandmother good, for she's weak and ill, and to bring back her strength.' 'Little Redcap, where does your grandmother live?' 'A good quarter of an hour further on in the forest. Beneath the three tall oak trees, that's where her house is. There are hazel-hedges below, surely you know that,' said Little Redcap. The wolf thought to himself: 'The tender young thing, she'll make a good meal and she'll taste even better than the old woman: use some guile when you go about it and you'll catch both of them.' So for a while he walked along at Redcap's side, then he said: 'Little Redcap, just see those pretty flowers all about; why don't you look round? I don't think you are listening at all to how sweetly the birds are singing. You're walking along wrapped up in yourself, as if you were going to school, and it's so bright and cheerful out here in the forest.'

Little Redcap opened her eyes wide, and when she saw how the sunbeams were dancing to and fro between the trees, and how everywhere was full of beautiful flowers, she thought: 'If I take grandmother a bunch of fresh flowers, that will give her pleasure too. It's so early in the day that I'll still arrive there in time.' So she strayed from the path into the forest, looking for flowers. And no sooner had she picked one than she thought there was another further on that was prettier, so she went after that, and wandered deeper and deeper into the wood. The wolf, on the other hand, went straight off to the grandmother's house and knocked at the door. 'Who's out there?' 'Little Redcap. I'm bringing cake and wine. Open the door.' 'Just lift the latch,' her grandmother called. 'I'm too weak, and I'm not able to get up.' The wolf lifted the latch, the door sprang open, and without saying a word he went straight to the grandmother's bed and swallowed her up. Then he dressed up in her clothes, put on her bonnet, got into her bed, and drew the curtains close.

As for Little Redcap, she had been chasing around after the flowers, and when she had gathered so many that she couldn't carry any more, she suddenly remembered her grandmother and made off towards her house. She was surprised that the door was standing open, and as she entered the parlour it seemed so strange to her in there that she thought: 'Lord, I feel so frightened today, and usually I like it so much at grandmother's!' She called out 'Good morning!' but received no answer. So she went up to the bed and drew back the curtains: there lay grandmother, with her bonnet pulled low on her face, and looking so odd. 'Oh grandmother, what big ears you have!' 'All the better to hear you.' 'Oh grandmother, what big eyes you have!' 'All the better to see you!' 'Oh grandmother, what big hands you have!' 'All the better to catch you!' 'But grandmother, what a terribly big mouth you have!' 'All the better to eat you up!' Scarcely had the wolf said this when he took one leap out of the bed and swallowed Little Redcap all up.

After the wolf had gratified his desires, he lay down in bed again, fell asleep, and began to snore noisily. The huntsman was just passing the house, and he thought: 'That old woman is snoring very loudly. I'd better see if anything's the matter with her.' So he went into the parlour, and as he reached the bed he saw that the wolf was lying in it. 'So this is where I find you, you old sinner,' he said. 'I've been looking for you for a long time.' He was about to aim his shotgun when it occurred to him that the wolf might have gobbled up the grandmother, and she might still be saved. So he didn't shoot, but took some shears instead and started to cut open the wolf's stomach. After he had made a few snips he saw the gleam of a little red cap, and then after a few more snips the girl leapt out, crying: 'Oh, how frightened I was! How dark it was inside the wolf!' And then the old grandmother emerged too, still alive and scarcely able to breathe. For her part Little Redcap quickly fetched some big stones, and they filled the wolf's stomach with them. When he woke up he tried to run away, but the stones were so heavy that he sank to the floor at once and fell down dead.

So they were all very happy; the huntsman skinned the wolf and went home with the pelt; the grandmother ate the cake and drank the wine Little Redcap had brought her, and was well again. As for Little Redcap, she thought: 'You'll never stray from the path into the forest by yourself again, not ever for the rest of your life, when your mother has told you not to.'

The tale is also told of how one day, when once again Little Redcap was taking a cake her mother had baked out to her grandmother, another wolf came up and chatted to her, trying to lead her away from the path. But Little Redcap was on her guard and went straight along and told her grandmother that she'd met the wolf, who had wished her a good morning but had peered at her with such a wicked look in his eyes: 'If it hadn't been on the public highway he'd have eaten me up.' 'Come,' said her grandmother, 'let's lock the door so that he can't get in.' Soon afterwards the wolf knocked at the door, calling: 'Open the door, grandmother, it's Little Redcap, bringing you cake.' But they stayed silently inside and didn't open the door. Old Grey-Hairs crept round the house a few times and at last jumped up onto the roof, intending to wait until Little Redcap set off for home that evening. Then he would creep after her and eat her up in the dark. But the grandmother could see what he had in mind. Now outside the house there stood a big stone trough, so she said to the child: 'Take the pail, Little Redcap. I boiled sausages yesterday, so pour the water they were boiled in into the trough.' Little Redcap carried the pail until the great big trough was full to the brim. The smell of the sausages rose up to the wolf's nostrils; he sniffed and peered down, and in the end he stretched his neck out so far that he couldn't hold on any longer and began to slide. He slid like this down from the roof into the big trough and drowned. As for Little Redcap, she went happily back home, and no one did her any mischief.

21. *The Bremen Town Band*

A MAN once had a donkey who had carried sacks to the mill for years without complaint. But now the poor beast's strength was failing, so that he grew less and less fit for work. Accordingly, his master thought he would cut back on his feed, but the donkey saw that this didn't promise well, so he ran away and took himself off towards Bremen: for there, he thought, he could play in the town band. When he had made his way for a while he came upon a hunting-hound lying in the road, panting like someone who had run himself into the ground. 'What are you panting like that for, Old Grip?' asked the donkey. 'Oh,' said the dog, 'because I'm old and getting weaker every day, and can't go hunting any more, my master wanted to put me down, so I took off. But how can I earn my bread now?' 'Do you know what?' said the donkey. 'I'm going to Bremen to play in the town band there. Come with me and join the band too. I'll play the lute and you can bang the drums.' The dog was pleased with the sugges-tion, and they went on their way. It wasn't long before they saw a cat sitting at the wayside with a face like a wet week. 'Well now, what's crossed you, old Sourpuss?' said the donkey. 'Who can be cheerful when their life's in danger?' answered the cat. 'Because I'm getting on and my teeth aren't so sharp, and I'd rather sit by the stove and spin than go hunting for mice, my mistress wanted to drown me. I ran away in time, it's true, but now I'm in need of good advice. Where shall I go?' 'Come to Bremen with us. After all, you know all about night-time serenading. Well, you can join the town band.' The cat liked the idea and went along with them. Soon the three runaways were passing a farmyard where the household cockerel was sitting on the gate and crowing with all his might. 'Your cries are cutting right through me,' said the donkey. 'What are you up to?' 'I've prophesied good weather,' said the cockerel, 'because it's Lady Day, when Our Lady washed the Christ-child's little shirt and wanted to dry it. But because tomorrow the farmer's wife has guests coming for Sunday lunch, she has shown no mercy and told the cook she wants to have me for soup tomorrow. So I'm to have my head chopped off this evening. Now I'm crowing at the top of my voice for as long as I'm still able.' 'Listen, you Redcrest,' said the donkey. 'Come away with us instead. We're going to Bremen. There's something better than death to be found everywhere. You've got a good voice, and if we make music together we're bound to do it in style.' The cockerel was pleased with the suggestion, and off they went all four of them together.

But they weren't able to reach the town of Bremen in one day, and by evening they had reached a forest where they thought they would pass the night. The donkey and the dog lay down under a tall tree. The cat and the cockerel took to the branches, but the cockerel flew right up to the treetop, where he would be safest. Before he went to sleep he looked about him once again towards all four points of the compass. It struck him that in the distance he could see a little spark flickering, and he called to his companions that a house couldn't be far away, for he could see a light. Said the donkey: 'Then we must set off and make for it, for this lodging isn't up to much.' The dog was of the view that a few bones with some meat on them would do him some good too. So they set off on the road towards the place the light was coming from, and soon they could see it shining brighter, and it grew bigger and bigger until they arrived outside a brightly lit robbers' den. The donkey, being the tallest, drew near the window and looked inside. 'What can you see, Greygrizzle?' asked the cockerel. 'What can I see?' answered the donkey. 'A table laid with wonderful food and drink, with robbers sitting round it having a good time.' 'That would suit us fine,' said the cockerel. 'Oh yes, would that we were there–her!' said the donkey. So the creatures put their heads together to see what they would have to do to drive the robbers out, and in the end they found a way to do it. The donkey was to stand with his front feet on the windowsill, the dog was to jump onto the donkey's back, the cat clamber onto the dog, and finally the cockerel would fly up and perch on the cat's head. When they had managed this, at a given signal they all of them began to make their music: the donkey brayed, the dog barked, the cat caterwauled, and the cockerel crowed. Then through the window and into the room they charged, making the panes rattle. The robbers jumped to their feet at this terrible howling: they could only think it was a ghost entering the room. Terrified, they fled out into the forest. Then the four companions sat down at the table, helped themselves to what was left, and ate as if they expected to go hungry for a month.

When the four minstrels had finished, they put out the light and looked for somewhere to sleep, each according to his nature and according to what was comfortable for him. The donkey lay down on the dung-heap, the dog behind the door, the cat on the hearth by the warm ashes, and the cockerel perched on the roost-beam; and because they were tired after the long way they had come, they soon fell asleep. When midnight was past, and the robbers saw from afar that there was no longer any light burning in the house and that everything seemed to be quiet, their chief said: 'We shouldn't have let ourselves be scared out of our wits like that,' and he told one of them to go and spy out the house. The scout found everything quiet and went into the kitchen to kindle a light. And because he thought the fiery glow of the cat's eyes were burning coals, he held a sulphur-match to them to light it. But the cat didn't see the joke and leapt at his face, spitting and scratching. He was mightily frightened at this, and ran to get out by the back door. But the dog, who was lying there, leapt up and bit him in the leg; and as he was racing across the yard past the dung-heap, the donkey gave him another hearty kick with his hind leg. For his part, the cockerel, who had been roused from his sleep by the commotion and had woken up all fresh and bright, crowed down from his beam: 'Cock-a-doodle-doo!' Then the robber ran as fast as he could back to his chief and said: 'Oh, there's a fearful witch sitting in the house. I felt her breath on me and she scratched my face with her long fingers. And at the door there's a man standing with a knife who stabbed me in the leg. And there's a black monster lying in the yard who hit out at me with a wooden cudgel. And up on the roof the judge is sitting, and he called out "Bring the rogue before me". So I upped and ran away.' From then on the robbers didn't dare enter the house ever again, but the four Bremen musicians were so delighted living there that they didn't want to leave it ever. And the last person who told this tale has her mouth still warm from the telling.

22. *The Singing Bone*

IN a certain country a great lamentation was once raised on account of a wild boar who grubbed up the farmers' fields, killed the cattle, and ripped up folks' bodies with its tusks. The king promised a rich reward to anyone who could free the land from this scourge, but the beast was so big and strong that no one dared venture near the forest where it lived. At last the king had it proclaimed that whoever caught or killed the wild boar should have his only daughter for wife.

Now there were two brothers living in that land, sons of a poor man. They came forward, determined to risk the enterprise. The elder, who was cunning and clever, did so out of pride; the younger, who was innocent and simple, did so out of his good heart. The king said: 'So that you are all the more certain of finding the beast, you should enter the forest from opposite sides.' So the elder went in from the west, and the younger from the east. And after the younger had been walking for a while, a little manikin came up to him. He was holding a black spear in his hand, and said: 'I shall give you this spear because your heart is innocent and good. You can use it to go after the wild boar with an easy mind; he will do you no harm.' He thanked the manikin, shouldered the spear, and went on his way without fear. Not long afterwards he caught sight of the beast, which ran at him. But he held the spear out towards it, and in its blind rage the boar ran onto it so violently that his heart was sliced in two. Then the boy took the monster on his shoulders and walked homewards, intending to bring it to the king.

As he came out on the other side of the forest, at its edge there stood a house where people were carousing with dancing and wine. His elder brother had gone inside, thinking that the boar wasn't going to run away, after all, and he wanted to drink himself into the right brave spirit first. But when he caught sight of his younger brother coming out of the forest laden with his spoils, his envious and malicious heart gave him no peace. He called to him: 'Come inside, dear brother, take a rest, and refresh yourself with a glass of wine.' The younger, who suspected no evil, went in and told him about the kind little man who had given him the spear he had used to kill the boar. The elder detained him until evening, when they went away together. But when they arrived in the dark at a bridge over a stream, the elder made the younger go ahead, and when he was halfway across the water he struck him a blow from behind, so that he fell dead. He buried him beneath the bridge, then he took the boar and brought it to the king, claiming that he had killed it. At this, he received the king's daughter as his wife. When there was no sign of his younger brother's return, he said: 'The boar will have ripped up his body,' and everyone believed him.

But because nothing remains hidden from God, even this black deed was to come to light. One day, many years later, a shepherd was driving his flock across the bridge, and he noticed in the sand below a little snow-white bone. He thought it would make a good mouth-piece, so he clambered down and picked it up, and he carved it into a mouthpiece for his horn. When he blew on it for the first time, to the shepherd's great amazement the little bone began to sing of its own accord.

> 'Shepherd, hear what I am saying,
> For that's my bone that you are playing:
> My brother struck me with a blow,
> Buried me by the bridge below,
> To claim he killed the fierce beast,
> And take his royal bride to their wedding feast.'

'What a strange little horn,' said the shepherd, 'singing of its own accord like that. I must take it to the king.' When he came before the king with it, the little horn began to sing its song once again. The king understood it perfectly and had the earth beneath the bridge dug up. Then the entire skeleton of the murdered brother came to light. The wicked brother couldn't deny his deed. He was sewn into a sack and drowned alive, but the bones of the boy who had been slain were laid to rest in a beautiful grave in the churchyard.

23. *The Devil With the Three Golden Hairs*

THERE was once a poor woman who bore a little son, and because he was born with a good-luck caul wrapped round him, it was foretold that in his fourteenth year he would have a king's daughter as his wife. Now it came about that soon afterwards the king came to the village, but no one knew that it was the king. When he asked what was new there, they answered: 'A few days ago there was a child born here with a good-luck caul, and whatever someone like that undertakes will always turn out luckily. It's also been foretold that in his fourteenth year he is to have the king's daughter as his wife.' The king, who had a wicked heart and was filled with anger at this prophecy, went to the parents and, pretending to be friendly, said: 'You poor people, hand your child over to me; I will take care of him.' At first they refused, but when the stranger offered solid gold in exchange and they thought: 'He's a good-luck child; after all, things are bound to work out well for him,' in the end they agreed and gave him the child.

The king put him in a casket and rode on further with it until he came to a deep river. Then he threw the casket into the water, thinking: 'I've saved my daughter from this unwelcome suitor.' But the casket didn't sink; instead, it sailed like a little ship, and not a drop of water made its way inside. It sailed on like this until it was two miles from the king's chief city. There was a mill here, where it got caught in the weir. A miller's apprentice, who by great good luck was standing nearby and noticed it, drew it towards him with a hook, thinking to find great treasures, but when he opened it, lying inside was a bonny boy, bright and happy. He took him to the miller and his wife, and because they had no children they were glad, saying: 'It is a gift to us from God.' They looked after the foundling well, and he grew up with all the virtues.

It happened that one day during a storm the king entered the mill. He asked the miller and his wife whether the tall lad was their son. 'No,' they answered, 'he's a foundling. Fourteen years ago he sailed up to the weir in a casket, and the miller's apprentice pulled him out of the water.' The king realized that this was no one else but the good-luck child he had thrown into the river, and he said: 'Good people, couldn't the lad take a letter to my lady the queen? I'll give him two pieces of gold as payment.' 'As my lord king commands,' they answered, and told the boy to make ready. Then the king wrote a letter to the queen, which said: 'As soon as the boy arrives with this letter he is to be killed and buried. It is all to be done before my return.'

The boy set off with this letter, but he lost his way, and in the evening came to a great forest. He saw a small light in the darkness, so he went towards it and arrived at a little house. When he went inside he saw an old woman all alone by the fire. She was frightened when she saw the boy, asking: 'Where do you come from, and where are you going?' 'I come from the mill,' he replied, 'and I'm on my way to my lady the queen, for I have to take her a letter; but because I've lost my way in the forest, I'd like to stay here for the night.' 'You poor boy,' said the woman, 'you've fallen into a robbers' den, and when they come home, they will kill you.' 'Whatever happens,' said the boy, 'I'm not afraid; but I'm so tired I can't go any further.' And he stretched out on a bench and fell asleep. Soon afterwards the robbers arrived, and asked angrily who was the young stranger lying there. 'Oh,' said the old woman, 'he's an innocent child. He lost his way in the forest and I took him in out of charity. He's supposed to be taking a letter to the queen.' The robbers broke open the letter and read it. It said that the boy was to be killed straight away as soon as he arrived. Then the hard-hearted robbers felt pity. Their chief tore up the letter and wrote another which said that as soon as the boy arrived he was to be married straight away to the king's daughter. Then they left him lying peacefully on his bench until the next day, and when he woke up they gave him the letter and put him on the right road. For her part the queen, once she had received the letter and read it, ordered a splendid wedding celebration and the good-luck child was married to the king's daughter; and, as the lad was handsome and kind, she lived with him happy and content.

After some time the king returned to his palace and saw that the prophecy had been fulfilled and the good-luck child was married to his daughter. 'How did this happen?' he said. 'In my letter I gave a very different command.' Then the queen handed him the letter, saying he could see for himself what was in it. The king read the letter and realized that it had been exchanged for another. He asked the young man what had happened to the letter he had entrusted to him, and why he had brought him a different one instead. 'I don't know anything about that,' he answered. 'It must have been exchanged in the night when I was asleep in the forest.' Full of rage, the king said: 'You shan't have it as easily as this. Anyone wanting to have my daughter must go down to Hell and fetch me three golden hairs from the Devil's head. If you bring me what I demand, you shall keep my daughter.' In setting this task, the king hoped to be rid of him for ever. But the good-luck child answered: 'I'll fetch the golden hairs for sure; I'm not afraid of the Devil.' After that he took his leave and began his travels.

His road led him to a great town, where the watchman at the gate questioned him closely, asking what sort of trade he practised and what he could do. 'I can do everything,' answered the good-luck child. 'Then you can do us a kindness,' said the watchman, 'if you can tell us why our market fountain, which used to flow with wine, has dried up and doesn't even run with water any more.' 'You shall learn why,' he answered, 'only wait until I return.' Then he went further and arrived outside another town. Again the watchman at the gate asked him what sort of trade he practised and what he could do. 'I can do everything,' he said. 'Then you can do us a kindness and tell us why a tree in our town, which used to bear golden apples, now doesn't even produce leaves.' 'You shall learn why,' he answered, 'only wait until I return.' Then he went further, and he reached a great river, which he had to cross. The ferryman asked him what sort of trade he practised and what he could do. 'I can do everything,' he answered. 'Then you can do me a kindness,' said the ferryman, 'and tell me why I have to ferry my boat to and fro endlessly, with never anyone to relieve me.' 'You shall learn why,' he answered, 'only wait until I return.'

When he had crossed the river, he found the entrance to Hell. It was black and sooty inside, and the Devil was not at home, but his grandmother was sitting there in a huge easy-chair. 'What do you want?' she said to him, but she didn't look all that wicked. 'I'd very much like three golden hairs from the Devil's head,' he answered, 'or else I won't be able to keep my wife.' 'That's asking a lot,' she said. 'If the Devil comes home and finds you, it'll cost you your life. But I feel sorry for you; I'll see if I can help you.' She turned him into an ant, saying: 'Creep into the fold of my skirt; you'll be safe there.' 'Yes,' he answered, 'that's all very well, but there are three things I'd still like to know: why a fountain, which used to flow with wine, has dried up and now doesn't even run with water any more; why a tree, which used to bear golden apples, no longer even produces greenery; and why a ferryman has to ferry his boat from one shore to the other endlessly without a relief.' 'Those are hard questions,' she answered, 'but just stay still and quiet, and attend to what the Devil says when I pull out the three golden hairs.'

When evening fell, the Devil came home. He had hardly stepped inside before he noticed a taint in the air. 'I smell, I smell human flesh,' he said. 'Something isn't right here.' Then he peered into every corner and looked about, but he could find nothing. His grandmother scolded him: 'The place has only just been swept,' she said, 'and everything's been tidied, and now you're turning it all upside-down. Your nose is always sniffing human flesh! Sit down and eat your supper.' When he had eaten and drunk he was tired, and his grandmother laid his head in her lap, saying she'd search his head for lice a while. It wasn't long before he fell asleep, puffing and snoring. Then the old woman took hold of one golden hair, pulled it out, and laid it at her side. 'Ouch!' cried the Devil, 'what are you up to?' 'I had a mysterious dream,' answered his grandmother; 'that's when I clutched at your hair.' 'What did you dream?' asked the Devil. 'I dreamed that a market fountain, which once used to flow with wine, had dried up and now wouldn't even run with water. What's causing it?' 'Ha! Wouldn't they like to know!' answered the Devil. 'There's a toad sitting under a stone in the fountain. If they kill that, the wine will flow again.' His grandmother went back to searching him for lice until he fell asleep, snoring so loud that the windows shook. Then she plucked out a second hair. 'Hey! What are you doing?' cried the Devil in a rage. 'Don't take it badly,' she answered; 'I did it while I was dreaming.' 'What did you dream this time?' he asked. 'I dreamed there was a kingdom where a fruit-tree stood which once used to bear golden apples and now wouldn't even produce greenery. What might be the reason for that?' 'Ha! Wouldn't they like to know!' answered the Devil. 'There's a mouse gnawing at the root. If they kill that, the tree will bear golden apples once more. But if it goes on gnawing, the tree will wither entirely. But leave me in peace, you and your dreams. If you disturb my sleep once again, you'll get a box on the ear.' His grandmother soothed him sweetly, and resumed searching his head for lice until he fell asleep, snoring away. Then she took hold of the third golden hair and plucked it out. The Devil leapt up with a shout and was about to do her a mischief, but she pacified him once more, saying: 'Who's answerable for their bad dreams!' 'What did you dream, then?' he asked—because he was curious, after all. 'I dreamed of a ferryman who complained that he had to ferry his boat to and fro endlessly and was never relieved. What might be causing it?' 'Ha! The dolt!' answered the Devil. 'If someone comes along and wants to be ferried across, he must put the pole into his hand. Then the other has to do the ferrying, and he is free.' As the grandmother had pulled out the three golden hairs and the three questions had been answered, she left the old monster in peace, and he slept until day broke.

When the Devil had sallied forth once more, the old woman drew the ant out of the fold in her skirt and restored the good-luck child back to his human shape. 'Here are the three golden hairs for you,' she said, 'and what the Devil said to your three questions you'll have heard for sure.' 'Yes,' he answered, 'I heard, and I'll keep it firmly in mind.' 'Well, you had some help,' she said, 'and now you can go on your way.' He thanked the old woman for her help in need, and was very pleased that everything had gone so well for him. When he reached the ferryman he was supposed to give him the promised answer. 'Ferry me across first,' said the good-luck child, 'and I will tell you how you can be relieved,' and when he reached the farther shore he gave him the Devil's advice: 'If someone else comes along, just put the pole into his hand.' He went on and reached the town where the barren tree stood and where the watchman also wanted an answer. So he told him what he'd heard the Devil say: 'Kill the mouse that is gnawing at its root, and it will bear golden apples once more.' The watchman thanked him, and as a reward gave him two donkeys laden with gold to follow after him. At last he reached the town whose fountain had dried up. So he said to the watchman what the Devil had said: 'There's a toad sitting in the fountain beneath a stone. You must look for it and kill it, and then the fountain will flow with wine aplenty.' The watchman thanked him, and likewise gave him two donkeys laden with gold.

At last the good-luck child arrived back home to his wife, whose heart was full of joy when she saw him again and heard how well everything had worked out for him. He took the king what he had demanded, the Devil's three golden hairs, and when the king saw the four donkeys with the gold, he was very pleased and said: 'Now all the conditions are fulfilled, and you may keep my daughter. But, my dear son-in-law, do tell me, where did all that gold come from? It's a mighty treasure!' 'I crossed a river,' he answered, 'and that's where I took it from. It was lying there on the bank instead of sand.' 'Can I get some for myself there too?' asked the king, who was very keen to find out. 'As much as you want,' he answered. 'There's a ferryman on the river. Have him ferry you over, and on the other side you can fill your bags full.' The greedy king set off with all speed, and when he came to the river he hailed the ferryman to take him across. The ferryman came and told him to get into his boat, and when they arrived on the far shore he put the punt-pole into the king's hand and leapt off and away. As for the king, he was forced to ferry the boat as a punishment for his sins.

'Is he still ferrying it?' 'What do you think? Nobody will have taken the pole from him.'

24. *The Girl With No Hands*

THERE was once a miller who, little by little, grew so poor that he had nothing left but his mill and the great apple-tree standing behind it. One day he had gone into the forest to fetch wood, when an old man he had never seen before came up to him and said: 'What are you plaguing yourself for, cutting wood? I'll make you rich if you promise me whatever is standing behind your mill.' 'That can't be anything but my apple-tree,' thought the miller, said yes, and pledged it to the strange man. But the stranger gave a mocking laugh, saying: 'After three years have gone by I shall come and fetch what belongs to me,' and he went away. When the miller returned home his wife met him, saying: 'Tell me, miller, where has this sudden wealth in our house come from? All at once the closets and cupboards are full, every one. Not a soul put it there, and I've no idea how it all happened.' He answered: 'It comes from a stranger who met me in the forest and promised me great riches. On my part I made a pact to give him whatever was standing behind the mill. We can surely give him the great apple-tree in return.' 'Oh, husband,' said the wife in terror, 'that was the Devil. He didn't mean the apple-tree; he meant our daughter. She was standing behind the mill brushing the yard.'

The miller's daughter was beautiful and devout, and in those three years she lived fearing God and without sin. When the time was up and the day came when the Evil One intended to carry her off, she washed herself clean and pure, and made a circle round herself with chalk. The Devil appeared very early, but he couldn't get near her. In fury he said to the miller: 'See that you take every drop of water away from her, so that she's no longer able to wash herself, or else I'll have no power over her.' The miller was afraid and did as he was told. The next day the Devil came again, but she had wept onto her hands and they were quite clean and pure. And again he was powerless to approach her, and in a rage he said to the miller: 'Chop off her hands, or else I won't be able to get hold of her.' The miller was horrified, and replied: 'How could I chop off the hands of my own child?' Then the Evil One threatened him, saying: 'If you don't do as I ask, you'll be mine yourself, and I'll come and carry you off.' The father was filled with fear, and he promised to obey him. Then he went to the girl and said: 'My child, if I don't chop off both your hands, the Devil will carry me off, and in my terror I promised him I would do it. Still, help me in my distress, and forgive me for the ill I am doing to you.' She answered: 'Dear father, do with me what you will; I am your child.' And she placed her hands down and let them be chopped off. The Devil came for the third time, but she had wept so long and so much upon the stumps that they were quite clean and pure. So he was forced to retreat, and lost all claim to her.

The miller said to her: 'I have gained so much because of you; I will keep you in luxury all your life.' But she replied: 'I cannot stay here. I shall go away; folk in their pity will give me as much as I need.' Then she had her maimed arms bound to her back, and at daybreak she set off on her way, walking the whole day long until night fell. Then she came to a royal garden, and in the moonlight she saw that there were trees growing there bearing beautiful fruit. She couldn't enter it, though, for there was a moat around it. And because she had been walking all day without a bite to eat and was tormented by hunger, she thought to herself: 'Oh, if only I were in that garden, so that I could eat some of the fruit—or else I shall perish.' Then she knelt down and called on the Lord God and prayed. All at once an angel came by and closed a sluice in the water so that the moat grew dry and she was able to walk across. Then she went into the garden, and the angel went with her. She saw a tree with fruit: they were beautiful pears, but they had all been counted. She went up to it, and to still her hunger she ate one of the pears from it with her mouth—but only one. The gardener saw her too, but because the angel was standing nearby he was afraid, thinking that the girl was a spirit, and kept silent, not daring to call out or speak to the spirit. When she had eaten the pear her hunger was satisfied, and she went and hid in the bushes. The king who owned the garden came down next morning. He counted and saw that one of the pears was missing. He asked the gardener what had become of it: it wasn't lying under the tree, but still, it was gone. Then the gardener answered: 'Last night a spirit came into the garden. It had no hands, and it ate a pear from the tree with its mouth.' The king said: 'How did the spirit cross the moat?' 'Someone in a snow-white gown came from Heaven. He closed the sluice and stopped the water so that the spirit could cross the moat. And because it must have been an angel, I was afraid, and I didn't ask any questions, and I didn't call out. Then, after the spirit had eaten the pear, it went away.' The king said: 'If it is as you say, I will keep watch with you tonight.'

When it grew dark, the king entered the garden, bringing with him a priest who was to address the spirit. All three sat down beneath the tree, on the lookout. At midnight the girl came creeping out of the bushes. She went up to the tree and again she ate a pear from it with her mouth; but next to her there stood the angel in the white robe. Then the priest stepped forward and said: 'Have you come from God or from the world? Are you spirit or mortal?' She replied: 'I am not a spirit, but a poor mortal, forsaken by all but God.' The king said: 'Though you have been forsaken by all the world, I shall not forsake you.' He took her with him into his royal palace, and because she was so beautiful and devout, he loved her with all his heart, and he had hands of silver made for her, and took her to be his consort.

A year later the king had to make a journey, so he commended the young queen to his mother, saying: 'When she is brought to bed, take care of her and tend her well, and write me a letter at once.' Then she bore a beautiful son. So his old mother promptly wrote a letter, sending him the joyful news. But on the way the messenger rested at the side of a brook, and being weary from the long journey, he fell asleep. Then the Devil, who had always been plotting to harm the devout queen, came up and exchanged the letter for another which said that the queen had brought a changeling into the world. When the king read the letter he was horrified and deeply troubled, but in reply he wrote that they should care for the queen and tend her well until he arrived. The messenger returned with the letter, rested at the same spot, and fell asleep again. Then the Devil came a second time and put a different letter into his pouch, which said they were to kill the queen together with her child. The old mother was filled with horror when she received the letter—she couldn't believe it, and wrote to the king once more. But the reply was no different, for each time the Devil foisted a false letter onto the messenger, and in the last letter it even said that they were to keep the queen's tongue and eyes as a token.

But the old mother wept that such innocent blood should be shed, and by night she sent for a hind, cut out its tongue and eyes, and kept them for the king. Then she said to the queen: 'I cannot have you killed, as the king commands—but you may not stay here any longer. Go with your baby out into the wide world and never come back again.' She bound the baby onto her back, and with eyes full of tears the poor woman went forth. She came to a great wild forest, where she knelt and prayed to God, and the angel of the Lord appeared to her and led her to a little house which had a sign on it with the words: 'Here all may dwell free.' Out of the house there came a snow-white maiden who said: 'Welcome, my Lady Queen,' and led her inside. Then she untied the little boy from her back and held him at her breast for him to drink, and after that she laid him in a beautiful little bed made ready for him. Then the poor woman said: 'How do you know that I was once a queen?' The white maiden replied: 'I am an angel, sent by God to look after you and your child.' So she stayed in the house for nearly seven years and was looked after well, and by God's mercy, because of her piety, the hands which had been chopped off grew once more.

At length the king returned home from his journey, and the first thing he desired was to see his wife with their child. Then his old mother began to weep, saying: 'You wicked man, how could you write to me telling me I should take the lives of two innocent souls?', and she showed him the two letters which the Evil One had forged. She went on to say: 'I have done as you commanded,' and showed him the tokens of tongue and eyes. Then the king began to weep for his poor wife and his little son so much more bitterly than she that his old mother took pity on him, saying: 'Be content. She is still alive. I had a hind slaughtered in secret, and I took the token eyes and tongue from her. But as to your wife, I bound the baby on her back and bade her go out into the wide world. She had to promise never to come back here because you were so angry with her.' Then the king said: 'I will go as far as the sky is blue. I will not eat or drink until I have found my dear wife and child again, if they have not been killed in the meantime or died of hunger.'

Then the king went wandering for seven long years, looking for her in every stony cliff and rocky cave. But he could not find her, and he thought she had perished. He neither ate nor drank throughout all this time, but God sustained him. At last he came to a great forest, and in it he found the little house which had the sign with the words: 'Here all may dwell free.' Then the white maiden came out, took him by the hand, and led him inside, saying: 'Welcome, my Lord King,' and asked him where he had come from. He replied: 'I have been wandering for almost seven years now, looking for my wife and her child. But I cannot find her.' The angel offered him food and drink, but he did not accept it and desired only to rest a little. Then he lay down to sleep and covered his face with a kerchief.

Then the angel went into the little room where the queen was sitting with her son, whom she was used to calling 'Full of Woe'. The angel said: 'Go out with your child; your husband has come.' Then she went out to where he was lying, and the kerchief fell from his face. Then she said: 'Full of Woe, pick up your father's kerchief and cover his face again.' The child picked it up and covered the king's face again. The king heard these words in his sleep, and gladly let the kerchief fall once more. Then the little boy grew impatient and said: 'Mother dear, how can I cover my father's face, when I haven't a father in the world? I've learned to pray "Our Father, which art in Heaven . . ." That was when you told me that my father was in Heaven and that he was the Lord God. How am I to recognize a wild man like this? He's not my father.' When the king heard this, he sat up and asked who she might be. Then she said: 'I am your wife, and this is your son, Full of Woe.' And he saw her living hands and said: 'My wife had hands of silver.' She answered: 'God in his mercy made my natural hands grow once more.' And the angel went into the inner room and fetched the silver hands and showed them to him. Only then did he see for sure that it was his dear wife and child, and he kissed them and was joyful, saying: 'A heavy stone has fallen from my heart.' Then the angel of God feasted them once more, and then they went home to his old mother. Everywhere there was great rejoicing, and the king and queen celebrated their wedding once again, and they lived happily until the end of their blessed days.

25. *Clever Hans*

HANS's mother asks: 'Where you off to, Hans?' Hans answers: 'To Gretel's.' 'Behave yourself, Hans.' 'I will. 'Bye, mother.' ' 'Bye, Hans.'

Hans goes to Gretel's. 'Good-day, Gretel.' 'Good-day, Hans. Brought me something nice?' 'Brought nothing. Like being given.' Gretel gives Hans a needle. Hans says: ' 'Bye, Gretel.' ' 'Bye, Hans.'

Hans takes the needle, sticks it in a hay cart, and walks home behind the cart. ' 'Evening, mother.' ' 'Evening, Hans. Where've you been?' 'Been at Gretel's.' 'What did you take her?' 'Didn't take. Got given.' 'What did Gretel give you?' 'Gave a needle.' 'Where've you put the needle, Hans?' 'Stuck it in the hay cart.' 'That was stupid of you, Hans. You should stick the needle in your sleeve.' 'No matter, better next time.'

'Where you off to, Hans?' 'To Gretel's, mother.' 'Behave yourself, Hans.' 'I will. 'Bye, mother.' ' 'Bye, Hans.'

Hans goes to Gretel's. 'Good-day, Gretel.' 'Good-day, Hans. Brought me something nice?' 'Brought nothing. Like being given.' Gretel gives Hans a knife. ' 'Bye, Gretel.' ' 'Bye, Hans.'

Hans takes the knife, sticks it in his sleeve, and goes home. ' 'Evening, mother.' ' 'Evening, Hans. Where've you been?' 'Been at Gretel's.' 'What did you take her?' 'Didn't take. Got given.' 'What did Gretel give you?' 'Gave a knife.' 'Where've you put the knife, Hans?' 'Stuck it in my sleeve.' 'That was stupid of you, Hans. You should put the knife in your pocket.' 'No matter, better next time.'

'Where you off to, Hans?' 'To Gretel's, mother.' 'Behave yourself, Hans.' 'I will. 'Bye, mother.' ' 'Bye, Hans.'

Hans goes to Gretel's. 'Good-day, Gretel.' 'Good-day, Hans. Brought me something nice?' 'Brought nothing. Like being given.' Gretel gives Hans a young goat. ' 'Bye, Gretel.' ' 'Bye, Hans.'

Hans takes the goat, ties her legs, and puts her in his pocket. By

the time he reaches home she has suffocated. ' 'Evening, mother.'
' 'Evening, Hans. Where've you been?' 'Been at Gretel's.' 'What did
you take her?' 'Took nothing. Got given.' 'What did Gretel give
you?' 'Gave a goat.' 'Where've you put the goat, Hans?' 'Put it in my
pocket.' 'That was stupid of you, Hans. You should tie the goat
round the neck with a halter.' 'No matter, better next time.'

'Where you off to, Hans?' 'To Gretel's, mother.' 'Behave yourself,
Hans.' 'I will. 'Bye, mother.' ' 'Bye, Hans.'

Hans goes to Gretel's. 'Good–day, Gretel.' 'Good–day, Hans.
Brought me something nice?' 'Brought nothing. Like being given.'
Gretel gives Hans a piece of bacon. ' 'Bye, Gretel.' ' 'Bye, Hans.'

Hans takes the bacon, ties it with a halter, and drags it behind him.
The dogs come and eat it up. When he comes home he has the halter
in his hand, but nothing left at the other end. ' 'Evening, mother.'
' 'Evening, Hans. Where've you been?' 'Been at Gretel's.' 'What did
you take her?' 'Took nothing. Got given.' 'What did Gretel give
you?' 'Gave a piece of bacon.' 'Where did you put the bacon, Hans?'
'Tied a halter, led home, dogs carried off.' 'That was stupid of you,
Hans. You should carry the bacon on your head.' 'No matter, better
next time.'

'Where you off to, Hans?' 'To Gretel's, mother.' 'Behave yourself,
Hans.' 'I will. 'Bye, mother.' ' 'Bye, Hans.'

Hans goes to Gretel's. 'Good–day, Gretel.' 'Good–day, Hans.
Brought me something nice?' 'Brought nothing. Like being given.'
Gretel gives Hans a calf. ' 'Bye, Gretel.' ' 'Bye, Hans.'

Hans takes the calf, puts it on his head, and the calf tramples on
his face. ' 'Evening, mother.' ' 'Evening, Hans. Where have you
been?' 'Been at Gretel's.' 'What did you take her?' 'Took nothing.
Got given.' 'What did Gretel give you?' 'Gave a calf.' 'Where did you
put the calf, Hans?' 'On my head. Trampled my face.' 'That was
stupid of you, Hans. You should lead the calf and tie it to the hay-rack.'
'No matter, better next time.'

'Where you off to, Hans?' 'To Gretel's, mother.' 'Behave yourself,
Hans.' 'I will. 'Bye, mother.' ' 'Bye, Hans.'

Hans goes to Gretel's. 'Good–day, Gretel.' 'Good–day, Hans.
Brought me something nice?' 'Brought nothing. Like being given.'
Gretel says to Hans: 'I'll come with you.'

Hans takes Gretel, ties a halter to her, leads her along, takes her to
the hay-rack, and fastens her there. Then Hans goes to his mother.

' 'Evening, mother.' ' 'Evening, Hans. Where've you been?' 'Been at Gretel's.' 'What did you take her?' 'Took nothing.' 'What did Gretel give you?' 'Gave nothing, came with me.' 'Where've you left Gretel?' 'Led on a halter, tied to the hay-rack, fed grass.' 'That was stupid of you, Hans. You should cast sheep's eyes at her.' 'No matter, better next time.'

Hans goes into the stall, pokes out the eyes of all the calves and sheep, and throws them into Gretel's face. Then Gretel gets angry, tears herself free and runs away, and is Hans's bride no more.

26. *Sensible Elsie*

THERE was once a man who had a daughter, and she was called Sensible Elsie. When she had grown up, her father declared: 'Time we found her a husband.' 'Yes,' said her mother, 'if only someone would turn up who would have her.' At last someone from a long way away did turn up. He was called Hans and he asked for her hand—but on condition that she should be really bright, too. 'Oho,' pronounced her father, 'that one is as bright as a button,' and her mother said: 'Oh, she can see the wind chase down the alley and hear the flies cough.' 'Yes,' said Hans, 'if she's not really bright, I won't have her.' Now when they were sitting at table after a meal, her mother said: 'Elsie, go down to the cellar and bring up some beer.' So Sensible Elsie took the pitcher from the wall and went down to the cellar, rattling sturdily with the lid on the way to pass the time. When she was down below, she fetched a little chair and placed it in front of the barrel so that she wouldn't need to bend and maybe hurt her back and be injured unexpectedly. Then she placed the can in front of her and turned the spigot. While the beer was running into the can, she didn't want her eyes to be idle so she looked up onto the wall. After much gazing to and fro she caught sight of a pickaxe right above her, left there accidentally by the masons. Then Sensible Elsie began to cry, saying: 'If I get Hans and we have a baby and she grows up and we send her down here into the cellar to draw beer, the pickaxe will fall on her head and strike her dead.' There she sat and wept and cried with all her might at the forthcoming calamity. The folk upstairs were waiting for their drink, but Sensible Elsie still did not come. So the wife said to the maid: 'Go down into the cellar, won't you, and see what's keeping Elsie.' The maid went and found her sitting in front of the barrel, howling noisily. 'Elsie, why are you crying?' asked the maid. 'Oh,' she answered, 'haven't I reason to cry? If I get Hans and we have a baby and she grows up and she's sent here to draw beer, perhaps the pickaxe will fall on her head and strike her dead.' At that the maid said: 'What a Sensible Elsie we have!' and sat down at her side and began to weep at the forthcoming calamity too. After a while, when the maid did not return and the folk upstairs were getting thirsty, the husband said to the house-servant: 'Go down into the cellar, won't you, and see what's keeping Elsie and the maid.' The servant went down; there sat Sensible Elsie and the maid, both of them crying together. So he asked: 'Why are you crying, then?' 'Oh,' said Elsie, 'haven't I reason to cry? If I get Hans and we have a baby and she grows up and she's sent here to draw beer, the pickaxe will fall on her head and strike her dead.' Then the servant said: 'What a Sensible Elsie we have!', sat down at her side, and he too began to bawl noisily. Upstairs they waited for the servant, but when he still did not come up the husband said to his wife: 'Go down into the cellar, won't you, and see what's keeping Elsie.' The wife went down and found all three lamenting. She asked what the reason was, and Elsie told her that her future baby would almost certainly be struck dead by the pickaxe if she grew up and had to draw beer and the pickaxe fell on her head. Then her mother, like the others, said: 'What a Sensible Elsie we have!', and sat down and joined in the weeping. Her husband upstairs waited a little while longer, but when his wife did not return and his thirst became stronger and stronger he declared: 'I'll have to go down into the cellar myself and see what's keeping Elsie.' But when he went into the cellar and there they were all sitting together weeping, and he heard the reason—that it was Elsie's baby's fault, the baby she might one day bring into the world, who could be struck dead by the pickaxe if she happened to be sitting under it to draw beer just at the moment it fell—he called out: 'What a Sensible Elsie!', and sat down and joined in the weeping too. The bridegroom remained upstairs alone for a long time. As no one showed any inclination to return, he thought: 'They'll be waiting for you down below. You must go down too and see what they have in mind.' When he went down, there sat the five of them howling and wailing quite pitifully, each outdoing the other. 'What kind of disaster has happened?' he asked. 'Oh, Hans dear,' said Elsie, 'if we marry and have a baby and she grows up and perhaps we send her down here to draw beer, and if the pickaxe left up there fell down, it could batter her on the head so that she's left lying for dead. Haven't we reason to cry?' 'Well,' said Hans, 'more brains than that aren't needed in my household. Because you're such a Sensible Elsie, I'll have you after all.' And he seized her by the hand and took her upstairs with him and they were wedded on the spot.

When Hans had had her for his wife for a while, he said: 'Wife, I'm going out to work and earn money for us. You go into the field and cut the corn for our bread.' 'Yes, Hans my dear, I'll do that.' After Hans had left she cooked herself a good porridge and took it with her to the field. Standing in front of the corn, she said to herself: 'What shall I do? Shall I cut it first or shall I sleep first? Hey, I'll sleep first.' So she lay down in the corn and went to sleep. Hans had come home long ago, but there was no sign of Elsie. 'What a Sensible Elsie I have,' he said. 'She's so hard-working that she doesn't even come home to eat.' But when she still failed to appear and evening had fallen Hans went out to see what she had cut. But nothing had been cut; on the contrary, she was lying in the corn sleeping. So Hans dashed home quickly and fetched a fowler's net with little bells on it and hung it round her; and she still went on sleeping. Then he ran home, locked the house door, and sat down on his chair and did some work. At length, when it was already quite dark, Sensible Elsie woke up, and when she stood up there was a clattering all round her and the little bells jingled at every step she took. Then she was frightened, and became confused over whether she really was Sensible Elsie or not, exclaiming: 'Is it me or isn't it?' But she didn't know what answer to give to that, and stood for a while in doubt. At last she thought: 'I'll go home and ask whether it's me or not—they'll know.' She ran to the door of her house, but it was locked, so she knocked on the window and called: 'Hans, is Elsie in there?' 'Yes,' answered Hans, 'she is in here.' At that she was frightened and said: 'Heavens, then it's not me out here,' and she went and tried another door. But when the people heard the jingling and tinkling they would not open up, and she could not find shelter anywhere. So she ran away from the village, and nobody has seen her since.

27. *The Table-Lay, the Gold-Donkey, and the Club in the Sack*

LONG years ago there was a tailor who had three sons, with only one goat between them. But because the goat provided all four of them with her milk, she had to be fed well and led out to pasture every day. The sons took turns to take her out. One day the eldest took her to the churchyard, where the finest grasses grew, and let her eat and jump about. In the evening, when it was time to go home, he asked: 'Goat, are you full?' The goat answered:

> 'So full of herbs and grass and hay
> I shan't want any more today, me–e–eh! me–e–eh!'

'Then let's go home,' said the boy, taking hold of her halter. He led her into her pen and tethered her fast. 'Well,' said the old tailor, 'did the goat have all the fodder she needs?' 'Oh,' answered his son, 'she's so full of herbs and grass and hay, she won't want any more today.' But his father wanted to make sure for himself. He went down into her pen, patted the dear creature, and asked: 'Goat, are you really full?' The goat answered:

> 'Why should I be full now, say?
> All I've done is jump today
> And found not a blade of grass or hay, me–e–eh! me–e–eh!'

'What's that?' cried the tailor. He ran upstairs and said to the boy: 'Oh, you young liar, telling me the goat was full and leaving her to go hungry!' And in his rage he took his yardstick from the wall and drove the boy out with buffets and blows.

Next day it was the second son's turn. He found a spot by the garden hedge where only the finest herbs were growing, and the goat ate them all right down to the ground. When evening came and he wanted to go home, he asked the goat: 'Goat, are you full?' The goat answered:

> 'So full of grass and leaves and hay
> I shan't want any more today, me–e–eh! me–e–eh!'

'Then let's go home,' said the boy, and he led her back and tethered her fast in her pen. 'Well,' said the old tailor, 'did the goat have all the fodder she needs?' 'Oh,' answered the son, 'she's so full of herbs and grass and hay, she won't want any more today.' This wasn't enough to convince the tailor, who went down into the pen and asked: 'Goat, are you really full?' The goat answered:

> 'Why should I be full now, say?
> All I've done is jump today
> And found not a blade of grass or hay, me-e-eh! me-e-eh!'

'You godless villain,' shouted the tailor, 'to let such a good creature go hungry!' He ran upstairs and with his yardstick he beat the boy out of the house.

Now the third son's turn came round. He wanted to do his job properly. He found a thicket of bushes with the richest leaves and let the goat graze on them. When evening came and he wanted to go home, he asked: 'Goat, are you really full?' The goat answered:

> 'So full of leaves and grass and hay
> I shan't want any more today, me-e-eh! me-e-eh!'

'Then let's go home,' said the boy, and he led her into her pen and tethered her fast. 'Well,' said the old tailor, 'did the goat have all the fodder she needs?' 'Oh,' answered the son, 'she's so full of grass and leaves and hay, she won't want any more today.' The tailor mistrusted this, went down, and asked: 'Goat, are you really full?' The wicked beast replied:

> 'Why should I be full now, say?
> All I've done is jump today
> And found not a blade of grass or hay, me-e-eh, me-e-eh.'

'Oh, the brood of liars!' shouted the tailor. 'One as godless and undutiful as the other! You shan't make a fool of me any longer!' And quite beside himself with rage, he bounded upstairs and thrashed the poor boy so mightily with his yardstick that he leapt out of the house.

Now the old tailor was alone with his goat. Next day he went down to her pen and patted her, saying: 'Come, my dear little creature, I'll take you to pasture myself.' He took her by the halter and led her to green hedges and to spots where yarrow was growing and other plants that goats enjoy. 'Now you can eat your fill to your heart's content,' he said to her, and let her graze till evening. Then he asked: 'Goat, are you full?' She answered:

> 'So full of herbs and grass and hay
> I shan't want any more today, me-e-eh! me-e-eh!'

'Then let's go home,' said the tailor and he led her into her pen and tethered her fast. As he was leaving, he turned round once more and said: 'Well, now you really *are* full.' But the goat didn't do any better by him, and cried:

> 'Why should I be full now, say?
> All I've done is jump today,
> And found not a blade of grass or hay, me-e-eh! me-e-eh!'

When the tailor heard this he was taken aback, and he realized that he had turned out his three sons without cause. 'Just wait,' he cried, 'you ungrateful creature, it's not enough just to drive you away. I'll mark you in such a way that you won't be able to show your face among respectable tailors ever again.' He bounded upstairs in haste, fetched his razor, lathered the goat's head, and shaved her as smooth as the palm of his hand. And because the yardstick would be too much of an honour, he fetched the whip and delivered such blows that she upped and leapt away with all her might.

As the tailor sat all alone in his house he fell into a great sadness. He would have gladly had his sons back, but nobody knew what had become of them. The eldest was apprenticed to a joiner, where he worked hard and cheerfully at learning the trade. And when the time had come for him to go journeying, his master made him a present of a little table, which certainly didn't look like anything special, and was made of common wood. But it had one good feature. If you set it up and said: 'Table, lay!', then at once the good little table was covered with a clean cloth and set with a plate and a knife and fork beside it, and jam-packed with dishes of stews and roasts and a tall glass glowing with red wine to gladden the heart. The young apprentice thought: 'This will be enough to last you your whole life.' He journeyed eagerly on in the wide world and was troubled not one bit whether an inn was good or bad or whether he could get a good meal there or not. If he pleased, he wouldn't put up at an inn at all, but would take his little table off his back in the open fields, in the forest, in a meadow, wherever he liked, and set it before him and command:

'Table, lay!', and everything his heart desired was there. At last it entered his head that he would go back to his father, for his anger would have cooled and he would receive his son gladly with the Table-Lay. It came about that on his way back home he arrived one evening at an inn that was full of guests. They bade him welcome and invited him to join them in their meal, for there was not much chance that he would get anything to eat otherwise. 'No,' the joiner replied, 'I won't rob you of your few mouthfuls. Instead, you shall be my guests.' They laughed, imagining he was just having a joke on them. But he set up his little wooden table in the middle of the parlour and commanded: 'Table, lay!' In a moment it was laid with fine food of a quality the innkeeper would not have been able to provide, and with a smell that rose sweetly to the guests' noses. 'Help yourselves, dear friends,' said the joiner, and when the guests saw that he meant it they didn't need to be asked twice, but drew up their chairs, got out their knives, and fell to with valour. And what amazed them most of all was, if one dish was emptied, then straight away another full one took its place. The innkeeper stood in a corner and gazed at the thing. He didn't know what to say, but he was thinking: 'You could certainly use a cook like that in your inn.' The joiner and his party made merry until late into the night. At last they lay down to sleep and the young journeyman too went to bed and put his little wishing-table against the wall. But the innkeeper's thoughts gave him no rest. It occurred to him that there was a little old table standing in his lumber-room that looked just like this one. He fetched it down very quietly and exchanged it for the wishing-table. Next morning the joiner paid the innkeeper for his stay, shouldered his little table without a thought that he had a false one, and went his way. At midday he arrived at his father's, who received him with great delight. 'Well now, my dear son, what trade have you learned?' 'Father, I've become a joiner.' 'A good trade,' responded the old man. 'But have you brought something back with you from your journeying?' 'Father, the best thing I've brought with me is this little table.' The tailor looked at it hard from all sides and said: 'You haven't made your masterpiece with this—it's a cheap old table.' 'But it's a Table-Lay,' answered the son. 'If I set it up and tell it to lay, straight away it will have the finest dishes on it, and a wine to go with them that will gladden your heart. Invite all our friends and relations for them to refresh and restore themselves, for the little table will make them all full.' When the guests were gathered together he set up his little table in the middle of the parlour and commanded: 'Table, lay.' But the little table didn't stir, and remained as empty as any other table that doesn't understand speech. Then the poor apprentice noticed that his table had been switched, and was ashamed at standing there like a liar. But his relations laughed at him and had to wend their way back home unfed and unwatered. The father got out his cloth again and went on tailoring, and as for the son, he went to work for a master-joiner.

The second son had gone to a miller and become an apprentice with him. When his serving-years were over the master-miller said to him: 'Because you've worked so well, I'll make you a present of a donkey of a very special kind. He doesn't pull a cart, nor carry sacks.' 'What's he good for, then?' asked the young apprentice. 'He spews gold,' answered the miller. 'If you stand him on a cloth and say "Bricklebrit", then the good beast will spew out gold pieces for you, front and back.' 'That's a fine gift,' said the apprentice, and he thanked his master and went out into the world. If he needed money, he had only to say to his donkey, 'Bricklebrit', and it rained gold pieces. All he had to do was to pick them up off the ground. Wherever he went, only the best was good enough for him, the dearer the better, for he always had a full purse. After he had looked around the world for a while, he thought: 'You must look your father up. When he sees the Gold-Donkey, he'll forget his anger and receive you kindly.' It came about that he happened upon the same inn where his brother's table had been switched. He was leading his donkey in by the bridle, and the innkeeper was about to take the beast from him and tether him up. But the young apprentice said: 'Don't trouble. I'll take my dapple grey to the stable myself and I'll tether him myself as well, for I have to know where he is.' This seemed odd to the innkeeper, and he reasoned that someone who had to look after his donkey himself didn't have much to spend. But when the stranger put his hand in his pocket and brought out two gold pieces and told him to go and buy something good for his supper, he opened his eyes wide, ran off, and chose the best he could get hold of. After his meal the guest asked what he owed. The innkeeper was minded to double the bill and said his guest would have to pay two gold pieces more. The apprentice put his hand in his pocket, but his gold had just run out. 'Wait a moment, mine host', he

said. 'I'll just go and fetch some gold'—and took the tablecloth with
him. The innkeeper had no idea what this was supposed to mean,
but he was curious and crept after him, and when his guest locked
the stable-door he peeped through a knot-hole in the wood. The
stranger spread the cloth out under the donkey, cried 'Bricklebrit',
and the beast began to spew out gold from back and front onto the
ground in a right downpour. 'Good Heavens!' said the innkeeper,
'that's the place for coining money fast! A purse like that one isn't so
bad!' The guest paid his reckoning and lay down to sleep, but during
the night the innkeeper crept down to the stable, led the Master of
the Mint away, and tied up another donkey in its place. Early next
morning the apprentice left with his donkey, imagining he had his
Gold-Donkey. At midday he arrived at his father's, who was
delighted when he saw him and received him gladly. 'What did you
become, my son?' asked the old man. 'A miller, father dear,' he
answered. 'What have you brought with you from your journeying?'
'Nothing more than a donkey.' 'There are donkeys enough here,'
said his father; 'I'd have preferred a good goat.' 'Yes,' answered his
son, 'but this is no ordinary donkey. It's a Gold-Donkey: if I say
"Bricklebrit", the good beast will spew a whole clothful of gold
pieces. Just invite all our relations here, and I'll make rich men of
them all.' 'I like the sound of that,' said the tailor, 'then I shan't need
to plague myself with the needle any longer,' so he ran off himself
and called his relations together. As soon as they had gathered the
miller told them to clear some space, spread out a cloth, and led the
donkey into the parlour. 'Now pay attention,' he said, and called
'Bricklebrit', but what fell wasn't gold pieces at all, and it soon
became clear that the beast had no idea of the art, for not every
donkey is that accomplished. Then the poor miller pulled a long
face; he saw that he had been cheated, and begged his relations to
forgive him, for they were going home as poor as they had arrived.
There was nothing left but for the old man to take up his needle
again and the young man to hire himself out to a miller.

The third brother had apprenticed himself to a turner, and
because it is an intricate craft, it took him longest to learn it. But his
brothers informed him in a letter of how badly things had gone for
them, and how on their last evening the innkeeper had robbed them
of their wonderful wishing objects. When the turner had finished his
apprenticeship and was to go journeying, because he had worked

so well his master made him a present of a sack, saying: 'It has a club inside.' 'I can hang the sack over my shoulder and it will serve me well, but what use is the club inside it? It will only make it heavy.' 'I'll tell you,' answered his master. 'If someone has done you any harm, then just say: "Club, out of the sack!", and the club will jump out amongst the folk and it will dance on their backs so merrily that they won't be able to move or stir for the next eight days; and it won't let up until you say: "Club, into the sack!" ' The apprentice thanked him and shouldered the sack. And if anyone came too close and threatened him, he would say: 'Club, out of the sack!', and straight away the club would jump out of the sack and beat one after another, right on the back of his coat or doublet, and wouldn't stop until it had stripped him of it; and this would happen so fast that before a fellow knew it, it was already his turn. One evening the young turner reached the inn where his brothers had been swindled. He put his haversack down on the table before him and began to tell of all the remarkable things he had seen in the world. 'Yes,' he said, 'it's true you can find a Table-Lay or a Gold-Donkey and suchlike; they're all of them good things and I certainly don't turn up my nose at them, but they're nothing compared with the treasure that I've come by and that I'm carrying about with me in that sack.' The innkeeper pricked up his ears. 'What on earth can that be?' he thought. 'The sack could be full of jewels, no less. It's only fair I should have that too, for all good things come in threes.' When it was time for sleep, the guest stretched out on the bench and laid his sack under his head for a pillow. The host, once he thought his guest was fast asleep, went up and pulled and tugged very gently and cautiously at the sack to see if he might perhaps be able to drag it away and slip another in its place. But the turner had been waiting for this for a long time and just as the innkeeper was about to give it a mighty jerk, he called: 'Club, out of the sack!' Straight away the little club leapt out, went for the innkeeper, and gave him a hiding in the way it knew how. The innkeeper cried for mercy, but the louder he cried the harder the club beat time on his back, until at last he fell to the ground exhausted. Then the turner spoke: 'If you don't give up the Table-Lay and the Gold-Donkey, the dance will start all over again.' 'Oh no!' cried the innkeeper, very meek and mild now. 'I'll return it all gladly, only send that accursed kobold crawling back into its sack.' Then the apprentice said: 'I will let mercy rule instead of justice, but watch out you don't do any harm again.' Then he called: 'Club, into the sack!' and let him be.

Next morning the turner made his way home to his father with the Table-Lay and the Gold-Donkey. The tailor was delighted when he saw him, and asked him too what trade he had learned out in foreign parts. 'Father dear,' he answered, 'I've learned to be a turner.' 'An intricate craft,' said his father. 'And what have you brought back with you from your journeying?' 'Something precious, father dear,' answered the son, 'a club in a sack.' 'What!' cried the father, 'a club? That's worth a lot of bother! It's something you could chop for yourself from any tree!' 'But not a club like this, father dear. If I say: "Club, out of the sack!", the club will jump out and if someone doesn't mean well by me, it will set him dancing under its blows, and it won't let up until he is lying on the ground begging for fair weather. Look, this club has helped me to get back the Table-Lay and the Gold-Donkey which that thieving innkeeper stole from my brothers. Call them both now and invite all our relations. I want to treat them to fine food and drink and fill their pockets with gold as well.' The old tailor was dubious, but he gathered his relations together all the same. Then the turner laid down a cloth in the parlour, led in the Gold-Donkey, and said to his brother: 'Now, dear brother, speak to him.' The miller said 'Bricklebrit', and in a moment the pieces of gold leapt down onto the cloth, as if it were raining torrents, and the donkey didn't let up until everyone had so much they couldn't carry any more. (I can see from the way you're looking that you'd like to have been there too.) Then the turner fetched the little table and said: 'Dear brother, now speak to it.' And scarcely had the joiner said: 'Table, lay,' than it was set and all covered with the most delicious dishes. Then such a feast was held as the tailor had never known in his house before, and all their relations stayed together until night, and they were all merry and content. The tailor locked up his needle and thread, yardstick and iron, in a cupboard and passed his life in joy and splendour with his three sons.

But what became of the goat, whose fault it was that the tailor drove away his three sons? I'll tell you. She was ashamed of her bald head and ran to a fox's den, where she crept inside. When the fox came home a pair of great big eyes glowed at him out of the dark, so that he was frightened and ran away. He was met by the bear, and as he looked so upset the bear said to him: 'What's the matter with you, brother fox. What a face you're making!' 'Oh,' answered the redcoat, 'a fierce beast is sitting in my den and it stared at me with eyes of fire.' 'We'll soon drive it out,' said the bear, who went along with the fox to his den and looked inside. But when he saw the eyes of fire he was seized by fear too: he didn't want to have anything to do with the fierce beast and took to his heels. He was met by the bee, who observed that he was looking very uneasy. She said: 'Bear, you're looking terribly out of sorts. What's happened to your cheery mood?' 'It's all very well for you,' answered the bear, 'there's a fierce beast with staring eyes sitting in the redcoat's house, and we can't drive it out.' The bee said: 'I'm sorry for you, bear. I'm only a poor weak creature you don't notice on your path, but I still believe I could help you.' She flew into the fox's den, settled on the goat's clean-shaven head, and stung her so mightily that she leapt up, crying 'Me-eh-eh! Me-eh-eh!', and rushed outside like a mad thing. And to this day no one knows where she has run to.

28. *Little Thumb*

THERE was once a poor farmer who sat one evening by the hearth, poking the fire, while his wife sat spinning. He said: 'Isn't it sad, that we have no children? It's so quiet here in our house, while it's so loud and lively in others'.' 'Yes,' answered his wife with a sigh, 'if we only had just one, and even if he were quite little, just as big as my thumb, I'd be content; we'd still love him with all our heart.' Now it happened that the woman grew sickly, and that after seven months she bore a child who was perfect in every limb, but was no bigger than a thumb. So they said: 'He is just as we wished, and he shall be our dear child,' and because he was so small they called him Little Thumb. They fed him well, but the child didn't grow any bigger, he just remained the size he was in his first hour; still, he looked out from intelligent eyes, and soon showed himself to be a clever, nimble little thing, while everything he took on turned out well.

One day the farmer was making preparations to go out into the forest and cut wood, and he said to himself: 'I do wish there was someone who could come after me with the cart.' 'Oh father,' called

Little Thumb, 'I'll bring you the cart, depend on it; it shall be in the forest at the appointed time.' Then the man laughed and said: 'How can you manage that? You're much too small to lead the horse by the reins.' 'That doesn't matter, father. If mother just hitches up the horse, I'll sit in his ear and tell him where he's to go.' 'Well,' answered his father, 'let's try it for once.' When the time came round, his mother hitched up the horse and sat Little Thumb in his ear. Then the little fellow gave the horse his orders how to pull the cart: 'Gee up! To the right—whoa there—now left!' And it went just as it should, as if a master-carter were driving, and the cart took the right road to the forest. Now it came about, just as the cart turned a corner and the little fellow called 'Gee up!', that two men, strangers to those parts, came by. 'Good Lord!' said one, 'what's this? There's a cart driving along and a carter calling to the horse and yet there's not a soul to be seen.' 'There's something peculiar going on,' said the other. 'Let's follow the cart and see where it stops.' But the cart drove deep into the forest and right to the place where the wood was being cut. When Little Thumb caught sight of his father, he called to him: 'You see, father, here I am with the cart. Now lift me down.' His father held the horse with his left hand, and with his right he lifted his son down from the horse's ear. Cheerfully, Little Thumb sat down on a stalk of straw. When the two strangers caught sight of him they were speechless with amazement. Then one of them took the other aside and said: 'Listen, that little fellow could make us a fortune if we put him on show for money in the big city; let's buy him.' They went up to the farmer and said: 'Sell us the little man; we'll look after him well.' 'No,' said the father, 'he's my heart of hearts, and I wouldn't sell him for all the gold in the world.' But when Little Thumb heard the deal, he clambered up the creases in his father's coat, perched on his shoulder, and whispered in his ear: 'Father, just hand me over: I'll come back.' So the father handed him over to the two men for a tidy sum of money. 'Where do you want to sit?' they asked him. 'Oh, just set me on the brim of your hat; I can stroll up and down there and look at the view without falling off.' They did as he wanted, and when Little Thumb had said goodbye to his father they took off with him. They walked along like this until twilight began to fall, when the little fellow said: 'Lift me down—it's urgent.' 'You just stay up there,' said the man whose head he was sitting on, 'I shan't mind—sometimes the birds leave their droppings on me too.' 'No,' said Little Thumb, 'I know my manners; just lift me down—quick.' The man took off his hat and set the little fellow down on some turf, where he jumped and crawled between the clods for a little way, then all of a sudden he slipped into a mouse-hole he had had his eye on. 'Goodnight, gentlemen—you can go home without me,' he called out, laughing at them. They ran up and prodded the mouse-hole with sticks, but in vain: Little Thumb crept further and further back, and as it soon grew very dark they were obliged to make their way back home, with anger and an empty purse.

When Little Thumb observed that they had gone he crept out from his underground tunnel once again. 'It's very dangerous, walking on turf in the dark,' he said, 'and very easy to break one's bones!' Fortunately he came upon an empty snail-shell. 'God be praised,' he said, 'I can pass the night there in safety,' and he settled down inside. It was not long, just as he was about to fall asleep, before he heard two men passing by. One of them was saying: 'How can we set about robbing that rich parson of his gold and silver?' 'I could tell you,' called Little Thumb from nowhere. 'What's that?' said one thief, in fright. 'I heard someone speaking.' They stopped and listened, so Little Thumb spoke again: 'If you take me with you, I'll help you.' 'Who are you then?' 'Look on the ground and find out where the voice is coming from,' he answered. The thieves found him at last and lifted him up high. 'Little lad, how can you help us?' they said. 'Listen,' he answered, 'I'll crawl in between the iron bars into the parson's storeroom and pass what you want out to you.' 'Very well,' they said, 'we'll see what you can do.' When they reached the parsonage Little Thumb crawled into the storeroom, but then he shouted out at once, at the top of his voice: 'Do you want everything that's here?' The thieves were alarmed and said: 'Speak softly, for goodness' sake, so as not to wake anyone.' But Little Thumb pretended he hadn't understood them, and shouted afresh: 'What are you after? Do you want everything that's here?' The cook, who slept in the next room, heard this and sat up in bed and listened. But in their alarm the thieves had run back part of the way; at last they took courage once again, thinking: 'The little fellow is just having a joke with us.' They came back and whispered to him: 'Now be serious and pass something out to us.' Then Little Thumb shouted once again, as loud as he could: 'I'll give you everything. Just reach your hands inside.' The listening maid heard that quite clearly, so she jumped out of bed and stumbled into the room. The thieves took off and ran as if the Wild Huntsman were after them; but as the maid couldn't see anything, she went off to light a candle. When she came back with it Little Thumb made off into the barn outside without being seen. But after the maid had searched every corner and found nothing she went back to bed at last, believing that she had only been dreaming with open eyes and ears after all.

Little Thumb had clambered up into the hay and found a comfortable place to sleep, where he intended to rest until it was day and then go home to his parents. But there were other experiences ahead of him! Oh indeed, there is much trouble and grief in the world! When day dawned the maid was already getting out of bed to feed the cattle. Her first errand was to the barn, where she gathered up an armful of hay, the very bundle where Little Thumb was lying asleep. But he was sleeping so soundly that he wasn't aware of anything, and didn't wake up until he was in the mouth of the cow who had picked him up with the hay. 'Oh Heavens,' he cried, 'what a fulling-mill I've fallen into!', but he soon realized where he was. Then he had to take care not to get between the cow's teeth and be crushed, though afterwards he couldn't prevent himself from slithering down into her stomach with the hay. 'They've forgotten to put the windows into this little parlour,' he said, 'and the sun doesn't shine into it; and they won't bring in a candle, either.' Altogether he didn't like these quarters at all, and the worst thing was that more and more hay was coming in at the door, and there was less and less room. So at last he called out in fear, at the top of his voice: 'Don't bring me any more fodder, don't bring me any more fodder!' The maid was milking the cow just at that moment, and when she heard these words spoken, without seeing anyone—and it was the same voice that she had heard in the night—she was so alarmed that she slipped off her little stool and spilt the milk. In the greatest haste she ran to her master, crying: 'Oh Heavens, parson, the cow talked!' 'You're crazy,' answered the parson, but he did go into the stable himself to see what was going on there. But he had hardly set foot in the stable when Little Thumb called out once more: 'Don't bring me any more fodder, don't bring me any more fodder!' At that the parson was alarmed himself; he imagined an evil spirit had entered into the cow, and ordered her to be killed. She was slaughtered, but her stomach, where Little Thumb was hidden, was thrown on the dung-heap. Little Thumb had great difficulty in working his way out; still, he'd got as far as to clear some space for himself, but just as he was about to thrust his head out a new misfortune arrived. A hungry wolf ran by and gobbled up the entire stomach in one gulp. Little Thumb did not lose courage. 'Perhaps', he thought, 'the wolf can be persuaded,' and he called to him out of his belly: 'Dear wolf, I know of a splendid meal for you.' 'Where can I get it?' said the wolf. 'In such and such a house. You'll have to crawl in through the drain and you'll find cake, ham, and sausage, as much as you can eat'—and Little Thumb gave the wolf an exact description of his father's house. The wolf didn't need to be told twice; that night he squeezed himself into the drain, and once in the pantry he ate to his heart's content. When he was full he wanted to leave, but he'd grown so fat that he couldn't go out by the same route. Little Thumb had counted on this, and he started to raise an almighty din inside the wolf and roared and shouted all he could. 'Be quiet,' said the wolf, 'you'll wake people up.' 'Go on,' said the little fellow, 'you've just eaten your fill; I want to have some fun too'—and he started all over again to shout with all his might. At last it woke his father and mother, who ran to the pantry and looked in through a crack. When they saw that a wolf was lodging there they ran off, and the husband fetched the axe and his wife the scythe. 'Stay behind me,' said the husband as they entered the pantry; 'if I've given him a blow and he hasn't yet died from it, you must chop him open and then cut him in pieces.' Then Little Thumb heard his father's voice and called: 'Father dear, I'm here; I'm hidden in the wolf's stomach.' Said his father, full of joy: 'God be praised, our dear child is found again,' and he told his wife to put away the scythe so as not to hurt Little Thumb. Then he lifted his axe and struck the wolf a blow on the head, so that he fell down dead. Then they fetched knife and scissors, cut open his body, and pulled out the little fellow. 'Oh,' said his father, 'how worried we've been for you!' 'Yes, father, I've been around a lot in the world; praise be that I can breathe fresh air once again.' 'Wherever have you been, then?' 'Oh father, I've been in a mouse's hole, in a cow's stomach, and in a wolf's belly. I'll stay with you now.' 'And we won't sell you again, not for all the riches in the world,' said his parents, and they hugged and kissed their dear Little Thumb. They gave him plenty to eat and drink, and they had new clothes made for him, for his old ones were quite ruined from the journey.

29. *Mrs Fox's Wedding*

THE FIRST TALE

THERE was once an old fox with nine tails, who believed his wife wasn't faithful to him so he wanted to lead her into temptation. He stretched out under the bench, stirred not a limb, and pretended that he was stone dead. Mrs Fox took to her room and locked herself in, and her maid, Missy Cat, sat by the hearth and did the cooking. When it became known that the old fox had died, the suitors began to turn up. The maid heard someone standing outside the house door and knocking; she went and opened it, and there was a young fox, who said:

> 'Pussycat, pussycat, what are you making?
> Perhaps you're asleep, perhaps you are waking?'

She replied:

> 'I'm certainly not asleep, but waking;
> Would you like to know what it is I'm making?
> I'm buttering beer and warming the cup;
> Would the gentleman like to sample a sup?'

'No thank you, missy,' said the fox. 'What is Mrs. Fox doing?' The maid replied:

> 'She's sitting alone upstairs in her room,
> Bewailing her grief and her sorrow and gloom;
> She's wept till her eyes are satiny-red,
> Because old Mister Fox is dead.'

'Just tell her, missy, that a young fox called by, with a will to woo her.' 'Very well, young sir.'

> The cat went up, trip trap, trip trap,
> And tapped on her door, tip tap, tip tap.
> 'Mrs Fox, are you in there?'
> 'Oh yes, my pussycat, I'm here.'
> 'You've a suitor outside, a younger fox.'
> 'Tell me, my dear, what d'you think of his looks?'

'Has he nine beautiful tails, like the late lamented Mr Fox?' 'Oh no,' answered the cat, 'only one.' 'Then I won't have him.'

Missy Cat went down and sent the suitor away. Soon afterwards there came another knock, and there was another fox at the door who wanted to court Mrs Fox; he had two tails; but he didn't fare any better than the first. After that more foxes came, always with one tail more, who were all turned down, until at last one arrived who had nine tails like old Mr Fox.

> 'Now open the doors and unbolt the locks
> And clear the yard of old Mr Fox.'

But just as the wedding was about to be celebrated, old Mr Fox bestirred himself under the bench, gave the whole pack of them a hiding, and drove them, as well as Mrs Fox, out of the house.

THE SECOND TALE

When old Mr Fox died, the wolf came wooing. He knocked at the door, and the cat, who was in service with Mrs Fox, opened it to him. The wolf greeted her, saying:

> 'Good morning, Miss Cat of Catterbrain Town.
> How is it that you are sitting alone?'

The cat replied:

> 'I'm crumbling my bread and milk in a cup.
> Would the gentleman like to sample a sup?'

'No thank you, Missy Cat,' answered the wolf. 'Isn't Mrs Fox at home?' The cat said:

> 'She's sitting upstairs in her room,
> Bewailing her grief and her sorrow and gloom,
> Bewailing her grief and her empty bed,
> Because old Mr Fox is dead.'

The wolf replied:

> 'If she wants to wed once more
> She only need come down the stair.'
> The cat then scampered up the stair,
> Waving her little tail in the air.
> She stopped when she came to the gallery floor,
> Tapped with her five golden rings at the door:
> 'Mrs Fox, are you in there?

If you want to wed once more,
You only need come down the stair.'

Mrs Fox asked: 'Is the gentleman wearing red breeches? And has he a pointed little mouth?' 'No,' answered the cat. 'Then he's no good for me.'

After the wolf was turned down there came a dog, a stag, a hare, a bear, a lion, and all the animals of the forest, one after another. But they always lacked one of the good features belonging to old Mr Fox, and the cat had to send the suitors away every time. At last a young fox arrived. Then Mrs Fox said: 'Is the gentleman wearing red breeches? And has he a pointed little mouth?' 'Yes,' said the cat, 'he does.' 'Then let him come up,' and she told the maid to prepare the wedding feast.

'Pussycat, brush the parlour floor,
And throw the old fox out of the door.
He caught so many plump, fat mice,
Ate them by himself alone,
But he never gave me one.'

Then the wedding was celebrated with young Mr Fox, and they cheered and they danced, and if they haven't stopped, they are dancing to this day.

30. *The Robber Bridegroom*

THERE was once a miller who had a beautiful daughter, and when she had grown up he wished for her to be provided for and well married. 'If a proper suitor comes along asking for her hand,' he thought, 'I'll give her to him.' It wasn't long before a suitor came by who seemed to be very rich, and since the miller could find no reason to object to him, he promised him his daughter. But the girl wasn't really fond of him, not as a girl should be fond of her betrothed, and she had no trust in him: whenever she looked at him or thought of him, she felt a shudder of fear in her heart. One day he said to her: 'You are to be my bride, and you haven't visited me once.' The girl replied: 'I don't know where your house is.' So her bridegroom said 'My house is out there in the dark forest.' The girl looked for excuses, and said she thought she wouldn't be able to find her way there. Her bridegroom said: 'Next Sunday you must come out to me. I've already invited the guests, and so that you can find the way through the forest I shall scatter ashes for you.' When Sunday came and the girl was to set out, she grew very scared—she herself didn't know why—and so that she could mark the path she filled both pockets with peas and lentils. At the entrance to the forest there was a scattering of ashes, so she followed them, but with every step she threw a few peas onto the ground. She walked for almost the whole day, until she came to the heart of the forest where it was darkest. There stood a lonely house, which she shrank from, for it looked so dismal and uncanny. She stepped inside, but there was nobody there, and a great silence prevailed. Suddenly a voice called:

> 'Turn back, young bride, and go no further,
> This is the house of murderers.'

The girl looked up and saw that the voice came from a bird who was hanging in a cage on the wall. Again he cried:

> 'Turn back, young bride, and go no further,
> This is the house of murderers.'

Then the pretty bride went on from one room to the next, and she went over the whole house, but it was quite empty, with not a human soul to be found. At last she reached the cellar too, where an ancient woman was sitting, her head trembling. 'Can you not tell me', the girl asked, 'if my bridegroom lives here?' 'Oh, you poor child,' answered the old woman, 'what have you fallen into! You are in a murderers' den. You imagine you're a bride soon to celebrate her wedding, but you'll hold your wedding with death. You see, I've had to put a great cauldron full of water on to boil, for when they have you in their power they will chop you up without mercy and eat you, for they eat human flesh. If I don't take pity on you and rescue you, you are lost.'

At that the old woman led her behind a huge barrel where she couldn't be seen. 'Be as quiet as a mouse,' she said. 'Don't stir and don't move, or else it's all over with you. In the night, when the robbers are asleep, we'll run away. I've been waiting for an opportunity for a long time.' She had scarcely hidden herself when the godless band came home. They had dragged another maiden back with them. They were drunk and paid no attention to her screams and whimpers. They gave her wine to drink, three glasses full, one glass of white, one glass of red, and one glass of yellow wine, and with this her heart burst in two. Then they tore off her dainty clothes, laid her on a table, chopped up her beautiful body into pieces, and sprinkled it with salt. The poor bride behind the barrel shivered and quivered, for she could see what kind of a fate the robbers had intended for her. One of them noticed a golden ring on the murdered girl's little finger, and when he couldn't remove it straight away he took an axe and hacked her finger off; but the finger bounded up high over the barrel and fell right into the bride's lap. The robber took a candle and tried to look for it, but he couldn't find it. Then another one said: 'Have you looked behind the big barrel as well?' But the old woman called: 'Come and eat, and leave your searching until tomorrow: the finger's not going to run away from you.'

Then the robbers said: 'The old woman's right', gave up the search, and sat down to their meal. The old woman trickled a sleeping draught into their wine, so that very soon they lay down in the cellar and fell asleep, snoring. When the bride heard them she came out from behind the barrel, and had to step over the sleeping robbers who were lying on the floor in rows, very fearful that she might wake one of them. But God helped her, and she came through without mishap. The old woman climbed the stairs with her and opened the door, and they sped off as quickly as they could away from the murderers' lair. The wind had blown away the scattered ashes, but the peas and lentils had sprouted and begun to grow, and showed them the way in the moonlight. They walked all through the night until they reached the mill in the morning. Then the girl told her father everything, just as it had happened.

When the day arrived for the wedding to be held, the bridegroom appeared, while the miller for his part had invited all his relatives and acquaintances. As they were sitting at table, each one was invited to tell a story. The bride sat quietly and said nothing. Then the bridegroom spoke to his bride: 'Now, my precious, don't you know any stories? Tell us a tale too.' She answered: 'Then I'll tell you a dream. I was walking alone through a forest, and at last I reached a house without a human soul inside. But on the wall there was a bird in a cage, who called:

"Turn back, young bride, and go no further,
This is the house of murderers."

And he called a second time. But sweetheart, I only dreamed it. And then I went through all the rooms, and they were all empty, and it was so uncanny there. At last I went down into the cellar, where an ancient woman was sitting, her head trembling. I asked her: "Does my bridegroom live in this house?" She answered: "Oh, my child, you've fallen into a robber's den. Your bridegroom does live here, but he will cut you up and kill you, and then boil you and eat you." But sweetheart, I only dreamed it. But the old woman hid me behind a huge barrel, and I'd scarcely been concealed before the robbers came home, dragging a maiden with them. They gave her three kinds of wine to drink, white, red, and yellow, and with this her heart burst in two. But sweetheart, I only dreamed it. At that they took off her dainty clothes, chopped her beautiful body up into pieces on a table, and sprinkled it with salt. But sweetheart, I only dreamed it. And one of the robbers noticed that there was still a ring on her ring-finger, and because it was hard to remove, he took an axe and chopped it off, but the finger bounded up high and behind the big barrel, where it fell into my lap. And here is the finger with the ring.' At these words, she took it out and showed it to the guests.

The robber, who had turned as while as chalk while she was telling her tale, leapt up and was about to flee, but the guests held him fast and handed him over to the courts. Then he and all his band were condemned to death for their wicked deeds.

31. *Godfather Death*

A POOR man had twelve children, and he had to work day and night just to be able to give them their bread. And when the thirteenth came into the world he did not know what to do in his distress, so he ran out onto the great highway intending to ask the first person he met to be godfather. The first to meet him was the good Lord, who already knew what was weighing on his heart, and said to him: 'Poor man, I'm sorry for you; I will lift your child from the font and take care of him and make him happy upon earth.' The man said: 'Who are you?' 'I am the good Lord.' 'Then I don't want you to be godfather,' said the man. 'You give to the rich and leave the poor to starve.' The man said this because he was ignorant of how wisely God distributes wealth and poverty. So he turned away from the Lord and went further along the road. Then the Devil came up to him and said: 'What are you looking for? If you'll take me to be godfather to your child, I will give him gold in plenty and all the pleasures of the world into the bargain.' The man asked: 'Who are you?' 'I am the Devil.' 'Then I don't want you to be godfather,' said the man. 'You deceive humankind and lead them astray.' He went further along the road, and bony-legged Death came striding towards him. He said: 'Take me for godfather.' 'You're the right one. You take the rich as well as the poor, without distinction. You shall be the godfather.' Death answered: 'I will make your child rich and famous, for someone who has me for his friend shall want for nothing.' The man said: 'The christening is next Sunday. Mind you come at the right time.' Death made his appearance as he had promised, and stood godfather in the proper way.

When the boy had grown up his godfather arrived one day and told him to come with him. He led him out into the forest and showed him a herb that was growing there, and said: 'Now you shall have your christening gift. I shall make you a famous physician. Whenever you are called to a sick patient, I will appear to you. If I am standing at the sick man's head, you can declare boldly that you can make him well again; and if you give him some of that herb, he will recover. But if I am standing at the sick man's feet, he is mine, and you must say that all help is in vain, and no doctor in the world could save him. But have a care that you do not use the herb against my will, for it could go badly for you.'

It was not long before the young man was the most famous physician in the whole world. 'He only needs to look at the sick man and he already knows the state of things, whether he will get well or whether he must die'—so it was said of him—and folk came to him from far and near, brought him to the patient, and gave him so much gold that soon he was a rich man. Now it happened that the king fell ill; the physician was summoned, and commanded to say whether his recovery was possible. But as he approached the king's bed Death was standing at his feet, and there was no herb growing that would cure him. 'If only I could outwit Death,' thought the physician. 'It's true, he will take it badly, but he is my godfather after all, so he'll probably turn a blind eye. I'll risk it.' So he took hold of the sick man and laid him top to tail, so that Death came to be standing at his head. Then he gave him some of the herb, and the king recovered and got better again. But Death came up to the physician and glowered darkly at him, threatened him with his finger, and said: 'You've pulled the wool over my eyes. This time I'll overlook it, but if you dare to do so once again it will cost you your life, and I'll come and take you away myself.'

Soon afterwards the king's daughter fell gravely ill. She was his only child, and he wept day and night until his eyes grew dim. He had it proclaimed that whoever saved her from death should become her consort and inherit the crown. When the physician came to the sick girl's bed he saw Death standing at her feet. He should have remembered his godfather's warning, but the great beauty of the king's daughter and the happy prospect of becoming her husband so besotted him that he threw all thought to the wind. He did not see the angry looks Death cast on him, raising his hand and threatening him with his dry fist; he lifted up the sick girl and laid her head where her feet had been lying. Then he gave her the herb, and at once her cheeks grew rosy and life stirred anew.

When Death saw that he had been cheated a second time out of claiming what was his, he advanced towards the physician with his long stride, and declared: 'It's over for you. It's your turn now,' seized him with his ice-cold hand so tightly that he could not fend him off, and led him to an underground cavern. There he saw how thousands upon thousands of candles were burning in countless rows, some tall, others half-sized, others small. Every moment some went out, and others burned high again, so that the flames seemed to shift to and fro in perpetual change. 'You see,' said Death, 'these are humanity's lamps of life. The tall candles belong to children, the half-sized ones to married couples in the prime of their lives, the small ones belong to the aged. But children too, and young folk, often have only a small light.' 'Show me my lamp of life,' said the physician, expecting that it would still be quite tall. Death pointed to a little stump which was just about to go out, and said: 'You see, there it is.' 'Oh, my dear godfather,' said the horrified physician, 'light me a new one; do it for my sake, so that I may enjoy my life, become king and consort to the king's beautiful daughter.' 'I cannot,' said Death. 'One has to be extinguished before another may be lit.'

'Then set the old one onto a new candle, so that it will burn right on when the old one is at an end,' begged the physician. Death pretended to grant his wish and reached for a fresh, tall candle; but because he wanted to have his revenge he deliberately blundered when changing the candles, and the little stump fell over and went out. At once the physician sank to the ground, and now he himself fell into the hands of Death.

32. *Thumbling's Travels*

A TAILOR once had a son who turned out to be tiny, indeed, no bigger than a thumb—which is why he was called Thumbling. But he had a brave spirit, and one day he said to his father: 'Father, I must and will go out into the world.' 'Very well, my son,' said the old man, taking a darning-needle and dabbing a knob of sealing-wax on the eye. 'Here's a sword for you to take with you on your way.' Now the little tailor wanted to take one more meal with his parents, so he hopped into the kitchen to see what his mother had been cooking for the last time. In fact, it was just served up, and the dish was standing on the hearth. 'Mother, what's there to eat today?' he asked. 'See for yourself,' said his mother. So Thumbling jumped on to the hearth and peeped into the dish; but because he craned his neck too far over, the steam from the food caught him up and carried him out through the chimney. For a while he rode the steam round about in the air, until at last he sank back down to earth. Now the little tailor was out in the wide world. He travelled about, and even went to work for a master-tailor, but the food was not to his liking. 'If you don't give us better food,' said Thumbling to his master's wife, 'I shall go away, and tomorrow morning early I'll chalk on your house door: "Potatoes too much! Meat too little! Farewell, Potato Prince!"' 'What are you after, grasshopper?' said the master's wife. She was cross, and picked up a duster to flick at him; my little tailor crept nimbly under a thimble, peeped out, and stuck out his tongue at the mistress of the house. She lifted the thimble and was about to pick him up but little Thumbling hopped into the duster, and when the master's wife shook it out to look for him he slid into a crack in the table. 'Ha, ha, mistress,' he called, popping his head out; and when she tried to flap the duster at him he jumped into the drawer. But all the same she caught him in the end, and chased him out of the house.

The little tailor went travelling and reached a great forest; there he encountered a band of robbers who were planning to steal the king's treasure. When they saw the little tailor they thought: 'A little fellow like that can crawl through a keyhole and he'll be useful to us as a picklock.' 'Hey there,' one of them called, 'Giant Goliath, will you come to the treasure-chamber with us? You can slip inside and throw us out the gold.' Thumbling thought hard; at length he said yes, and went with them to the treasure-chamber. There he inspected the doors at the top and the bottom to see if they hadn't a crack. It was not long before he discovered one wide enough to let him creep inside. Indeed, he was about to go in at once, but one of the two sentries standing outside the door noticed him and said to the other: 'What ugly sort of a spider is crawling there? I'll squash it dead.' 'Let the poor creature go,' said the other, 'it hasn't done you any harm.' Then Thumbling slipped through the crack into the treasure-chamber without mishap. He opened the window and, seeing the robbers standing below, he tossed out one gold coin after another to them. As the little tailor was in the swing of things he heard the king coming, wishing to inspect his treasure-chamber, so he quickly crept away and hid. The king noticed that a lot of solid gold coins were missing, but could not understand who might have stolen them, for the locks and bolts were in good order and everything seemed well secured. So he went away again, saying to the two sentries: 'Watch out; someone is after the money.' Now when Thumbling began his work afresh they heard the money inside shift about, jingling: ring-a-ding, ring-a-ding. They hurried swiftly inside, intending to catch a thief. But the little tailor, who had heard them coming, was swifter still. He leapt into a corner and hid under cover of a gold coin, so that none of him could be seen. As he did so he went on teasing the sentries, calling: 'Here I am.' The sentries ran towards him, but as they approached he had already hopped into another corner beneath a gold coin, calling: 'Ha! Here I am.' And in this way he made fools of them, driving them round and round the treasure-chamber until they were weary and went away. Then little by little he threw out all the coins. He sent the last one on its way with all his might, hopped nimbly on to it himself, and flew out of the window down to the robbers. They sang his praises, saying: 'You're a mighty hero—do you want to be our chief?' Thumbling thanked them, but said he wanted to see the world first. They shared out the loot, but the little tailor demanded only one groat, because he couldn't carry any more.

After that he girded on his sword once more, bade the robbers good-day, and took to the road again. He went to work for a number of master-tailors, but they were not to his liking; in the end he hired himself out as a serving-man at an inn. But the maids could not stand him, for while they could not see him he could see everything they were up to on the sly, and he would tell the innkeeper what they took from the plates or fetched for themselves from the cellar. So they said: 'Just wait, we'll make you pay for it,' and they arranged to play a trick on him. Soon afterwards, when one of the maids was scything the grass in the garden, she saw Thumbling jumping about and scrambling up and down the plants, and she quickly mowed him down with the grass, tied it all up in a big cloth, and threw it down in secret in front of the cows. Now there was one big black cow among them and she swallowed him down with the grass—without hurting him. But he did not like it down below at all, for it was completely dark, and there wasn't a candle burning either. When the cow was being milked, he called out:

> 'Pail, poll, pull,
> Will the bucket soon be full?'

But with the noise from the milking, no one understood. Then the landlord went into the stalls and said: 'Tomorrow that cow is to be slaughtered.' Thumbling became so frightened that he called out in a high voice: 'Let me out first—I'm shut up inside.' The landlord certainly heard this, but had no idea where the voice was coming from. 'Where are you?' he asked. 'Inside the black one,' came the answer, but the landlord did not understand what that meant, and went away.

Next morning the cow was slaughtered. Fortunately, in all the cutting and carving not a stroke hacked Thumbling, but he did find himself amid the sausage-meat. Then, when the butcher set to and started work, he cried with all his might and main: 'Don't chop too deep, don't chop too deep, I'm here inside.' But the chopping-knives were making so much noise that not a soul heard it. Now poor Thumbling was really in trouble, but need means speed, and he leapt so nimbly between the chopping-knives that not one of them touched him, and he managed to survive in one piece. But he still could not escape. There was no other way out: he was forced to submit to being stuffed into a blood-sausage together with the bits of bacon-fat. It made a rather tight lodging, and on top of that he was hung up in the chimney for smoking, where the time dragged on tediously. At last, in winter, he was brought down, because the sausage was to be served to a guest. Now, while the landlady was slicing the sausage he was careful not to stretch his head out too far, so that his neck would not be sliced as well; at last he saw a good moment, drew a deep breath, and jumped out.

But the little tailor did not want to stay any longer in a house where he had fared so badly, so he took off on his travels once again instead. But his freedom did not last long. In the open fields he met a fox on his way, who snapped him up without thinking. 'Hey, Mister Fox,' called the little tailor, 'it's me, stuck in your throat; let me out.' 'You're right,' answered the fox, 'there's not much on you for me to eat; if you promise me the hens in your father's yard, I'll let you go'. 'With all my heart,' answered Thumbling, 'you shall have all the hens, I promise you.' So the fox let him go once more, and carried him home himself. When his father saw his beloved little son again he gladly gave the fox every hen he possessed. 'In return I've brought you a fine gold piece,' said Thumbling, and offered him the groat he had earned on his travels.

'But why did the fox get the poor chickens to eat?' 'Oh, you silly, your father would surely love his child more than all the chickens in his yard.'

33. *Fitcher's Bird*

THERE was once a warlock who took on the shape of a poor man and went from house to house begging, and took pretty girls captive. No one knew where he took them, for they never came to light again. One day he appeared at the door of a man who had three beautiful daughters. He looked like a poor, feeble beggar, and he carried a basket on his back as if he wanted to collect alms in it. He begged for a bite to eat, and when the oldest daughter came out and was about to offer him a piece of bread, he just touched her and she was forced to jump into his basket. Then he sped away with long, strong strides and carried her to his house which stood in the midst of a dark forest. Inside the house everything was magnificent. He gave her whatever she wished for, saying: 'My precious, you will enjoy yourself here with me. You have everything your heart desires.' This went on for a few days, until he said: 'I have to go away on a journey and leave you alone for a short time. Here are the keys to the house. You may go everywhere and look at everything, only not into one small room, which this little key here will unlock. This I forbid you on pain of death.' He also gave her an egg, saying: 'Look after this egg for me with great care; it would be better to have it with you constantly, for if it were to be lost a great calamity would come of it.' She took the keys and the egg and promised to attend to everything properly. When he was gone she walked about the house from top to bottom, inspecting everything. The rooms shone with silver and gold, and she thought she had never seen such great splendour. At last she also came to the forbidden door; she wanted to go past it, but her curiosity gave her no peace. She looked at the key. It looked like any other; she put it in the lock and gave it a little turn, and the door sprang open. But what did she see as she went in? A huge blood-stained basin was standing in the middle of the room, and in it there lay human beings, dead and chopped in pieces; next to it there stood a block of wood with a bright axe lying on it. She was so terrified that the egg, which she was holding in her hand, fell into the basin. She took it out and wiped off the blood, but in vain: it reappeared in the twinkling of an eye. She wiped and she scoured, but she couldn't get rid of it.

It wasn't long before the man came back from his journey, and the first things he demanded were the key and the egg. She held the egg out to him, but she was trembling as she did so, and he saw at once from the red stain that she had been in the bloody chamber. 'Since you went into the chamber against my will,' he declared, 'you shall go into it now against your own. Your life is at an end.' He threw her down, dragged her in by the hair, struck off her head on the block, and chopped her up so that her blood flowed onto the floor. Then he threw her into the basin with the others.

'Now I'll fetch me the second,' said the warlock, and again he went to the house door in the shape of a poor man, and begged. Then the second daughter brought him a piece of bread, and like the first he made her captive by merely touching her and carried her off. She fared no better than her sister; she allowed herself to be tempted by her curiosity, opened the bloody chamber and looked inside, and on his return she was forced to pay for it with her life. Then he went and fetched the third daughter, but she was clever and crafty. After he had given her the keys and the egg, and had left on his journey, first she carefully put away the egg; then she looked over the house, and lastly she went into the forbidden chamber. Alas, what did she see! Her two dear sisters lying there in the basin, pitifully murdered and chopped in pieces! But she set to and gathered their limbs together and put them to rights, head, body, arms and legs. And when nothing more was missing, the limbs began to stir and join together, and both girls opened their eyes and were alive once more. Then they were full of joy, and they kissed and hugged one another. On his return, the man at once demanded key and egg, and as he was unable to discover any trace of blood on it, he declared: 'You have passed the test. You shall be my bride.' But now he no longer had any power over her and was forced to do what she demanded. 'Very well,' she replied, 'before that you must take a basketful of gold to my father and mother and carry it on your back yourself; meantime I will arrange the wedding.' Then she ran to her sisters, hidden by her in a little room, and said: 'This is the moment when I can rescue you: the villain shall carry you home himself. But as soon as you are home, send help to me.' She put them both into a basket and covered them completely with gold so that nothing of them could be seen; then she called the warlock in and told him: 'Now be off with the basket, but see that you don't stop and rest on the way, for I shall look out of my little window and keep watch.'

The warlock lifted the basket onto his back and went off with it. But it weighed on him so heavily that the sweat ran down his face. So he sat down, wanting to rest a little, but at once someone in the basket called: 'I'm looking out of my little window and I can see you resting. On you go.' He thought it was his bride calling, and went on his way again. Once again he was about to sit down, but straight away there came a cry: 'I'm looking out of my little window, and I can see you resting. On you go.' And whenever he stopped there was a cry, and so he had to go on until at last, groaning and out of breath, he brought the basket with the gold and the two girls to their parents' house.

But back in his home the bride was arranging the wedding feast, and she invited the warlock's friends to attend. Then she took a death's head with grinning teeth, decked it with jewellery and a garland of flowers, and carried it up to the attic window and made it look out. When everything was ready she got into a barrel of honey, cut open the feather-bed, and rolled in it, so that she looked like a very strange bird and no one could recognize her. Then she walked out of the house and was met on the way by some of the wedding guests, who asked her:

> 'Where have you come from, Fitcher's bird?'
>   'From Fitcher's house, haven't you heard?'
> 'What is the young bride doing there?'
>   'She's cleaned the house: attic, cellar, and stair,
> And she's peering from the attic down at you here.'

At last she met the bridegroom wandering slowly back. Like the others he asked:

> 'Where have you come from, Fitcher's bird?'
>   'From Fitcher's house, haven't you heard?'
> 'What is my young bride doing there?'
>   'She's cleaned the house: attic, cellar, and stair,
> And she's peering from the attic down at you here.'

The bridegroom looked up and saw the bedizened death's head. He imagined it was his bride, and he nodded to her and greeted her in a friendly way. But when he had gone inside together with all his guests, the brothers and relatives of the bride, who had been sent to rescue her, reached the house. They locked all the doors so that no one could escape, and then they set fire to it so that the warlock, together with all his retainers, could not help burning to death.

34. *The Tale of the Juniper Tree*

A LONG time ago now, perhaps two thousand years, there was a rich man who had a fair and godly wife, and they loved each other very much. But they had no children, and they greatly wished for some. The wife prayed for a child day and night, but they did not and they did not get one. In front of their house there was a yard where a juniper tree grew, and one day in winter the wife was standing beneath it peeling an apple, and as she was peeling the apple she cut her finger and the blood fell onto the snow. 'Oh,' said the wife, sighing deeply as she saw the blood before her on the snow, and she grew so downcast, 'if only I had a child as red as blood and as white as snow.' And as she said this her heart was filled with happiness, for she felt as if it was to be. Then she went indoors; and after a month had passed the snow melted; in two months the earth grew green; in three months the flowers sprang from the earth; in four months all the trees put out their shoots and the green branches grew into one another; then the birds sang so that the whole wood resounded and the blossoms fell from the trees; then the fifth month had passed, and she stood beneath the juniper tree, which smelt so sweet that her heart leapt for joy, and she fell upon her knees and could not restrain herself; and when the sixth month had passed, the fruits were plump and firm, and she grew very still; and in the seventh month she reached for the juniper berries and ate them so greedily that she grew sad and sick. Then the eighth month passed and she called her husband, and wept, and said: 'If I die, bury me beneath the juniper tree.' Then she was quite comforted and glad until the next month passed, when she had a child as white as snow and as red as blood, and when she saw that, she was so full of joy that she died.

Then her husband buried her beneath the juniper tree, and began to weep greatly. After a while his weeping grew a bit quieter, and after he had wept a bit more he arose, and after a while longer he took another wife.

With the second wife he had a daughter, but the child of his first wife was a little son, who was as red as blood and as white as snow. When the wife looked on her daughter she loved her greatly, but then she would look at the little boy and it pierced her heart, for she imagined he stood in her way wherever she turned, and she was always thinking how she might divert all the wealth towards her daughter. And the Evil One put it in her mind to turn very cruel towards the little boy, pushing him from one corner to another, cuffing him here and buffeting him there, so that the poor child went in constant fear. As soon as he came out of school there was no place where he could be at peace.

One day the wife went up to the storeroom, and her little daughter came up too, and said: 'Mother, give me an apple.' 'Yes, my child,' said the woman, and gave her a beautiful apple from the chest. But the chest had a great heavy lid with a great sharp iron lock. 'Mother,' said the little daughter, 'shan't my brother have one too?' This annoyed the woman, but she said: 'Yes, when he comes from school.' And when she saw from the window that he was coming, it was just as if the Evil One came upon her, and she snatched the apple and took it away from her daughter and said: 'You shan't have one before your brother.' Then she flung the apple back into the chest and closed it. When the little boy came in at the door, the Evil One put it into her head to say to him, all friendly: 'My son, would you like an apple?' but she looked at him harshly. 'Mother', said the little boy, 'how cruelly you are looking at me! Yes, give me an apple.' Then it was as if she was compelled to speak to him: 'Come with me,' she said, and lifted the lid, 'fetch your own apple.' And as the little boy stooped inside, the Evil One told her what to do. Crash! She slammed the lid shut, so that his head flew off and fell in among the red apples. Then she was overcome by fear, and thought: 'If only I can shift the blame from myself!' So she went upstairs to her room, and from the topmost drawer of her closet she took a white cloth and fastened his head back onto his neck, and she bound the neckerchief round so that nothing could be seen and sat him on a chair outside the door and put the apple into his hand.

Then Marleenken came into the kitchen to her mother, who was standing by the fire holding a pan of hot water in front of her, all the time stirring it. 'Mother,' said Marleenken, 'my brother is sitting outside the door looking all white with an apple in his hand. I asked him to give me the apple, but he didn't answer me. I was very frightened.' 'Go back to him,' said her mother, 'and if he doesn't want to answer you, give him one over the ear.' So Marleenken went and said: 'Brother, give me the apple.' But he remained silent, so she gave him one over the ear. His head fell off then, which made her so frightened that she began to cry and howl, and she ran to her mother and said: 'Oh, mother, I've knocked my brother's head off,' and she cried and she cried and was not to be consoled. 'Marleenken,' said her mother, 'what have you done! But just keep quiet, so that no one notices, for there's nothing to be done about it; we'll make him into a stew.' So the mother took the little boy and hacked him in pieces, put him in the pan, and made him into a stew. But Marleenken stood nearby and cried and cried, and her tears all fell into the pan, and they had no need of any salt at all.

Then the father came home and sat down at table and said: 'Where's my son, then?' At that the mother served up a big, big dish of stew, and Marleenken cried and couldn't stop. Then the father said again: 'Where's my son?' 'Oh,' said the mother, 'he's gone to the country, to his mother's great-uncle. He'll stay there a while.' 'What's he doing there? And he didn't even say goodbye!' 'Oh, he wanted to go. And he asked me if he could stay six weeks. He'll be well looked after.' 'Oh,' said the man, 'I'm very sad; it's not right; he really should have said goodbye.' With that he began to eat, and said: 'Marleenken, why are you crying? Your brother will come back, for sure.' 'Well, wife,' he said, 'what is it makes my meal taste so good? Give me some more!' And the more he ate, the more he wanted, and he said: 'Give me some more; you shall have none of it; it's as if it all belonged to me.' And he ate and he ate, and he threw all the bones under the table until he had eaten it all up. But Marleenken went to her trunk and from the bottom-most drawer she took her best silk kerchief and gathered up all the little bones from under the table, and tied them in the silk kerchief and carried them outside the door and wept her tears of blood. There she lay down in the green grass beneath the juniper tree, and after she had lain there, all at once she felt light of heart and she wept no longer. Then the juniper tree began to stir, and the branches parted and then closed again, just as if someone were clapping their hands for joy. At the same time there rose a kind of mist from the tree, and deep in the mist there burned a fire, and out of the fire there flew such a beautiful bird which sang so splendidly and flew high up into the air, and after it had gone the juniper tree was as it had been before, and the kerchief with the bones was gone. But Marleenken was as light of heart and glad as if her brother were still alive. Then she went back into the house and ate her dinner.

But the bird flew away and settled on a goldsmith's house and began to sing:

> 'It was my mother who butchered me,
> It was my father who ate me,
> My sister, little Marleen,
> Found all my little bones,
> Bound them in a silken cloth,

And laid them under the juniper tree.
Peewit, peewit, what a beautiful bird am I!'

The goldsmith was sitting in his workshop making a golden chain when he heard the bird sitting and singing up on his roof, and sounding so beautiful to his ears. He got up, but as he was crossing the threshold he lost a slipper. But he went right on up the street all the same, in one slipper and one sock; he was wearing his leather apron; in one hand he was holding the gold chain and in the other his tweezers; and the sun shone bright on the street. Then he went and stood still and spoke to the bird: 'Bird,' he said, 'how beautifully you can sing. Sing me that song again.' 'No,' said the bird, 'I shan't sing it twice for nothing. Give me the gold chain, and I'll sing it again.' 'Right,' said the goldsmith, 'here's the gold chain for you. Now sing it again.' So the bird came and took the gold chain in his right claw and went and perched in front of the goldsmith and sang:

> 'It was my mother who butchered me,
> It was my father who ate me,
> My sister, little Marleen,
> Found all my little bones,
> Bound them in a silken cloth,
> And laid them under the juniper tree.
> Peewit, peewit, what a beautiful bird am I!'

Then the bird flew to a shoemaker's, and settled on his roof and sang:

> 'It was my mother who butchered me,
> It was my father who ate me,
> My sister, little Marleen,
> Found all my bones,
> Bound them in a silken cloth,
> And laid them under the juniper tree.
> Peewit, peewit, what a beautiful bird am I!'

The shoemaker heard this, and ran outside his door in his shirt-sleeves. He looked up at his roof and had to hold his hand before his eyes, so that the sun shouldn't blind him. 'Bird,' he said, 'can't you sing beautifully!' Then he called indoors: 'Wife, come outside, there's a bird here. Look at him; he can sing beautifully, that's for sure.' Then he called his daughter and her children and his apprentices, maids, and lads, and they all came up the street to see how beautiful the bird was, and he had bright red and green feathers, and round his neck they were like sheer gold, and his eyes glistened in his head like stars. 'Bird,' said the shoemaker, 'sing me that song again.' 'No,' said the bird, 'I shan't sing it twice for nothing; you must give me something as a gift.' 'Wife,' said the man, 'go up to the loft; on the topmost shelf there's a pair of red shoes; bring them down.' So his wife went up and fetched the shoes. 'Right, bird,' said the man, 'now sing it again.' So the bird came and took the shoes in his left claw and flew back up onto the roof and sang:

> 'It was my mother who butchered me,
> It was my father who ate me,
> My sister, little Marleen,
> Found all my little bones,
> Bound them in a silken cloth,
> And laid them under the juniper tree.
> Peewit, peewit, what a beautiful bird am I!'

And when he had finished singing he flew away, the chain in his right claw and the shoes in his left, and he flew far away towards a mill, and the mill went clip clap, clip clap, clip clap. And inside the mill were twenty miller's lads who were hewing a millstone, and they hacked, hick hack, hick hack, hick hack, and the mill went clip clap, clip clap, clip clap. Then the bird went and settled on a linden tree which stood in front of the mill, and he sang:

> 'It was my mother who butchered me,'

then one of them stopped working,

> 'It was my father who ate me,'

then two more stopped working and listened,

> 'My sister, little Marleen,'

then four more stopped,

> 'Found all my little bones,
> Bound them in a silken cloth,'

then only eight were still hacking,

> 'And laid them under'

then only five,

'the juniper tree.'

now only one,

'Peewit, peewit, what a beautiful bird am I!'

Then the last one stopped working, and he had heard only the last of the bird's song. 'Bird,' he said, 'how beautifully you sing! Let me hear your song too; sing it to me again.' 'No,' said the bird, 'I shan't sing it twice for nothing; give me the millstone and I'll sing it again.' 'Yes,' he said, 'if it belonged to me alone you should have it.' 'Yes,' said the others, 'if he'll sing it again, he shall have it.' Then the bird came down, and the millers, all twenty of them, set to with a beam and raised the stone, hu-u-up, hu-u-up, hu-u-up! Then the bird stuck his neck through the hole and wore it like a collar, and flew up onto the tree again and sang:

> 'It was my mother who butchered me,
> It was my father who ate me,
> My sister, little Marleen,
> Found all my little bones,
> Bound them in a silken cloth,
> And laid them under the juniper tree.
> Peewit, peewit, what a beautiful bird am I!'

And when he had finished singing he spread his wings, and in his right claw he had the chain, and in his left claw the shoes, and around his neck he had the millstone. And he flew far away to his father's house.

In the parlour the father, the mother, and Marleenken were sitting at table, and the father said: 'Oh, how glad, how light of heart I feel.' 'No,' said the mother, 'I feel very frightened, just as if a great storm were coming.' For her part Marleenken sat and cried and cried, then the bird came flying up, and as he settled on the roof the father said: 'I feel so happy, and the sun is shining outside so brightly, I feel as if I'm about to see an old friend.' 'No,' said the wife, 'I feel so frightened, my teeth are chattering, and it burns like fire in my veins.' And she tore at her corsets and the rest, but Marleenken sat in a corner and cried, and she had her plate in front of her eyes and cried her plate quite wet. Then the bird settled high on the juniper tree and sang:

> 'It was my mother who butchered me,'

At that the mother covered her ears and shut her eyes and would neither see nor hear, but there was a roaring in her ears like the fiercest storm, and her eyes burned and darted like lightning.

> 'It was my father who ate me,'

'Oh mother,' said the man, 'there's a beautiful bird. It is singing so splendidly, the sun is shining so warm, and there's a smell just like cinnamon.'

> 'My sister, little Marleen,'

Then Marleenken laid her head upon her knees and wept her eyes out, but the man said: 'I'm going outside. I must look at the bird from nearby.' 'Oh, don't go,' said the wife, 'I feel as if the whole house were tottering and on fire.' But the man went outside and looked at the bird.

> 'Found all my little bones,
> Bound them in a silken cloth,
> And laid them under the juniper tree.
> Peewit, peewit, what a beautiful bird am I!'

With this the bird dropped the gold chain, and it fell right round the man's neck so neatly that it fitted exactly. Then he went inside and said: 'Look what a beautiful bird that is; he's given me this fine gold chain and he looks so beautiful.' But the woman was frightened and she fell, measuring her length in the parlour, and her cap fell off her head. Then the bird sang once again:

> 'It was my mother who butchered me,'

'Oh, if only I were a thousand feet below ground, and might not hear it!'

> 'It was my father who ate me,'

Then the woman fell down as if she were dead.

> 'My sister, little Marleen,'

'Oh,' said Marleenken, 'I'll go outside too and see if the bird will give me a present.' So she went outside.

> 'Found all my little bones,
> Bound them in a silken cloth,'

Then he dropped the shoes down to her.

> 'And laid them under the juniper tree.
> Peewit, peewit, what a beautiful bird am I!'

Then she was so light-hearted and glad. And she wore her new red shoes and danced and tripped back inside. 'Oh,' she said, 'I was so sad when I went outside, and now I'm so happy. He's a splendid bird for sure, giving me a pair of red shoes.' 'No,' said the wife, jumping up, with her hair standing on end like flames of fire, 'I feel as if the world is coming to an end; I'll go outside too, to see if my heart will be lighter.' And as she came out of the door, crash! The bird dropped the millstone onto her head, so that she was squashed to a pulp. The father and Marleenken heard it and went outside. Then smoke and flames and fire rose from the spot, and when that was over there stood her little brother. And he took his father and Marleenken by the hand and they were all three so happy, and they went into the house and sat down at table and ate their dinner.

35. *Old Sultan*

A FARMER once had a faithful dog called Sultan, who had grown old and had lost all his teeth, so he was no longer able to grip anything fast. One day the farmer was standing at the door of their house talking to his wife, and he said: 'Tomorrow I'll shoot old Sultan: he's no use any more.' His wife, who was sorry for the faithful creature, answered: 'As he's served us for so many years and stayed true to us, we could surely provide for him in his old age.' 'Go on,' said her husband, 'you're a fool; he hasn't a tooth left in his head and no thief is going to be scared of him. It's time he was put down. True, he's served us well—but he's been well fed in return.'

The poor dog, who was lying stretched out in the sun not far away, had overheard everything and was sad that tomorrow was to be his last day. He had a good friend, the wolf, and that evening he slipped out to the forest to see him, and bewailed the fate that awaited him. 'Listen, brother,' said the wolf, 'I'll help you out of your trouble. I've thought of something. Early tomorrow morning your master will be going haymaking with his wife, and they'll be taking their baby with them, because there's no one left behind in the house. While they are working they usually lay the baby behind the hedge in the shade: you lie down next to him, just as if you wanted to guard him. Then I'll come out of the wood and steal the child: you must chase after me eagerly, as if you were trying to get the baby back from me. I'll let him drop and you can take him back to his parents. Then they'll believe that you've saved him and they'll be far too grateful to do you any harm. On the contrary, you'll be in their good graces, and they'll see to it that in future you lack for nothing.'

The dog was delighted with this suggestion, and as it had been planned so it was carried out. The father gave a cry when he saw the wolf running across the field with his child, but when old Sultan brought him back he was overjoyed and patted the dog, saying: 'Not a hair on your back shall be touched; we'll provide for you in your old age for as long as you live.' As for his wife, he told her: 'Go home right away and make old Sultan a bread-porridge—he won't need to chew it—and fetch the pillow from my bed: he shall have it to sleep on.' From then on old Sultan lived as comfortably as he could possibly wish. Not long afterwards the wolf paid him a visit, and was delighted that everything had gone so well. 'But brother,' he said, 'you'll turn a blind eye, won't you, if I carry off one of your master's fat sheep on occasion? It's a struggle to make a living these days.' 'Don't count on it,' answered the dog. 'I'm still faithful to my master. I can't agree to that.' The wolf thought he didn't mean it and came slipping in at night, intending to take the sheep for himself. But the farmer, to whom faithful Sultan had revealed what the wolf had in mind, lay in wait and gave the wolf a terrible thrashing with his flail. The wolf had to run for it, but he shouted at the dog: 'Just wait, you wicked fellow, you'll pay for this.'

Next morning the wolf sent the boar to challenge the dog to come out to the forest, where they would settle the affair. The only second Sultan could find was a cat with just three legs, and as they went out together the poor cat was limping along, at the same time stretching her tail straight up in pain. The wolf and his second were already at the appointed place, but when they saw their opponent coming they imagined he was bringing a sword with him, for that is what they took the cat's upright tail to be. And while the poor creature was bobbing along on its three legs, all they could think was that it was picking up a stone each time, intending to throw it at them. They both became frightened: the wild boar crept into the undergrowth and hid; the wolf leapt up into a tree. When the dog and the cat arrived they were surprised that no one could be seen. But the wild boar had not been able to conceal himself in the undergrowth completely; his ears were still sticking out. As the cat was looking around cautiously, the boar twitched his ears; the cat, imagining it was a mouse stirring, leapt over and gave a hearty bite. At that the boar reared up with an almighty squeal and ran away, calling: 'Up in the tree—that's where the culprit is sitting.' The dog and the cat looked up and caught sight of the wolf; he was ashamed at appearing so timid, and accepted the dog's offer of peace.

36. *The Six Swans*

A KING once went hunting in a great forest, and he went in such eager pursuit of one deer that none of his huntsmen could follow him. As evening drew near he stopped and looked about him, and saw that he was lost. He searched for some way out of the forest, but could find none. Then he saw an old woman with trembling head approach—but she was a witch. 'Good woman,' he addressed her, 'can you show me the way through the forest?' 'Oh yes, my lord king,' she answered, 'indeed I can, but there is one condition, and if you do not fulfil it you will never leave the forest and must needs starve to death.' 'What kind of condition do you mean?' asked the king. 'I have a daughter,' said the old woman, 'who is so beautiful that you will never find her like in all the world, and who is indeed worthy to be your consort. If you make her your lady queen, I will show you the way out of the forest.' The king consented, his heart full of fear, and the old woman led him to her cottage, where her daughter was sitting by the fire. She received the king as if she had been expecting him, and he saw that she was indeed very beautiful, but even so she was not to his liking, and he could not look on her without a secret shudder of fear. After he had lifted the girl up onto his horse the old woman showed him the way, and the king arrived at his palace once more, where their wedding was celebrated.

The king had already been married once, and by his first wife he had seven children, six boys and one girl, whom he loved more than anything in the world. Now, because he was afraid that their stepmother would not treat them well, and even do them harm, he took them to a lonely castle in the midst of a forest. It lay so hidden, and the way there was so hard to find, that he would not have been able to find it himself if a wise-woman had not made him the gift of a ball of yarn which had magical powers: if he threw it forward it would unwind of its own accord and show him the way. But the king went out so often to see his beloved children that the queen soon noticed his absence; she became curious and wanted to know what he was doing out there all alone in the forest. She gave a great deal of money to his servants, and they betrayed his secret to her; they also told her of the ball of yarn that could show the way on its own. From then on she did not rest until she had found out where the king kept the ball. When she did, she made little shirts of white silk and, as she had learned the arts of witchcraft from her mother, she sewed a spell into them. And one day, when the king had ridden out to hunt, she took the shirts and went into the forest; and the ball of yarn showed her the way. The children, seeing someone coming from afar, thought their beloved father had come to them and ran, full of joy, to meet him. But over each of them she flung one of the little shirts, and the moment the shirts touched their bodies they were turned into swans and flew high over the forest and away. The queen went home delighted, believing she was rid of her stepchildren, but the girl had not run out with her brothers to meet her, and the queen knew nothing about her. Next day the king came to visit his children, but he found no one there but the girl. 'Where are your brothers?' he asked. 'Oh father dear,' she replied, 'they've gone, and left me alone.' And she told him how she had watched from her little window and seen her brothers flying away over the forest, and she showed him the feathers they had shed in the courtyard, which she had gathered up. The king grieved, but he didn't think that the queen had committed this wicked deed, and because he was afraid that the girl too would be stolen from him he wanted to take her with him. But she was afraid of her stepmother, and begged the king to allow her to stay just this one night longer in the castle in the forest.

The poor girl thought: 'This is no longer a place for me to stay. I will go and look for my brothers.' So when night fell she fled, going deep into the forest. She walked without stopping all night long and all through the next day, until she could go no further, she was so weary. Then she saw a hunters' lodge, so she climbed up and found a room with six little beds, but she did not venture to lie down on any of them, but crept underneath one and lay down on the hard ground, intending to pass the night there. But just as the sun was about to sink she heard a whirring sound, and saw six swans come flying in at the window. They settled on the floor and blew at one another, and blew off all their feathers; and they slipped off their swan's skin like a shirt. The girl looked at them and recognized her brothers. She was overjoyed, and crept out from under the bed. The brothers were no less joyful when they caught sight of their little sister, but their joy was short-lived. 'This is no place for you to stay,' they told her. 'This is a refuge for robbers. If they come home and find you, they'll kill you.' 'Can't you protect me, then?' their little sister asked. 'No,' they answered, 'for we can only cast off our swan's skin for a quarter of an hour every evening, when we have our human form, but after that we are turned into swans once again.' Their sister wept and asked: 'Can't you be released from the spell, then?' 'Oh no,' they answered, 'the conditions are too hard. For six long years you may not speak or laugh, and during that time you must sew six shirts out of star-flowers. If you utter a single word, all your work will be in vain.' And when the brothers had said this the quarter of an hour was over, and they flew out of the window as swans once again.

As for the girl, she firmly resolved to rescue her brothers, even if it cost her her life. She left the hunters' lodge, went into the depths of the forest, then climbed a tree and passed the night there. Next morning she went out and gathered star-flowers and began to sew. She could not talk to anyone, and had no desire to laugh; she sat there and had eyes only for her work. One day, when she had already been there a long time, it happened that the king of that land was hunting in the forest, and his huntsmen came upon the tree where the girl was sitting. They called to her, asking: 'Who are you?' But she gave no answer. 'Come down to us,' they said. 'We won't hurt you.' She just shook her head. When they went on pestering her with more questions, she took the golden chain from her neck and threw it down to them, thinking that would satisfy them. But they persisted, so she threw them down her belt, and when that was no use either, she threw down her garters, and bit by bit she threw down everything she had on and could do without, until she kept nothing more than her shift. But the huntsmen refused to be sent away like this; they climbed the tree, lifted her down, and led her before the king. The king asked: 'Who are you? What are you doing in that tree?' But she didn't answer. He asked her in all the languages he knew, but she remained as silent as a fish. But because she was so beautiful, the king's heart was touched and he fell in love with her. He wrapped her in his cloak, set her before him on his horse, and took her to his palace. Then he had her clad in rich garments, and she shone in her beauty like the bright day—but not a word could she be brought to utter. He seated her by his side at table, and her unassuming demeanour and her modesty were so greatly to his liking that he said: 'This is the girl I wish to marry, and no one else in all the world.' And in a few days he married her.

But the king had a wicked mother, who was not satisfied with this marriage and spoke ill of the young queen. 'Who knows where that unspeaking wench comes from,' she said. 'She is not worthy of a king.' A year later, when the queen brought her first child into the world, the old woman took it away from her and smeared her mouth with blood while she was asleep. Then she went to the king and accused the queen of being one who ate human flesh. The king would not believe it, and would not suffer anyone to do her harm. The next time she bore another bonny boy her false mother-in-law practised the same deception, but the king could not bring himself to believe what she said. He declared: 'She is too devout and good to do something like that; if she were not mute and could defend herself, her innocence would come to light.' But when the old woman stole the newborn child for a third time and accused the queen—who uttered not a word in her own defence—the king could not do otherwise than hand her over to the court, which condemned her to death by fire.

When the day arrived for the sentence to be carried out, it was also the last day of the six years she was forbidden to speak or laugh, and she had released her dear brothers from the power of the spell. The six shirts were finished, only the last one still lacked the left sleeve. As she was being led to the stake she laid the shirts over her arm; and as she was standing there and the fire was just about to be lit, she looked about her, and six swans came winging their way through the air. So she saw that the time of their deliverance was drawing near, and her heart stirred with joy. The swans whirred towards her and sank down so that she could throw the shirts over them; and as soon as they were touched by the shirts their swan's skin fell from them, and her brothers stood before her as their own bodily selves, handsome and young; only the youngest was lacking his left arm; instead, he had a swan's wing on his back. They hugged and kissed one another, and the queen went up to the king, who was utterly astonished, and she began to speak, saying: 'My dearest husband, now I may speak and reveal to you that I am innocent and that I have been falsely accused,' and she told him of the ruse practised by the old woman, who had stolen her three children and hidden them away. Then to the king's great joy the children were brought in, and as a punishment the wicked mother-in-law was bound to the stake and burned to ashes. But the king and the queen with her six brothers lived for many long years in peace and happiness.

37. *Briar-Rose*

IN days gone by there lived a king and a queen who every day would say: 'Oh, if only we had a child!', but they never had one. Then it happened one day, when the queen was bathing, that a frog crawled out of the water onto land and told her: 'Your wish will be fulfilled. Before a year goes by you will bring a daughter into the world.' What the frog had said to her indeed came about, and the queen bore a little girl who was so beautiful that the king could not contain his joy, and he ordered a great feast. He invited not only his relatives, friends, and acquaintances but the wise-women as well, so that they would be gracious and well-disposed towards the child. There were thirteen of them in his kingdom, but because he had only twelve golden platters for them to eat from, one of them had to stay at home. The feast was celebrated with great splendour, and when it was at an end the wise-women presented the child with their magical gifts: the one with virtue, the other with beauty, the third with riches, and in this way with everything in the world that could be wished for. Eleven of them had just uttered their spells when suddenly the thirteenth made her entrance. She wanted to take her revenge for not being invited, and without a greeting or even a glance at anyone she called out in a loud voice: 'In her fifteenth year the

king's daughter shall prick herself on a spindle and fall down dead.'
And without another word, she turned and left the hall. Everyone
was horrified. Then the twelfth wise-woman stepped forward; she
still had her wish left, and because she had no power to annul the
wicked spell, but could only lessen its force, she said: 'It shall not be
death: instead, the king's daughter shall fall into a deep sleep which
shall last one hundred years.'

The king, who wanted to save his child from this calamity,
commanded that all the spindles in the entire kingdom should be
burned. As for his daughter, the gifts the wise-women had made
were all fulfilled, for she was so beautiful, virtuous, kind, and sensible that everyone who looked at her could not but love her. Now it
happened that on the very day she had just passed fifteen, the king
and queen were not at home and the girl stayed behind in the palace
all on her own. So she wandered around everywhere, inspecting
parlours and bedchambers at her pleasure, until at last she came to
an old tower. She climbed the narrow, winding stair and reached a
little door. In the lock there was a rusty key; when she turned it the
door flew open, and sitting there in a little room was an old woman
with a spindle, busily spinning her flax. 'Good morning, granny,'
said the king's daughter, 'what are you doing there?' 'I'm spinning,'
said the old woman, nodding her head. 'What kind of thing is that,
bobbing about so merrily?' asked the girl, taking the spindle, for she
wanted to spin herself. But scarcely had she touched the spindle
when the magic spell was fulfilled and she pricked her finger on it.

But the very moment she felt it prick her she fell onto the bed that
was standing there and lay in a deep sleep. And this sleep spread over
the entire palace: the king and the queen, who had just come home
and entered the hall, started to fall asleep, and the entire court with
them. Then the horses in the stables fell asleep, and the dogs in the
yard, the pigeons on the roof, the flies on the wall, even the fire
flickering in the hearth grew still and went to sleep, and the meat
on the spit stopped sizzling, and the cook, who was about to pull the
kitchen-boy's hair because he had made some mistake, let go of him
and slept. And the wind dropped, and on the trees outside the palace
not a leaf would stir any more.

But around the palace a hedge of thorns began to grow, which
grew taller every year, until at last it surrounded the entire palace
and grew over it so that nothing at all could be seen of it any longer,

not even the banner on the roof. But the rumour of the beautiful, sleeping Briar-Rose—for that is what the king's daughter was called—went about the land, so that from time to time there came princes who tried to force their way through the hedge to the palace. But it could not be done, for the thorns clung tightly together as if they had hands, and the young men were left hanging in the hedge, unable to free themselves, and they died a wretched death. After long, long years had passed, a king's son once again came to the land and he heard an old man tell of the hedge of thorns: how a palace was said to stand behind it, where a wondrously beautiful princess, called Briar-Rose, had been sleeping for a hundred years, and sleeping with her were the king and the queen and the entire court. His grandfather had also told him that many princes had already come and tried to force their way through the hedge of thorns, but they had remained hanging on it and had died a sad death. Then the young man said: 'I am not afraid. I will go forth and see the fair Briar-Rose.' However much the good old man tried to dissuade him, he did not listen to his words.

But now the hundred years had just passed, and the day had come when Briar-Rose was to awaken again. As the king's son drew near the hedge of thorns it was nothing but huge and beautiful flowers which parted of their own accord and let him through unharmed, and then, a hedge once more, it closed again behind him. In the palace courtyard he saw the horses and the pied hunting-hounds lying asleep; the pigeons were sitting on the roof with their little heads tucked beneath their wings. And when he went into the house the flies were asleep on the wall, and the cook in the kitchen was still raising his hand as if he were on the point of setting about the boy, and the maid was sitting in front of the black hen she was supposed to be plucking. Then he went further and saw the entire court lying asleep in the hall, and up near the throne lay the king and the queen. Then he went still further, and everything was so quiet you could hear yourself breathe, and at last he reached the tower, and he opened the door to the little room where Briar-Rose was sleeping. There she lay, and she was so beautiful that he could not take his eyes off her, and he bent over and gave her a kiss. As he touched her with his kiss Briar-Rose opened her eyes, awoke, and looked at him with a welcoming gaze. Then they went down together, and the king woke up, and the queen, and the entire court, and they stared at one another in amazement. And the horses in the courtyard stood up and shook themselves, and the hunting-hounds leapt up and wagged their tails; the pigeons on the roof drew their heads out from under their wings, looked around, and flew out into the fields; the flies on the walls went on crawling; the fire in the kitchen rose, flickered, and cooked the meal; and the cook gave the boy such a box on the ear that he yelled; and the maid finished plucking the hen. And then the prince's wedding with Briar-Rose was celebrated with great splendour, and they lived happily to the end of their days.

38. *Foundling-Bird*

THERE was once a forester who went into the forest to hunt, and as he entered it he heard crying, as if it were a little child. He followed the cries and came at last to a tall tree, and high up in the tree there was a little child sitting. For his mother had fallen asleep under the tree with the child, and a bird of prey had seen the child on her lap. It had flown down to them, picked up the child in its beak, and set it down in the tall tree.

The forester climbed up, brought the child down, and thought to himself: 'Take the child home with you and bring him up together with your Lenchen.' So he took him home, and the two children grew up together. But because the boy had been found in a tree, and because a bird had carried him away, he was called Foundling-Bird. Foundling-Bird and Lenchen loved each other so much, oh so much, that if one of them didn't see the other, each of them would grow sad.

But the forester had an old cook, and one evening she took two buckets and began to carry water; she went out to the well not once, but many times. Lenchen watched her, and said: 'Tell me, old Sanne, why are you carrying so much water?' 'If you won't repeat it to a soul, I'll tell you.' Then Lenchen said no, she wouldn't repeat it to a soul, so the cook said: 'Early tomorrow morning, when the forester has gone hunting, I shall boil the water, and when it's simmering in the cauldron I shall throw Foundling-Bird in and cook him in it.'

Very early next morning the forester got up and went hunting, and as he left, the children were still in bed. Then Lenchen said to Foundling-Bird: 'Just as you won't leave me, I won't leave you.' So

Foundling-Bird replied: 'Not now, not ever.' Then Lenchen said: 'Then I'll tell you: yesterday evening old Sanne carried so many buckets of water into the house. I asked her why she was doing that, and she said if I wouldn't tell a soul, she would tell me. I said I wouldn't tell a soul for sure; then she said, tomorrow morning early, when father was out hunting, she would boil the cauldron of water, throw you in, and cook you. But let us get up quickly, dress ourselves, and run away together.'

So the two children got up, dressed themselves, and ran away. Now when the water in the cauldron was boiling, the cook went up to the bedroom, intending to fetch Foundling-Bird and throw him in. But when she entered and went towards the beds, the two children were off and away. At this she became terribly afraid, and said to herself: 'What shall I say when the forester comes home and sees that the children are gone? Follow them quickly, so that we can get hold of them again.'

So the cook sent three farmhands after them, telling them to run and catch up with the children. But the children were sitting at the edge of the forest, and when they saw the three farmhands coming from far off Lenchen said to Foundling-Bird: 'Just as you won't leave me, I won't leave you.' So Foundling-Bird replied: 'Not now, not ever.' Then Lenchen said: 'You turn into a rose-tree, and I'll turn into a rose growing on it.' When the three farmhands came to the edge of the forest there was nothing but a rose-bough with one rose growing on it, but the children were nowhere. So they said: 'There's nothing doing here,' and went home and told the cook they had seen nothing at all, only a rose-tree with one rose growing on it. Then the old cook scolded them: 'You simpletons, you should have cut the rose-tree in two and picked the rose and brought it home. Quick, go and do it now.' So they had to go out and look a second time. But the children saw them coming from far off, so Lenchen said: 'Foundling-Bird, just as you won't leave me, I won't leave you.' Foundling-Bird replied: 'Not now, not ever.' Said Lenchen: 'So you turn into a church, and I'll turn into the crown inside it.' By the time the three farmhands arrived there was nothing to be seen but a church with a crown inside. So they said to one another: 'What are we doing here? Let's go home.' When they reached home the cook asked whether they had found anything, and they said no, they'd found nothing but a church, and there was a crown inside. 'You fools,' scolded the cook, 'why didn't you break into the church and bring the crown home with you?' So the old cook herself started out and went after the children with the three farmhands. But the children saw the three farmhands coming from far off, with the cook tottering behind. Then Lenchen said: 'Foundling-Bird, just as you won't leave me, I won't leave you.' And Foundling-Bird replied: 'Not now, not ever.' Said Lenchen: 'Turn into a pond, and I'll turn into the duck upon it.' But the cook arrived, and when she saw the pond leaned over it, intending to drink it dry. But the duck came swimming up fast, seized her by the head with her beak, and pulled her into the water: there the old witch had to drown. Then the children went home together and they were very, very happy. And if they haven't died, they are living still.

39. *Snow-White*

ONCE upon a time in midwinter, when the snowflakes were falling from the sky like down, a queen was sitting and sewing at a window which had a frame of black ebony. And as she sewed at the window and glanced up at the snow, she pricked her finger with her needle and three drops of blood fell onto the snow. And because the red looked so beautiful on the white snow, she thought to herself: 'If only I had a child as white as snow, as red as blood, and as black as the wood in the window-frame.' Not long afterwards she had a little daughter who was as white as snow, as red as blood, and with hair as black as ebony, and because of that she was called Snow-White. And as the child was born, the queen died.

A year later the king took another wife. She was a beautiful woman, but she was proud and arrogant and could not endure it that anyone should surpass her in beauty. She had a marvellous mirror, and when she stood in front of it and gazed at herself, she would say:

> 'Mirror, mirror on the wall,
> Who is the fairest one of all?'

And the mirror would answer:

> 'Lady, you are the fairest one of all.'

Then she was satisfied, for she knew that the mirror was telling the truth.

But Snow-White was growing up, becoming more and more beautiful, and when she was seven years old she was as fair as the bright day and fairer than the queen herself. One day, when the queen asked her mirror:

> 'Mirror, mirror on the wall,
> Who is the fairest one of all?'

The mirror answered:

> 'Lady, you are the fairest here,
> But Snow-White is a thousand times more fair.'

This horrified the queen, who turned yellow and green with envy. From that hour, whenever she saw Snow-White her heart would turn over in her body, she hated the girl so much. And envy and arrogance grew in her heart like a weed, taller and taller, so that day and night she no longer had any peace. So she called a huntsman to her and told him: 'Take the child out into the forest. I don't want to set eyes on her again. You are to kill her, and bring me her lungs and liver as a token.' The huntsman obeyed and led the child out into the forest. And just as he had drawn his hunting-knife and was about to stab Snow-White in her innocent heart, she began to cry, saying: 'Oh, huntsman dear, spare my life; I'll run away into the wild wood and never come home again.' And because she was so fair, the huntsman took pity on her and said: 'Run away then, you poor child.' 'The wild animals will soon have eaten you up,' he thought, but even so he felt as if a stone had been lifted from his heart because he didn't need to kill her. And as a young boar-piglet came leaping by just at that moment, he stabbed him, took out his lungs and liver, and brought them to the queen as a token. The cook was commanded to stew them in salt, and the wicked woman ate them up, imagining it was Snow-White's lungs and liver she had eaten.

Now the poor child was all alone in the great forest, and she grew so frightened that she gazed at all the leaves on the trees and didn't know what to do to save herself. And so she began to run, and she ran over the sharp stones and through the thorns, and the wild animals leapt past her, but they did her no harm. She ran for as long as her feet could carry her, until it was nearly evening. Then she saw a little house, and she went inside to rest. Everything in the little house was very small, but I just can't tell you how neat and clean it was. There was a little table with a white cloth, laid with seven little plates, each plate with its little spoon, seven little knives and forks as well, and seven little cups. Against the wall there were seven little beds, arranged side by side and covered with sheets as white as snow. Because Snow-White was so hungry and thirsty she ate some bread and greens from each little plate, and drank a drop of wine from each little cup, for she didn't want to take it all from just one. Afterwards, because she was so tired, she lay down on one of the little beds, but none of them was the right size for her: this one was too long, that one too short, until at last the seventh was just right. So she remained lying on that one, entrusted herself to God, and fell asleep.

When it had grown quite dark the masters of the little house arrived. They were the seven dwarves who dug and mined for ore in the mountains. They lit their seven little lanterns, and as it grew bright in the little house they saw that somebody had been there, for everything was not in the order they had left it in. The first said: 'Who's been sitting on my chair?' The second: 'Who's been eating from my plate?' The third: 'Who's taken some of my bread?' The fourth: 'Who's eaten some of my greens?' The fifth: 'Who's been using my fork?' The sixth: 'Who's been using my knife?' The seventh: 'Who's been drinking from my cup?' Then the first turned round and, seeing that there was a little dent on his bed, he said: 'Who's tried out my bed?' The others ran up, and cried: 'Somebody's been lying in my bed too.' But when the seventh looked at his bed, he saw Snow-White lying there asleep. Then he called the others, who came running up, and they cried out in amazement. They fetched their seven little lanterns and threw their light on Snow-White. 'Oh, good Lord! Good Lord!' they cried. 'What a beautiful child!' And they were so joyful that they didn't wake her up, but let her go on sleeping in the little bed. As for the seventh dwarf, he slept with his fellows, an hour apiece with each of them. And so the night passed.

When morning came Snow-White woke, and when she saw the seven dwarves she was startled. But they were friendly, asking: 'What's your name?' 'My name is Snow-White,' she replied. 'How did you come to be in our house?' the dwarves asked again. Then she told them the story of how her stepmother had wanted to have her killed, but the huntsman had spared her life, and then she had run and run all day long until at last she had found their little house. The dwarves said: 'If you will keep house for us, cook and make the beds, wash and sew and knit, and if you will keep everything tidy and clean, you can stay with us and you shall lack for nothing.' 'Yes,' said Snow-White, 'with all my heart,' and she stayed with them. She kept their house in order; in the mornings they went out into the mountains in search of ore and gold; in the evenings they came back and their meal had to be ready for them. Throughout the day the girl was on her own, so the good little dwarves warned her: 'Beware your stepmother. She'll soon find out that you're here; don't, don't let anyone in.'

As for the queen, once she believed she had eaten Snow-White's lungs and liver she had no other thought but that she was once again the first and foremost and most beautiful of all. So she came and stood in front of her mirror and said:

'Mirror, mirror on the wall,
Who is the fairest one of all?'

Then the mirror answered:

'Lady, you are the fairest here,
But Snow-White, living far away
With the seven dwarves this day,
Is still a thousand times more fair.'

At that she was horrified, for she knew that the mirror did not lie, and she realized that the huntsman had deceived her and that Snow-White was still alive. And then she racked her brains again and again to think how she could kill her, for as long as she was not the fairest one of all her envy would not leave her in peace. And when at last she had thought of a plan, she stained her face and dressed up like an old pedlar-woman, and she was quite unrecognizable. In this shape she crossed the seven mountains to the seven dwarves, knocked on their door, and called: 'Fine wares for sale! Going cheap! Going cheap!' Snow-White peeked out of the window and called: 'Good morning, good woman! What have you for sale?' 'Good wares, fine wares,' she answered. 'Laces for your bodice in every colour,' and she produced one woven of brightly coloured silk. 'I can let this good woman in,' thought Snow-White. She unbolted the door and bought herself a set of pretty laces. 'My child,' said the old woman, 'what a sight you are! Come, I'll lace your bodice properly!' Snow-White wasn't suspicious, stood in front of her, and allowed herself to be laced up with the new laces. But the old woman laced fast and she laced so tight that Snow-White lost her breath and fell down as if she were dead. 'Now you *were* once the fairest of all,' said the old woman, and hurried out.

Not long afterwards, at eventide, the seven dwarves came home, but how horrified they were when they saw their dear Snow-White lying on the ground. She didn't stir or move, as if she were dead. They lifted her up, and because they saw that her lacing was too tight, they cut her laces. Then she began to breathe a little, and bit by bit she came back to life. When the dwarves heard what had happened they declared: 'That old pedlar-woman was no one but the godless queen. Take care and don't let anybody in if we are not here with you.'

As for the wicked woman, when she came home she went before her mirror and asked:

> 'Mirror, mirror on the wall,
> Who is the fairest one of all?'

And it replied, as it always did:

> 'Lady you are the fairest here,
> But Snow-White, living far away
> With the seven dwarves this day,
> Is still a thousand times more fair.'

When she heard that, all the blood drained from her heart, she was so horrified, for she realized that Snow-White had come back to life. 'But now,' she said, 'I'll think up something that shall destroy you.' And with the black arts she commanded she made a poisoned comb. Then she disguised herself, taking on the shape of another old woman. In this guise she crossed the seven mountains to the seven dwarves, knocked at the door, and called: 'Good wares going cheap, going cheap!' Snow-White looked out and said: 'Go your ways, I mustn't let anyone in.' 'Surely you're allowed to look,' said the old woman, taking out the poisoned comb and holding it up. The girl liked it so much that she let herself be fooled and opened the door. When they had agreed on the sale the old woman said: 'Now I'll comb your hair properly.' Poor Snow-White suspected nothing, and let the old woman have her way. But the comb had hardly touched her hair before the poison in it took effect and the girl fell down unconscious. 'You paragon of beauty,' said the wicked woman, 'it's over with you now,' and off she went. But as luck would have it, it was nearly evening, when the seven little dwarves would come home. When they saw Snow-White lying on the ground as if she were dead they suspected her stepmother at once, so they looked carefully and found the poisoned comb. They had scarcely drawn it out before Snow-White revived and told them what had happened. Then they warned her once again to be on her guard and to open her door to no one.

Back home, the queen stood before her mirror and said:

> 'Mirror, mirror on the wall,
> Who is the fairest one of all?'

Then it answered, as it had before:

> 'Lady, you are the fairest here,
> But Snow-White, living far away
> With the seven dwarves this day,
> Is still a thousand times more fair.'

When she heard the mirror speaking like this she shook and shuddered with rage. 'Snow-White shall die,' she cried, 'even if it costs my own life.' And straight away she went off to the most secret, lonely little room, where no one came, and there she made a poisonous, poisonous apple. On the outside it looked lovely, white with rosy cheeks, so that the sight of it would make you want to take a bite, but whoever ate one morsel of it would be bound to die. When the apple was ready the queen stained her face and disguised herself as a peasant woman; in this guise she crossed the seven mountains to the seven dwarves. She knocked at their door. Snow-White put her head out of the window and said: 'I'm not allowed to let anyone at all inside; the seven dwarves have forbidden it.' 'That's all right by me,' answered the peasant woman, 'I want to be rid of my apples. There—I'll give you one.' 'No,' said Snow-White, 'I'm not allowed to accept anything.' 'Are you afraid of being poisoned?' said the old woman. 'Look, I'm cutting the apple in two; you shall eat the red cheek and I'll eat the white.' But the apple had been made so cleverly

Snow-White

that only the red cheek were poisoned. Snow-White's mouth watered for the lovely apple, and when she saw the peasant woman eating a part of it she could no longer resist, but stretched out her hand and took the half that was poisoned. But she had scarcely taken a morsel of it in her mouth when she fell to the ground dead. Then the queen gazed at her with terrifying eyes, uttered a piercing laugh, and said: 'White as snow, red as blood, black as ebony! This time the dwarves won't be able to wake you up again.' And when, back at home, she questioned the mirror:

> 'Mirror, mirror on the wall,
> Who is the fairest one of all?',

it answered her at last:

> 'Lady, you are the fairest one of all.'

So her envious heart was at peace—as far as an envious heart can be at peace.

The little dwarves, when they arrived home that evening, found Snow-White lying on the ground, and she breathed not a breath, and she was dead. They lifted her up, looking for something poisonous, loosened her bodice, combed her hair, washed her with water and wine, but all in vain; the dear girl was dead, and she remained dead. They laid her on a bier and took their places around it, all seven of them, and they shed tears over their loss, and they wept for three days. Then they were about to bury her, but she still looked as fresh as a living being, and still had her lovely red cheeks. 'We can't lower her into the black earth,' they said, and they had a transparent coffin of glass made, so that she could be seen from all sides. They laid her in the coffin and in letters of gold they wrote her name upon it, and that she was a king's daughter. Then they placed the coffin out on the mountain-side, and one of them always remained there to watch over it. And the animals, too, came up and wept for Snow-White, first of all an owl, then a raven, and last of all a dove.

Now Snow-White lay in her coffin for a long, long time, and she did not moulder, but looked as if she were asleep, for she was still as white as snow, as red as blood, with hair as black as ebony. But it happened that a king's son entered the forest and arrived at the dwarves' house, wanting to stay there for the night. He saw the coffin on the mountain-side, with the lovely Snow-White within, and read what was written in letters of gold upon it. Then he said to the dwarves: 'Let me have the coffin. I'll give you whatever you want in exchange.' But the dwarves answered: 'We won't give it for all the gold in the world.' So he said: 'Then grant it to me as a gift, for I cannot live without the sight of Snow-White. I will honour and revere her as my dearest prize.' As he spoke in this way, the good little dwarves took pity on him and gave him the coffin. The king's son then had it borne away on the shoulders of his servants. Then it happened that they stumbled over a branch, and the morsel of poisoned apple that Snow-White had bitten was shaken out of her throat. It was not long before she opened her eyes, lifted the cover of the coffin, sat up, and was alive again. 'Great Heavens, where am I?' she cried. Full of joy, the king's son said: 'You are with me', and he told her what had happened, declaring: 'I love you more than everything in the world; come with me to my father's palace; you shall become my consort.' So Snow-White loved him, and went with him, and preparations for their wedding were made with great splendour and magnificence.

As for Snow-White's godless stepmother, she too was invited to the celebration. When she had dressed herself in fine array, she stepped before the mirror and said:

> 'Mirror, mirror on the wall,
> Who is the fairest one of all?'

The mirror answered:

> 'Lady, you are the fairest here
> But the young queen is a thousand times more fair.'

At that the wicked woman uttered a curse, and she was filled with fear, such fear, that she didn't know what to do with herself. At first she didn't want to go to the wedding at all, but that gave her no peace: she had to go and see the young queen. And when she entered she recognized Snow-White, and she stood there in fear and terror, unable to stir. But iron slippers had already been set over a fire of coals, and they were carried in with tongs and placed before her. Then she was forced to put her feet into the red-hot shoes and dance until she fell to the ground dead.

40. *Knapsack, Hat, and Horn*

THERE were once three brothers who had fallen deeper and deeper into poverty, and at length their distress was so great that they were bound to starve, with nothing left to eat or drink. So they said: 'It can't go on like this. It will be better if we go out into the world and seek our fortune.' So they set off, and had already walked many a long road and trodden countless blades of grass, but still their fortune had not come to meet them. One day they reached a great forest, and in its midst there was a mountain; as they drew nearer they saw that it was made all of silver. At that the eldest said: 'Now I have found the good fortune I wished for, and I shall ask for nothing more.' He took as much of the silver as he could carry, turned round, and went back home. But the other two said: 'We want something more of our good fortune than mere silver,' and didn't touch it, but went on their way. After they had been walking for a couple of days they came to a mountain which was made all of gold. The second brother stood and thought hard, and was quite uncertain: 'What am I to do?' he said. 'Shall I take as much gold for myself as will be enough for the rest of my life, or shall I continue on my way?' At last he came to a decision, crammed his pockets with as much as they would hold, said goodbye to his brother, and went home. But the third said: 'Silver and gold—that leaves me cold. But I don't want to turn my fortune down; perhaps I'll be granted something better.' He continued on his way, and after walking for three days he reached a forest that was even bigger than the last and seemed to go on for ever; and as he found nothing to eat or drink, he was close to dying of starvation. So he climbed a tall tree to see if he could make out where the forest ended, but as far as his eyes could reach there was nothing but treetops in sight. So he set about climbing back down the tree, but he was tormented by hunger and thought: 'If only I could eat my fill just once more.' When he reached the ground, to his astonishment he saw beneath the tree a table richly laid with dishes whose steam rose to meet him. 'This time', he declared, 'my wish has come true at the right moment,' and without questioning who had brought the food or who had cooked it, he went up to the table and ate eagerly until his hunger was satisfied. When he had finished, he thought: 'It would be a real pity if this dainty little tablecloth were to be spoiled here in the forest,' so he folded it neatly and put it in his pocket. Then he continued on his way, and that evening, when his hunger stirred once again, he wanted to put his little tablecloth to the test. So he spread it out, saying: 'I wish that once again you were laid with good food,' and the wish had hardly left his lips when there appeared as many dishes as there was room for on the cloth, all filled with the most delicious food. 'Now,' he said, 'I can tell which kitchen has been cooking for me: tablecloth, you shall be dearer to me than a mountain of silver or gold,' for he realized that it was a wishing-cloth. All the same, the little cloth wasn't enough for him to settle down peacefully at home; he would sooner wander about in the world still and continue to try his luck. One evening in a lonely forest he came upon a charcoal-burner, black with soot, who was burning charcoal and had potatoes roasting in the fire for his dinner. 'Good evening, blackbird,' he said. 'How are things with you in this solitary place?' 'One day just like the next,' replied the charcoal-burner, 'and potatoes every evening. Be my guest, if you like.' 'Many thanks,' answered the traveller, 'I won't rob you of your dinner, for you didn't reckon with a guest, but if you'll put up with my company let me invite you.' 'Who'll serve up for you?' asked the charcoal-burner. 'I can see you've brought nothing with you, and there's no one round about within a couple of hours' distance who could give you anything.' 'All the same,' the traveller answered, 'it shall be a meal better than any you have ever tasted.' He took his little cloth from his knapsack, spread it on the ground, and said: 'Tablecloth, lay,' and at once there stood roast meat and stewed, as warm as if it had just come from the kitchen. The charcoal-burner opened his eyes wide; he needed no further asking but set to, cramming bigger and bigger gobbets into his black mouth. When they had eaten it all up he grinned with pleasure and said: 'Listen, I approve of your little cloth—it would be something to suit me here in the forest, where no one cooks me a good meal. What if we made an exchange? Hanging in the corner over there is a soldier's knapsack. It's true, it looks old and nothing special, but it has marvellous powers. I don't need it any longer, so I'll exchange it for your little cloth.' 'First I have to know what sort of marvellous powers they are,' the traveller rejoined. 'I'll tell you,' answered the charcoal-burner. 'Every time you tap it with your hand, up will come a corporal with six men armed from head to foot, and whatever you command they will do.' 'Fine by me,' the traveller said, 'if that's the way it is, let's exchange.' So he gave the charcoal-burner the little cloth, took the knapsack from its peg, slung it over his shoulder, and took his leave. After he had walked a stretch of the road he wanted to try out his knapsack's marvellous powers, so he tapped on it. At once the seven warriors stood before him, and the corporal asked: 'What does my lord and master require?' 'March at the double to the charcoal-burner and demand the return of my wishing-cloth.' They wheeled left, and it wasn't long before they returned, bringing back what he had demanded; they hadn't asked any questions, but just taken it from the charcoal-burner. The traveller ordered them to dismiss and went on his way, hoping that his luck would shine on him even more cheerfully. At sunset he came upon another charcoal-burner who was preparing his supper by the fire. 'If you'd join me in my meal,' said the grimy fellow, '—it's potatoes with salt, but no butter—sit down here with me.' 'No,' the traveller answered, 'this time you shall be my guest,' and he set out his little cloth, which was promptly laid with the finest dishes. They ate and drank together and were in high good humour. After their meal the charcoal-burner said: 'Up there on the bench there's a worn-out old hat, which has strange qualities: if you put it on your head and turn it round, the cannons will go off as if twelve were firing at once, and they'll shoot everybody down, so that no one can hold out against them. The hat's no use to me, and I'd be glad to give it away in exchange for your little cloth.' 'I like the sound of that,' the traveller answered, and took the little hat. He put it on his head and left his little cloth behind. But he had hardly gone some way when he tapped on his knapsack and ordered his soldiers to bring him back his cloth. 'Things are happening one after the other,' he thought, 'and I feel as if my luck isn't over yet.' His thoughts had not deceived him, either. Again, after walking for a day, he came upon a third charcoal-burner who invited him, like the others, to potatoes with no butter. For his part, the traveller had him share a meal from his wishing-cloth, and the charcoal-burner enjoyed it so much that at last he offered him a little horn in exchange. Its qualities were quite different from those of the hat. If you blew it, walls and fortifications, and in due course towns and villages, would all fall down. The traveller did indeed give the charcoal-burner his cloth in exchange, but afterwards sent his troops to demand it back, so that in the end he had knapsack, hat, and horn all together. 'Now,' he said, 'I'm a made man, and it's time for me to go home and see how my brothers are doing.'

When he reached home he found his brothers had built a fine house with their silver and gold, and were living it up. He went in to them, but because he arrived wearing a ragged coat, with the shabby hat on his head and the old knapsack on his back, they refused to recognize him as their brother. They jeered and said: 'You're claiming to be our brother, who scorned silver and gold and wanted a better fortune for himself; he's sure to arrive in all his splendour as a mighty king, not as a beggarman'—and they turned him out. This made him furious; he tapped on his knapsack for as long as it took for a hundred and fifty soldiers to stand in rank and file before him. He ordered them to surround his brothers' house, and two of them were to take hazel-switches with them and tan the hide of the haughty pair into glove-leather until they knew who he was. A tremendous row broke out, folk gathered together and tried to give the two brothers some support in their distress, but they could do nothing against the soldiers. At last word of it reached the king, who grew angry and dispatched a captain and his company with orders to turn the disturber of the peace out of town; but the man with the knapsack had soon gathered a bigger troop together who drove back the captain and his men, so that they had to withdraw with bloody noses. The king declared: 'That vagabond still has to be brought to heel,' and next day he sent an even greater company against him—but they could do even less. The man sent even more of his people against the king's men, and to get it over more quickly he turned the hat round a couple of times on his head; then the heavy guns started their game, and the king's men were beaten and driven to flight. 'Now I shan't make peace,' he declared, 'until the king gives me his daughter to be my wife and I rule the whole kingdom in his name.' He sent this message to the king, who said to his daughter: ' "Must" is a hard nut: what else is there left for me but to do what he demands? If I want to make peace and keep the crown on my head, I must give you up to him.'

So the wedding was celebrated, but the king's daughter was annoyed that her consort was a common man in a shabby hat with an old knapsack slung on his shoulder. She would gladly have been rid of him, and racked her brains day and night to think how she could bring this about. Thinking to herself: 'Perhaps his magic powers might be hidden in the knapsack,' she pretended affection and caressed him, and when his heart had softened she said: 'If only you would take off that nasty old knapsack—it spoils your looks and makes me ashamed of you.' 'Dear little thing,' he answered, 'this knapsack is my greatest treasure. As long as I have it, I'm not afraid of any force in the world'; and he revealed to her what marvellous powers he possessed. Then she flung her arms about his neck as if she were about to kiss him, but instead she deftly removed the knapsack from his shoulder and ran off with it. As soon as she was alone she tapped on it and ordered the warriors to take their former lord prisoner and lead him out of the royal palace. They obeyed, and the wicked woman sent more of her people after him to drive him right out of the country. He would have been lost if he hadn't had the hat. Scarcely were his hands free but he turned it round a couple of times; at once the cannons began to thunder and mowed them all down. The king's daughter had to come herself and beg for mercy. Because she begged so movingly and promised to be better in future, he let himself be persuaded and granted her peace. She behaved sweetly towards him, pretending to love him dearly, and she was clever enough to fool him into confiding to her after a while that even if someone had the knapsack in his power, they could do nothing against him as long as the old hat was still his. Once she knew the secret she waited until he had fallen asleep, then she took the hat from him and had him thrown out onto the street. But he still had his horn left, and in his anger he blew it with all his might. At once everything fell down—walls, fortifications, towns, and villages, and they struck the king and the king's daughter down dead. And if he hadn't put the horn down and had gone on blowing just a little longer, everything would have been destroyed and not a stone left on top of another. After that no one opposed him, and he set himself up as king over the whole kingdom.

41. *Rumpelstiltskin*

THERE was once a miller who was poor, but he had a beautiful daughter. Now it so happened that he came to speak with the king, and to make himself seem important he said to him: 'I have a daughter who can spin straw into gold.' The king said to the miller: 'That's an art much to my liking; if your daughter is as skilful as you say, bring her to my palace tomorrow and I will put her to the test.' Now when the girl was brought to him he led her into a room which was filled up with straw, gave her spinning-wheel and reel, and declared: 'Set to work at once, and if by morning you haven't spun this straw into gold, you shall die.' Then he locked the room himself, and she was left there alone.

The poor miller's daughter sat there, and for the life of her she didn't know what to do; she had no idea how you could spin straw into gold, and she grew more and more afraid, so that in the end she began to cry. Then all at once the door opened and a little manikin stepped inside, saying: 'Good evening, Miss Miller, why are you crying so much?' 'Oh dear,' replied the girl, 'I'm supposed to spin straw into gold, and I don't know how to do it.' Said the little man: 'What will you give me if I spin it for you?' 'My necklace,' said the girl. The little man took the necklace, sat down at the wheel, and whirr, whirr, whirr, three times the thread was drawn—and the bobbin was full. Then he put on another, and whirr, whirr, whirr, three times the thread was drawn—and the second one was full; and so it went on until morning, and there was all the straw spun and all the bobbins were full of gold. As soon as the sun rose the king came, and when he saw the gold he was astonished and delighted, but his heart grew still more gluttonous for gold. He had the miller's daughter taken to another room full of straw which was much bigger, and he commanded her to spin that overnight as well, if her life was dear to her. The girl didn't know what to do and began to cry; then the door opened again and the little manikin appeared, saying: 'What will you give me if I spin the straw into gold for you?' 'The ring on my finger,' answered the girl. The little man took the ring, began whirring again with the wheel, and by morning he had spun all the straw into shining gold. The king was delighted beyond bounds by the sight; but he still did not have his fill of gold, but had the miller's daughter taken to an even bigger room full of straw, and he said: 'You must spin this yet again tonight: but if you get it done, you shall become my consort.' 'Even if she is a miller's daughter,' he thought, 'I shan't find a richer wife in the whole world.' When the girl was alone the little man came again for the third time, saying: 'What will you give me if I spin the straw for you this time too?' 'I have nothing more I can give you,' answered the girl. 'Then promise me, when you are queen, your first child.' 'Who knows how things will turn out?' thought the miller's daughter, and in her distress she had no idea what else she could do; so she promised the little man what he desired, and in return the little man once again spun the straw into gold. And when the king came in the morning and found everything as he had wished it, he celebrated his wedding with her, and the beautiful miller's daughter became a queen.

A year later she brought a beautiful child into the world, and she no longer gave a thought to the little man; then suddenly he stepped into her chamber, saying: 'Now give me what you promised.' The queen was stricken with fear, and offered the little man all the riches of the kingdom if he would leave her child with her. But the little man said: 'No, I would rather have a living creature than all the treasure in the world.' Then the queen began to weep and wail so sorrowfully that the little man took pity on her. 'I'll give you three days,' he declared, 'and if by that time you know what my name is, you shall keep your child.'

All night long the queen called to mind all the names she had ever heard, and she sent a messenger far and wide throughout the land to find out what other names there might be. Next day, when the little man came, she began with Kaspar, Melchior, Balzar, and listed all the names she knew, one after another, but at each one the little man declared: 'That's not what I'm called.' The second day she enquired all round the neighbourhood to find out what names people were called there, and recited the strangest and most peculiar names to the little man. 'Are you called Skinnyribs perhaps, or Sheepshanks, or Pegleg?' But each time he answered: 'No, I'm not.' On the third day the messenger came back and told her: 'I couldn't find out a single new name, but as I came upon a high mountain round the forest corner by the back of beyond, I saw a little house, and in front of the house a fire was burning, and over the fire the funniest little man was leaping and hopping on one leg and crying:

> "Today I'll bake, tomorrow I'll brew,
> The next I'll fetch the queen's new child;
> Still no one knows it just the same
> That Rumpelstiltskin is my name."'

You can imagine how glad the queen was when she heard the name, and when soon afterwards the little man stepped in and asked: 'Well, Lady Queen, what's my name?' she asked first of all: 'Is your name Tom?' 'No.' 'Is your name Dick?' 'No.'

'Might your name perhaps be Rumpelstiltskin?'

'The Devil told you, the Devil told you,' shrieked the little man, and in his anger he stamped his right foot so deep into the earth that he sank down as far as his waist; then he seized his left foot with both hands in a rage, and tore himself right down the middle into two.

42. *The Golden Bird*

LONG, long ago there was a king who had a beautiful pleasure garden behind his palace. In it there grew a tree which bore apples of gold. As the apples ripened they were counted, but on the very next day one was always missing. The king was informed of this, and he commanded that every night a watch should be kept beneath the tree. Now the king had three sons, and when night fell he sent the eldest into the garden. But when midnight came he could not help falling asleep, and next morning another apple was missing. On the following night the second son had to keep watch, but he did not fare any better: when it had struck twelve he fell asleep, and in the morning an apple was missing. Now it was the third son's turn to keep watch. He was ready to do so too, but the king didn't believe he was up to much and thought he would achieve even less than his brothers; at last, though, he did allow it. So the young man lay down beneath the tree, kept watch, and did not allow himself to succumb to sleep. As it struck twelve something came rustling through the air, and in the moonlight he saw a bird flying up, with plumage shining bright with gold. The bird settled on the tree, and it had just pecked off an apple when the young man shot an arrow at it. The bird flew away, but the arrow had struck its plumage and one of its golden feathers fell to earth. The young man kept it, and next day he took it to the king and told him what he had seen during the night. The king called his council together, and everyone declared that one feather like this was worth more than the entire kingdom. 'If the feather is so precious,' declared the king, 'then just this one is no use to me. I want the whole bird. I must have it.'

The eldest son set off, relying on his intelligence and certain that he would find the golden bird. When he had walked some distance he saw a fox sitting at the edge of a forest. He raised his gun and took aim. The fox called out: 'Don't shoot; I'll give you some good advice in return. You're on your way in search of the golden bird: this evening you'll come to a village where two inns face each other on opposite sides of the road. One is brightly lit, and there'll be lively goings-on inside—but don't put up there; instead, go into the other one, even though it looks in a poor way.' 'How can such a silly creature give me any sensible advice?' thought the king's son, pressing the trigger; but he missed the fox, who stretched his tail and sped swiftly into the forest. After that the king's son continued on his way, and in the evening he came to the village with the two inns. There was singing and dancing going on in the one, while the other had a miserable, gloomy look. 'I'd be a fool', he thought, 'if I went into that shabby tavern and ignored the good one.' So he went into the cheery inn, lived it up there, and forgot the bird, his father, and the words of the wise.

After some time had passed and the eldest son still hadn't come home, the second son set out in search of the golden bird. Like the eldest he encountered the fox, who gave him his good advice which the son did not heed. He arrived at the two inns. His brother was standing at the window of the one where the lively noise was coming from, and called to him. He couldn't resist but went inside, and from then on just lived for his pleasures.

Again some time passed, and the youngest of the king's sons wanted to set out and try his luck, but his father would not permit it. 'It will be useless,' he said, 'he'll be even less successful in finding the golden bird than his brothers, and if he meets with some mishap he won't know what to do; he doesn't have what it takes.' But in the end, when he had no peace from the boy, he let him set out. Again the fox sat at the edge of the forest and gave his good advice. The young man was good-natured, and said: 'Don't worry, little fox, I shan't do you any harm.' 'You won't regret it,' answered the fox, 'and so that you get along faster, climb up behind on my tail.' And he had scarcely seated himself before the fox began to run. And off they raced over hill and dale, so fast that his hair whistled in the wind. When they arrived in the village the young man dismounted, followed the fox's good advice, and without looking round went into the mean little inn, where he put up for the night undisturbed. Next morning, when he reached the fields, the fox was already sitting there and said: 'I'll tell you what else you have to do. Keep going straight ahead, and at last you will come to a castle with a whole host of soldiers lying in front of it; but don't worry about them, because they'll all be sleeping and snoring. Go right through them and straight into the castle; make your way through all the rooms, and last of all you will come to a chamber where a golden bird is hanging in a wooden cage. Nearby is an empty cage of gold for show, but take care that you don't remove the bird from his humble cage nor put him in the splendid one, otherwise things might go badly for you.' After these words the fox stretched out his tail again and the king's son mounted it; then off they raced over hill and dale, so fast that his hair whistled in the wind. When he reached the castle he found everything as the fox had said. The king's son entered the chamber where the golden bird was sitting in the wooden cage, and a golden cage stood nearby; and as for the three golden apples, they were lying about in the room. He thought it would be ridiculous to leave the golden bird in the mean and ugly cage, so he opened the cage door, caught hold of the bird, and put him into the golden cage. But that very moment the bird uttered a piercing shriek. The soldiers woke up, rushed in, and led him to prison. Next morning he was taken before a court of justice, and as he had confessed everything he was condemned to death. Nevertheless the king said he would grant him his life under one condition, which was that he should fetch him the golden horse which ran even faster than the wind. And then, if he could do that, he could keep the golden bird as well as a reward.

The king's son set off, but he was sad and he sighed, for where was he to find the golden horse? Then all at once he saw his old friend the fox sitting by the wayside. 'You see,' said the fox, 'that happened because you didn't listen to me. But be of good heart: I'll help you and tell you how you can get to the golden horse. You must go on straight ahead, and you will come to a castle where the horse is standing in the stables. The grooms will be lying outside the stables, but they will be sleeping and snoring and you'll be able to lead the horse out undisturbed. But one thing you must heed: put the poor saddle of wood and leather on his back and not the golden saddle hanging nearby, otherwise things will go badly for you.' Then the fox stretched out his tail, the king's son mounted it, and off they raced over hill and dale, so fast that his hair whistled in the wind. Everything was exactly as the fox had said. He went into the stable where the golden horse was standing; but as he was about to put the poor saddle on the horse, he thought: 'Such a fine beast would be disgraced if I didn't put on the good saddle that suits him.' But the good saddle had scarcely touched it before the horse began to neigh loudly. The grooms woke, seized the young man, and threw him into prison. Next morning he was condemned to death by the court of justice, but the king promised to grant him his life and the golden horse as well if he could bring him the king's fair daughter from the golden castle.

With a heavy heart the young man set out on his way, but fortunately for him he soon came upon the faithful fox. 'I should really leave you to your ill luck,' said the fox, 'but I'm sorry for you, and I'll help you out of your trouble once more. Your way will take you straight to the golden castle; you will reach it in the evening, and at night, when all is quiet, the king's fair daughter goes to the bath-house to bathe. Now, as she is going in, jump out at her and give her a kiss; then she will follow you, and you'll be able to carry her off with you; only do not let her bid her parents farewell beforehand, otherwise things could go badly for you.' Then the fox stretched his tail, the king's son mounted it, and off they raced over hill and dale, so fast that his hair whistled in the wind. When he arrived at the golden castle it was just as the fox had said. He waited until around midnight when everyone was fast asleep and the fair maiden was going to the bath-house. Then he jumped out and gave her a kiss. She said she would gladly go with him, but begged and pleaded with him, and with tears, to allow her to bid her parents farewell first. To begin with he resisted her pleas, but as she wept more and more and fell at his feet, he finally gave in. But the maiden had scarcely gone up to her father's bed before he and everyone else in the castle too woke up and the young man was arrested and thrown into prison.

Next morning the king said to him: 'Your life is forfeit, and you can only be pardoned if you can remove the mountain that lies in front of my windows, blocking my view. This you must bring about within eight days. If you succeed you shall have my daughter as your reward.' The king's son began to dig and delve without stopping, but after seven days, seeing how little he had achieved and that all his labour had been for nothing, he was overcome by great sadness and gave up all hope. But on the evening of the seventh day the fox appeared and said: 'You don't deserve my help—but just go to bed and sleep; I'll do the work for you.' Next morning, when he woke up and looked out of the window, the mountain had disappeared. Full of joy, the young man rushed to the king and announced that his condition was fulfilled, and whether he would or not, the king must keep his word and give him his daughter.

Now the two set out together, and it wasn't long before the faithful fox came up to them. 'True, you've won the best of all,' he said, 'but the maiden from the golden castle needs a golden horse to match.' 'How am I to get that?' asked the young man. 'I'll tell you,' answered the fox. 'First take the fair maiden to the king who sent you to the golden castle. They will be overjoyed, and will be glad to give you the golden horse and will lead it out to you. Now mount it straight away, giving your hand to everyone in farewell, last of all to the fair maiden. And once you have her by the hand, swing her up onto the horse and race away. Nobody will be able to catch you up, for that horse can run faster than the wind.'

Everything was carried out successfully, and the king's son rode away with the fair maiden. The fox didn't stay behind, but told the young man: 'Now I'll help you to the golden bird as well. When you draw near the castle where the bird is to be found, let the maiden dismount, and I'll take care of her. Then ride with the golden horse into the courtyard of the castle; they will be delighted at the sight, and will bring the bird out to you. The moment the cage is in your hand, race back to us and take the maiden up on the horse again.' When the plan had worked and the king's son was about to ride home with his treasures, the fox said: 'Now you are to reward me for my support.' 'What do you ask for?' said the young man. 'When we go into that forest over there, shoot me dead and cut off my head and my paws.' 'That would be a fine act of gratitude,' said the king's son. 'I can't possibly grant you that.' Said the fox: 'If you don't want to do it, I shall have to leave you. But before I go I will give you one piece of advice more. Beware of two things: never buy gallows-meat, and never sit on the edge of a well.' So saying, he ran into the forest.

The young man thought: 'That's a very odd creature, with the strangest fancies. Who would buy gallows-meat! And I've never had a great desire to sit on the edge of a well.' He rode on with the fair maiden, and his way led him once more through the village where his two brothers had stayed on. There was a great deal of clamour and commotion going on, and when he asked what was up, they said two people were to be hanged. As he drew closer he saw that it was his brothers, who had been up to all sorts of misdeeds and had squandered everything they owned. He asked if they could not be set free. 'If you'll pay for them,' the people answered, 'but what do you want to waste your money for, setting these good-for-nothings free?' But he didn't think twice and paid for them, and when they had been set free they continued the journey together.

They came to the forest where they had first met the fox, and because it was cool and sweet-smelling there, and the sun was blazing hot, both brothers said: 'Let us rest a while by this well, and eat and drink.' He agreed, and while they were talking he forgot and sat down on the edge of the well, suspecting no ill. But the two brothers pushed him backwards into the well, took the maiden, the horse, and the bird and made their way home to their father. 'We're not just bringing you the golden bird,' they said, 'we've also captured the golden horse and the maiden from the golden castle.' Everyone was overjoyed—but the horse would not eat, the bird would not sing, and the maiden sat and cried.

As for the youngest brother, he did not perish. Fortunately the well was dry, and he fell on soft moss without harming himself. But he couldn't get out. Nor did the faithful fox desert him in this trouble either. He came leaping down to him and scolded him for forgetting his advice. 'Even so, I can't give over now,' he said. 'I'll help you up into the light of day once more.' He told him he should grasp him by the tail and hold on tight. And then he pulled him up to the top. 'You're still not out of danger,' said the fox. 'Your brothers weren't sure you were dead, and they have surrounded the forest with sentries, who are to kill you if they catch sight of you.' Now there was a poor man sitting at the wayside. The young man exchanged clothes with him, and in this way he reached the king's court. No one recognized him, but the bird began to sing, the horse began to eat, and the fair maiden stopped crying. In amazement the king asked: 'What does it mean?' Then the maiden spoke: 'I don't know; but I was so sad, and now I am so happy. I have a sense that my rightful bridegroom has come.' The king sent for all the people who were in his palace, and the young man came too, dressed as a poor man in his ragged clothes. But the maiden recognized him at once and flung her arms around his neck. The godless brothers were seized and executed, but the youngest was married to the fair maiden and declared the king's heir.

But what happened to the poor fox? Long afterwards the king's son went into the forest once more. He was met by the fox, who said: 'Now you have everything you could wish for. But there is no end to my misfortune; and remember, it is in your power to deliver me.' And again he begged and pleaded with the king's son to shoot him dead and cut off his head and paws. So he did—and the deed was scarcely done before the fox turned into a human being, and he was none other than the brother of the king's fair daughter, delivered at last from the spell that had been cast on him. And now their happiness was complete, for as long as they lived.

43. *The Golden Goose*

THERE was once a man who had three sons. The youngest was called Silly-Billy and he was mocked and jeered at and put down at every opportunity. It happened that the eldest was about to go into the forest to cut wood, and before he left his mother gave him a fine rich cake and a bottle of wine to take with him so that he should not suffer from hunger or thirst. When he went into the forest he was met by a little old grey man who bade him good-day and said: 'Will you give me a piece of the cake in your pouch and let me drink a mouthful of your wine? I'm so hungry and thirsty.' But the clever son answered: 'If I give you my cake and my wine, I'll have nothing for myself. Away with you!'—and he left the little man standing and went on. But when he began to chop at a tree it wasn't long before he made a false stroke and the axe cut his arm, so that he had to go home and have it bandaged. This happened on account of the little grey man.

After that the second son went into the forest, and as with the eldest, his mother gave him a cake and a bottle of wine. He too was likewise met by the little old grey man, who begged him for a little piece of his cake and a drink of wine. But the second son too said, quite sensibly: 'Whatever I give to you, I'll have that much less for myself. Away with you!'—and he left the little man standing and went on. His punishment wasn't slow in coming. He had only aimed a few strokes at a tree when he struck his own leg, so that he had to be carried home.

Then Silly-Billy said: 'Father, let me go out for once and cut wood.' Answered his father: 'Your brothers have hurt themselves cutting wood; don't touch it; you don't understand anything about it.' But Silly-Billy begged for so long that in the end he said: 'Off you go, then. You'll learn wisdom the hard way.' His mother gave him a cake that had been made with water and cooked in the ashes and a bottle of sour beer to go with it. When he went into the forest he was likewise met by the little old grey man, who greeted him and said: 'Give me a piece of your cake and a drink from your bottle. I'm so hungry and thirsty.' Answered Silly-Billy: 'All I have is cake from the ashes and sour beer, but if you don't mind those, let's sit down and eat.' So they sat down, and when Silly-Billy took out his ash cake it was a fine rich cake, and the sour beer was a good wine. They ate and drank, and afterwards the little man said: 'Because you've a good heart and were glad to share what you had, I will give you a present that will bring you luck. There's an old tree standing over there. If you cut it down you'll find something in its roots.' And the little man took his leave.

Silly-Billy went and chopped down the tree, and as it fell he saw in its roots a goose which had feathers of pure gold. He lifted it out and took it with him to an inn, where he planned to stay overnight. But the innkeeper had three daughters, who saw the goose and were curious to find out what kind of weird and wonderful bird it was, and they would have loved to have one of its golden feathers. The eldest thought: 'There'll soon be an opportunity for me to pull out a feather.' And when Silly-Billy went outside for a moment she caught hold of the goose by its wing, but her fingers and hand stuck to it. Soon afterwards the second daughter came, and her only thought was to take a golden feather for herself; but she had hardly touched her sister before she stuck to her. Finally the third daughter too came along with the same thing in mind; the other two screamed: 'Keep off, for Heaven's sake, keep off!' But she didn't understand why she should keep off, thinking: 'If they're with the goose, I'll be with the goose too,' and she bounced over to them. And the moment she touched her sister, she stuck to her. That's how they had to pass the night with the goose.

Next morning Silly-Billy took the goose under his arm and went off, without a care for the three girls hanging on to it. They had to run along behind him all the time, now to the right, now to the left, as his legs took him. Deep in the countryside they were met by the parson, and when he saw the procession, he said: 'Shame on you, you wicked girls, why are you chasing through the fields after the young fellow? Is that proper?' As he was speaking he seized the youngest by the hand and was about to pull her away; but the moment he touched her he too was stuck, and he had to run along behind them himself. It wasn't long before the sexton came by and saw the Reverend following on the heels of the three girls. He was astonished, and called out: 'Hey, Reverend, where are you off to so fast? Don't forget we've still got a christening to do today.' And he ran up to him and seized him by the sleeve, but he too remained stuck. As the five were trotting along like this, one after the other, two farm-labourers came from the fields carrying their hoes. The parson called to them and begged them to free himself and the sexton. But they'd hardly touched the sexton before they were stuck, so now there were seven of them running after Silly-Billy and the goose.

Next he came to a town which was ruled by a king with a daughter who was so solemn that nobody was able to make her laugh. So he had proclaimed a law saying that whoever could make her laugh should marry her. When Silly-Billy heard this, he went with his goose and its train, into the presence of the king's daughter, and when she saw the seven figures running, one after the other all the time, she began to laugh very loudly, and wouldn't stop at all. Then Silly-Billy asked for her hand in marriage, but this son-in-law was not to the king's liking. He raised all sorts of objections, and said that first he would have to bring him a man who was able to drink a whole cellar of wine dry. Silly-Billy thought of the little grey man, who could surely help him. He went out into the forest and saw a man sitting at the place where he had cut down the tree, with a very gloomy expression on his face. Silly-Billy asked what he was taking to heart so badly. He answered: 'I have such a great thirst, and it's impossible for me to quench it. I can't stomach cold water. I've just emptied a barrel of wine, but that's just a drop in the ocean.' 'I can help you there,' said Silly-Billy. 'Just come along with me, and you shall drink yourself full.' So he led him to the king's cellar, where the man set about the huge barrels and drank and drank until his belly hurt, and before one day was over he had drunk the whole cellar dry. Once again Silly-Billy asked for his bride's hand, but the king was annoyed that a low-born fellow everybody called a simpleton should win his daughter. He set fresh conditions: he should first find a man who was able to eat a mountain of bread. Silly-Billy didn't think for long, but went straight away out into the forest: there on the same spot sat a man who was tightening a belt round his body. With a sullen grimace, he said: 'I've just eaten a whole ovenful of crusty bread, but what good is that if you've a hunger as great as mine: my stomach is still empty, and I have to tighten my belt if I'm not to die of hunger.' Silly-Billy was delighted to meet him, and said: 'Up you get and come with me. You shall eat your fill.' He led him to the royal court, where the king had commanded all the flour in all the realm to be collected and baked into an enormous mountain. But the man from the forest stationed himself in front of it and began to eat; and in one day the entire mountain had vanished. For the third time Silly-Billy asked for his bride's hand, but once again the king looked for an excuse and demanded a ship that could travel on land and on water. 'The moment you come sailing up in it,' he said, 'you shall have my daughter for your wife.' Silly-Billy went straight to the forest, and sitting there he saw the little old grey man he had given his cake to. The little man said: 'I've drunk for you and eaten for you, and I'll give you the ship as well—and all because you took pity on me.' Then he gave him the ship that could travel on land and on sea, and when the king saw it he couldn't refuse him his daughter any longer. Their marriage was celebrated, and after the king's death Silly-Billy inherited the realm and lived long and happily together with his wife.

44. *Coat o' Skins*

THERE was once was a king who had a wife with golden hair, and she was so beautiful that there was none her like on earth. It happened that she lay ill, and when she felt that she would soon die she called the king and said: 'If you would marry again after my death, then take no one who is not as beautiful as I am, and who doesn't have such golden hair as mine: you must promise me that.' After the king had promised this, she closed her eyes and died.

For a long time the king was inconsolable, and he had not a thought of taking a second wife. At last his counsellors spoke to him: 'There is only one step to be taken: the king must marry again, so that we have a queen.' Now messengers were sent far and near to look for a bride who would be the dead queen's equal in beauty. There was none to be found in the whole world, and even if they had found her, there was still no one who would have had such golden hair. So the messengers returned, their task unfulfilled.

Now the king had a daughter who was just as beautiful as her dead mother, and she had the same golden hair, too. When she had grown up the king looked at her one day and saw that she was the equal of his dead consort in every way, and suddenly he felt a passionate love for her. So he declared to his counsellors: 'I will marry my daughter, for she is the very image of my dead wife, and in any case I cannot find any other bride who is her equal.' When the counsellors heard this they were horrified, and declared: 'It is forbidden by God for a father to marry his daughter; no good can come of this sin, and the kingdom will be dragged down into ruin with him.' His daughter was even more horrified when she heard her father's decision, but she hoped she could still persuade him out of his intent. So she said to him: 'Before I fulfil your wish I must first have three gowns, one as golden as the sun, one as silvery as the moon, and one as brilliant as the stars; as well as these I want a coat made of a thousand different kinds of fur and pelt, and every animal in your kingdom must contribute a piece of his skin to it.' But to herself she was thinking: 'It will be completely impossible to obtain these things, and so I will be able to persuade my father out of his wicked thoughts.' But the king persisted, and the most skilful maidens in his kingdom were set to weave the three gowns, one as golden as the sun, one as silvery as the moon, and one as brilliant as the stars; and his huntsmen were set to catch all the animals in the entire kingdom and take a piece of their skin; from the pieces a coat of a thousand different kinds of skin was made. At last, when, everything was finished, the king had the coat brought to him, spread it out before her, and declared: 'Tomorrow our wedding shall take place.'

Now when the king's daughter saw that there was no more hope of changing her father's heart, she decided to run away. At night, when everyone was asleep, she got up, and from among her treasures she took three things: a gold ring, a little gold spinning-wheel, and a little gold reel; she packed her three gowns of sun, moon, and stars in a nutshell, put on her many-skinned coat, and blackened her face and hands with soot. Then she commended herself to God and went away. She walked all night long until she reached a great forest. And because she was weary, she settled down inside a hollow tree and fell asleep.

The sun rose, and she went on sleeping. And still she went on sleeping until far into the day. Now it so happened that the king who owned this forest was hunting there. When his dogs came up to the tree they sniffed and ran around it barking. Said the king to his huntsmen: 'Go and see what kind of game is hiding there.' The huntsmen followed his command, and on returning they told him: 'There's a strange animal lying in the hollow tree; we've never seen one like it before; its skin has a thousand different kinds of fur on it: but it's lying on the ground and sleeping.' The king told them: 'See whether you can capture it alive; then tie it down in the cart and bring it with us.' When the huntsmen seized the girl she woke in terror and cried to them: 'I'm a poor girl, deserted by my father and mother. Have pity on me and take me with you.' Then they said: 'Coat o' Skins, you'll be useful in the kitchen; just come with us and you can clear out the ashes.' So they sat her on the cart and drove home to the royal palace. There they showed her a little cubby-hole under the stairs, where no daylight came, and they said: 'Furry little creature, that's where you can live and sleep.' Then she was sent into the kitchen, where she carried wood and water, raked the fire, plucked the fowls, sorted the vegetables, cleared the ashes, and did all the heavy work.

Coat o' Skins lived a wretched life there for a long time. Alas, beautiful king's daughter, what is to become of you! But it happened once that a great festivity was being celebrated in the palace, so she said to the cook: 'May I go up for a while and look on? I'll stand outside the door.' Answered the cook: 'Yes, go ahead. But in half an hour you must be back to gather up the ashes.' So she took her little oil-lamp, went to her cubby-hole, took off her coat of skins, and washed the soot from her face and hands so that all her beauty came to light once more. Then she opened the nut and lifted out the gown that shone like the sun. And when that was done she went up to the festivities, and everyone made way for her, for they could only think that she was a king's daughter. As for the king, he came towards her, offered his hand, and danced with her, thinking in his heart: 'My eyes have never seen anyone so beautiful before.' When the dance was over she curtsied, and as the king was looking round she vanished, and no one knew where. The sentries standing outside the palace were called and questioned, but no one had caught sight of her.

She herself had run back to her cubby-hole. Quickly taking off her gown, she blackened her face and hands and put on her furry coat and was Coat o' Skins once more. As she came into the kitchen and was about to start her work and clear out the ashes, the cook said: 'Leave it till tomorrow and cook the king's soup for me: I want to go up for a while just this once and take a peep. But don't drop the slightest hair in it, on else in future you won't get any more to eat.' So the cook went off and Coat o' Skins made the soup for the king. She made a bread soup, as skilfully as she was able, and when she had finished she fetched her gold ring from her cubby-hole and put it in the dish in which the soup was served. When the ball was over the king sent for his soup and enjoyed it: it tasted so good that to his mind he had never had a better soup. But when he reached the bottom he saw a gold ring lying in the bowl, and he couldn't understand how it had got there. So he commanded the cook to come before him. The cook was alarmed when he heard the command, saying to Coat o' Skins: 'I'm sure you've dropped a hair into the soup: if that's true, you'll get a hiding.' When he came before the king, the king asked him who had made the soup. Answered the cook: 'I made it.' But the king said: 'That's not true, for it was cooked in a different style from usual, and much better too.' Answered the cook: 'I have to confess: I didn't cook it. It was the furry creature.' Said the king: 'Go and send her up.'

When Coat o' Skins came, the king asked: 'Who are you?' 'I'm a poor child who no longer has a father or mother.' He questioned further: 'How do you make yourself useful in my palace?' She replied: 'I'm no use for anything but having the boots thrown at my head.' He questioned further: 'Where did you get the ring that was in my soup?' She replied: 'I don't know anything about a ring.'

So the king wasn't able to find anything out, and had to send her away again.

Some time later more festivities were held, and as before Coat o' Skins asked the cook for permission to go and watch. He replied: 'Yes, but come back in half an hour and make the king the bread soup he enjoys so much.' So she ran to her cubby-hole, quickly washed herself, and from the nutshell she lifted the gown that was as silvery as the moon and put it on. Then she went up, looking like a king's daughter. The king came towards her, overjoyed to see her again, and because the dance was just striking up, they danced together. But when the dance was over she vanished again, so quickly that the king was unable to see where she went. For her part she leapt back to her cubby-hole and turned herself into the furry creature again; then she went into the kitchen to cook the bread soup. While the cook was upstairs she fetched the gold spinning-wheel and put it into the dish, so that the soup served was covering it. After that it was brought to the king, who enjoyed it, and it tasted as good as before. He sent for the cook, who had to confess this time too that Coat o' Skins had made the soup. So again Coat o' Skins came before the king, but she answered as before that she was only good for having the boots thrown at her head, and that she knew nothing about the little gold spinning-wheel.

When the king arranged festivities on a third occasion, things went just as they had before. True, the cook did say: 'You're a witch, furry creature, always putting something in the soup which makes it so good that the king enjoys it better than the soup I prepare,' but because she begged him he allowed her to go up for the agreed time. This time she put on the gown that was as brilliant as the stars and entered the hall wearing it. Again the king danced with the beautiful maiden, and in his eyes she had never been so beautiful. And while he danced he put a gold ring onto her finger without her noticing, and he had commanded that the dance should go on for a long time. When it was over he wanted to hold her fast by the hands, but she tore herself away and sprang so quickly among the throng of people that she vanished before his eyes. She ran as fast as she could to her cubby-hole under the stairs, but because she had been so long, staying over half an hour, she was unable to take off her beautiful gown but could only throw her coat of fur over it, and in her haste she didn't make herself altogether sooty: one finger remained white.

Then Coat o' Skins ran into the kitchen, made the king's bread soup, and, as the cook was away, she put in the gold reel. When the king found the reel at the bottom of the dish he sent for Coat o' Skins; then he caught sight of her white finger and saw the ring he had put on it during the dance. At that he seized her by the hand and held it fast, but when she tried to break free and run away the furry coat fell open a little and her starry gown shimmered through. The king seized her coat and tore it off. Then her golden hair poured down, and she stood there in all her glory and she couldn't hide any longer. And when she had wiped the soot and ashes from her face she was more beautiful than anyone had ever seen upon earth. As for the king, he declared: 'You are my beloved bride, and we shall nevermore part from each other.' After that their wedding was celebrated, and they lived happily to the end of their lives.

45. *Jorinda and Joringel*

THERE was once an ancient castle in the middle of a great, dense forest, and within it there lived an old woman all alone who was a sorceress of sorceresses. By day she turned herself into a cat or a night-owl, but in the evening she would take on the form of a proper human being once more. She knew how to lure the deer and the birds, and then she would slaughter them and boil them and roast them. If anyone came within a hundred paces of her castle he was forced to stand still, unable to move from the spot until she raised the spell. But if a chaste maiden entered this circle the sorceress would turn her into a bird and lock her in a basket-cage, and carry off the cage into a room in the castle. She had about seven thousand such cages in the castle, holding such rare birds.

Now there was once a maiden called Jorinda who was more beautiful than all other girls. She was promised to a very handsome young man called Joringel, and he to her. They were in the first days of their betrothal, and took the greatest delight in each other. So that they could talk intimately together for once, they went walking in the forest. 'Take care', said Joringel, 'that you don't go too near the castle'. It was a lovely evening; through the tree trunks the sun shone bright onto the dark green of the forest, and on the ancient birches the turtle-dove sang her mournful song.

Jorinda cried now and then. She sat down tearfully in the sunshine, and Joringel sat tearfully too. They were as distressed as if they were going to die; they looked about them, not sure where they were, and they did not know which way to take to go home. The sun was sinking, still half above the mountain, half below. Joringel looked through the bushes and saw the ancient walls of the castle close to him; he shrank back, full of deathly fear. Jorinda was singing:

> 'My little bird with his ring so red
>   Sings sorrow, sorrow, sorrow:
> He sings to the dove that he will be dead,
>   Sings sorrow, sorr—jug jug, jug jug.'

Joringel looked at Jorinda: she had been turned into a nightingale, and she was singing 'jug jug, jug jug'. A night-owl with glowing eyes flew round her thrice, and thrice shrieked: to-whit to-whoo. Joringel could not move. He stood there like a stone, unable to weep or speak or stir hand or foot. By now the sun had sunk completely; the owl flew into a thicket, and straight afterwards a crooked old woman came out, sallow and gaunt, with huge, red-rimmed eyes and a hooked nose with a point reaching down to her chin. She muttered something, caught the nightingale, and bore her away on her hand. Joringel could say nothing, nor move from the spot; the nightingale was gone. At last the woman came back, and said in a hollow voice: 'Greetings, Zachiel. When the moon shines into the cage, unbind him, Zachiel, at once.' And Joringel was set free. He fell on his knees before the old woman and begged her to restore his Jorinda to him, but she said he should never have her again, and went away. He called, he wept, he cried, but all in vain. 'Alas, what is to become of me?' Joringel went away, and at length he came to an unknown village. For a long time he herded sheep there. He often walked around the castle, but not too close to it. At length he dreamed one night that he found a blood-red flower with a large and beautiful pearl in its heart. He plucked the flower and went up to the castle with it: everything he touched with the flower was released from the spell; he also dreamed that he recovered his Jorinda in this way. In the morning, when he woke, he began to search over hill and over dale to see if he could find such a flower. He searched until the ninth day, when he found the blood-red flower early in the morning. In its heart was a large dewdrop, as big as the most beautiful pearl. He carried this flower day and night until he drew near the castle. He was not frozen fast, but went on as far as the gateway. Joringel was overjoyed. He touched the gate with the flower and it leapt open. He entered it, crossed the courtyard, and listened out for the sound of many birds; at last he heard them. He went and found the hall; the sorceress was there, feeding the birds in their seven thousand cages. When she saw Joringel she grew angry, very angry, railed at him with bile and bane, but could get no nearer to him than two paces. He took no notice of her, and instead went and looked closely at the cages with the birds. But there were hundreds of nightingales. How was he to find his Jorinda again? While he was looking in this way, he noticed that the old woman was secretly removing one cage with a bird in it, and taking it towards the door. At once he leapt after her, touched the cage with the flower—and the old woman too, who no longer had the power to cast spells—and there stood Jorinda; she put her arms around his neck, as beautiful as she had been before. Then he turned all the other birds back into maidens and went home with his Jorinda, and they lived long and happily together.

46. *The Three Children of Fortune*

A FATHER once called his three sons before him, and gave the first a cockerel, the second a scythe, and the third a cat. 'I'm an old man now,' he said, 'and my death is near, so I want to provide for you before my end. Money I do not have, and what I am giving you now does not seem to be worth much; it simply depends on whether you use it prudently. Just find a country where such things are still unknown, and your fortune is made.' After his father's death the eldest set out with his cockerel, but wherever he went the cockerel was already well known: he could already see it from afar in the towns, perched on the towers and turning with the wind; in the villages he heard more than one crowing, and no one was inclined to wonder at the creature, so it did not look as if he would make his fortune with it. Even so, at last he did succeed in arriving on an island where the people had no knowledge of cockerels, and

didn't even know how to divide up their time. They knew perfectly
well when it was morning or evening, but at night, if they didn't
sleep it away, no one knew how to work out the time. 'Look,' he
said, 'what a proud creature! He has a ruby-red crest on his head
and he wears spurs like a knight. He will call you at a given time
three times in the night, and when he calls for the last time it will
soon be sunrise. But if he calls in broad daylight, then be prepared,
for the weather will certainly change.' The people were greatly
pleased with this, once they spent a whole night without sleeping,
and listened with delight to the cockerel calling the time loud and
clear at two and four and six o'clock. They asked him whether the
bird might be for sale, and how much he wanted for him. 'About as
much as a donkey can carry in gold,' he answered. 'A ridiculous
sum for such a valuable creature,' they all cried and gladly gave
him what he had asked.

When he came home with this wealth his brothers were astonished,
and the second said: 'Then I will set off after all, and see if my scythe
will do as well.' But it did not look as if it would, for everywhere he
encountered farmers who had just as good a scythe on their shoulder
as he had. But at last he too prospered on an island where the people
had no knowledge of scythes. When the corn was ripe there they
would post cannons at the edge of the fields and shoot it down. That
was a pretty uncertain affair: some would overshoot the field, or
another would shoot the ears of corn instead of the stalks and shoot
them away; a great deal of corn was ruined in the process, and on top
of that there was a dreadful noise. So the man took up position and
mowed the corn so quietly and so quickly that the people gaped with
open mouths in amazement. They were willing to give him whatever
he wanted for it, and he received a horse laden with as much gold as
it could carry.

Now the third brother wanted to match his cat to the right taker
too. He fared as the others had: as long as he remained on the
mainland there was nothing to be done. There were cats everywhere,
and there were so many of them that the newborn kittens were
mostly drowned in the pond. At last he had himself ferried to an
island, and fortunately it so happened that a cat had never been seen
there before, and the mice had got the upper hand so completely that
they would dance on the tables and benches, whether the master
of the house was at home or not. The people lamented mightily at

the plague; the king himself did not know how to protect himself against them in his palace. Mice were squeaking in every nook and cranny, and gnawing whatever they could get their teeth into. Then the cat began her hunt, and in no time she had cleared two great halls, and the people begged the king to buy the animal for the kingdom. The king was glad to give what was asked, which was a mule laden with gold—and the third brother came home with the greatest treasure of all.

The cat had a high old time with the mice in the royal palace, and she bit so many of them to death that it was no longer possible to count them. At last she became very hot from her labours and grew thirsty; she stopped, raised her head, and wailed: 'Miaw, miaw!' The king and all his people who heard the cry were terrified at the strange wailing, and in their fear they all ran out of the palace. Down below the king held a council to discuss the best thing to do; at last it was decided to send a herald to the cat and demand that she should leave the palace or expect force to be used against her. The counsellors said: 'We would rather be plagued by the mice—we are used to that affliction—than put our lives at the mercy of such a monster.' A noble page had to go up and ask the cat whether she would leave the castle of her own free will. But the cat, who had become even thirstier, merely answered: 'Miaw, miaw!' The noble page understood her to say: 'Absolutely, absolutely not,' and conveyed the answer to the king. 'Well,' said the counsellors, 'she shall yield to force.' Cannons were mounted and the building set on fire. When the flames reached the hall where the cat was sitting, she leapt out of the window without mishap. But the besiegers did not stop until the entire palace was bombarded to smithereens.

47. *Six Make Their Way Through the Whole World*

THERE was once a man who was master of all trades; he served in the war, where he conducted himself boldly and well, but when the war was over he was dismissed and sent on his way with three farthings for his keep. 'Just you wait,' he said, 'I'm not putting up with this. If I find the right followers, the king will have to hand over the treasures of the entire land.' Full of rage, he walked into the forest, and there he saw a man standing who had just pulled up six trees as if they had been stalks of corn. Said he to him: 'Will you be my servant and come along with me?' 'Yes,' he answered, 'but I want to take this bundle of wood back home to my mother first'—and he took one of the trees and bound it round the other five, lifted the faggot onto his shoulder and carried it off. Then he came back and went along with his master, who said: 'We two should make our way through the whole world very nicely.' After they had been walking for a little while they met a huntsman, who was kneeling with gun raised and taking aim. Said the master to him: 'Huntsman, what are you shooting at?' He answered: 'Two miles from here there's a fly sitting on the bough of an oak tree; I want to shoot out his left eye.' 'Oh, come with me,' said the man. 'If we three are together we should make our way through the whole world very nicely.' The huntsman was ready, and went along with him. They came to seven windmills, whose sails were turning round very fast, though no wind was blowing to left or right, and not a leaf was stirring. The man said: 'I don't know what's driving these windmills—there's no breeze blowing,' and he went on with his servants. When they had been walking for two miles they saw a man sitting up a tree, who was holding one nostril closed and blowing out of the other. 'Heavens, what are you doing up there?' asked the man. He answered: 'Two miles from here are seven windmills. Look, I'm blowing at them for their sails to turn.' 'Oh, come with me,' said the man. 'If we four are together we should make our way through the whole world very nicely.' So the blower climbed down and went with them. After a while they saw a man who was standing on one leg; he had unbuckled the other and put it down beside him. The master said: 'You've found a comfortable way of resting.' 'I'm a runner,' he answered, 'and so that I don't stride out too fast, I've unbuckled one leg; if I run with both legs I go faster than a bird can fly.' 'Oh, come with me. If we five are together we should make our way through the whole world very nicely.' So he went along with them, and before very long they met a man who had a hat on, but was wearing it entirely over one ear. The master said to him: 'Manners! Manners! Don't put your hat on one ear, please, you look like Tom Fool.' 'I must,' said the other, 'for if I put my hat on straight there'll be an almighty frost, and the birds beneath the heavens will freeze and fall dead to earth.' 'Oh, come with me,' said the master. 'If we six are together we should make our way through the whole world very nicely.'

Now the six entered a town where the king had let it be proclaimed that whoever would run a race with his daughter and carry off the victory should become her consort; but if he lost he should lose his head. The man put himself forward, but said: 'I'll have my servant run on my behalf, though.' The king answered: 'In that case you must pledge his life too, that is, your life and his will stand surety for the victory.' When this was agreed and contracted, the man buckled the runner's other leg on him, saying: 'Now, swift as you can, and help us to win.' It was settled, though, that the winner was to be the one who was the first to bring water back from a far-distant well. The runner was given a pitcher, and so was the king's daughter, and they started to run at the same time; but in a moment, when the king's daughter had run only a very short length, none of the spectators could see the runner any more—it was as if the wind had rushed by. In a short time he reached the well, filled his pitcher with water, and turned round. But halfway back he was overcome by weariness, so he set down his pitcher, lay down, and fell asleep. But he had made a pillow of a horse's skull that was lying on the ground, so that his bed would be hard and he would wake soon. Meanwhile the king's daughter, who could also run well, as well as any ordinary human could, had reached the well and was hastening back with her pitcher full of water. When she saw the runner lying there asleep she was delighted, and declared: 'The enemy has been delivered into my hands,' and she emptied his pitcher and ran on. Now all would have been lost if the sharp-eyed huntsman had not by good luck been standing high up in the palace and seen everything. So he said: 'The king's daughter shan't get the better of us,' loaded his gun, and aimed so skilfully that he shot the horse's skull from under the runner's head without hurting him. At that the runner woke, jumped up, and saw that his pitcher was empty and the king's daughter already far ahead. But he did not lose heart: he ran back to the well with his pitcher, filled it with water again, and was back home ten minutes before the king's daughter. 'You see,' he said, 'it's only now I've really stretched my legs; before that you couldn't call it running at all.'

But the king was offended, and his daughter still more so, that she should be won by a common discharged soldier like him. They consulted together about how they could be rid of him and his companions as well. Then the king said to her: 'I've found a remedy. Never fear, they shan't come back home a second time.' And to them he said: 'Now you shall be merry together, and eat and drink,' and he led them to a room which had a floor of iron; its doors too were made of iron and the windows were secured by iron bars. There was a table in the room, laid with fine food. The king told them: 'Go in and enjoy yourselves.' And once they were inside he had the doors locked and bolted. Then he sent for the cook and ordered him to keep a fire going beneath the room until the iron became red-hot. The cook did so, and it began to heat up. While the six were sitting at table they grew very warm and thought it was on account of the food; but as it grew hotter and hotter and they wanted to get out but found the doors and windows locked, they realized that the king meant ill by them and intended them to suffocate. 'But he shan't succeed,' said the one with the hat. 'I'll summon up a frost that will make the fire ashamed and want to crawl away.' So he put his hat on straight, and at once there fell such a frost that all the heat vanished and the food in the dishes began to freeze. After a couple of hours had passed, and the king believed they had perished in the heat, he had the doors unlocked, for he wanted to see for himself. But as the doors opened there they stood, all six of them, fresh and fit and saying it would be to their liking if they could come out, because it was so cold in the room that the food in the dishes had frozen solid. At that the king went down to the cook in a rage, berated him, and asked why he had not done as he had been ordered. But the cook answered: 'There's heat enough—see for yourself.' Then the king saw that a tremendous fire was burning beneath the iron room, and realized that this was not the way to finish off the six.

Now once again the king thought hard about how he could be rid of these badly behaved guests. He sent for their master and said: 'If you will accept money and give up your claim on my daughter, you shall have as much as you wish.' 'Oh yes, my lord king,' he answered, 'give me as much as my servant can carry, and I won't ask for your daughter.' The king was content with this, but the man went on: 'I'll come and fetch it in fourteen days' time.' Then he summoned all the tailors in the whole kingdom and made them sit for fourteen days sewing at one sack. When it was ready, the strong man—the one who could pull up trees—was told to take the sack on his shoulder and go to the king with it. Then the king said: 'What kind of a mighty fellow is this, to carry a bale of linen as big as a house?' He was horrified, thinking: 'What an amount of gold that one will cart off!' So he ordered a ton of gold to be brought out; sixteen of the strongest men had to carry it up, but the strong man seized it with one hand, stuffed it into the sack, saying: 'Why don't you fetch some more now? This hardly covers the bottom of the sack.' So bit by bit the king had his entire treasure brought up; the strong man pushed it into the sack, and the sack was still barely half full. 'Fetch more,' he called, 'these few bits and pieces aren't filling it up.' So seven thousand wagons laden with gold had to be brought together from the entire kingdom; the strong man shoved them all into his sack, as well as the oxen pulling them. 'I won't take time inspecting it,' he declared, 'I'll take what comes—just so that the sack is filled.' Though there was already so much inside, there was still room for a lot more, but he said: 'I'll make an end of it now; once in a while you can tie up a sack, even if it isn't quite full yet.' Then he humped it onto his back and went off with his companions.

Now when the king saw how this one man was carrying away the wealth of his entire kingdom, he was filled with anger and commanded his cavalry to mount: they were to ride after the six with orders to take the sack away from the strong man. Two regiments soon caught up with them and called: 'You are our prisoners. Put down the sack with the gold or you'll be crushed to pieces.' 'What's that you say?' said the blower. 'We're your prisoners? You'll be dancing in the air sooner, every one of you.' He held one nostril closed and with the other he blew at both regiments. They were driven apart, scattered high into the blue sky, over the hills and far away, some here, some there. One sergeant cried for mercy: he'd been wounded nine times and was a decent fellow who didn't deserve such disrespect. So the blower let up a little so that he could descend without harm, and then said to him: 'Now go home to the king and tell him he has only to send more cavalry and I'll blow them all up into the air.' The king, on hearing the message, declared: 'Let the fellows go. They've certainly got spirit.' So the six took their wealth home, shared it amongst themselves, and lived happily to the end of their days.

48. *Grandfather and Grandson*

THERE was once an old man, as old as the hills, whose eyes had grown dim, who had become deaf, and who trembled in the knees. When he sat at table he could hardly hold the spoon and he would spill his soup on the tablecloth and some of it would dribble from his mouth as well. His son and his son's wife were disgusted at this, so in the end the old grandfather was made to sit in the corner behind the stove, and they gave him his food in a little earthenware basin, with not enough to feed him either. Then he would gaze sadly towards the table, and his eyes would grow moist. On one occasion his trembling hands were not able to hold his basin, and it fell to the floor and broke in pieces. The young wife scolded him, but he said nothing, only sighed. So she bought him a little wooden bowl for a few farthings, and from then on he had to eat from that. As they were sitting there like this, his little four-year-old grandson was fitting some small boards together on the floor. 'What are you making there?' his father asked him. 'I'm making a little trough,' the child answered, 'it's for father and mother to eat from when I'm grown up.' Then man and wife looked at each other for a while, and at length they began to weep. Straight away they brought the old grandfather to the table, and from then on they always had him to eat with them. And they said nothing either, when he spilled a little.

49. *The Tale of Little Hen's Death*

LITTLE HEN once went with Little Cock to the Nut Mountain, and they agreed that whoever found a kernel was to share it with the other. Now Little Cock found a big, big nut—but he said nothing about it, wanting to eat the kernel by himself. But the kernel was so big that he couldn't swallow it down and it stuck in his throat, so that he was afraid he would choke. So he called: 'Little Hen, I beg you, run as fast as you can and fetch me some water, or else I'll choke.' Little Hen ran as fast as she could to the well and said: 'Source, you must give me some water: Little Cock is lying on the Nut Mountain;

he's swallowed a huge kernel and he'll choke.' The well answered: 'First run to the bride and have her give you some red silk.' Little Hen ran to the bride: 'Bride, you must give me some red silk: I'll give the red silk to the well; the well will give me some water, the water I'll take to Little Cock, who is lying on the Nut Mountain and has swallowed a huge kernel, and he'll choke on it.' The bride answered: 'First run and bring me my garland, which is still hanging on a willow-tree.' So Little Hen ran to the willow-tree and took the garland down from the branch and brought it to the bride, and the bride gave her some red silk in return, which Little Hen took to the well, who gave her some water in return. Then Little Hen took the water to Little Cock, but by the time she arrived Little Cock had choked and lay there dead without moving. Little Hen was so sad that she cried out loud, and all the animals came and mourned Little Cock. Six mice built a little cart to drive Little Cock to his grave. When the cart was ready they harnessed themselves in front of it, and Little Hen was the driver. But on the way the fox turned up: 'Where are you going, Little Hen?' 'I'm going to bury my Little Cock.' 'May I ride with you?'

> 'Yes, but sit in the cart behind;
> In front is too much for my horses, you'll find.'

So the fox sat at the back of the cart, followed by the wolf, the bear, the stag, the lion, and all the beasts of the forest. And so the journey continued until they came to a brook. 'How are we to cross?' said Little Hen. Near the brook there lay a blade of straw, who said: 'I'll lie over it crossways, and you can drive across on me.' But as the six mice were stepping onto the bridge the blade of straw slipped and fell into the water, and the six mice all fell in and drowned. So their distress broke out anew. A lump of charcoal said: 'I'm big enough; I'll lie across, and you can ride over me.' The charcoal did indeed lie across the water, but unfortunately she touched it just a bit, hissed, went out, and was dead. When a stone saw this he took pity on Little Hen and wanted to help her, and *he* lay across the water. This time Little Hen pulled the cart herself, but now that she had it on the far side and was on dry land with Little Cock, deceased, she was about to pull over the others, who were riding behind. But there were just too many of them for her, and the cart fell back and they all fell into the water together and drowned. Now Little Hen was alone with Little Cock. She dug him a grave and laid him in it, and made a hillock over it, and then she sat down and grieved until she died too; and then they were all dead.

50. *Hans in Luck*

HANS had served his master for seven years, so he said to him: 'Master, my time is up, and now I would like to go back home to my mother; give me my wages.' His master answered: 'You have served me faithfully and honestly, and as your service was, so shall be your reward'—and he gave him a nugget of gold as big as Hans's head. Hans took his neckerchief from his pocket, wrapped up the lump of gold in it, placed it on his shoulder, and set off on the road home. As he was walking along like this, all the time planting one foot in front of the other, he caught sight of a rider trotting by, fresh and cheerful on a lively horse. 'Oh,' said Hans, loud enough to be heard, 'it's a great thing to be riding. Perched up there as if you're sitting on a chair, not stumbling on the stones, saving your shoe-leather and arriving in no time.' The horseman, who had heard him, stopped and called: 'Hi, Hans, why are you going on foot, then?' 'I have to,' he answered, 'I have this nugget to carry. True, it's gold, but I can't keep my head up straight with it, and it's heavy on my shoulder too.' 'Do you know what?' said the rider. 'Let's exchange. I'll give you my horse and you give me your nugget.' 'With all my heart,' said Hans, 'but I warn you, you'll be lugging a load.' The rider dismounted, took the gold, and helped Hans up, putting the reins firmly into his hands and saying: 'If you're to go really fast, you just have to click your tongue and call "gee-up, gee-up".'

Hans was in heaven, sitting there riding the horse so free and easy. After a little while it occurred to him that it ought to go faster, so he began to click his tongue and call 'gee-up, gee-up'. The horse changed to a fast trot, and before he knew it Hans had been thrown off and was lying in a ditch that separated the fields from the highway. The horse would have run away too, if it hadn't been stopped by a farmer who was walking along, driving a cow ahead of him. Hans gathered himself together and got up on his feet again. But he was cross, and he said to the farmer: 'It's no joke riding, especially when you're landed with a nag like this, which bucks and throws you off so that you could break your neck; I'll never mount another one again, not ever! There's nothing to compare with that cow of yours! You can walk behind her without worrying, and on top of that you're sure of your daily milk, butter, and cheese. What wouldn't I give to have a cow like that!' 'Well,' said the farmer, 'if it will oblige you all that much, I'll exchange my cow for your horse.' Hans agreed eagerly, with a thousand thanks; the farmer swung himself up on the horse and rode off—fast.

Hans drove his cow placidly ahead of him, ruminating on the deal he had made. 'If I have just a piece of bread—and I shan't lack for that—then I can eat it with butter and cheese as often as I want. If I'm thirsty, I'll milk the cow and drink her milk. Heart, what more can you desire?' When he reached an inn he stopped, and in his great delight at his deal he ate everything he had brought with him, his lunch *and* his supper, all up, and with his last couple of farthings he treated himself to half a glass of beer. Then he drove the cow on further, always towards his mother's village. The heat grew more oppressive the closer to noon it became, and Hans found himself on a heath which was still about an hour's walk away. He became so hot that his tongue was sticking to his gums with thirst. 'I can do something about this,' he thought. 'I'll milk my cow now, and refresh myself with her milk.' He tied her to a dry tree and, as he had no bucket, he put his leather cap below her—but however much he laboured, not a drop of milk appeared. And because he was so clumsy at it, in the end the impatient creature gave him such a kick with one of her hind legs that he tumbled to the ground and for a while couldn't remember where he was. Fortunately a butcher came along just then, with a young pig lying in a barrow. 'What a trick to play!' he exclaimed, helping our good Hans to his feet. Hans told him what had happened. The butcher offered him his bottle, saying: 'Have a drink. You'll feel better. I doubt if that cow will give any milk. She's an old beast, fit to pull a cart at best, or to be slaughtered.' 'Oh dear, oh dear,' said Hans, smoothing down his hair, 'who would have thought it? True, it's good to be able to take a creature like that home for slaughter—the amount of meat! But I'm not so fond of beef; it's not tender enough for me. Now, a young pig . . . That's more to my taste—and think of the sausages too.' 'Listen, Hans,' said the butcher, 'I'll do you a favour and exchange my pig for your cow.' 'God reward you for your friendship,' exclaimed Hans. He handed over the cow, while the butcher untied the little pig from the barrow and put the rope that was binding it into Hans's hand.

Hans went on his way, pondering how everything had gone like a dream: if he encountered anything troublesome it was put right straight away. Later he was joined by an apprentice who was carrying a fine white goose under his arm. They bade each other good-day, and Hans began to tell him of his good luck, and how he had always made an exchange on such good terms. The apprentice told him that he was taking the goose to a christening feast. 'Try lifting her,' he went on, seizing her by the wings, 'see how heavy she is—but then, she's been fattening for eight weeks. Anyone eating roast meat from this one will have to wipe the fat from both sides of his mouth.' 'Yes,' said Hans, weighing her with one hand, 'she's certainly heavy—but my pig isn't hogwash either.' Meanwhile the apprentice had been looking all about him very suspiciously and shaking his head. 'Listen,' he said, 'there may be something a bit dodgy about your pig. In the village I've just come through one had just been stolen from the mayor's pigsty. I'm afraid, I'm afraid you have it there, at the end of your rope. They've sent folk out after it, and it would be a bad business if they caught you with that pig; throwing you into the dungeon is the least they'd do.' Our good Hans grew fearful. 'Oh Heavens,' he said, 'help me out of this trouble. You know your way around in these parts better than I do. Take my pig here and leave me your goose.' 'I'm taking a risk,' answered the apprentice, 'but I don't want it to be my fault if you get into trouble.' So he took the rope in his hand and drove the pig off along a side alley—fast. As for our good Hans, rid of his burden of cares he walked on with the goose under his arm towards home. 'If I consider it aright,' he told himself, 'I've still done better out of the exchange: first a good roast; then the amount of goose grease oozing out of it—that will yield enough bread and dripping for a year's quarter; and lastly the fine white down I'll have stuffed in my pillow—I shan't need rocking to sleep. Won't my mother be delighted!'

As he was walking through the last village a knife-grinder was standing there with his cart. His wheel was humming and he was singing along with it:

> 'I'll sharpen your shears as I'm turning my wheel,
> And to every fair wind I will trim my sail.'

Hans stopped and looked at him. At last he spoke to him, saying: 'All's well with you—you're getting on with your sharpening so cheerfully.' 'Yes,' answered the knife-grinder, 'a good trade is founded on solid gold. Your true knife-grinder is a man who will find money whenever he puts his hand in his pocket. But where did you buy that fine goose?' 'I didn't buy it; I exchanged it for my pig.' 'And the pig?' 'I got it in place of a cow.' 'And the cow?' 'I got it for a horse.' 'And the horse?' 'I gave a nugget of gold as big as my head for it.' 'And the gold?' 'Oh, that was my wages for seven years' service to my master.' 'You've known how to look after yourself each time,' said the knife-grinder. 'If you could get as far as hearing the money jingling in your pocket when you get up, you'll have made your fortune.' 'How am I to do that?' asked Hans. 'You must become a knife-grinder like me. Really, all you need is a whetstone—the rest will follow of its own accord. I have one here. It's a bit damaged, it's true, but all you need give me for it is your goose. Do you want it?' 'How can you ask?' answered Hans. 'I'll become the luckiest man on earth; if I have money whenever I put my hand in my pocket, I shan't have another care in the world.' He handed over the goose and accepted the whetstone. 'Well now,' said the knife-grinder, lifting an ordinary heavy boulder lying near him, 'here's a good, hard-wearing stone for you into the bargain. It's good for hammering on; you can beat your old nails straight on it. Take it, and look after it.'

Hans loaded up the stone and went his way with delight in his heart, his eyes shining with joy. 'I must have been born in a good-luck caul,' he cried. 'Everything I wish for happens to me as if I were a Sunday's child.' Meanwhile, because he'd been up and about since dawn, he began to get tired; he was also plagued by hunger, because he had eaten up all his provisions at once, in his joy over the cow he had bargained for. In the end he could make his way further only with toil and trouble, and he had to stop every minute, for the stones were weighing him down pitifully. He couldn't help thinking how good it would be if he didn't need to carry them just now. Like a snail, he crawled up to a well in the fields. He intended to rest and refresh himself with a drink of cool water. He didn't want to damage his stones as he sat down, so with great care he put them by him on the edge of the well. Then he sat down himself and was bending over to drink when, by mistake, he gave them a little knock—and both stones fell with a splash to the bottom. When Hans saw them sink to the depths with his own eyes, he leapt up in joy; then he fell on his knees and thanked God, with tears in his eyes, that He had shown him this mercy as well, for He had freed him of those heavy stones which were the only things slowing him down, and in such a gracious way that Hans had no need to blame himself. 'There is nobody under the sun', he cried, 'as lucky as I am.' Light of heart and free of every burden, he now ran all the way until he reached home and his mother's house.

51. *The Fox and the Geese*

THE fox once came to a meadow where a flock of fine, fat geese were sitting. He laughed and said: 'I've come just at the right moment. Here you are sitting pretty, all of you; I can eat you all up, one after the other.' The geese qua-quacked in fright, leapt up, and began to wail and beg pitifully for their lives. But the fox was deaf to their pleas, saying: 'There is no mercy. You must die.' At length one of them plucked up her courage and said: 'If we poor geese must leave our fresh young lives, show us mercy in one thing and grant us a last prayer, so that we do not die with our sins upon us. After that we will line up in a row, so that each time you can choose the fattest for yourself.' 'Yes,' said the fox, 'that's fair of you, and a pious request. Go ahead and pray, and I'll wait.' So the first began a very long prayer, always 'qua, qua!', and because there was no sign that she would come to an end, the second did not wait until it was her turn, but also started up: 'qua, qua!' The third and the fourth followed her, and soon they were all qua-quacking together. (And when they've finished their prayer, I'll finish telling the story. But for the moment, they're still praying.)

52. *The Singing, Soaring Lark*

THERE was once a man who was about to go on a long journey, and on parting he asked his three daughters what he should bring them back as a present. The eldest wanted pearls, the second wanted diamonds, but the third said: 'Father dear, my wish is for a singing, soaring lark.' Her father said: 'Yes, if I can get one, you shall have it.' He kissed all three and set off. Later, when the time came round and he was on his way back home, he had bought pearls and diamonds for his two eldest daughters, but he had looked everywhere in vain for the singing, soaring lark for the youngest. This made him sorry, for she was his dearest child. His way led him through a forest, and in the middle of the forest stood a splendid palace, and near the palace stood a tree, and right at the top of the tree he saw a lark singing and soaring. 'Aha, you've turned up just in time for me, little lark,' he said, very pleased, and told his serving-man to climb up and catch the little creature. But as he stepped up to the tree a lion leapt out from beneath it, shook himself, and gave such a roar that the leaves trembled on the trees. 'Anyone who tries to steal my singing, soaring lark,' he growled, 'I eat for my dinner.' The man said: 'I didn't know the bird belonged to you. I'll make good the wrong I've done you and pay my ransom in solid gold, if only you will spare my life.' 'The only thing that can save you', said the lion, 'is if you promise to give me for my own whatever first comes to meet you at home; but if you are willing to do this, I will grant you your life— and the bird for your daughter as well.' But the man refused, saying: 'That could be my youngest daughter. She loves me best, and always runs to meet me when I come home.' But his serving-man was fearful, and said: 'Does it have to be your daughter who comes to meet you?—It could be a cat or a dog just as well.' So the man let himself be persuaded, took the singing, soaring lark, and promised to give the lion for his own whatever would meet him first when he arrived home.

When he reached home and entered his house, the first person to meet him was none other than his youngest daughter. She came running, kissed him and hugged him, and when she saw that he had brought a singing, soaring lark she was beside herself with joy. But her father could not rejoice; instead he began to weep, saying: 'My dearest child, I have bought that little bird at a great price. I have had to promise you to a wild lion in exchange, and once he has you he'll tear you to pieces and eat you up.' And he told her everything that had happened and begged her not to go to the forest, whatever might follow. But she consoled him, saying: 'Dearest father, what you promised must be kept. I will go there, and I'm sure

to pacify the lion so that I come back to you safe and sound.' Next
morning she made him show her the way, bade him farewell, and
walked confidently into the forest. Now the lion was really a king's
son who had been put under a spell: by day he was a lion, and all
his retinue were also turned into lions; but at night they took on
their natural, human shape. When she arrived she was welcomed
kindly and led into the palace. When night came he was a handsome
man, and their wedding was celebrated in splendour. They lived
happily together, spending their nights awake and sleeping in the
daytime. One day he came and said: 'Tomorrow there will be a
celebration in your father's house because your eldest sister is getting married; if you would like to attend, my lions shall lead you
there.' So she said yes, she would love to go and see her father
again, and rode there, accompanied by the lions. There was great
joy when she arrived, for everyone believed she had been torn to
pieces by the lion and had died long ago. But she told them what a
handsome husband she had and how well she fared. She remained
with them for as long as the wedding celebrations went on, and
then she rode back into the forest once again. When the second
daughter was to be married and she was invited to the wedding, she
said to the lion: 'This time I don't want to be alone; you must come
with me.' But the lion said it would be too dangerous for him, for if
he were to be touched by the blaze of light shed by a burning torch
or candle while he was there, he would be turned into a dove and
would be compelled to fly with the doves for seven years. 'Oh,' she
said, 'do come with me. I'll watch over you, and shield you from
light of every kind.' So they set off together, and took their little
child with them as well. There, in a hall, she had walls built which
were so strong and thick that no light could penetrate them. He was
to sit there when the wedding lights were set ablaze. But the door
was made of green wood, which split and made a little crack which
no one noticed. The wedding was celebrated in splendour, but
when the procession came back from church with so many torches
and lights and passed the hall, a ray of light no more than a hair in
breadth fell upon the king's son, and the moment the ray touched
him he was transformed. When she came in and looked for him, she
didn't see him—but there sat a white dove. The dove said to her:
'For seven years I must fly away and out into the world; but every
seven paces I will let fall a red drop of blood and a white feather;

they are to show you my way, and if you can follow my trail you will be able to release me.'

Then the dove flew out of the door and she followed it, and every seven paces a red drop of blood and a white feather fell, showing her the way. She went on and on like this, out into the wide world, without looking round or pausing to rest until the seven years were almost done. She rejoiced, thinking they would soon be released— but that was still far off. One day, as she was walking along with these thoughts, a feather no longer fell, nor the red drop of blood, and when she opened her eyes the dove had vanished. And because she thought to herself: 'No human being can help you in your search,' she climbed up to the sun and said to her: 'You are able to shine into every crack and over every peak; have you seen a white dove flying?' 'No,' said the sun, 'I haven't. But I will give you a little casket. Open it when you are in great trouble.' So she thanked the sun, and walked on until it was evening and the moon was shining. She asked the moon: 'You shine all night, and across all the fields and forests; have you seen a white dove flying?' 'No,' said the moon, 'I haven't; but I will give you an egg. Break it when you are in great trouble.' She thanked the moon and walked on until the night wind came along and blew on her. So she said to him: 'You waft over all the trees and under all the leaves; have you seen a white dove flying?' 'No,' said the night wind, 'I haven't, but I will ask the other three winds. Perhaps they have seen it.' The east wind and the west wind arrived, but they had seen nothing. But the south wind said: 'I have seen the white dove. He has flown to the Red Sea, where he has turned back into a lion, for the seven years are done. The lion is doing battle there with a winged serpent, but the serpent is a king's daughter who has been bewitched.' Then the night wind said to her: 'I will give you some advice: go to the Red Sea. On the right bank you will find tall canes growing. Count them, and cut down the eleventh and strike the serpent with it. Then the lion will be able to defeat her, and both will recover their human bodies. After that, look around and you will see the griffin who broods over the Red Sea. Swing yourself up onto his back with your best-beloved: the bird will carry you home over the sea. Here is a nut for you as well. When you are halfway across the sea, drop it. It will open at once and a huge nut-tree will grow out of the water, and the griffin will be able to rest on it. For if he could not rest, he would not be strong enough to carry you over. And if you forget to drop the nut he will let you fall into the sea.'

So she went there, and she found everything as the night wind had said. She counted the canes by the sea and cut down the eleventh. She struck the winged serpent with it, and the lion overpowered the creature. Straight away both had their human bodies restored. But when the king's daughter, once a serpent, was released from the spell, she took the young man by the arm, seated herself on the griffin, and carried the prince's son off with her. There stood the poor girl who had journeyed so far, forsaken once more, and she sat down and wept. But at last she took heart and said: 'I will go as far as the wind blows and for as long as the cock crows until I find him.' And she went on, a long, long way, until at last she came to the palace where both were living together; there she heard that a celebration would soon be held, when they intended to hold their wedding. But she said: 'God will help me yet,' and she opened the little casket that the sun had given her. Inside there was a gown which shone as brightly as the sun itself. She took it out and put it on, and went up into the palace and all the people and the bride herself looked at her in wonder. The gown pleased the bride so much that she thought it could make her wedding dress, so she asked if it was for sale. 'Not for money, nor for goods,' answered the girl, 'but in return for flesh and blood.' The bride asked what she meant by that. She said: 'Let me sleep for one night in the bedroom where the bridegroom sleeps.' The bride was unwilling, but even so she still wanted to have the gown, so at last she consented, but told the serving-man he had to give the king's son a sleeping draught. When it was night and the young man was already asleep, the girl was taken into his bedroom. Then she sat down at his bedside and said: 'I followed after you for seven years; I went to the sun and the moon and the four winds asking after you, and I helped you against the serpent: will you forget me completely?' But the king's son was sleeping so deeply that it only seemed to him as if the wind were whispering in the fir-trees outside. When morning dawned she was led out again, and she had to yield up her golden gown. And when that too was no help, she grew sad and went out to a meadow where she sat down and wept. And while she was sitting there so forlorn, she remembered the egg that the moon had given her. She broke it open and out came a hen with twelve chickens, all of gold, which ran around cheeping and creeping back under the old hen's wings so that there was nothing prettier to be seen in the whole world. Then she stood up and drove them in front of her on the meadow, until the bride looked out of the window. The little chicks pleased the bride so much that she came down at once and asked if they were for sale. 'Not for gold nor for goods, but in return for flesh and blood. Let me sleep one night more in the bedroom where the bridegroom sleeps.' The bride said yes, intending to deceive her as she had on the previous evening. But as the king's son was going to bed he asked his serving-man what the murmuring and whispering in the night had been. At that the serving-man told him everything: how he had been made to give him a sleeping draught because a poor girl had been sleeping in his bedroom in secret, and tonight he was supposed to give him another. Said the king's son: 'Pour away the drink next to my bed.' At night she was taken in again, and when she began to tell the story of how sadly she had fared, at once he recognized his beloved wife by her voice. He leapt up, crying: 'Now at last I am truly released. It is as if I've been in a dream, for the stranger princess bewitched me so that I was forced to forget you, but God has delivered me from my beguilement in time.' So that night they both left the palace in secret, for they feared the princess's father, who was a sorcerer. They seated themselves on the griffin's back, who bore them over the Red Sea, and when they were halfway across she let the nut drop. At once a huge nut-tree rose up, and the griffin rested on it. Then he carried them back home where they found their child, who had grown tall and handsome, and from that day onwards they lived happily until the end of their days.

53. *The Goose-Girl*

THERE once lived an old queen whose husband had died long years ago, and she had a beautiful daughter. When the daughter grew up she was promised to a king's son who lived in a country far away. Now when the time came for them to be married and for the daughter to journey to the unknown kingdom, the old queen packed up for her a great many precious utensils and vessels finely wrought, gold and silver, goblets and jewels—in short, everything fit for a royal dowry, for she loved her child with all her heart. She also assigned her a waiting-maid who was to ride with her and deliver the bride into the hands of the bridegroom. Each of them was given a horse for the journey; the princess's horse was called Falada, and he was able to talk. Now when the hour for parting arrived the old mother went into her bedroom, took a little knife, and cut her fingers so that they bled. She held a white napkin beneath them and let three drops of blood fall onto it. She gave them to her daughter, saying: 'My dear child, guard them well; you will need them on your way.'

So the two bade each other a troubled farewell; the king's daughter hid the napkin in her bosom, mounted her horse, and rode away to her bridegroom. After they had been riding for an hour she felt very thirsty, and said to her waiting-maid: 'Get down from your horse and fill the goblet you brought for me with water from the brook, for I would like to drink.' 'If you're thirsty,' said the waiting-maid, 'get down yourself, lie at the water's edge to drink, for I shan't be your maidservant.' So in her great thirst the king's daughter got down from her horse, bent over the water of the brook, and drank, for the girl would not let her drink from the golden goblet. Then she said: 'Oh, heavens!' and the three drops of blood answered: 'If your mother knew of this, the heart in her breast would break in two.' But the royal bride was humble, said nothing, and mounted her horse again. They rode on for some miles in this way, but the day was warm, the sun was scorching, and soon she was thirsty again. When they came to a river she called to her waiting-maid once more: 'Get down from your horse and give me some water to drink from my golden goblet,' for she had long ago forgotten the girl's unkind words. But the waiting-maid said even more haughtily: 'If you want a drink, get it yourself; I shan't be your maidservant.' So in her thirst the king's daughter got down from her horse, lay down over the flowing water, and wept, saying: 'Oh, heavens!' And again the drops of blood answered: 'If your mother knew of this, the heart in her breast would break in two.' And as she drank like this, leaning too far over the water, the napkin with the three drops fell from her bosom and was carried away by the water, though in her great fear she did not notice it. But the waiting-maid had seen, and she rejoiced at having the bride in her power: for in losing these drops of blood she had become weak and powerless. When she tried to mount her horse again, the one called Falada, the waiting-maid said:

'*I* belong on Falada, and you belong on my nag'; and she had to put up with it. Then with harsh words the waiting-maid ordered her to take off her royal garments and put on the serving-girl's poor clothes, and in the end she was forced to vow beneath the open heavens that when they reached the royal court she would not breathe a word about it to a human soul; for if she had not sworn this oath she would have been killed on the spot. But Falada saw it all and bore it firmly in mind.

The waiting-maid then mounted Falada and the rightful bride the poor horse, and they rode on like this until at last they came to the royal palace. There was great rejoicing at their arrival, and the king's son rushed to meet them and lifted the serving-maid from her horse, believing she was his consort; she was led up the stairway, but the rightful princess had to stay below. Then the old king looked out of the window and saw her standing in the courtyard, and he saw how delicate she was, tender and most fair. He went into the royal chamber at once and asked the bride about the girl she had with her, standing there below in the courtyard, and who she was. 'Oh her—I brought her with me for company on the way; give the serving-girl some work to do, so that she doesn't stand around idle.' But the old king had no work for her, and all he could think of was to say: 'I've a little serving-boy who looks after the geese. She can help him.' The boy was called Curdy, short for Conrad, and the rightful bride was obliged to help him look after the geese.

But it was not long before the false bride said to the young king: 'My dearest husband, I beg you, do me a favour.' 'Gladly,' he answered. 'Well, send for the knacker, then, and have him cut off the head of the horse I rode to come here, for it displeased me on the way.' But really she was afraid that the horse might speak, and tell what she had done to the princess. Now things had gone so far that this was to be carried out and faithful Falada was to die, when the news also reached the ears of the rightful princess. In secret she promised the knacker money, which she would pay him if he would do her a small service: in the town there was a great and gloomy gateway which she had to pass through with the geese evening and morning; would he nail Falada's head beneath the gate so that she could still see him again more than just once? So the knacker's man promised to do this; he cut off the head and nailed it fast beneath the gloomy gateway.

Early next morning, as she and Curdy were driving the geese out under the gate, she said as she went past:

'Oh Falada, that you should hang there.'

Then the head replied:

'Oh maiden queen, that you should walk there.
If your mother knew,
Her heart would break in two.'

Then she went on walking further out of the town in silence, and they drove the geese into the open country. And when they reached the meadow she sat down and unbound her hair. It was pure gold, and Curdy gazed at it, delighting in its sheen, and he tried to pull out a few strands. So she said:

'Wind, wind, blow today,
Blow Curdy's little hat away,
And send him chasing after it
Until I've braided up my hair
And found another place to sit.'

And there came such a strong wind that it blew Curdy's little hat far across the fields and he had to run after it. By the time he came back she was finished with combing and braiding, and he couldn't pull a single strand. Then Curdy was cross and wouldn't speak to her; and that's how they looked after the geese until evening came. Then they went home.

Next morning, as they were driving the geese under the gloomy gate, the maiden said:

'Oh Falada, that you should hang there.'

Falada replied:

'Oh maiden queen, that you should walk there.
If your mother knew,
Her heart would break in two.'

And out in the country she sat down in the meadow once more and began to comb her hair; and Curdy ran and tried to grab at it, so, very quickly, she said:

'Wind, wind, blow today,
Blow Curdy's little hat away,

And send him chasing after it
Until I've braided up my hair
And found another place to sit.'

Then the wind blew, and it blew his hat off his head and far away so that Curdy had to run after it; so that by the time he came back she had long since tidied her hair and he couldn't manage to steal a single strand. And that's how they looked after the geese until evening came.

But in the evening, after they had come home, Curdy went before the old king and said: 'I don't want to look after the geese with that girl any longer.' 'Why not?' asked the old king. 'Oh, she plagues me all day long.' Then the old king ordered him to tell him what she had been up to. Then Curdy said: 'In the mornings, when we take the flock under the gloomy gateway, there's a horse's head nailed to the wall, and she speaks to it:

"Falada, that you should hang there."

Then the head replies:

"Oh you maiden queen, that you should walk there.
If your mother knew,
Her heart would break in two." '

And in this way Curdy went on to tell him what happened on the goose-meadow and how he had to run after his hat in the wind.

The old king commanded him to drive the geese out again the next day, and when morning came he himself sat down behind the gloomy gateway and heard her speaking with the horse's head; and after that he followed her into the countryside and hid in a bush in the meadow. Then he soon saw with his own eyes how the goose-girl and the goose-boy drove in the flock, and how after a while she sat down and loosened her hair, which shone in its glory. Straight away she repeated:

'Wind, wind blow today,
Seize Curdy's little hat away,
And send him chasing after it
Until I've braided up my hair
And found another place to sit.'

Then a gust of wind came and carried away Curdy's hat so that he had to run a long way after it, while the maid went on quietly combing and braiding her hair—all of which was observed by the old king. After that he went back unnoticed, and when the goose-girl came home that evening he called her aside and asked her why she behaved in that way. 'I mustn't tell you, and I mustn't cry my grief to any human soul, for I swore it beneath the open heavens, because I would have lost my life else.' He urged her to tell, and gave her no peace, but he could get nothing out of her. Then he said: 'If you won't tell me anything, then cry your grief to that iron stove,' and he went away. So she crept into the stove and began to weep and wail; she poured out her heart, saying: 'Here I am, sitting abandoned by all the world, and after all I am a king's daughter, and a false waiting-maid used her power to bring me to this pass, where I've had to cast off my royal garments, and she's taken my place next to my bridegroom and I have to perform menial tasks as a goose-girl. If my mother knew, the heart in her breast would break in two.' Now the old king was standing outside by the stove-pipe, listening secretly, and he heard what she spoke. Then he came in again and told her to come out of the stove. She was given royal garments to wear and it seemed a miracle, she was so beautiful. The old king summoned his son and revealed to him that the bride he had was false: she was merely a waiting-maid, but the rightful bride was standing here, the sometime goose-girl. The young king's heart was full of joy when he saw her beauty and virtue, and a great feast was arranged to which all the people and good friends were invited. The bridegroom sat at the head with the king's daughter on one side of him and the waiting-maid on the other, but the waiting-maid was blinded and no longer recognized the other in the radiance of her jewels. When they had eaten and drunk and were in high good humour, the old king set the waiting-maid a riddle: what would a person deserve who had deceived their lord in such and such a way—and he told the whole story and asked: 'What judgement does this person merit?' Then the false bride said: 'She doesn't deserve any better than to be stripped naked and put in a barrel barbed inside with nails; and two white horses should draw it and drag her down alley after alley to her death.' 'You are that person,' said the old king, 'and you have pronounced your own sentence. It shall be passed on you accordingly.' And when the sentence was carried out the young king married his rightful bride, and together they ruled their kingdom in peace and happiness.

54. *The Young Giant*

A FARMER had a son who was only the size of a thumb—and who didn't get any bigger. And after some years he still hadn't grown the least bit bigger, not even by the breadth of a hair. Once, when the farmer was about to go out into the fields to plough, the little fellow said: 'Father, I want to come out with you.' 'You want to come out too?' said his father. 'You stay here. You're no use out there; and I might lose you, at that.' Then the little thumbkin began to cry, so for the sake of peace his father put him in his pocket and took him with him. Out in the field he took him out and sat him down in a fresh furrow. While he was sitting there like that a huge giant came striding along. 'You see that big bogeyman over there?' said his father, wanting to frighten the little fellow into being good. 'He's coming to fetch you.' But the giant had hardly taken a few steps with his long legs before he had reached the furrow. He lifted the little thumbkin up carefully, looked at him hard, and without saying a word went off with him. The father stood by, unable to utter a sound for sheer terror, thinking only that his child was lost to him and that he would never set eyes on him again, not for all his days.

In fact, the giant took him home and let him suckle at his breast, and the thumbkin grew and became big and strong after the way of the giant's kind. After two years had passed the old giant went with him into the forest; he wanted to put him to the test, and said: 'Pull up a twig for yourself.' Already the boy was so strong that he tore a young sapling out of the ground, together with its roots. But the giant's opinion was: 'That's not good enough,' so he took him home and suckled him for another two years. When he tried him out again, his strength had already increased so much that he was able to pull up a fully grown tree out of the ground. That was still not enough for the giant, so he suckled him again for another two years, and after that, when he took him into the forest, saying: 'Now for once pull up a proper twig,' the boy pulled up the broadest oak-tree out of the ground with a great tearing noise—and it was just child's play to him. 'Now, that's it,' said the giant. 'You've learned enough.' And he led him back to the field where he had once carried him off. His father was standing behind the plough, and the young giant went up to him, saying: 'Look, father, what a man your son has grown to be.' The farmer was terrified, and said: 'No, you're not my son. I don't want you. Get away from me.' 'Indeed I am your son. Let me do the work. I can plough as well as you, and better.' 'No, no, you're not my son. And you don't know how to plough. Get away from me.' But because he was afraid of this huge man, he dropped the plough, took a step back, and sat down on the edge of the field. So the young giant took the plough and pushed on it with just one hand, but the pressure was so powerful that the plough went deep into the earth. The farmer couldn't bear the sight and shouted at him: 'If you want to plough, you shouldn't press so hard—that'll make for bad work.' So instead, the boy unharnessed the horses, took the plough himself, and said: 'Just go home, father, and tell mother to cook a big dish of food; meanwhile, I'll turn the soil over.' So the farmer went home and arranged for the food with his wife; and as for the boy, he ploughed the field, two acres of it, by himself, and then he harnessed himself before the harrow, and harrowed everything with two harrows at once. When he was finished he went into the forest and tore up two oak trees, laid them over his shoulders, with one harrow fore and one aft and one horse fore and one aft, and he carried it all as if it were a bundle of straw back to his parents' house. When he reached the yard his mother didn't recognize him, and asked: 'Who is this terrible huge man?' The farmer said: 'It's our son.' 'No,' she declared. 'That can't be our son. We never had a son that big. Ours was a little thing.' She shouted at him: 'Go away, we don't want you.' The boy was silent. He led his horses to the stable, gave them their oats and hay, all quite properly. When he had finished he went into the parlour, sat down on the bench, and said: 'Mother, I'd like to eat now. Will it be ready soon?' So she said 'yes,' and brought in two big, big dishes full—she and her husband could have eaten their fill from them for eight days. But the boy ate them all up by himself, and asked if she couldn't serve up some more. 'No,' she said, 'that's all we have.' She did not dare contradict him, but went and put a huge cauldron on the fire to cook a pig, and when it was done she carried it in. 'At last a few crumbs more,' he said and ate it all up—but it was still not enough to satisfy his hunger. Then he said: 'Father, I can see that I shan't have enough to eat my fill here with you. If you will get me a staff of iron, a strong one that I can't break across my knee, I'll go out into the world.' The farmer was glad. He harnessed his two horses to the cart and brought a staff from the blacksmith which was so big and thick that only the two horses could haul it. The boy took it across his knee and—crack!—broke it in half like a beanpole. The father harnessed four horses and fetched a staff so big and thick that only the four horses could haul it. The son bent this in half across his knee too, and threw it away, saying: 'Father, this is no use to me. You'll have to do better than these horses to bring me a stronger staff.' So the father harnessed eight horses and brought a staff so big and thick that only the eight horses could cart it back. When the son took this one into his hand, straight away he snapped a piece off the top, and said: 'Father, I see you can't find me the sort of staff I need, so I won't stay with you any longer.'

So he went away, and made out that he was a blacksmith's apprentice. He came to a village where there was a blacksmith who was a real skinflint: he grudged folk everything and wanted to have it all for himself. The boy walked into this man's smithy and asked him if he needed an apprentice. 'Yes,' said the smith, who looked at him and thought: 'That's a sturdy fellow. He'll strike the first blow well and earn his bread.' He asked: 'How much do you want for wages?' 'I don't want any at all,' he answered, 'only every fourteen days, when the other apprentices get their wages paid, I'll give you two blows— but you'll have to put up with them.' The skinflint was heartily content with this, for he thought he would save a lot of money that way. Next morning the stranger apprentice was to be the first to strike, but when the master presented the red-hot rod and the boy struck the first blow, the iron flew into pieces and the anvil sank into the ground, so deep that they couldn't get it out again. The skinflint grew angry at this, saying: 'What the . . . I can't use you. You strike much too hard. What do you want for that one stroke?' He said: 'I'll only give you just a very little blow, nothing more'—and he lifted his foot and gave him a kick which sent him flying over four cartloads of hay. And then he picked out the thickest iron rod in the smithy, took it in his hand and used it as a stick—and went on his way.

After he had been walking for a while he came to a farm and asked the bailiff if he needed a foreman. 'Yes,' said the bailiff, 'I can use one. You look like a sturdy fellow who can get things done. How much do you want for a year's wages?' Again he replied that he didn't want any wages at all, but every year he would give him three blows, and he'd have to put up with them. The bailiff was content with this, for he was a skinflint too. Next morning the farmhands were supposed to go into the woods; the other hands were already up, but he was still lying in bed. So one of them shouted at him: 'Get up; it's time; we want to go into the woods, and you have to come with us.' 'Oh,' he said, very rude and stubborn, 'go ahead; I'll be back again sooner than you lot all together.' So the others went to the bailiff and told him the foreman was still lying in bed and wouldn't go with them to the woods. The bailiff said they should wake him again and tell him to harness the horses to the carts. But the foreman said, as before: 'Go ahead; I'll be back again sooner than you lot all together.' And he remained lying in bed for another two hours. Then at last he rose from his featherbed, but first he fetched two bushels of peas from the cellar, cooked a porridge for himself, and calmly ate it. Then, when that was done, he harnessed the horses to the cart and drove into the woods. Not far outside the woods there was a narrow pass he had to go through; first he drove the cart forward; then he made the horses stand still and went behind the cart, pulling up trees and brushwood and making a great barrier of branches so that no horse could get through it. As he arrived at the edge of the woods the others were just leaving with their carts laden, wanting to go home, so he said to them: 'Just go on ahead; I'll still get home sooner than you do.' He didn't drive very far into the wood at all, but straight away tore up two of the biggest trees out of the ground, threw them onto the cart, and turned round. When he reached the barrier the others were standing there, unable to get through. 'You see,' he said, 'if you'd stayed with me, you'd have got home just as quickly and could have had another hour's sleep.' He wanted to drive on then, but his horses couldn't manage to make their way through, so he unharnessed them, put them on the top of the cart, took the shafts into his own hands, and—hup!—he dragged everything through. And it went as easily as if he had loaded his cart with feathers. When he was on the other side he said to the others: 'You see, I got through quicker than you,' and drove on, while the others had to stay where they were. Back in the farmyard he took a tree in his hand and showed it to the bailiff, saying: 'Isn't that a fine cord of wood?' At that, the bailiff said to his wife: 'He's a good farmhand. Even if he does sleep long, he's still back sooner than the others.'

So he served the bailiff for one year. When that was over and the other hands were receiving their wages, he said it was time for him to

take his wages too. But the bailiff was afraid of the blows he was due
to get and begged him fervently to consider them as given, he'd
rather become the foreman himself and he should be the bailiff. 'No,'
he said, 'I don't want to become a bailiff; I'm a foreman and a
foreman I'll stay; but I will hand out what we agreed.' The bailiff
wanted to give him whatever he asked for, but it was no use: the
foreman said 'no' to everything. At that, the bailiff didn't know what
to do, and begged him for fourteen days' grace, for he wanted to
think up something. The foreman pronounced that he should have
the fourteen days. The bailiff summoned all his clerks and told them
they should think hard and give him their advice. The clerks pondered for a long time, and at last they said that no one's life was safe
from the foreman, who could strike a man dead as easily as a fly. The
bailiff should tell him to climb into the well to clean it out, and while
he was down below they would roll one of the millstones lying about
and drop it onto his head—and then he would never return to the
light of day. This advice pleased the bailiff, and the foreman was
ready to climb down into the well. When he was below and standing
on the bottom of the well, they rolled the biggest millstone, thinking
his head would have been smashed, but he called up: 'Chase the hens
away from the well—they're scratching in the sand up there and
dropping the grains into my eyes, so that I can't see.' So the bailiff
called: 'Shoo! Shoo!' pretending to scare off the hens. When the
foreman had finished his work he climbed up and said: 'Look,
haven't I found a fine collar?'—and there was the millstone, and he
was wearing it round his neck! The foreman wanted to take his wages
there and then, but once again the bailiff begged for fourteen days'
time to think it over. The clerks assembled and advised the bailiff to
send the foreman to the haunted mill at night, to grind corn there,
for no one had come out of there next morning alive. This suggestion pleased the bailiff; he called the foreman the same evening and
told him to drive eight pecks of corn to the mill and grind it that
night, for they needed it urgently. So the foreman went to the barn
and put two pecks in his right pocket and two in his left; he took four
pecks crossways in a double-sack, half on his back and half on his
chest, and laden like this, he went to the haunted mill. The miller
told him that he could grind corn perfectly well by day but not at
night, for then the mill had a curse on it and anyone who had entered
it had been found dead there in the morning. He said: 'I'll be all

right. You just be off and put your head down.' At that, he went into
the mill and poured in his grain. Towards eleven o'clock he went
into the miller's parlour and sat down on the bench. After he had
been sitting there for a little while, all at once the door opened and in
came a great big table, and on the table appeared wine and roast meat
and a lot of good things to eat—all of their own accord, for nobody
was there serving it up. And after that the chairs moved to the
table—but nobody came in, until all at once he saw fingers handling
the knives and forks and putting food onto the plates, but he could
see nothing besides. Being hungry, and seeing the food, he sat down
at the table, joined in the meal, and enjoyed it greatly. When he had
eaten his fill and the others had emptied their dishes too, the lights
were all suddenly snuffed out—he heard it quite clearly. And now,
when it was pitch-dark, he got something like a cuff on the ear. So he
said: 'If something like that happens again, I'll give it back.' And
when he got a cuff on the ear for the second time he hit back in
return. And it went on like this all night long: he took nothing for
nothing, but gave back what he got with interest, and wasn't shy in
lashing out. But at dawn everything ceased. When the miller rose he
wanted to see how he had fared, and was amazed that he was still
alive. He explained: 'I ate my fill, got cuffed about the ear, but I
handed out a few knocks too.' The miller was delighted, saying that
the mill was now free of the curse, and he wanted to give him a great
deal of money. But he replied: 'I don't want money—I have enough.'
Then he took his flour on his back and went home. There he told the
bailiff that he'd done the job and now he wanted his wages as agreed.
When the bailiff heard this he really did become frightened: he
didn't know what to do. He walked up and down the room and drops
of sweat were running from his brow. Then he opened the window
for some fresh air, but before he could turn round the foreman had
given him such a kick that he flew out of the window up into the air,
on and on, until he couldn't be seen any more. Then the foreman
said to the bailiff's wife: 'If he doesn't come back you'll have to take
the other blow.' 'No, no,' she cried, 'I can't accept it,' and she opened
the other window, for the drops of sweat were running down her
brow. Then he gave her such a kick that she flew out of the window
like her husband, but because she was lighter she flew even higher
than he did. 'Come to me,' her husband called, but in return she
called: 'You come to me—I can't reach you.' And there they floated

high in the air, and neither one could reach the other. And whether they're floating there still, I don't know; but the young giant took his iron staff and went on his way.

55. *The King of the Golden Mountain*

A MERCHANT once had two children, a boy and a girl, who were both still little and couldn't yet walk. Now he had two richly laden ships on the high seas, carrying his entire fortune, and while he was thinking they would gain him a great deal of money the news arrived that they had sunk. So instead of being a rich man he was now a poor man, and he had nothing left but an acre of land outside the town. To rid his thoughts of his misfortune for a while he went out to his land, and as he was walking up and down, all at once, standing by his side, was a little black manikin, who asked why he was so sad and what he was taking so much to heart. The merchant said: 'If you could help me, I would certainly tell you.' 'Who knows?' answered the little black man. 'Perhaps I will.' So the merchant told him that all his wealth had been lost at sea, and he had nothing left but this acre of land. 'Don't worry,' said the little man, 'if you promise that in twelve years' time you will bring me, here to this place, whatever first comes and bumps against your legs at home, you shall have as much money as you wish.' The merchant thought: 'That couldn't be anything but my dog.' But he didn't think of his little boy, and said yes, gave the black manikin his seal and signature to it, and went home.

When he came home his little boy was so glad to see him that he clung on to the benches and toddled over and clutched him fast by the legs. His father was horrified, for he remembered his promise and realized now what he had pledged; but because he found his coffers and cupboards were still empty of money, he thought the little man must only have been joking. A month later he went up to the attic, intending to look out some old pewter to sell, when he saw a huge pile of money lying there. Now he was back in good spirits; he traded, and became a bigger merchant than before, unmindful of the future. Meanwhile the boy was growing, and he was clever and intelligent as well. But the nearer the twelve years loomed, the more troubled the merchant became, so that you could see the fear in his

face. His son asked him one day what was the matter; his father
didn't want to say, but the boy persisted until at last he told him that
without knowing what he was promising he had agreed terms with a
little black manikin, and received a great deal of money in return. He
had put his signature and seal to it, and now, when twelve years were
over, he would have to deliver his son up to him. At that his son
declared: 'Oh father, don't be afraid; it will work out well. The black
creature has no power over me.'

The son asked the priest to bless him, and when the hour came he
and his father went out together to the acre of land, and the son drew
a circle and stood inside it with his father. Then the little black
manikin arrived and said to the old man: 'Have you brought what
you promised me?' The father was silent, but the son asked: 'What
do you want here?' The little black man said: 'I'm talking to your
father, not you.' The son answered: 'You have deceived and deluded
my father. Give me the signed document.' 'No,' said the little black
man, 'I shan't give up my rightful claim.' They argued between
themselves for a long time, and at last they agreed that the son—
because he belonged neither to his old enemy nor, any longer, to
his father—should board a little ship which was floating on a river
flowing by, and that his father should push it off with his own foot.
The little ship turned over, so that its keel was on top and its deck in
the water. And the father, believing that his son was lost, went home
and mourned for him.

But the ship did not sink: it floated on undisturbed, with the boy
sitting safe inside. It floated on in this way for a long time, until at
last it ran aground on an unknown shore. He stepped out onto land,
and seeing a fine palace in front of him, he headed straight for it. But
when he entered he found it had been laid under a spell. He walked
through all the rooms, but they were empty, until he came to the last
chamber. Inside it there lay a snake, coiling and curling. But the
snake was a maiden under a spell, who rejoiced when she saw him,
saying: 'Have you come, my saviour? I have been waiting for you for
twelve years. This kingdom is under a spell, and you must release it.'
'How can I do that?' he asked. 'Tonight twelve black men will come
to this place, hung with chains. They will ask you what you are doing
here, but remain silent and do not answer them, and let them do with
you what they will. They will torment you, beat you, stab you; allow
it all to happen—only do not speak. At twelve o'clock they have to go

away. And on the second night twelve more will come, on the third twenty-four, who will chop off your head; but at twelve o'clock their power will be at an end, and if you have held out and not uttered a single little word, I shall be released from the spell. I shall come to you with the Water of Life in a flask; I will sprinkle you with it, and you shall be alive and well, as you were before.' Then he said: 'I will gladly release you.' It all happened as she had said. The black men were unable to force a single word from him, and on the third night the serpent became a beautiful princess, who came bearing the Water of Life and brought him back to life. Then she flung her arms around his neck and kissed him, and there was rejoicing and happiness in the whole palace. Then their wedding was held, and he was the king of the Golden Mountain.

So they lived happily together, and the queen bore a bonny boy. Eight years had already passed when he thought of his father. His heart was moved, and he was filled with the wish to visit him at home one day. But the queen did not want to let him leave, saying: 'I know it will be my misfortune.' But he gave her no peace until she consented. As he departed she gave him a wishing-ring, saying: 'Take this ring and put it on your finger, and straight away you will be transported to wherever you wish to be; only you must promise me that you will never use it to wish me away from this place to your father.' He promised this, put the ring on his finger, and wished himself home outside the town where his father lived. In the twinkling of an eye he found himself there. He was about to enter the town, but when he arrived outside the gate the watchmen would not let him in because the clothes he had on were so strange, and yet so rich and splendid. So he went to a mountain where a shepherd was guarding his flock, and exchanged clothes with him. He put on the old smock and entered the town without being stopped. When he came to his father's house he revealed who he was, but his father would not believe that this was his son, saying that it was true he had once had a son, but he was long dead; still, as he could see that he was a poor and needy shepherd, he would give him a plate of food to eat. At that the shepherd said to his parents: 'I am truly your son. Don't you know some mark on my body you can recognize me by?' 'Yes,' said his mother, 'our son had a strawberry-mark under his right arm.' He pushed up his shirt and they saw the strawberry under his right arm, and no longer doubted that this was their son.

Then he told them that he was the king of the Golden Mountain, and his consort was a king's daughter, and they had a beautiful son, seven years old. At that his father said: 'That can't be true, not now, not ever. A fine king, going around in a ragged shepherd's smock!' The son was angered by this and, without heeding his promise, he turned his ring round and wished for the two, his spouse and his son, to come to him. And they were there in the twinkling of an eye, but the queen wept and lamented, saying he had broken his word and brought misfortune upon her. He said: 'I did it without thinking, not out of ill will,' and he tried to persuade her; and she made a show of yielding, but she had mischief in mind.

He led her outside the town to the acre of land and showed her the river where the little ship had been launched. Then he said: 'I am tired. Sit, for I would sleep a while in your lap.' So he laid his head in her lap and she groomed it for lice for a little until he fell asleep. Once he was asleep she first drew the ring off his finger, then she drew her foot from under him, leaving only her slipper behind; next she took her child in her arms and wished herself back in her kingdom. When he woke up he was lying there utterly forsaken; his wife and child had gone, and the ring from his finger too, only the slipper still lay there as a token. 'You can't go back home to your parents,' he thought, 'they would say you were a warlock. You must just rouse yourself and make your way back to your kingdom.' So he set off, and came at length to a mountain where three giants were standing, quarrelling among themselves because they did not know how they were to divide up their inheritance. When they saw him walking by, they called to him: 'Little people—big brains,' saying that he should share out their inheritance. But the inheritance consisted first of a sword—if someone took it in their hand and said: 'All heads off, except mine', everyone's head was lying on the ground; secondly, of a cloak—anyone who put it on was invisible; and thirdly of a pair of boots—anyone who put them on and wished themselves away in some other place was there in the twinkling of an eye. He said: 'Give me all three, so I can try them out and see if they are in good shape.' So they gave him the cloak, and as soon as he had put it round his shoulders he was invisible and turned into a fly. Then he took on his own shape once more, saying: 'The cloak is good. Now give me the sword.' But they said: 'No, we won't give it to you. If you were to say: "All heads off, except mine", all our heads would be off, and you would be the only one to keep yours.' Even so they did give it to him, on condition that he should try it out on a tree. This he did, and the sword cut through the trunk of a tree as if it were a blade of straw. Then he wanted to have the boots too, but they said: 'No, we won't give them away. If you were to put them on and wish yourself up on the mountain, we'd be standing down here without a thing.' 'No,' he said, 'I won't do that.' So they gave him the boots as well. Now that he had all three, his only thoughts were of his wife and child, and he murmured aloud to himself: 'Ah, if only I were on the Golden Mountain,' and straight away he vanished before the giants' eyes— so that's how their inheritance was shared out. When he was near the palace he heard shouts of rejoicing and the music of fiddles and flutes; the servants told him that his wife was celebrating her wedding to another. At that he grew angry, saying: 'The false creature, she deceived me and deserted me when I fell asleep.' So he hung his cloak around his shoulders and went into the palace, invisible. When he entered the hall he saw a great table, laid with the choicest dishes, and the guests were eating and drinking, laughing and joking. As for the queen, she sat in their midst on a regal throne, dressed in splendour and wearing the crown on her head. He took his place standing behind her, seen by no one. When they served a piece of meat onto her plate, he took it away and ate it; and when they poured her a glass of wine, he took it away and drank it; and still they kept on serving her, and still she had nothing, for plate and glass kept vanishing in the twinkling of an eye. She was dismayed and ashamed, and she rose and went to her chamber and wept. As for him—he followed her. She said: 'Has the Devil crept up on me, or did my saviour never come?' At that he struck her in the face, saying: 'Did your saviour never come? He is standing over you, you deceiver. Have I deserved this of you?' He made himself visible, went into the hall, and called: 'The wedding is over! The rightful king has come!' The kings, princes, and counsellors assembled there jeered and laughed at him; but he said bluntly: 'Will you leave, or won't you?' At that they made to take him prisoner and crowded round him, jostling, but he drew his sword, saying: 'All heads off, except mine!' So all their heads rolled onto the ground, and he alone was the victor, and he was once more king of the Golden Mountain.

56. *The Water of Life*

THERE was once a king who lay sick, and no one believed he would survive. Now he had three sons who were much distressed by this, and they went down into the palace garden and wept. There they were met by an old man, who asked them why they were grieving. They told him their father was so sick that he was likely to die, for there was nothing that would help him. Then the old man told them: 'I know of one more remedy, the Water of Life; if he drinks of it he will recover; but it is hard to find.' The eldest said: 'I will find it, that's for sure,' and he went to the sick king and begged for his permission to go out in search of the Water of Life, for that alone could cure him. 'No,' said the king, 'the danger is too great. I would sooner die.' But his son begged for so long that the king gave his consent. In his heart the prince was thinking: 'If I can bring him the water, I shall be my father's dearest son, and I shall inherit the kingdom.'

So he set out, and after he had been riding for some time, there in his path stood a dwarf, who called to him, saying: 'Where are you off to so fast?' 'Foolish little fellow,' said the prince, very proud, 'you don't need to know,' and he rode on. But the little manikin had become angry, and wished him ill fortune. Soon afterwards the prince found himself in a mountain glen, and the further he rode the closer the mountains drew together, until at last the path became so narrow that he could go no further; it was impossible to turn his horse round or dismount from the saddle, and he sat there as if he were imprisoned. The sick king waited long for him, but he did not come. So the second son said: 'Father, let me go out in search of the Water of Life,' thinking to himself: 'If my brother is dead, the kingdom will fall to me.' At first the king did not want to let him go either, but at last he gave in. So the prince rode off along the same path his brother had taken, and he too encountered the dwarf, who stopped him and asked where he was bound for in such haste. 'Little fellow,' said the prince, 'you don't need to know,' and without a backward glance he rode on. But the dwarf put a curse on him, and like his brother he found himself in a mountain glen, unable to move forwards or back. That's what happens to the proud.

When the second son stayed away too, the youngest pleaded that he might go out and fetch the water, and at last the king had to let him go. When he met the dwarf, and the dwarf asked him where he was bound for in such haste, he stopped and answered his question, explaining: 'I'm in search of the Water of Life, for my father is sick unto death.' 'And do you know where it is to be found?' 'No,' said the prince. 'Because your manners are gentle, not arrogant like your false brothers, I will pass on my knowledge and tell you the way you must take to reach the Water of Life. It springs from a fountain in the courtyard of a castle that lies under a spell. But you will not be able to enter it unless I give you an iron rod and two little loaves of bread. Strike three times with the rod on the iron gate to the castle and it will fall open. Inside there are two lions who will open their jaws wide, but if you throw a loaf of bread into their mouths they will lie still. Then hurry and help yourself to the Water of Life before it strikes twelve, or else the gate will slam shut again, and you will be locked in.' The prince thanked him, took the rod and the bread, and set off. And when he arrived everything was as the dwarf had said. The gate fell open at the third blow from the rod, and after he had quieted the lions with the bread he went into the castle and entered a fine great hall; princes were seated there bound by the spell, and from their fingers he took their rings. A sword was lying there and a loaf of bread, and these he took away with him. He went further and reached a room where a beautiful maiden was standing, who was overjoyed when she saw him. She kissed him and told him that he had released her from the spell and should have her entire realm. And if he came back in a year's time, their wedding would be held. She also told him where the fountain with the Water of Life was to be found—but he would have to hurry to help himself to the water before it struck twelve. So he went on and came at last to a room in which a fine, freshly made bed was standing, and because he was tired he wanted to rest a little first. So he lay down and fell asleep. When he woke it was striking a quarter to twelve. At that he leapt up in alarm, ran to the fountain, and drew water from it with a goblet standing nearby. Then he hastened to get away. Just as he was leaving by the iron gate, it struck twelve, and the gate slammed shut so hard that it took off a piece of his heel.

But he was happy to have obtained the Water of Life. He rode homewards, and once again passed the dwarf on his way. When the dwarf saw the sword and the bread he said: 'You've gained a great possession in these: with the sword you can defeat a whole army, and as for the bread, it will never run out.' The prince did not want to go home to his father without his brothers, so he said: 'Dear dwarf, can you tell me where my two brothers are? They set off in search of the Water of Life earlier than I did and they have never returned.' 'They are stuck, confined between two mountains,' said the dwarf. 'I sent them there with my spells, because they were so arrogant.' Then the prince pleaded and pleaded until the dwarf set them free once again, but he warned him, saying: 'Beware of them; they have wicked hearts.'

When his brothers arrived he was overjoyed, and he told them what had happened to him: how he had found the Water of Life and brought back a goblet of it with him, and how he had released a beautiful princess from a spell, who was going to wait for him for a year and then their wedding was to be held and he was to rule over a great realm. After that they rode on together and came upon a land where famine and war reigned; its king already believed he would be ruined, so great was the distress. So the prince went to him and gave him the loaf of bread; with this the king was able to feed his entire realm to the full; the prince also gave him the sword, and with this the king smote his enemies' armies and from then on was able to live in peace, undisturbed. After that the prince took back his loaf of bread and his sword, and the three brothers rode on. Then they reached two more countries where famine and war reigned, and each time the prince gave their kings his loaf of bread and his sword, so that by now he had rescued three kingdoms. And after that they boarded a ship and journeyed over the seas. On the crossing the two elder brothers spoke together in secret: 'It was the youngest who found the Water of Life, not we; in return the king will give him the kingdom that is our due, and rob us of our good fortune.' They grew vengeful, and agreed between themselves that they would destroy him. They waited until he was fast asleep one evening, when they poured the Water of Life out of his goblet and kept it for themselves. Into the goblet itself they poured bitter sea-water.

Now when they arrived home the youngest took his goblet to the sick king for him to drink from it and regain his strength. But scarcely had the king drunk a sip of the bitter sea-water when he became even more ill than before. And as he was lamenting over this, the two elder sons came and accused the youngest of intending to poison the king; they had brought him the true Water of Life, they said, offering it to him. He had scarcely drunk a sip when he felt his sickness vanish, and he became as strong and healthy as he had been in his young days. Afterwards the two of them went to the youngest and mocked him, saying: 'There's no doubt you found the Water of Life—but you had the trouble and we have the reward. You should have been cleverer and kept your eyes open. We took it from you while you were asleep on the ship, and when the year is out one of us will go and fetch the beautiful king's daughter. But mind you don't reveal any of this. Father won't believe you anyway, and if you say a single word you shall lose your life as well. But if you are silent you shall keep it.'

The king was angry with his youngest son, and believed he had plotted against his life. So he summoned the court together for them to pronounce sentence upon him: he was to be shot in secret. Now one day, when the prince was going hunting and suspected no ill, the king's huntsman was ordered to accompany him. When they were out in the forest alone the huntsman was looking so sorrowful that the prince asked him: 'Good huntsman, what is the matter?' The huntsman said: 'I may not tell you, but even so, I should.' So the prince said: 'Out with it, whatever it is, I will forgive you.' 'Oh,' said the huntsman, 'I am supposed to shoot you dead. The king has commanded me.' The prince was startled at this, and said: 'Good huntsman, let me live. I will give you my royal garments; in return give me your humble clothes.' The huntsman said: 'I'll do so gladly. I could not have shot at you anyway.' So they exchanged clothes and the huntsman went home; as for the prince, he went deeper into the forest.

After some time three carriages arrived at the old king's court with gold and precious stones for his youngest son. They were sent by the three kings who had defeated their enemies with the prince's sword and fed their lands with his bread, and they wanted to show their gratitude. At that the old king thought: 'Could it be that my son was innocent?' And he spoke to his men: 'If only he still lived! How sorry I am that I had him killed.' 'He is still alive,' said the huntsman. 'I could not bring myself to carry out your command,' and he told the king what had happened. A weight fell from the king's heart, and he had it proclaimed in all the kingdoms round about that his son's return was permitted, and that he should be welcomed with mercy.

As for the king's daughter, she had a road built before her palace all golden and glittering, and she told her servants that the suitor who came riding over it straight towards her was the rightful one, and they were to let him in, but whoever came riding along to the side of the road was not the rightful one, nor should they let him in. Now when the year had almost passed the eldest son thought he would hasten and go to the king's daughter and claim to be her saviour; then he would have her as his wife—and her realm as well. So he rode off, and when he reached the palace and saw the splendid golden road, he thought to himself: 'It would be such a pity if you were to ride on that,' turned his horse, and rode along to the right-hand side of the road. But when he came up to the gate the servants told him he was not the rightful one and should go away. Soon afterwards the second son set off, and when he came to the golden road and his horse set his hoof on it, he thought: 'It would be such a pity; it could crush something,' turned his horse, and rode along to the left-hand side of the road. But when he came up to the gate the servants told him he was not the rightful one and should go away. Now when the year had wholly passed, the third son wanted to leave the wood and ride out to his best-beloved and forget his sorrows in her company. So he set off, always thinking of her and looking forward to being with her, and he did not see the golden road at all. He rode his horse straight down the middle, and when he came up to the gate it was opened for him and the king's daughter received him with joy, and said he was her saviour and lord of the realm. And with great happiness their wedding was celebrated. And when it was over she told him that his father had sent for him and had forgiven him. So he rode to his father and told him everything: how his brothers had deceived him and how nevertheless he himself had kept silent about it. The old king wanted to punish them, but they had boarded a ship and sailed away over the seas, and never returned as long as they lived.

57. *The Bearskin Man*

THERE was once a young fellow who got himself recruited as a soldier; he bore himself bravely and was always to the fore when it was raining bullets. As long as the war lasted all went well, but when peace was made he was dismissed, and the captain told him he could go wherever he wanted. His parents were dead and he no longer had a home, so he went to his brothers and asked them to support him until the war broke out again. But his brothers were hard-hearted, and said: 'What are we to do with you? We've no use for you. Look to it that you make your own way.' The soldier had nothing left but his gun, which he shouldered, and set off out into the world. He came to a great heath where nothing was to be seen but a circle of trees. He sat down sadly beneath them and pondered his fate. 'I've no money,' he thought, 'I've learnt no trade except soldiering, and now, because peace has been made, they don't need me any more; I foresee I shall starve.' All at once he heard a roaring, and when he looked round an unknown man was standing before him wearing a green coat and looking very grand, but showing an ugly cloven foot. 'I know what you need,' said the man. 'You shall have wealth and possessions, as much as you can get through, however wildly you spend, but I must know in advance whether you are faint-hearted, so that I don't throw away my money in vain.' 'A soldier and fear, what sort of a match is that?' he answered. 'You can put me to the test.' 'Very well,' answered the man, 'look behind you.' The soldier turned round and saw a huge bear growling and trotting towards him. 'Oho,' cried the soldier, 'I'll tickle you on the nose—and you won't enjoy growling after that', and he took aim and shot the bear on the muzzle so that it collapsed and did not move. 'I can see you don't lack courage,' said the stranger, 'but there's still one condition that you have to fulfil.' 'As long as it doesn't put my salvation at risk,' answered the soldier, who had understood perfectly well who it was he had before him. 'If it does, I won't have anything to do with it.' 'That you shall see for yourself,' answered Greencoat: 'For the next seven years you may not wash, nor comb your hair nor your beard, nor cut your nails, nor say the Lord's Prayer. And I will give you a coat and a cloak which you must wear for this span of time. If you die in the course of these seven years you are mine, but if you stay alive you shall be free—and rich for the rest of your life into the bargain.' The soldier thought of the dire plight he was in, and as he had gone to meet his death so often, he was ready to risk it now too, and he agreed. The Devil took off his green coat and offered it to the soldier, saying: 'If you're wearing this coat and you put your hand in the pocket, you'll always have your hand full of money.' Then he stripped the bear of its skin and said: 'This shall be your cloak and your bed as well, for you must sleep on this, and may not lie on any other. And on account of this garb you shall be called the Bearskin Man.' So saying, the Devil vanished.

The soldier put on the coat, and straight away thrust his hand in the pocket—and he found that the thing really worked. Then he draped the bearskin round him and went out into the world. He was cheerful, and did not abstain from anything that would raise his spirits and lower his money. In the first year things went well enough, but in the second he was already looking like a monster. His hair covered his face almost completely, his beard resembled a piece of rough felt, the ends of his fingers had claws, and his face was so covered with dirt that if you'd sowed it with cress, the seeds would have sprouted. Anyone who saw him ran away, but because he gave money to the poor everywhere to pray for him, to plead that he might not die in the course of the seven years, and because he paid well for everything, he was always given shelter all the same. In the fourth year he came to an inn where the landlord would not take him in and would not even give him a place in the stable because he feared it would frighten the horses. But when the Bearskin Man put his hand in his pocket and drew out a handful of ducats the landlord was persuaded, and gave him a room in an outhouse. But he had to promise not to show himself, to avoid getting the inn a bad reputation.

When the Bearskin Man was sitting alone that evening, wishing with all his heart that the seven years were over, he heard a loud lamenting in a room nearby. He had a compassionate heart, and when he opened the door he saw an old man who was weeping vehemently, and beating his hands together above his head. The Bearskin Man came closer, but the man leapt to his feet and was about to run away. At last, hearing a human voice, he let himself be brought round, and by kindly persuasion the Bearskin Man prevailed on him to reveal the cause of his grief. His wealth had gradually disappeared, he and his daughters were bound to starve, and he was so poor that he could not even pay the landlord and was due to be thrown into prison. 'If that's all you're worried about,' said the Bearskin Man, 'I have money enough.' He sent for the landlord, paid him, and slipped another bag of gold into the unfortunate man's pocket.

When the old man realized he was free of his cares, he did not know how he could show his gratitude. 'Come with me,' he said to the Bearskin Man. 'My daughters are wonders of beauty. Choose one of them to be your wife. When she hears what you have done for me, she will not refuse. It's true, you do look a little strange, but she'll soon tidy you up.' The Bearskin Man was pleased by the suggestion, and went along with the old man. When the eldest daughter caught sight of him, she was so dreadfully appalled at his countenance that she gave a scream and ran away. The second did stand and look him up and down hard, but then she spoke: 'How can I take a husband who no longer has a human form? The shaven bear who was once on show here pretending to be a human being was more to my liking: at least he was wearing a hussar's fur jacket and white gloves. If he was merely ugly, I could get used to him.' As for the youngest daughter, she said: 'Father dear, he must be a good man to have helped you out of your distress. If you have promised him a bride in return, your word must be kept.' It was a shame that the Bearskin Man's face was covered with dirt and hair, otherwise you could have seen how his heart laughed within him when he heard these words. He took the ring from his finger and broke it in two; he gave her one half and kept the other for himself. He wrote his name in her half and wrote her name in his own, and begged her to take good care of her half. Then he took his leave, saying: 'I must go on travelling for three years more. If I do not return you are free, because then I shall be dead. But beg God to keep me alive.'

The poor bride dressed all in black, and whenever she thought of her betrothed tears came into her eyes. From her sisters she received nothing but scorn and derision. 'Take care,' said the eldest, 'if you offer him your hand, he'll strike it a blow with his paw.' 'Watch out,' said the second, 'bears are fond of sweet things, and if you're to his liking, he'll eat you up.' 'You must always do as he wishes,' the eldest started up again, 'or else he'll begin to growl.' And the second went on: 'But the wedding will be fun: bears are such good dancers.' The bride was silent, but did not let them upset her. As for the Bearskin Man, he wandered about in the world from one place to another, did good where he was able, and gave amply to the poor for them to pray for him. At length, when the last day of the seven years dawned, he went out once again onto the heath and sat down beneath the circle of trees. It was not long before the wind roared and the Devil stood before him, looking at him sourly; then he threw him his old coat and demanded his green coat back. 'We haven't got that far yet,' answered the Bearskin Man. 'You must clean me first.' Whether he would or no, the Devil had to fetch water, wash the Bearskin Man down, comb his hair, and cut his nails. After that he looked like a brave warrior, and he was much handsomer than ever before.

When the Devil had taken off without mishap, the Bearskin Man's heart was light. He went into town, put on a splendid velvet coat, seated himself in a carriage drawn by four white horses, and drove to the house of his bride. No one recognized him. Her father thought he was a high-born general and led him into the room where his daughters were sitting. He was made to sit down between the two elder girls; they poured wine out for him, set the most delicious food before him, and thought they had never seen a handsomer man in the world. When at last he asked their father whether he would give him one of his daughters to be his wife, the two elder girls jumped up and ran to their rooms, meaning to put on splendid dresses, for each of them imagined she was the chosen one. As soon as he was alone with his betrothed, he took out the half-ring and dropped it into a goblet of wine, which he offered her across the table. She took it, but when she had drunk the wine and found the half-ring at the bottom of the goblet her heart began to pound; she took the other half, which she wore on a ribbon round her neck, matched it against his, and it became clear that both parts fitted each other perfectly. Then he said: 'I am your betrothed bridegroom whom you saw wearing a bearskin, but by God's grace I have received my human shape again and become pure and clean once more.' He went up to her, embraced her, and gave her a kiss. Meanwhile the two sisters entered in full fig, and when they saw that the handsome man had fallen to their younger sister's share, and when they heard that he was the Bearskin Man, they ran out full of rage and fury. The one drowned herself in the well, the other hanged herself on a tree. That evening someone knocked on the door, and when the bridegroom opened it there stood the Devil in the green coat, who declared: 'You see, now I have two souls in exchange for your one.'

58. *Tales of Toads and Adders*

I

THERE was once a little boy whose mother gave him a little bowl of white bread and milk every afternoon, and the child would sit out in the yard to eat it. But whenever he began to eat the house adder would come creeping out of a crack in the wall, lower her little head into the milk, and share it. The child took pleasure in this, and if he was sitting there with his little bowl and the adder did not come straight away, he would call to her:

> 'Adder, padder, hear me sing:
> Come on out, you little thing,
> Your milk is waiting here for you,
> Enjoy it as you always do.'

Then the adder would come out quick and find it good to drink. She showed her gratitude too, for she brought the child all sorts of pretty things from her secret treasures, bright stones, pearls, and toys of gold. But the adder would only drink milk, and would leave the bread. So one day the child took his little spoon and hit her gently on the head with it, saying: 'Thing, eat the bread too.' His mother, who was standing in the kitchen, heard the child talking to someone, and when she saw that he was hitting at an adder with his spoon, she ran out with a log of wood and killed the good creature.

From that time on a change took place in the child. As long as the adder had been eating with him he had grown big and strong, but now he lost his bonny red cheeks and grew thinner. It was not long before the bird of death began to cry at night and the redbreast to gather twigs and leaves for a funeral wreath, and soon afterwards the child was lying on the bier.

II

An orphan child was sitting and spinning by the town wall when she saw an adder creeping out from a gap low down in the wall. Quickly she spread out her blue silk kerchief at her side, for adders are mightily fond of these, creeping on nothing else. As soon as the adder saw it she turned round and came back, carrying a little golden crown. She laid it on the kerchief and then went away again. The girl put the crown on her head. It glittered, and was made of delicate gold filigree. Not long after, the adder came back a second time; but when she could no longer see the crown she crawled up to the wall, and in sorrow struck her head against it for as long as she had strength, until in the end she lay dead. If the girl had only left the crown lying on the kerchief, the adder would probably have brought even more of her treasures out of her hole.

III

Paddock calls: 'Huhu, huhu'; child says: 'Come on out.' The toad comes out and the child asks her about his little sister: 'Have you seen Red-Stocking?' Paddock says: 'Nor me neither: what about you? Huhu, huhu, huhu.'

59. *The Jew in the Thorn Bush*

THERE was once a rich man who had a servant who served him diligently and honestly; he was the first to get up every morning and the last to go to bed at night, and if there was hard work that no one wanted to tackle, he was always the first to get down to it. And he didn't complain either, but was content with everything and always cheerful. When his year of service was over his master didn't give him his wages, thinking to himself: 'That's the canniest thing to do. I'll save a bit that way and he won't leave me, but he'll stay in my service, which will suit me very nicely.' His man didn't protest, did his work for a second year as he had the first, and when it came to an end and once again he didn't get his wages, he put up with it and stayed on longer. When his third year too was over his master stopped to think, put his hand in his pocket—but took nothing out of it. At last the servant started to speak: 'Sir, I've served you honestly for three years. Be so kind as to give me my rightful due: I would like to be off and look about me in the world outside.' Then the skinflint replied: 'Yes, my good servant, you have served me patiently, and for that you shall be liberally rewarded.' He put his hand in his pocket again, and one by one counted out three farthings for his man. 'There's one farthing for each year for you; that's an ample wage and generous. There aren't many masters you'd receive that from.' The good servant, who didn't know much about money, accepted his capital, thinking: 'Now you've your full pay in your pocket, you don't need to bother to slave away with hard work.'

So he set off, uphill and down, singing and skipping to his heart's content. Now it happened that as he was passing a thicket of bushes, a little manikin stepped out of them and called to him: 'Where are you off to, my cheerful friend? You're carrying your cares lightly, I see.' 'Why should I be sad?' replied the servant. 'I've been paid in full. Three years' wages are jingling in my pocket.' 'How much does your wealth come to then?' asked the little man. 'How much? Three farthings in cash, counted out aright.' 'Listen,' said the dwarf, 'I'm a poor man in need. Give me your three farthings. I can't work any longer, but you're young; you can easily earn your bread.' And because the servant had a good heart and felt sorry for the little man, he gave him his three farthings, saying: 'In God's name, I can manage without them.' Then the little man said: 'I can see you've a good heart, so I'll grant you three wishes, one for each farthing, and you shall find they'll come true.' 'Aha,' said the servant, 'you're one of those conjurors. Very well, if it's to be so, I'll wish first for a fowling-piece that will hit everything I aim at; second for a fiddle that will make everyone hearing its tune dance the moment I play it; and third, that if I make a request of anyone, he may not refuse.' 'You shall have them all,' said the little man, and he reached into the bushes, and—just think—there lay the fowling-piece and the fiddle all ready for use, as if they had been produced to order. He gave them to the servant, saying 'Whatever you ask, nobody in the world shall refuse you.'

'Heart, what more can you desire?' said the servant to himself, and went cheerfully on his way. Soon afterwards he met a Jew with a long goatee beard who was standing listening to the song of a bird sitting high up in the top of a tree. 'God's miracle!' he cried. 'Such a little creature with such a monstrous mighty voice! If only it were mine! If someone could just put salt on his tail!' 'If that's all,' said the servant, 'the bird shall come down in no time,' took aim and hit the target, and the bird fell down into the thorn hedge. 'Go on, you rogue,' he said, 'and fetch the bird out for yourself.' 'Oh my,' said the Jew, 'if the kind sir will leave out the rogue, the dog will come running; I'll retrieve the bird now that you've hit it,' and he bent down onto the ground and began to work his way into the bushes. Just as he was right in the midst of the thorn bushes, the good servant was overcome with mischief and he unstrapped his fiddle and began to play. Straight away the Jew began to kick up his legs and leap in the air; and the more the servant played, the better went the dance. But the thorns tore his shabby coat, combed his goatee beard, and pricked him and pierced him all over his body. 'Oh my!' cried the Jew. 'What good is this fiddling to me? Stop playing, kind sir, I've no wish to dance!' But the servant didn't listen, thinking 'You've taken it out of folk long enough; this time the thorn hedge shan't treat you any better,' and he struck up afresh so that the Jew had to leap higher and higher and the tatters of his coat hung from the prickles. 'Oy weh,' cried the Jew, 'I'll give the good sir whatever he asks for; a whole purse full of gold, if only he stops playing the fiddle.' 'If you're so free with your money,' said the servant, 'I'll stop playing my music, but I must compliment you: you dance to it with real style'—at which he took the purse and went his way.

The Jew stood there and watched him going, and said nothing until the servant was far away and out of sight. Then he yelled with all his might and main: 'You miserable minstrel, you tavern–fiddler: you just wait till I get you on your own! I'll chase you till you lose the soles of your shoes: you rascal, put another farthing in your mouth to make you a pennyworth!' And he went on ranting and reviling with all the insults he could let loose. That made him feel a bit better, and when he'd got his breath back he ran into town to find the judge. 'Oy weh, Mister Judge sir, look at how some godless person has robbed me on the public highway, and look what a dreadful state he's left me in: a stone on the ground would have pity. My clothes in tatters! My body stabbed and jabbed! My poor wealth taken as well as the purse! Good ducats all of them, each one finer than the other: for Heaven's sake, throw the man into prison.' Said the judge: 'Was it a soldier who put you in this plight with his sword?' 'God forbid!' said the Jew. 'He didn't have a bare blade, but he did have a fowling–piece hanging at his back and a fiddle round his neck; the villain is easy to recognize.' The judge sent his men out after him, and they found the good servant, who had been making his way along very slowly, and they also found the purse with gold on him. When he was taken before the court he said: 'I didn't touch the Jew, and I didn't take the money from him. He offered it to me of his own free will for me to stop playing my fiddle, because he couldn't abide my music.' 'God forbid!' yelled the Jew. 'He picks up lies like flies on the wall!' The judge didn't believe him either, saying: 'That's a miserable excuse. No Jew would do that,' and he condemned the good servant, because he had committed a robbery on the public highway, to the gallows. And as he was being led away the Jew still yelled after him: 'You layabout, you swine of a musician, now you're getting the wages you deserve.' Very calmly the servant climbed the ladder with the hangman, but on the last rung he turned round and addressed the judge: 'Grant me one last request before I die.' 'Yes,' said the judge, 'as long as it's not your life you're asking for.' 'Not my life,' answered the servant. 'Let me, I beg you, at the last play on my fiddle just once more.' The Jew raised a hullabaloo: 'For Heaven's sake, don't allow it, don't allow it!' However, the judge said: 'Why should I deny him the brief pleasure. It is granted—and that's an end to the matter.' In any case, he couldn't refuse on account of the wish that had been granted the servant. But the Jew cried: 'Oy weh, oy weh! Tie me up! Tie me fast!' Then the good servant took his fiddle from round his neck, tucked it under his chin, and as he struck up the first note everyone began to shuffle and sway, the judge, the clerk, and the servants of the court; and the rope fell from the hand of the one who was about to tie up the Jew; at the second note they all kicked up their legs, and the hangman let go of the good servant and made ready for the dance; at the third note everyone leapt into the air and began to dance, the judge and the Jew to the fore dancing best of all. Soon everyone who had come to the market-place out of curiosity was dancing too, old and young, fat folk and thin, pell-mell; even the dogs who had come running reared up on their hind feet and hopped along too. And the longer he played, the higher the dancers leapt, until they were bumping into one another's heads and beginning to cry piteously. At last, quite out of breath, the judge called out: 'I'll grant you your life—only just stop fiddling!' The good servant took pity on them, set down his fiddle, hung it back round his neck, and climbed down the ladder. There he went up to the Jew, who was lying on the ground gasping for breath, and he said: 'You rogue, now confess how you came by the money, or I'll take my fiddle from round my neck and begin to play again.' 'I stole it, I stole it,' the Jew cried, 'but you earned it honestly.' So the judge had him led to the gallows and hanged as a thief.

60. *The Bright Sun Brings It To Light*

A TAILOR's prentice once journeyed abroad in the world practising his craft, but at one time he could find no work, and his poverty was so great that he had not a farthing for his keep. At this time he met a Jew on the way, and thought: 'He's got plenty of money on him,' and he drove God from his heart and went for the Jew, saying: 'Give me your money, or I'll beat you to death.' The Jew said: 'Spare my life. I have no money—no more than eight farthings.' But the tailor replied: 'I say you do have money—out with it!'—and he used violence on the Jew and beat him up until he was near to death. And as the Jew was about to die, he uttered his last words: 'The bright sun will bring it to light!' and with that he died. The tailor's prentice searched his pockets looking for money, but he found no more than eight farthings, as the Jew had said. So he grabbed the Jew, threw him behind a bush, and went on his way, following his trade. Then, after he had been journeying for a long time, he reached a town where he went to work for a master-tailor who had a pretty daughter. He fell in love with her, married her, and lived with her in a good, contented marriage.

In time, when they already had two children, his father-in-law and mother-in-law died and the young folk had the household to themselves. One morning, as the husband was sitting on his table before the window, his wife brought him his coffee. He poured it into the saucer and was just about to drink when the sun shone onto it and the reflection darted to and fro, making ringlets and curlicues on the wall. The tailor looked up and said: 'Yes, it does want to bring it to light, but it can't!' His wife said: 'My dear husband, what's this? What do you mean?' 'I can't tell you,' he answered. But she said: 'If you love me, you must tell me,' and she assured him with her fairest words that no one else should learn of it—and she gave him no peace. So he told her how, many years ago when he had been journeying, with his clothes all in rags and no money at all, he had killed a Jew, and how in the fear of death the Jew had uttered the words: 'The bright sun will bring it to light!' Now the sun had just tried to bring it to light, reflecting onto the wall and making ringlets, but it wasn't able to. Afterwards he begged her particularly to tell no one, or else he would lose his life—which indeed she promised. But once he had sat down to work she went to her good neighbour and confided the story to her—but she was to pass it on to nobody. Before three days were past, though, the whole town knew it, and the tailor was taken before the court of law and tried. So the bright sun did bring it to light after all.

61. *The Wilful Child*

THERE was once a wilful child who did nothing his mother wanted. That is why the Good Lord took no delight in him and let him become ill. No doctor was able to help him, and in a short time he was lying on his deathbed. Then, when he was lowered into his grave and the earth covered him over, all at once his little arm emerged and reached upwards. And when they put it back and covered it with fresh earth, it was no use, and the little arm emerged again and again. So the mother herself had to go to the grave and strike the arm with a switch, and once she had done this it withdrew into the grave, and only then was the child at peace beneath the earth.

62. *The Devil and His Grandmother*

THERE was once a great war, and the king had very many soldiers fighting for him, but he gave them so little pay that they could not live on it. So three of them got together and planned to desert. One of them said to the others: 'If we're caught, they'll hang us on the gallows-tree—how shall we set about it?' Said the other: 'You see that great cornfield over there? If we hide in it, not a soul will find us. The army is not allowed to go through it, and tomorrow it has to march on further.' They stole into the corn, but the army did not march on; it remained in camp round about instead. Two days and two nights they stayed in the corn, becoming so hungry that they might almost have died. But if they came out of the field, their death was certain. 'What good has deserting done us?' they said. 'We're bound to die a miserable death here.' Meanwhile a fiery dragon came flying through the air and descended towards them and asked why they were hiding there. 'We're three soldiers,' they answered, 'and we took off because our pay was short; now we're bound to die here of hunger, or else we must swing on the gallows if we come out.' 'If you will serve me for seven years,' said the dragon, 'I will lead you right through the army without anyone catching you.' 'We have no choice; we must accept,' they answered. At that, the dragon seized them in his claws, carried them through the air high above the army, and set them down on earth again far away from it. But the dragon was none other than the Devil himself. He gave them a switch, saying: 'Crack this whip, and as much gold as you ask for will come bouncing around you: you'll be able to live like great lords, keep horses, and ride in coaches—but after seven years have passed, you are mine.' Then he held out a book in which they all had to put their signatures. 'But before I claim you,' he said, 'I will also ask you a riddle. If you can guess the answer you shall be free and released from my power.' Then the dragon flew away and they journeyed on with their little whip. They had gold in plenty, they dressed in grand clothes, and travelled about in the world. Wherever they went they lived in pleasure and in splendour, they rode by coach and horse, ate and drank—but they did nothing wicked. Time passed quickly for them, and when the seven years were drawing to an end two of them were filled with mighty fear and dread, but the third made light of it, saying: 'Brothers, don't be afraid. I haven't fallen on my head; I'll guess the riddle.' They went out into the country, and sat, and the two had an anxious look on their faces. An old woman came by who asked why they were so sad. 'Oh, what's it to you? You can't help us.' 'Who knows?' she answered. 'Just tell me your trouble.' So they told her they had been the Devil's servants for almost seven years; he had provided them with bags of money, but they had signed themselves away to him and would be his if, at the end of the seven years, they were not able to solve a riddle. 'If you are to be helped,' the old woman said, 'one of you must go into the forest, where he will come to a fallen cliff that looks like a little house. He must go inside, and there he will find help.' The two gloomy ones thought: 'That won't help us,' and stayed sitting where they were; the third, though, the cheerful one, set out and went deep into the forest until he found the cottage in the cliff. And there, sitting in the house, was an ancient crone who was the Devil's grandmother. She asked him where he came from, and what he wanted there. He told her all that had happened, and because she liked the look of him, she took pity on him and said she would help. She lifted up a great flagstone that lay above a cellar, and said: 'Hide down there. You'll be able to hear every word that's spoken up here; just sit still and don't move. When the dragon comes I'll ask him about the riddle: he'll tell me everything; and then pay attention to his reply.' At twelve o'clock that night the dragon came flying in and demanded his dinner. His grandmother laid the table and served up food and drink to please him, and they ate and drank together. Then, in conversation, she asked him how his day had gone and how many souls he had snared. 'I didn't have much luck today,' he answered, 'but I have caught three soldiers—I'm sure of them.' 'Ah yes, three soldiers,' she said, 'they've got their wits about them; they could still escape you.' 'They're mine,' said the Devil scornfully. 'I asked them a riddle too, which they'll never be able to guess.' 'What kind of a riddle?' she asked. 'I'll tell you: in the great North Sea there lies a dead ape—that is to be their roast meat; and a whale's rib—that is to be their silver spoon; and an old, hollow horse's hoof—that is to be their wineglass.' When the Devil had gone to bed the old grandmother lifted the flagstone and let the soldier out. 'Did you attend to everything he said?' 'Yes,' he answered, 'I know enough now—and the rest I'll see to myself.' After that he had to leave in secret by a different way through the window, and return with all speed to his companions. He told them how the Devil had been outwitted by the old grandmother and how he had heard the solution to the riddle. Then they were all glad and full of high spirits; they took their switch and whipped up so much money that it bounced on the ground. When the seven years were fully over the Devil arrived with his book and showed them their signatures, saying: 'I will carry you off to hell, and there you shall have a meal; if you can guess what kind of roast meat you will have to eat, you shall go free, released from my power—and you can keep the whip.' Then the first soldier began: 'In the great North Sea there lies an ape—that's the roast, I suppose.' The Devil was annoyed, went 'Hm, hm, hm!' and asked the second: 'But what's to be your spoon, eh?' 'A whale's rib—that's to be our silver spoon.' The Devil made a face, growled 'Hm, hm, hm!' again three times and said to the third: 'And do you also know what's to be your wineglass?' 'An old horse's hoof, that's to be our wineglass.' Then with a loud cry the Devil flew away, and had power over them no longer; but the three kept the switch, whipped up as much money as they wanted, and lived happily to the end of their days.

63. *One-Eye, Two-Eyes, and Three-Eyes*

THERE was once a woman who had three daughters. The eldest was called One-Eye, because she had only one eye in the middle of her forehead. The middle daughter was called Two-Eyes, because she had two eyes, just like everyone else; and the third was called Three-Eyes, because she had three eyes, and her third eye, like her eldest sister's, was in the middle of her forehead. But because Two-eyes looked no different from other human souls, her sisters and her mother couldn't stand her. 'You and your two eyes,' they told her, 'you're no better than common folk. You don't belong to us.' They pushed her around, and gave her shabby cast-offs to wear and no more than the leftovers to eat, and they were as unkind to her as they could be.

It came about that Two-Eyes had to go out into the fields to tend the goat, but she was still very hungry, because her sisters had given her so little to eat. So she sat down on a ridge and began to cry. And she cried so much that two little streams poured from her eyes. And when she looked up in her grief, there stood a woman before her who asked: 'Two-Eyes, why are you crying?' Two-Eyes answered: 'Because I have two eyes like everyone else, my sisters and my mother can't stand me, they push me from pillar to post, give me cast-offs to wear and nothing but the leftovers to eat. Today they gave me so little that I'm still very hungry.' Then the wise-woman told her: 'Two-Eyes, dry your face. I'll tell you something so that you'll never go hungry again. Just recite to your goat:

> Goat, neigh,
> Table, lay,

and a fresh-laid table will stand before you with the tastiest food upon it, so that you can eat as much as you want. And when you've eaten enough and don't need the table any longer, just recite:

> Goat, neigh,
> Table, away,

and it will vanish from your sight.' At that, the wise-woman went away. Two-Eyes for her part thought: 'I must try it at once, to see if what she said is true, for I'm so hungry,' so she recited:

> 'Goat, neigh,
> Table lay,'

and she'd scarcely uttered the words before a little table was standing before her, covered with a little white cloth and on it a plate with knife and fork and silver spoon, laid about with the most delicious dishes, steaming and still warm, as if they had just come from the kitchen. Then Two-Eyes said the shortest grace she knew: 'Lord God, be our guest allway, Amen,' set to, and enjoyed her meal. And when she had had enough, she recited, as the wise-woman had taught her:

> 'Goat, neigh,
> Table, away.'

At once the table with everything on it vanished. 'That's the way to keep house,' thought Two-Eyes, very happy and light of heart.

That evening, when she came home with her goat, she found a little earthen bowl with food which her sisters had put down for her, but she didn't touch it. Next day she went out again with her goat, leaving the few scraps they had offered her uneaten. The first time and the second time the sisters didn't think anything of it, but when it happened every time, they sat up and took notice, saying. 'There's something not right with our Two-Eyes, she's always leaving her food. She always used to eat everything up; she must have found another source.' So that they could get at the truth, One-Eye was to go along too when Two-Eyes drove the goat to the meadow, and she was to look out for what her sister was up to out there, and see whether anyone was bringing her food and drink.

So when Two-Eyes set off once again, One-Eye went up to her and told her: 'I'll come along with you to the fields and see that the goat is properly tended and taken to pasture.' But Two-Eyes spotted what One-Eye had in mind, so she drove the goat out into the tall grass, saying: 'Come, One-Eye, let's sit down and I'll sing you a song.' One-Eye sat down, tired from the unaccustomed walk and the heat of the sun, and all the time Two-Eyes sang:

> 'One-Eye, are you waking?
> One-Eye, are you sleeping?'

Then One-Eye closed her one eye and fell asleep. And when Two-Eyes saw that One-Eye was sleeping fast and couldn't tell on her, she recited:

> 'Goat, neigh,
> Table, lay,'

and sat down at her little table and ate and drank until she'd had enough. Then she called once again:

> 'Goat, neigh,
> Table, away,'

and everything vanished in a moment. Then Two-Eyes woke One-Eye, telling her: 'One-Eye, you wanted to tend the goat and now you fall asleep over it. Meanwhile the goat's been able to roam all over the place. Come on, let's go home.' So they went home, and once again Two-Eyes left her little bowl untouched, and One-Eye wasn't able to tell her mother why her sister didn't want to eat, saying as her excuse: 'I fell asleep out there.'

Next day her mother told Three-Eyes: 'This time you shall go along and watch out to see whether Two-Eyes is eating out there, and whether someone is bringing her food and drink, for she must be eating and drinking in secret.' So Three-Eyes went up to Two-Eyes and told her: 'I'll come along with you and see whether the goat is properly tended and taken to pasture.' But Two-Eyes spotted what Three-Eyes had in mind, so she drove the goat out into the tall grass, saying: 'Let's sit down, Three-Eyes, and I'll sing you a song.' Three-Eyes sat down, tired from the long walk and the heat of the sun, and once again Two-Eyes began singing the little song she'd sung before:

> 'Three-Eyes, are you waking?'

But instead of singing, as she should:

> 'Three-Eyes, are you sleeping?'

without thinking, she sang:

> '*Two-Eyes*, are you sleeping?'

and all the time she sang:

'Three-Eyes, are you waking?
Two-Eyes, are you sleeping?'

Then two of her sister's three eyes closed and went to sleep, but the third, because the little spell had not been directed at it, did not. True, Three-Eyes shut it, but only out of cunning, as if that eye were asleep too. But she peeped, and could see everything perfectly well. And when Two-Eyes imagined Three-Eyes was fast asleep, she recited her little spell:

'Goat, neigh,
Table, lay,'

and ate and drank to her heart's content and then bade the table go away once more:

'Goat, neigh,
Table, away,'

and Three-Eyes saw it all too. Then Two-Eyes came up to her and woke her, telling her: 'Oh, Three-Eyes, did you fall asleep? You're a good one to tend the goat! Come on, let's go home.' And when they came home Two-Eyes ate nothing again, and Three-Eyes told her mother: 'Now I know why the stuck-up thing isn't eating. Out there, when she tells the goat:

"Goat, neigh,
Table lay,"

there's a table standing before her, laid with the finest things to eat, much better than we have here. And when she's had enough, she says:

"Goat, neigh,
Table, away,"

and everything vanishes; I saw it all exactly as it happened. She sent only two of my eyes to sleep with a little spell, but luckily the one in my forehead stayed awake.' Then the envious mother cried: 'Do you mean to be better off than we are? You shan't have that pleasure any longer!' She fetched a butcher's knife and plunged it into the goat's heart, so that it fell down dead.

When Two-Eyes saw this she went out, full of sorrow, sat down on the edge of the field, and wept bitter tears. Then all at once the wise-woman was standing next to her, saying: 'Two-Eyes, why are you crying?' She answered: 'The goat who laid the table so beautifully for me every day when I recited your little spell has been stabbed to death by my mother. Now I shall have to endure hunger and distress again.' The wise-woman said: 'Two-Eyes, I'll give you some good advice: ask your sisters to give you the innards of the slaughtered goat, and bury them in the ground in front of the house door, and it will bring you luck.' Then she vanished, and Two-Eyes went home and said to her sisters: 'Sisters dear, please give me something left from my goat. I'm not asking for anything especially good. Just give me the innards.' Then they laughed and told her: 'You can have them, if that's all you want.' So Two-Eyes took them and buried them secretly that evening in front of the house door, as the wise-woman had advised.

Next morning, when they all of them woke and stepped outside the door of the house, there stood a marvellous, magnificent tree, with leaves of silver and fruit of gold hanging among the branches, so that there was nothing more beautiful and precious in all the wide world. But they had no idea how the tree had arrived there in the night. Only Two-Eyes spotted that it had grown out of the goat's innards, for it was growing on the very place where she had buried them in the earth. Then their mother said to One-Eye: 'Climb up, my child, and pick some fruit from the tree for us.' One-Eye climbed up, but as she was about to take hold of one of the golden apples the branch drew away from her hand; and that happened each time, so that she couldn't pick a single apple, however much she tried. Then their mother said: 'Three-Eyes, you climb up, you can look around with your three eyes better than One-Eye.' One-Eye slid down and Three-Eyes climbed up. But Three-Eyes wasn't any more adept, and look around as she would, the golden apples always shrank back. At last their mother grew impatient and climbed up herself, but she couldn't take hold of the fruit any better than One-Eye or Three-Eyes, and each time she snatched at thin air. Then Two-Eyes spoke: 'I'll try going up; perhaps I'll be more successful.' Of course the sisters cried out: 'You and your two eyes, what are you after?' But Two-Eyes climbed up, and the golden apples didn't draw away from her but slipped into her hand of their own accord, so that she was able to pluck one after another and brought a whole apronful back down with her. The mother took them from her, and instead of treating poor Two-Eyes better, as she, One-Eye, and Three-Eyes should, they just became jealous that she was the only one who was able to pick the fruit, and they dealt with her even more harshly.

It came about, when they were once standing near the tree together, that a young knight came by. 'Quick, Two-Eyes,' the sisters called, 'crawl under this, we don't want you to shame us,' and they hurriedly upended an empty barrel standing just by the tree over poor Two-Eyes, and they shoved the golden apples she had picked underneath the barrel as well. Now as the knight drew nearer—he was a handsome lord—he paused, admired the splendid tree of gold and silver, and said to the two sisters: 'Who is the owner of this fine tree? Anyone who would give me a branch from it could ask whatever he wished for in return.' Then One-Eye and Three-Eyes answered that the tree belonged to them, and they would certainly pluck him a branch. They both made great efforts to do so, too, but they were quite unable to, for every time the branches and fruit drew back from them. Then the knight said: 'That's very odd—that the tree belongs to you, but it's not in your power to pluck anything from it.' They insisted that the tree was their property. But even as they were saying this, Two-Eyes rolled a couple of golden apples from the barrel, so that they ran up to the knight's feet, for Two-Eyes was cross that One-Eye and Three-Eyes were not telling the truth. When the knight saw the apples he was amazed, and asked where they were coming from. One-Eye and Three-Eyes replied that they did have another sister, but she wasn't allowed to show herself because she only had two eyes, like other common folk. But the knight demanded to see her, and called: 'Two-Eyes, come out.' So Two-Eyes came out cheerfully from under the barrel, and the knight wondered at her great beauty, saying: 'Two-Eyes, can you really pluck a branch from the tree for me?' 'Yes,' answered Two-Eyes, 'of course I can, for the tree belongs to me.' And she climbed up. With no trouble at all she broke off a branch with its silver leaves and golden fruit and offered it to the knight. Then the knight said: 'Two-Eyes, what shall I give you in return?' 'Oh,' answered Two-Eyes, 'I have to suffer hunger and thirst, want and neglect, from early morning to late at night: if you would take me with you and rescue me, then I'd be happy.' So the knight lifted Two-Eyes onto his horse and took her home to his father's palace. There he gave her beautiful clothes, food and drink to her heart's content, and

because he loved her so greatly they were married in church and
their wedding was celebrated with great joy.

Now when Two-Eyes was led away by the handsome knight, the
two sisters really did envy her good fortune. 'All the same, we still
have the marvellous tree,' they thought. 'Even if we can't pick
any fruit from it, everybody will still stop in front of it and visit us
and admire it—who knows when our ship will come in!' But next
morning the tree had disappeared and their hopes departed. And
when Two-Eyes looked out from her little chamber, there it was
standing outside it, to her great joy, for it had followed her.

Two-Eyes lived long and happily. One day two poor women came
to her at the palace, begging for alms. Two-Eyes looked at them
closely and recognized her sisters One-Eye and Three-Eyes, who
had fallen into such poverty that they had to wander and beg their
bread from door to door. But Two-Eyes bade them welcome and was
kind to them and looked after them, so that they were both sorry in
their hearts for all the wrongs they had done their sister when they
were young.

64. *The Shoes That Were Danced To Tatters*

THERE was once a king who had twelve daughters, each more
beautiful than the other. They slept together in one grand room,
their beds standing side by side, and in the evenings, when they were
in bed, the king would lock the door and bolt it. But in the mornings
when he unlocked it, he would see that their shoes were danced to
tatters, and no one was able to discover how this had come about. So
the king had it proclaimed that whoever was able to find out where
they were dancing at night might choose one of them to be his wife,
and be king after his death; but whoever put himself forward and
still, after three days and nights, was not able to find out was to
forfeit his life. It was not long before a king's son came forward and
volunteered to risk the venture. He was made welcome, and that
evening he was led to a room adjoining the bedroom. A bed was
made up for him there, and he was to keep watch to see where they
went dancing; and so that they couldn't get up to anything in secret

or slip off somewhere else outside, the door leading to their bedroom was also left open. But his eyelids weighed like lead upon his eyes and he fell asleep. And when he woke next morning all twelve had been dancing, for their shoes were lying there with their soles in tatters. On the second evening and the third it was no different, so his head was cut off without mercy.

After that many more came and volunteered for the adventure, but all of them were obliged to lose their lives. Now it came about that a poor soldier who had been wounded and could no longer serve in the army found himself on the road to the town where the king lived. There he met an old woman who asked him where he was bound for. 'I don't rightly know myself,' he said, adding as a joke: 'I might fancy finding out where the king's daughters wear their shoes out dancing, and then becoming king.' 'That's not so difficult,' said the old woman. 'Take care you don't drink the wine they bring you in the evening, and you must pretend that you've fallen fast asleep.' Then she gave him a little cloak, saying: 'If you put this on you'll be invisible, and you'll be able to slip out after the twelve.' Once the soldier had received this good advice he took the venture seriously, so that he plucked up his courage and went before the king and offered himself as a suitor. He was made as welcome as the others, and clad in regal garments. At bedtime that evening he was led into the ante-room, and when he was about to go to bed the eldest daughter came and brought him a goblet of wine; but he had tied a sponge under his chin and let the wine trickle into that, drinking not a drop. Then he lay down, and after a little while began to snore as if he were fast asleep. The twelve royal daughters heard him and laughed, and the eldest said: 'This one might have spared himself his life too.' After that they got up and opened cupboards, chests, and closets and lifted out magnificent gowns; they did themselves up in front of the mirror, skipped about, and looked forward to the dance. Only the youngest said: 'I don't know what it is: you're all looking forward to the dance, but I've such a strange feeling: I'm sure something bad is going to happen to us.' 'You're a timid goose,' said the eldest, 'always afraid of something. Have you forgotten how many king's sons have already been here to no avail? I didn't even need to have given the soldier a sleeping draught—that clod wouldn't wake up anyway.' Only when they were all ready did they look at the soldier to make sure, but he had closed his eyes and didn't move or stir, so they believed they were safe. Then the eldest went up to her bed and tapped on it; straight away it sank into the ground and they went down through the opening, one after the other, the eldest in the lead. The soldier, who had been watching everything, didn't hesitate for long, but put on his little cloak and went down with them, behind the youngest. Halfway down the stairs he trod on the edge of her gown, which alarmed her, and she called out: 'Who's there? Is someone holding my dress?' 'Don't be so silly,' said the eldest. 'You've just caught it on a nail.' So they went all the way down, and once they were below they were standing in a marvellous avenue of splendid trees. All their leaves were of silver, and glittered and gleamed. The soldier thought: 'You'd better take back some proof,' and he broke off a bough from one of them. At that a mighty cracking sound came from the tree. Again the youngest called: 'Something's not right. Did you hear that noise?' But the eldest said: 'They're firing shots of joy, because soon we shall have released our princes from the spell.' Then they came to an avenue of trees where all the leaves were of gold, until finally they came to a third, whose leaves were made of bright diamonds; the soldier plucked a bough from each, and each time there came a cracking sound, which made the youngest jump with fright; but the eldest insisted they were shots of joy being fired. They went on and came to a vast lake where twelve little ships were anchored, and in each ship there sat a handsome prince who had been waiting for the twelve. Each took one of them into his ship. As for the soldier, he joined the youngest in her ship. Then her prince said: 'I don't know what it can be: the ship is much heavier today. I shall have to row with all my might if I'm to move it.' 'It must be because of the warm weather,' said the youngest, 'I'm feeling quite warm myself today.' On the far side of the water there stood a fine, brightly lit palace, sending forth the lively music of drums and trumpets. They rowed across the water and entered the palace, where each prince danced with his beloved. As for the soldier, he joined in the dance too— invisibly, and if one of the princesses was holding a goblet of wine, he would drink it up so that when it reached her lips it was empty. This too alarmed the youngest, but each time the eldest shushed her. They danced until three o'clock in the morning, when all their shoes were worn out with dancing and they were forced to stop. The princes led them back across the water, and this time the soldier sat in the front ship with the eldest. On the bank they bade their princes farewell and promised to return the next night. When they reached the stairs, the soldier ran ahead of them and got into his bed, and when the twelve came tripping up slowly and wearily he was snoring again loud enough for them all to hear, and they said: 'We're quite safe from him.' Then they took off their beautiful dresses, packed them away, put their worn shoes under their beds, and lay down. Next morning the soldier said nothing, for he wanted to watch the strange goings-on again, and he joined them for the second and the third night. It was all just like the first time, and each time they danced until their shoes were in tatters. The third time, though, he took a goblet away with him as proof. When the hour had come when he was to make his report he took the three boughs and the goblet and went into the king's presence; as for the twelve, they were standing behind the door, listening out for what he would say. When the king put the question: 'Where have my twelve daughters been dancing their shoes to tatters at night?' he answered: 'With twelve princes in an underground palace,' and he reported what had happened and produced his proofs. Then the king sent for his daughters and asked them whether the soldier had told the truth, and when they saw that they had been betrayed and that there was no use denying it, they had to confess everything. Then the king asked the soldier which daughter he wanted for his wife. He answered: 'I'm not so young any longer, so give me the eldest.' So the wedding was held that very day, and he was promised the kingdom after the king's death. As for the princes, they were spellbound again for as many days still as the nights they had danced with the twelve.

65. *Iron John*

THERE was once a king who had a great forest near his palace, teeming with all kinds of game. One day he sent out a huntsman to shoot a roe deer, but the huntsman never returned. 'Perhaps he has met with some mishap,' said the king, and next day he sent out two other huntsmen to look for him—but they too did not come back. So on the third day he sent for all his huntsmen, saying: 'Search the whole forest, and do not give up until you have found all three.' But out of all these huntsmen, not one came home, and of the pack of hounds they took with them none was seen again. From that time on no one would venture into the forest again, and it stood there silent and solitary, while from time to time an eagle or hawk was seen flying over it. This went on for many years, when one day an unknown huntsman came before the king looking for a position, who offered to enter the perilous forest. But the king was reluctant to give him permission, saying: 'It is eerie in there. I fear you will fare no better than the others and will not come out again.' The huntsman answered: 'Sire, I will take the risk. I know nothing of fear.'

So the huntsman made his way into the forest with his hound. It wasn't long before the hound came upon the scent of a deer and wanted to chase after it; but he had hardly started to run before he found himself standing in front of a deep pool, unable to go further. A naked arm reached out of the water, grabbed him, and dragged him under. When the huntsman saw this, he went back and brought along three men with buckets who had to empty the pool of water. When they reached the bottom they could see a wild man lying there whose body was brown as rusted iron and whose hair fell over his face and down to his knees. They bound him with cords and led him away. There was great wonderment in the palace at the wild man; the king had him put in an iron cage out in the courtyard and forbade anyone, on pain of death, to open the cage door, and the queen herself was obliged to take the key into her keeping. From then on everyone was able to enter the forest in safety again.

Now the king had a son who was eight years old. Once when the boy was playing in the courtyard his golden ball fell into the cage. He ran up to it and said: 'Give me back my ball.' 'Not until you have opened the door for me,' answered the man. 'No,' said the boy, 'I won't do that. The king has forbidden it.' And he ran off. Next day he came back and demanded his ball; the wild man said: 'Open my door,' but the boy didn't want to. On the third day the king had gone hunting, and the boy turned up once again and said: 'Even if I wanted to, I can't open your door; I haven't got the key.' At that the wild man told him: 'It's lying under your mother's pillow. You can go and fetch it.' The boy, who wanted to have his ball back, threw all caution to the winds and went and brought the key. The door swung open heavily, and he jammed his finger in it. Once it was open, the wild man stepped out, gave him back his golden ball, and sped off. The boy grew frightened; he cried and called after the man: 'Oh, wild man, please, don't go away. If you do, they'll beat me.' The wild man turned, lifted him up and set him on his shoulder, and strode off with all speed into the forest. When the king came home he noticed the empty cage and asked the queen what had happened. She knew nothing about it and looked for the key: it was gone. She called the boy, but no one answered. The king sent his men out to search the countryside, but they couldn't find him. It was easy for him to guess what had happened, and great grief reigned at the royal court.

When the wild man arrived back in the dark wood, he lifted the boy down from his shoulder and said to him: 'You will not see your father and mother again, but I will keep you to live with me, for you set me free, and I am sorry for you. If you do everything I tell you, you shall live well. I've treasure and gold enough—more than anyone in the world.' He made the boy a bed of moss, where he fell asleep. Next day the man led the boy to a spring and said: 'Look, the golden well is bright and clear as crystal; you must sit by the spring and see that nothing falls in, for that would defile it. I shall come every evening and see whether you have obeyed my command.' The boy sat down at the edge of the spring, and saw how sometimes a golden fish, sometimes a golden snake would appear in the water, and he took care that nothing fell in. Once, when he was sitting like this, his finger was hurting so keenly that without meaning to he put it into the water. He drew it out again swiftly, but saw that it was all covered with gold, and however hard he tried to wipe it off, it was all in vain. That evening Iron John returned. He looked at the boy and asked: 'What happened to the spring?' 'Nothing, nothing,' answered the boy, hiding his finger behind his back so that Iron John shouldn't see it. But the man said: 'You've dipped your finger into the water. This time I'll let it pass, but take care that you don't let anything fall in again.' Next morning very early the boy was already sitting by the spring and keeping watch. His finger was hurting him again, so he ran his hand through his hair, when unluckily one hair fell into the spring. Iron John arrived, and he already knew what had happened. 'You've dropped a hair into the spring,' he said. 'I'll overlook it once more, but if it happens a third time, the spring is profaned and you cannot stay with me any longer.' On the third day the boy was sitting at the well, not moving his finger, even though it was really hurting. But time seemed to go slowly, and he gazed at his face mirrored on the water's surface. And as he did so, he bent further and further over to look himself straight in the eyes, and his long hair fell down from his shoulders into the water. Hastily he sat up straight, but already all the hair on his head was covered with gold and shining like the sun. You can imagine how frightened the poor boy was all of a sudden. He took his handkerchief and tied it round his head so that the man shouldn't see it. When he came, he knew everything already, and said: 'Take off your kerchief.' Then the boy's golden hair poured down onto his shoulders. Make what excuses he might, it was no use. 'You have not stood the test, and you cannot stay here any longer. Go out into the world; there you will learn how poverty fares. But because you have a good heart and because I mean well by you, I will grant you one thing: if you are in distress, go to the forest and call "Iron John" and I will come to your aid. My power is great, greater than you think, and I have gold and silver in plenty.'

So the king's son left the forest and walked on and on along roads paved and unpaved, until at last he came to a great town. He looked for work there, but could find none, and he had learnt no trade which might have helped him along. At last he went to the palace and asked if they would take him on. The court servants had no idea how he could be useful to them, but he pleased them, so they said he could stay. In the end the cook took him into his service, saying he could carry wood and water and clear out the ashes. One day, just when no one else was at hand, the cook told him to carry the food up to the royal table. But as he did not want to let his golden hair be seen, he kept his little hat on his head. Such a thing had never happened to the king before, and he exclaimed: 'When you approach the royal table you must doff your hat.' 'Oh Sire,' answered the boy, 'I can't. I have a nasty scab on my head.' At that the king sent for the cook and berated him, asking how he could take a boy like that into his service; he should throw him out at once. But the cook was sorry for him, and exchanged him for the gardener's lad.

The lad now had to plant and water, dig and delve, and endure wind and weather. Once, in the summer, when he was working alone in the garden, the day was so hot that he took off his little hat for the air to cool his brow. As the sun shone on his head his hair gleamed and glittered so brightly that the rays from it lit up the bedroom of the king's daughter, who leapt out of bed to see what it was. She caught sight of the gardener's lad and called to him: 'You, lad, bring

me a spray of flowers.' Hastily he put on his hat and picked some
wild flowers of the field and bound them together. As he was going
up the steps, the flowers in his hand, he was met by the gardener,
who protested: 'How can you take the king's daughter a bunch of
such homely flowers? Quick—fetch some others, and pick out the
rarest and fairest.' 'Oh no,' said the lad, 'the wild flowers have a
stronger, sweeter scent; they'll please her more.' When he came into
her room the king's daughter said: 'Doff your little hat; it's not
proper to keep it on your head in my presence.' Again he answered:
'I mustn't: I have a scabby head.' But she grabbed at his little hat and
pulled it off, and his golden hair fell down onto his shoulders, a
splendid sight! He wanted to run away, but she held him by the arm
and gave him a handful of ducats. He went away with them, paying
no heed to the gold. He took them to the gardener, saying: 'Here's
a present for your children. They can play with them.' Next day
the king's daughter called to him again to bring her a bunch of wild
flowers, and when he brought them into her room she promptly
snatched at his hat, wanting to take it away from him. But he held it
fast with both hands. Again she gave him a handful of ducats, but
he didn't want to keep them and gave them to the gardener as a
plaything for his children. On the third day it was just the same: she
couldn't rob him of his hat, and he didn't want her ducats.

Not long afterwards the land was plunged into war. The king
mustered his people, not knowing if he would be able to resist the
enemy, who was very powerful and in possession of a great army.
Then the gardener's lad said: 'I'm grown up now and I want to go to
the war too; just give me a horse.' The others laughed and said:
'When we're gone, go and find one: we'll leave one for you in the
stable.' After they had marched off he went into the stable and led
out the horse: it was lame in one foot and limped along, hobbledyclip
hobbledyclop. Even so, the lad got on his back and rode away to the
dark forest. When he reached the forest's edge, he called out 'Iron
John' three times, so loud that it echoed through the trees. At once
the wild man appeared and asked 'What is your desire?' 'I need a
strong charger, for I want to go to war.' 'That you shall have, and
more.' Then the wild man went back into the forest, and it was not
long before a groom emerged leading a charger with flaring nostrils,
which was scarcely to be mastered. It was followed by a great band of
warriors, all armoured in iron, their swords flashing in the sunlight.

The young man handed his three-legged horse over to the groom, mounted the other, and rode at the head of his troop. As he drew near the battlefield a great part of the king's men had already fallen, and it would not have taken much for those who were left to be forced to retreat. The young man drove forward with his iron troop, passed like a storm over the enemy, and struck down all who opposed him. They tried to flee, but the young man followed hard on their heels, without giving over until not a soldier was left. But instead of going back to the king, he led his band along byways to the forest once again, and summoned Iron John. 'What is your desire?' asked the wild man. 'Take back your charger and your troop, and give me my three-legged horse once again.' Everything he asked was done, and he rode home on his three-legged horse. When the king returned to his palace his daughter came to meet him and congratulate him on his victory. 'I am not the one who carried off the victory,' he said, 'but an unknown knight who came with his troop to my aid.' His daughter wanted to know who the unknown knight was, but the king had no idea. 'He went in pursuit of the enemy, and I haven't seen him since,' he said. She asked the gardener for news of his lad, but he laughed and said: 'He's just come home on his three-legged horse, and the others have been jeering at him, calling: "Here's our Hobbledyclip-clop turning up!" and asking him: "What hedge have you been sleeping under all the while?" But he told them: "I did best of all; if it hadn't been for me, things would have gone badly." Then they laughed at him even more.'

The king said to his daughter: 'I will proclaim a great celebration. It shall go on for three days, and you shall throw a golden apple; perhaps the unknown knight will be present.' When the celebration was announced the young man went out to the forest and called Iron John. 'What is your desire?' he asked. 'To catch the princess's golden apple.' 'You've as good as caught it already,' said Iron John, 'and you shall have a suit of red armour for the occasion, and ride a proud bay.' When the day came the young man galloped up, placed himself among the knights, and was recognized by no one. The king's daughter stepped out and threw a golden apple towards the knights. No one caught it but the red knight alone. However, as soon as he had it in his hand he dashed away. On the second day Iron John equipped him as a white knight and gave him a white horse for his mount. Again he was the only one to catch the apple, but he did not linger for a moment, only dashed away with it. The king grew angry, declaring: 'This is not permitted; he must appear before me and speak his name.' He commanded that if the knight who caught the apple rode off yet again the king's men were to pursue him, and if he did not return of his own accord, they were to strike him down and run him through. On the third day he was given a suit of black armour by Iron John, and a black horse for his mount, and again he caught the apple. But when he dashed away with it the king's men pursued him, and one of them came so close that he wounded him in the leg with the point of his sword. Even so he escaped them, but his horse gave such a mighty leap that his helmet fell off and they all could see that he had hair of gold. They rode back and reported everything to the king.

Next day the king's daughter asked the gardener about his lad. 'He's working in the garden. The odd fellow has been at the festivities too, and only got back yesterday evening. And he showed my children three golden apples that he'd won.' The king summoned the young man into his presence, and he appeared, wearing his little hat once more. But the king's daughter went up to him and took it off, and his golden hair fell down to his shoulders, and everyone marvelled at how handsome he was. 'Are you the knight who came every day to the festivities, each time wearing a different colour, who caught the three golden apples?' asked the king. 'Yes,' he answered, 'and here are the apples.' And he brought them from his pocket and held them out to the king. 'If you need more proof, you can see the wound your men made in my leg when they pursued me. But I am also the knight who helped you to victory over your enemies.' 'If you are capable of such deeds, you are not a gardener's lad; tell me, who is your father?' 'My father is a powerful king, and I have gold in plenty, as much as I desire.' 'I owe you my thanks, I see,' declared the king. 'Is there some service I can do for you?' 'Yes,' he answered, 'indeed you can. Give me your daughter to be my wife.' At that the maiden laughed and said: 'He doesn't stand on ceremony, but his golden hair already told me that he's no gardener's lad.' And she went up to him and kissed him. His father and his mother came to the wedding, full of joy, for they had given up all hope of seeing their beloved son again. And as they were sitting at the wedding feast the music suddenly fell silent, the doors swung open, and in strode a proud king with a great retinue. He went up to the young man and embraced him, declaring: 'I am Iron John. A spell was cast on me, turning me into a wild man, but you have delivered me. All the treasures that I own shall be your possessions.'

66. *The Lord's Beasts and the Devil's*

THE Lord God had created all the beasts and chosen the wolves to be his hounds; but he had forgotten to create the goat. So the Devil bestirred himself, intending to do some creating too, and he made the goats, with elegant long tails. But when they went to graze they usually caught their tails in the thorn hedges, and the Devil had to go and with great difficulty disentangle them. At last he was fed up with it, so in the end he went and bit the tail off every goat, as you can see to this day from the stumps.

Now, of course, he could let them graze on their own, but it came to pass that the Lord God saw how they would gnaw at a flourishing tree one moment, damage the fine grapes the next, and spoil more tender plants at another. This grieved him so much that, of his goodness and mercy, he set his wolves upon them, who soon tore the goats straying there to pieces. When the Devil heard of this he went before the Lord, saying: 'Your creature has torn mine in pieces.' The Lord answered: 'But what harm you created it to do!' The Devil said: 'I was bound to. Just as it is my purpose to do harm, anything I created could not possibly have a different nature—and you'll have to pay me for this.' 'I will pay you as soon as the oak-leaves fall; come to me then; your money is already counted.' When the oak-leaves had fallen the Devil came and demanded what was owed him. But the Lord said: 'In Constantinople in the church there stands a tall oak which is still bearing all its leaves.' Raging and cursing, the Devil departed and went in search of the oak-tree. For six months he wandered in the wilderness before he found it, and by the time he returned all the other oaks were in full green leaf again. So he had to abandon his claim, and in his anger he put out the eyes of all the other goats, and replaced them with his own.

So that is why all goats have the eyes of the Devil and stumpy, bitten tails, and why the Devil likes to assume their shape.

67. *The Little Shepherd Boy*

THERE was once a little shepherd boy who was famous far and wide because of the wise answers he gave to every question. The king of that land also heard of this, but did not believe it. Rather, he sent for the boy and said to him: 'If you are able to answer three questions I shall put you, I will regard you as my own child and you shall live with me in my royal palace.' Said the little boy: 'What are the three questions?' The king said: 'The first is this: how many drops of water are in the Great Ocean?' The little shepherd boy answered: 'My Lord King, dam up all the rivers on earth so that not a drop I haven't first counted runs into the sea—and then I will tell you how many drops there are in the ocean.' Said the king: 'The second question is: how many stars are there in the sky?' The shepherd boy said: 'Give me a big piece of white paper.' And then he took a pen and made so many little dots with it that you could hardly make them out and certainly couldn't count them, and your eyes were dazzled if you looked at them. Then he said: 'There are as many stars in the sky as there are dots on this paper. Just count them.' But no one was able to do so. Said the king: 'The third question is: how many seconds are there in eternity?' Then the little shepherd boy said: 'In Further Pomerania the Diamond Mountain is to be found: it is two miles high, two miles wide and two miles deep; every hundred years a little bird comes and sharpens his beak on it, and when the whole mountain has been worn away with sharpening, the first second of eternity will have passed.'

Said the king: 'You have solved the three questions like a wise man, and from now on you shall live with me in my royal palace, and I will regard you as my own child.'

68. *The Starry Coins*

THERE was once a little girl whose father and mother had died, and she was so poor that she no longer had a little room to live in nor a little bed to sleep in, and at last she had nothing left but the clothes on her back and a scrap of bread in her hand which some charitable soul had given her. But she was good and devout. And because she had been abandoned thus by all the world, she put her trust in the Good Lord and went out into the open country. There she met a poor man, who said: 'Oh, give me something to eat—I'm so hungry.' She offered him all of her piece of bread, saying: 'God bless it for you,' and went on her way. Then a child came by, whimpering and saying: 'Oh, my head is so cold—give me something I can cover it with.' So she took off her cap and gave it to her. And after she had gone a while further there came another child, who had no bodice to wear, and was freezing. So she gave the child her own. And further on a child begged her for a jacket and she gave that away too. At last she reached a forest, and it had already grown dark when yet another child came and begged for a petticoat. The good girl thought: 'It's a dark night; no one will see you, you can surely give away your petticoat,' and she took off her petticoat and gave that away too. And as she was standing like that, with nothing left to her at all, all at once the stars fell down from heaven, and they were all solid shining coins of money; and even though she had just given away her petticoat, she was wearing a new one—and it was made of the very finest linen. So she gathered up the coins into her petticoat and was rich for the rest of her life.

69. *The Stolen Farthing*

A FATHER was sitting at table one midday with his wife and children, and a good friend who had come on a visit was eating with them. And as they were sitting there it struck twelve, and the stranger saw the door open and a little child come in, very pale and dressed in clothes as white as snow. She did not look round, nor say a word, but went straight into the next room. Soon afterwards she came back and went just as silently out through the door again. On the second and the third day she came again, in just the same way. So at last the stranger asked the father whose was the pretty child who came into the room each midday. 'I haven't seen her,' he answered, 'and I've no idea whose she is.' Next morning, when she came once again, the stranger pointed her out to the father, but he could not see her, nor could the mother, nor the children either. Then the stranger stood up, went to the door of the next room, opened it a little, and looked in. There he saw the child sitting on the floor, busily burrowing and digging in the cracks in the floorboards; but when she saw the stranger, she vanished. When he told them what he had seen, describing the child closely, the mother recognized her and said: 'Oh, that's my dear child who died four weeks ago.' They broke open the floorboards and found two farthings which the child had once been given by her mother to give to a poor man. But she had thought: 'You can buy a cake for yourself with that,' and kept the farthings, hiding them in the floorboard cracks. But she had had no peace in her grave and had come each midday to look for the farthings. So her parents gave the money to a poor man, and after that the child was never seen again.

70. *Reviewing the Brides*

THERE was once a young shepherd who dearly wanted to get married. Of three sisters he knew, each one was as beautiful as the other, so that he found it very hard to choose and couldn't decide which he should favour. So he asked his mother for advice, and she declared: 'Invite them, all three. Serve them with a cheese, and pay attention to the way they cut it.' This the young man did. As for the first, she ate up the cheese, rind and all. The second hastily cut away the rind from the cheese, but as she was in such a hurry she left a lot of good cheese still on it and threw that away with the rind. The third pared the rind off neatly, not too much and not too little. The shepherd told his mother all about it, and she pronounced: 'Take the third to be your wife.' He did so, and passed his life with her in happiness and contentment.

71. *The Tale of Cockaigne*

IN the time of old Cockaigne, I went about and saw Rome and the Vatican hanging on a fine silken thread, and a man with no feet outrunning the speediest horse, and a bittersharp sword slicing through a bridge. Then I saw a young donkey with a silver nose who was chasing two swift hares, and a broad linden-tree bearing hot griddle-cakes. Then I saw a skinny old goat carrying all of a hundred cartloads of lard on her body and sixty loads of salt. Aren't those big enough lies? Then I saw a plough sink its teeth into the ground without horse or oxen, and a one-year-old child throw four millstones from Regensburg to Trier and from Trier down into Strasburg, and a hawk was swimming across the Rhine—which he had a perfect right to do. Then I heard the fishes making such a racket all together that the sound rose up to high heaven, and sweet honey flowed like water from a deep valley to a high mountain-top; these were strange stories. There were two crows mowing a meadow, and I saw two gnats at work building a bridge, and two pigeons were plucking a wolf to pieces, and there were two children who brought forth two young goats, and two frogs who were threshing grain together. I saw two mice ordain a bishop and two cats who scratched out a bear's tongue. Then a snail came running by and struck two wild lions dead. A barber was standing there shaving a woman's beard, and two suckling infants bade their mother be quiet. Then I saw two greyhounds retrieving a mill from the water, and a poor old nag stood by and said they were doing fine. And in the farmyard there were four horses threshing corn with might and main, and two goats stoking the oven and a red cow was sliding bread into it. Then a cockerel called: 'Cock-a-doodle-doo, that's the end of the tale, cock-a-doodle-doo.'

72. *A Tall Tale From Diethmarsch*

I'LL tell you something. I saw two roast chickens flying. They were flying fast and had turned their bellies towards Heaven, their backs towards Hell. And an anvil and a millstone were swimming across the Rhine, nice and slow and smooth, and a frog was sitting on the ice at Whitsun eating a ploughshare. There were three fellows walking on crutches and stilts who wanted to catch a hare. One was deaf, the second dumb, the third blind, and the fourth couldn't stir a step. Do you want to know how they did it? First the blind man saw the hare trotting across the field; the dumb fellow called out to the cripple and the cripple grabbed it by the collar. Some folk wanted to go sailing on dry land. They set their sails to the wind and went seafaring over wide fields; then they sailed over a high mountain-top, where they couldn't help drowning miserably. A crayfish drove a hare to flight, and high on the rooftop there lay a cow who had climbed up there. In that country the flies are as big as the goats are here. Open the window for the lies to fly out.

73. *A Riddling Tale*

THREE women were turned into flowers growing in the field. However, one of them was allowed to stay in her house at night. Once, as day was drawing near and she had to return to her playfellows in the field and become a flower again, she said to her husband: 'If you come this morning and pick me, I shall be set free and stay with you from then on'—and that did indeed happen. Now the question is: how did her husband recognize her, when the flowers were all alike and indistinguishable? Answer: 'Because she stayed in her house at night and not out in the field, the dew didn't fall on her as it did on the other two—that's how her husband recognized her.'

74. *Snow-White and Rose-Red*

A POOR widow once lived in a lonely little cottage; at the front she had a garden where there were two rose-trees growing; one bore white roses and the other red. And she had two children who were like the two rose-trees in their looks; one was called Snow-White and the other Rose-Red. But they were as devout and good, as hard-working and sweet-tempered as two children have ever been in all the world; only Snow-White was quieter and gentler than Rose-Red. Rose-Red would rather skip about in the fields and meadows, pick the flowers, and catch the birds of summer; but Snow-White would sit at home with their mother and help her about the house, or read to her if there was nothing to do. The two children were so fond of each other that they always walked hand in hand whenever they went out together. And when Snow-White would say: 'We won't ever leave each other,' Rose-Red would answer: 'Not for as long as we live,' and their mother would add: 'Always share what you have between you.' They often ran about in the forest on their own, gathering red berries, but no creature did them any harm, but came up to them trustingly: the rabbit would eat a cabbage-leaf out of their hands, the roe deer would graze at their side, the stag would leap past cheerfully, and the birds would remain on the branch and sing every song they knew. No mishap befell them: if they had lingered too late in the forest and night came upon them, they would lie down close to each other on the moss and sleep until morning came. Their mother knew this, and did not worry for them. Once, when they had slept the night in the forest and were wakened by the sun at dawn, they saw a beautiful child in a shining white robe sitting near their mossy bed. She stood up and looked at them with friendly eyes, but said nothing, and went into the forest. And when they looked round they saw that they had been sleeping right next to a pit, and if they had gone a few steps further they would surely have fallen in. Their mother told them that it must have been the angel who watches over good children.

Snow-White and Rose-Red kept their mother's cottage so clean that it was a pleasure to look inside. In summer Rose-Red would look after the house, and every morning before their mother woke she would put flowers at her bedside, a rose from each of the little rose-trees. In winter Snow-White would light the fire and hang the kettle on the hook above it; the kettle was made of brass, but it shone like gold, it had been scoured so clean. In the evening, when the snow-flakes fell, their mother would say: 'Snow-White, go and bolt the door,' and then they would sit by the hearth and their mother would put on her spectacles and read from a big book and the two girls would listen as they sat spinning. Near them a little lamb lay on the floor, and on a perch behind them there sat a white dove, her head tucked beneath her wing.

One evening, as they were sitting cosily together, there came a knock on the door, as if someone wanted to be let in. Their mother said: 'Quickly, Rose-Red, open the door. It will be a traveller, looking for shelter.' Rose-Red went and pushed back the bolt, thinking it would be a poor man. But it wasn't. It was a bear, who pushed his broad black head in at the door. Rose-Red screamed aloud and jumped back; the lamb bleated, the dove fluttered her wings, and

Snow-White hid behind her mother's bed. But the bear began to talk, saying: 'Don't be afraid. I won't harm you. I'm half-frozen, and I just want to warm myself a little by your fire.' 'You poor bear,' said their mother, 'lie down by the fire, and just take care that your fur doesn't singe.' Then she called, 'Snow-White, Rose-Red, come out. The bear won't hurt you; he means well.' So they came towards him, and bit by bit the lamb and the dove drew near too, no longer afraid of him. The bear spoke: 'Children, brush the snow from my coat a little,' so they fetched the broom and brushed his fur clean; for his part, he stretched out before the fire, growling comfortably with pleasure. It wasn't long before they grew confident and started romping about their ungainly guest. They ruffled his coat with their hands, put their feet up on his back, and rolled him to and fro; or they would take a hazel switch and beat him, and if he growled they would laugh. But the bear was content to put up with it, only if they went too far he would call: 'Children, spare my life:

> Snow-White, Rose-Red,
> Will you strike your suitor dead?'

When it was time for sleep and the two were going to bed, their mother said to the bear: 'You can stay here by the hearth, for the Good Lord's sake; that way you'll be sheltered from the cold and the harsh weather.' As soon day dawned the two children let him out, and he trotted off over the snow into the forest. From then on the bear came every evening at the appointed time, lay down by the hearth, and allowed the children to play with him as much as they wanted; and they were so used to him that the door would not be bolted until their black companion had arrived.

When the spring arrived and everything was green outside, the bear said to Snow-White one day: 'I must go away now, and I may not come back all through the summer.' 'Where are you going then, bear dear?' asked Snow-White. 'I have to go into the forest and guard my treasures against the wicked dwarves; in winter, when the earth is frozen hard, they have to stay underground and they can't work their way through, but now, when the sun has brought the thaw and warmed the earth, they will break through and climb up; they will ransack and steal; and once anything falls into their hands it won't come out into the light of day so easily.' Snow-White was very sad at his departure, and when she unbolted the door for him and as he squeezed his way out, his fur caught on the door-latch and a piece of his coat tore off, and it seemed to Snow-White as if she had seen gold shimmering through, but she couldn't be sure. The bear ran swiftly away and soon disappeared into the trees.

After a while their mother sent the children into the forest to gather withies. They found a huge tree out there, fallen onto the ground, and near the trunk something was jumping up and down in the grass, though they couldn't make out what it was. When they drew nearer they saw it was a dwarf, with an ancient, withered face and a snow-white beard as long as your arm. The end of his beard was caught in a cleft of the tree and the little fellow was jumping to and fro like a dog on a rope, not knowing what to do. He stared at the girls with his fiery red eyes and shrieked at them: 'What are you standing there for? Can't you come and help me?' 'What have you been doing, little manikin?' asked Rose-Red. 'You silly, nosy little goose,' answered the dwarf, 'I wanted to split the tree, to chop kindling for the kitchen; if I use the big logs the little meals our kind needs will burn: we don't gobble down as much as you greedy guzzling folk. I'd already driven the wedge in nicely and it would all have gone according to plan, but the cursed piece of wood was too slippery and jumped out all of a sudden, and the cleft in the tree snapped shut so quickly that I couldn't pull out my lovely white beard in time. And now the cream-faced loons are laughing! Ugh! What a nasty pair!' The children tried and tried, but they weren't able to pull out his beard, it was stuck too fast. 'I'll run and fetch someone,' said Rose-Red. 'Stupid blockhead!' snarled the dwarf. 'Where's the point in fetching someone? You're already two too many for me! Can't you think of a better idea?' 'Don't be so impatient,' said Snow-White. 'I'll do something about it.' She took her little scissors from her pocket and cut off the end of his beard. As soon as the dwarf felt he was free he grabbed at a sack which was hidden beneath the roots of the tree and was full of gold. He lifted it out, growling to himself: 'Ill-mannered pack, cutting off a piece of my proud beard! The devil repay you!' So saying, he swung his sack onto his back and went off, without even giving the children another glance.

Some time afterwards Snow-White and Rose-Red were going to catch fish for supper. When they were near the stream they saw something that looked like a large grasshopper hopping towards the water, as if it meant to jump in. They ran up and recognized the dwarf. 'Where are you going?' asked Rose-Red. 'You surely don't want to go into the water?' 'I'm not such a fool!' shrieked the dwarf. 'Can't you see that that cursed fish wants to pull me in?' The little man had been sitting there fishing when the wind had unfortunately tangled up his beard with his fishing-line; just then a big fish had bitten, and the feeble little creature didn't have the strength to haul him out. The fish was keeping the upper hand and dragging the dwarf towards him. Of course the dwarf clung on to every rush and reed, but that wasn't much use. He was forced to follow the movements of the fish and was in constant danger of being pulled into the water. The girls arrived just in time. They held him fast and tried to untie his beard from the line, but in vain: beard and line were tangled up tight in each another. The only thing to be done was to take out the little scissors and cut his beard—which shortened it by a little. When the dwarf saw this he shrieked at them: 'Is that manners, you little toad, to ruin someone's looks like that? Not content with clipping the end of my beard, now you've gone and cut off the best part of it: how can I show myself in front of the other dwarves? May you run the thorny road with no soles to your shoes!' Then he fetched a sack of jewels which was lying in the reeds and, without saying another word, dragged it away and vanished behind a stone.

Now it came about that soon afterwards their mother sent the girls into town to buy needles and thread, ribbons and laces. Their path led them across a heath strewn with mighty boulders. They saw a huge bird hovering in the air, circling slowly above them, sinking lower and lower, at last landing not far from them on a rock. Straight afterwards they heard a piercing, pitiful scream. They ran up and saw with horror that the eagle had seized their old acquaintance the dwarf, and was about to carry him off. Full of compassion, the children promptly held on tight to the little man, and tugged away at him in contest with the eagle until the bird dropped his prey. When the dwarf had recovered from his first fright he shrieked in his shrill voice: 'Can't you treat me more gently? You've torn at my poor thin jacket; look—it's in tatters and full of holes, blundering, ham-fisted pair that you are!' Then he picked up a sack of precious stones and slipped back into his cave beneath the rock. The girls were used to his ingratitude by now; they continued on their way and carried out their errand in the town. When they reached the heath once more on their way home they surprised the dwarf, who had emptied out his sack of precious stones on a clear patch of ground, not thinking that anyone would be coming by at such a late hour. The evening sun shone on the brilliant stones, which glittered and gleamed so splendidly, in such bright colours, that the children stopped to watch. 'What are you standing there for, gawping?' shrieked the dwarf, his ashen face turning vermilion with rage. He was about to carry on telling them off when a loud growling could be heard and a black bear came trotting out of the forest. The dwarf leapt up in alarm, but he couldn't reach his hidey-hole, the bear was already too close. In terror he cried: 'Dear Bear, sir, have mercy, I'll give you all my treasures. Look at those beautiful jewels lying there. Spare my life. I won't make much of a meal—I'm too small and skinny. There, look, grab those two godless girls, they'll make a tender mouthful for you, plump as young partridges—eat them, for God's sake.' The bear paid no attention to his words, but gave the spiteful creature a single blow with his paw—and the dwarf never stirred again.

The girls had run away, but the bear called after them: 'Snow-White, Rose-Red, don't be afraid, wait, I'll come with you.' Then they recognized his voice and stopped, and suddenly, when he joined them, his bear's skin fell away from him, and he stood there in the form of a handsome young man, clad all in gold. 'I am a king's son,' he told them. 'The godless dwarf who stole my treasure laid a spell on me: I was to roam the forest in the shape of a wild bear until his death delivered me. Now he has received the punishment he richly deserved.'

Snow-White was married to the king's son, and Rose-Red to his brother, and they shared between them all the rich treasures that the dwarf had gathered in his cave. Their old mother lived peacefully and happily with her children for many long years. As for the two little rose-trees, she took them with her, and they stood outside her window, every year bearing the most beautiful roses, white and red.

75. *Sharing Joy and Sorrow*

THERE was once a tailor who was an ill-tempered soul, and in his eyes his wife, who was a good, hard-working, devout woman, could never do anything right. Whatever she did, he was still dissatisfied:

he would growl and rail and batter and beat her. When the authorities finally heard of this they sent for him and put him in prison, for him to mend his ways. He remained in jail on bread and water for a time; then he was set free, but had to promise not to beat his wife any more but to live with her in peace, sharing joy and sorrow, as befits married folk. For a while all went well, but then he reverted to his old ways, ill-tempered and cantankerous. And because he was forbidden to beat her, he tried to grab her hair and pull it. His wife escaped him and ran out into the yard, but he darted after her with yardstick and scissors and whatever was to hand. When he hit her he laughed, and when he missed her he raged and thundered. He carried on so long that the neighbours came to his wife's aid. The tailor was summoned before the authorities once again and reminded of his promise. 'Gentlemen,' he answered, 'I have kept my promise. I haven't beaten her, but I have shared joy and sorrow with her.' 'How can that be,' said the judge, 'when she has brought another serious complaint against you?' 'I didn't beat her, but because she was looking so peculiar, I only tried to comb her hair with my hand; but she got away from me and maliciously deserted me. So I went after her fast and, so that she should return to her duty, I threw whatever was to hand after her, as a well-meant reminder. And I have shared joy and sorrow with her too, for whenever I managed to hit her it made me glad and made her sad, but if I missed, she was glad and I was sad.' The judges were not content with this answer, though, but had him paid the reward he deserved.

76. *The Moon*

LONG, long ago there was a land where the night was always dark and the sky was spread over it like a black cloth, for the moon never rose there, and not a star twinkled in the gloom. When the world was created there had been enough light for the night. Three lads once left this land to go on their travels; they came to another kingdom where at evening, when the sun had vanished behind the mountains, there rested on an oak-tree a shining globe which radiated a gentle light far and near. Even though it was not as bright as the sun, it was possible to see everything and make it out very well. The travellers stood still and asked a farmer driving past with his cart what kind of light it was. 'That's the moon,' the farmer answered; 'our mayor bought it for three talers and fastened it on the oak-tree. He has to pour oil into it every day and keep it clean, so that it burns bright. He gets one taler every week from us for doing it.'

When the farmer had driven off one of them said: 'We could use this lamp; we have an oak-tree at home which is just as tall, and we could hang it on that. How glad we would be not to have to grope our way around in the dark at night.' 'Do you know what?' said the second. 'Let's fetch a cart and horses and carry off the moon. Folk here can buy another for themselves.' 'I'm a good climber,' said the third, 'I'll bring it down.' The fourth managed to find a cart and horses and the third climbed the tree. He bored a hole in the moon, drew a rope through it, and lowered it down. When the shining globe lay in the cart, they covered it with a cloth so that no one should notice its theft. They took it to their country without mishap and hung it on a tall oak-tree. Old and young rejoiced when the new lamp shed its radiance over all the fields and filled parlours and bedrooms with its light. The dwarves emerged from their rocky caves and the little elves in their red coats danced in a ring in the meadows.

The four supplied the moon with oil, cleaned the wick, and received their taler every week. But they grew old, and when one of them became ill and foresaw his death, he laid down in his will that, as his property, the fourth part of the moon should be buried with him. When he died the mayor climbed the tree, and with a hedge-shears cut away a quarter, which was then laid in the coffin. The light from the moon was reduced, but not noticeably as yet. When the second died the second quarter was buried with him, and the light diminished. It grew still weaker after the death of the third, and when the fourth was laid in his grave the old gloom set in once more. If folk went out at evening without a lantern, they bumped their heads together.

But when the four parts of the moon were united again in the Underworld, where darkness had always reigned, the dead became restless and woke from their sleep. They were amazed that they could see again: the moonlight was sufficient for them, for their eyes had grown so weak that they would not have been able to bear the brilliance of the sun. They rose and grew cheerful, and they took up their old way of life again. Some of them went gambling and dancing, others dashed into the taverns where they demanded wine, got drunk, blustered and quarrelled, and finally raised their cudgels and went for one another with them. The din got noisier and noisier until at last it reached up to Heaven.

St Peter, who guards the Gate of Heaven, believed the Underworld had mutinied, and called the heavenly hosts together to drive back the Devil in case he and his comrades were trying to storm the abode of the blessed. But since they didn't come, he mounted his horse and rode through the Gate of Heaven down to the Underworld. There he calmed down the dead, bade them lie in their graves once more, and took the moon away with him. Then he hung it up in the sky.

77. *The Messengers of Death*

LONG, long ago a giant was once travelling on the great highway when suddenly an unknown man leapt to meet him, crying: 'Stop! Not a step further!' 'What?' exclaimed the giant. 'You wretch, I can squash you between finger and thumb—you want to bar my way? Who are you, to speak so boldly?' 'I am Death,' replied the other; 'no one withstands me, and you too must obey my commands.' But the giant refused and began to wrestle with Death. It was a long and furious struggle, and in the end the giant gained the upper hand and struck Death down with his fist, so that he collapsed next to a stone. The giant went his ways, and Death lay there defeated, so weak he could not rise again. 'What is to come of this,' he said, 'if I just stay lying here in the corner? No one in the world will die any more, and it will become so crowded with folk that they will no longer have room to stand side by side.' Meanwhile a young man came along the road, fit and fresh, singing a song and glancing this way and that. When he caught sight of the man half-fainting, he went up to him out of fellow-feeling, poured a drink from his own flask down his throat to restore him, and waited till he recovered his strength. 'And do you know', asked the stranger, 'who I am and who it is you have helped back onto his feet?' 'No,' answered the young man, 'I've never met you.' 'I am Death,' he declared, 'and I cannot make an exception, even of you. But so that you see that I am grateful, I promise I will never take you by surprise, but will send my messengers first before I come and fetch you.' 'Very well,' said the young man, 'there's some gain in knowing when you are coming, and that at least I'll be safe from you until then.' Then he went on his way. He was cheerful and in good spirits and lived only for the day. But youth and health did not last long. Soon illnesses and pains arrived to plague him by day and rob him of his rest by night. 'I shan't die,' he said to himself, 'for Death will send his messengers first; I only wish these bad days of sickness were over.' As soon as he felt better, he began to enjoy life again. Then one day someone tapped him on the shoulder: he looked round, and Death was standing behind him, saying: 'Follow me, the hour of your departure from the world has come.' 'What?' answered the man. 'Would you break your word? Didn't you promise me that before you came yourself you would send your messengers? I have seen none.' 'Be silent,' replied Death. 'Haven't I sent you one messenger after another? Didn't the fever come to clutch you and shake you and cast you down? Didn't the dizziness make your head swim? Didn't the gout pinch you in all your limbs? Wasn't there a roaring in your ears? Didn't the toothache gnaw at your jaw? Haven't your eyes grown dim? Beyond all this, hasn't my very brother, sleep, reminded you of me every evening? Didn't you lie at night as if you were already dead?' The man did not know what to reply, yielded to his fate, and went away with Death.

78. *The Unequal Children of Eve*

WHEN Adam and Eve were driven out of Paradise they had to build themselves a house on barren ground, and they ate their bread in the sweat of their brows. Adam dug the fields and Eve span wool. Each year Eve brought a child into the world, but the children were unequal: some were beautiful, others ugly. After a long time had passed God sent an angel to the two, announcing that he would come and take a look at their household. Delighted that the Lord was so gracious, Eve cleaned her house busily, decked it with flowers, and strewed rushes on the floor. Then she called her children to her, but only the beautiful ones. She washed and bathed them, combed their hair, put freshly washed shirts on them, and warned them to behave like well-brought-up children in the Lord's presence. They were to bow nicely before him, offer him their hand, and answer his questions modestly and sensibly. But the ugly children were to keep out of his way. One hid beneath the hay, another under the roof, the third in the straw, the fourth in the stove, the fifth in the cellar, the sixth underneath a tub, the seventh underneath the wine-barrel, the eighth under Eve's old fur, the ninth and tenth under the cloth she used for making their clothes, and the eleventh and twelfth under the leather she cut out to make their shoes. She was just ready when there was a knock at the front door. Adam peered through a crack and saw that it was the Lord. With reverence he opened the door, and the Heavenly Father entered. There stood the beautiful children all in a row; they bowed, offered their hand, and knelt down. For his part, the Lord began to bless them. He laid his hands upon the head of the first one, saying: 'You shall become a mighty king,' likewise saying to the second: 'You shall become a prince,' to the third: 'You an earl,' to the fourth: 'You a knight,' to the fifth: 'You a gentleman,' to the sixth: 'You a townsman,' to the seventh: 'You a merchant,' to the eighth: 'You a scholar.' So he bestowed upon them all the wealth of his blessings. When Eve saw that the Lord was so charitable and gracious, she thought: 'I will call my ill-favoured children here. Perhaps he will give them his blessing too.' So she ran and fetched them out of the hay, straw, stove, and wherever else they were hidden. Then the whole uncouth, grubby, scabby, grimy crew arrived. The Lord smiled and looked at them all thoughtfully, saying: 'These too I will bless.' He laid his hands upon the head of the first one, saying to him: 'You shall become a farmer,' to the second: 'You shall become a fisherman,' to the third: 'You a blacksmith,' to the fourth: 'You a tanner,' to the fifth: 'You a weaver,' to the sixth: 'You a shoemaker,' to the seventh: 'You a tailor,' to the eighth: 'You a potter,' to the ninth: 'You a carter,' to the tenth: 'You a sailor,' to the eleventh: 'You a messenger,' and to the twelfth: 'You shall be a house-servant all your life long.'

When Eve had also listened to all this, she said: 'Lord, how unequally you share out your blessings! After all, they are all my children, born to me; your mercy should rain upon them all equally.' But God replied: 'Eve, you do not understand. It is my duty and my due to provide the whole world with your children. If they were all princes and lords, who should sow the corn, thresh it, grind it, and bake it? Who should forge the iron, weave the cloth, shape the timber, build, dig, sew, and stitch? Each one shall represent his estate, so that one may support another and all be nourished, as the members of the body are.' Then Eve answered and said: 'Oh Lord, forgive me. I was too hasty in protesting. Thy will be done, even upon my children.'

79. *The Golden Key*

ONCE, in the winter-time, when deep snow was lying on the ground, a poor lad had to go out and fetch wood on a sledge. After he had gathered it and loaded the sledge, he was frozen so cold that he had no wish to go straight back home, but instead wanted to light a fire first to warm up a little. So he scraped away the snow, and when he had cleared the ground he found a little golden key. Now he thought that where there was a key there must also be a lock to match, so he dug in the earth and found a little iron casket. 'If only the key fits!' he thought. 'There are precious things in this casket, for sure.' He looked, but there was no keyhole. At last he discovered one, but it was so small it could scarcely be seen. He tried the key and it fitted sweetly. Then he turned it once—and now we must wait until he has unlocked it completely and lifted the lid, and then we shall find out what marvellous things were in the casket.

* * *

CHILDREN'S LEGENDS

80. *St Joseph in the Forest*

THERE was once a mother who had three daughters: the eldest was ill-mannered and wicked; the second was a good deal better, though she too had her faults; but the youngest was a good, devout child. But their mother was so peculiar that it was the eldest daughter she loved best and the youngest she could not stand. So she often sent the poor girl out into a great forest just to get rid of her, for she thought the girl would lose her way and never come back. But the girl's guardian angel—which every devout child has—did not desert her, but again and again put her on to the right way. But her little guardian angel once behaved as if he were not on hand, and the child was not able to find her way out of the forest. She walked and walked until evening fell, when she saw a little light burning in the distance. She ran towards it and found herself outside a little cottage. She knocked; the door opened, and she came to a second door, where she knocked again. An old man with a snow-white beard and venerable appearance opened to her, and it was none other than St Joseph. He spoke very kindly: 'Come, my dear, sit by the fire on my chair and warm yourself. I'll bring you some clear water if you are thirsty, but here in the forest I've nothing for you to eat but a few roots, which you will have to peel and cook for yourself first.' So St Joseph held the roots out to her, which she scraped clean; then she brought out the little bit of pancake and the bread her mother had given her, put it all together in a little cauldron on the fire, and made herself a vegetable stew. When it was ready, St Joseph said: 'I'm so hungry. Give me some of your food.' The child was willing, and gave him more than she kept for herself, but God's blessing was upon her, so that she was filled. After they had eaten St Joseph said: 'Now let us go to bed. But I have only one bed; you take it and I'll lie on the straw on the ground.' 'No,' she answered, 'you lie in it; the straw is soft enough for me.' But St Joseph picked up the child in his arms and carried her to the little bed, where she said her prayers and went to sleep. Next morning, when she woke up, she wanted to say good morning to St Joseph, but she did not see him. So she got up and looked for him, but she couldn't find him anywhere. At length she noticed a bag of money behind the door, so heavy that she could only just carry it. A note written on it said that it was for the child who had slept there that night. So she took the bag and sped off with it, and she returned to her mother without mishap. And because the child gave her all the money, her mother could not but be content with her.

Next day the second child wanted to go into the forest too. Her mother gave her a much bigger slice of pancake and bread to take with her. She fared exactly as the first child had. That evening she arrived at St Joseph's little cottage, who gave her roots to make a stew. When it was ready, he said to her, as he had before: 'I'm so hungry. Give me some of your food.' The child answered: 'Share and share alike.' Afterwards, when St Joseph offered her his bed, she answered: 'No, you get into bed with me; there's enough room for both of us.' St Joseph picked her up in his arms, put her to bed, and lay down in the straw. In the morning, when the child woke up and looked for St Joseph, he had vanished, but behind the door she found a small bag of money with a note written on it that it was for the child who had slept there that night. So she took the little bag and ran home with it and gave it to her mother—but on the sly she kept a few coins for herself.

The eldest daughter was now filled with curiosity, and next morning she wanted to go out into the forest too. Her mother gave her as many pancakes to take with her as she wanted, and bread and cheese as well. That evening she found St Joseph in his cottage, just as the other two had. When the stew was ready and St Joseph said: 'I'm so hungry, give me some of your food,' the girl answered: 'Wait until I'm full, and then you shall have what I leave.' But she ate up almost everything, and St Joseph was forced to scrape the plate clean. Afterwards the good old man offered her his bed and was ready to lie on the straw. She accepted this without protest, lay down in the bed, and left the straw to the old man. Next morning, when she woke, St Joseph was not to be found, but that did not worry her: she was looking behind the door for a bag of money. It seemed to her that something was lying on the ground, but because she could not make out clearly what it was, she bent down—and bumped her nose on it. But it stuck to her nose, and when she straightened up she saw to her horror that it was a second nose clinging on to the first. Then she started to cry and bawl, but that was no help: she was forced to look down her nose and see how far it stuck out. So she ran away screaming until she met St Joseph. She fell at his feet and implored him until he removed the nose out of pity, and gave her two pennies as well. When she arrived home her mother was standing at the door. She asked her: 'What sort of present did you get?' At that the girl lied, answering: 'A big bag full of money—but I lost it on the way.' 'Lost it!' cried her mother. 'Then we'll go and find it,' and she took her daughter by the hand and was about to go and look for it with her. At first the girl began to cry, and she did not want to go. At last she did go with her mother, but on the way they were attacked by so many lizards and snakes that they could not save themselves. In the end the creatures stung the wicked child to death, and they stung her mother in the foot because she had not brought her up better.

81. *The Rose*

THERE was once a poor woman who had two children. Every day the youngest had to go into the forest and fetch wood. Now once, when she had gone a long way in search of it, a child came up to her, that small, but very sturdy, and busily helped her to gather the wood, and even carried it as far as the house. And then, before a moment went by, the child vanished. The girl told her mother, who wouldn't believe it at first. But in the end she brought a rose in with her and told her mother that the pretty child had given it to her, saying that when it was in full bloom, he would come again. Her mother put the rose in water. One morning the child didn't stir from her bed. Her mother went up to the bed and found the child dead, and lying there that graciously. And the same morning the rose came into full bloom.

82. *Our Lady's Goblet*

A DRAYMAN's cart, which was heavily laden with wine, was once stuck so fast that, for all his efforts, he could not pull it clear. Now just at that moment Our Lady came along that way, and when she saw the poor man's distress she said to him: 'I am tired and thirsty; give me a glass of wine, and I will free your cart.' 'Gladly,' answered the drayman, 'but I have no glass I could give you to hold the wine.' Then Our Lady picked a small white, red-striped, flower, which is called wild bindweed and looks very like a goblet, and she handed it to the drayman. He filled it with wine and Our Lady drank it, and in that moment the wagon was freed and the drayman was able to drive on. The flower is still called Our Lady's Goblet to this day.

APPENDIX A
Selected Earlier Versions

The King's Daughter and the Enchanted Prince (1810)

[THE first item is the opening, under a different title, of the tale that
the brothers chose to open the collection, 'The Frog King, or Iron
Henry', as it was sent in manuscript, in Wilhelm's hand, to Brentano in
1810. The tales from the manuscript, here 1, 19, and 37, appear to be
drafts varying in fullness and written down with little attention to
style, often with abbreviated forms, insertions, and minimal punctu-
ation. These have been normalized. The second item is the opening of
the tale as presented in Vol. I of the first edition (1812). The major
revision of the text took place in the third edition of 1837, and though
Wilhelm continued to tinker with it through subsequent editions—in
each he tried out a different formulation for the transformation—the
literary version in the third edition is essentially the final text. See note.]

The king's youngest daughter went out into the forest and sat down by a
cool well. Then she took a golden ball and was playing with it when it
suddenly rolled down into the well. She watched it falling into the depths,
and stood at the well and was very sad. All at once a frog reached his head
out of the water and said: 'Why are you wailing so much?' 'Oh! You nasty
frog,' she answered, 'my golden ball has fallen into the well.' Then the
frog said: 'If you will take me home with you and I can sit next to you, I'll
fetch your golden ball for you.' And when she had promised this, he dived
down and soon came back up with the ball in his mouth, and threw it onto
land.

1. *The Frog King, or Iron Henry* (1812)

There was once a king's daughter who went out into the forest and sat
down by a cool well. She had a golden ball which was her favourite toy; she
would throw it up high and catch it again in the air, and enjoyed herself as
she did. One day the ball had risen very high; she had already stretched
out her hand and curled her fingers ready to catch it when it bounced past
onto the ground quite close to her and rolled and rolled straight into the
water.

The king's daughter gazed after it in dismay, but the well was so deep that the bottom was not to be seen. Then she began to cry piteously and lament: 'Oh, if only I had my ball again, I'd give everything, my clothes, my jewels, my pearls, and whatever the world might hold.' While she was lamenting like this a frog popped his head out of the water and said: 'King's daughter, why are you wailing so plaintively?' 'Oh,' she said, 'you nasty frog, what can you do to help me! My golden ball has fallen into the well.' The frog said: 'I don't want your pearls, nor your jewels, nor your clothes, but if you will take me to be your companion and let me sit next to you and eat from your little golden plate and sleep in your little golden bed, and if you will honour me and love me, I will bring your golden ball back to you.' The king's daughter thought: 'What nonsense that silly frog is chattering—after all, he is bound to stay in the water, but perhaps he can fetch me my ball, so I'll just say yes,' so she said: 'Yes, if you like, only get me back my golden ball, and I'll promise you everything.'

11. *Rapunzel* (1812)

[THIS, in translation, is the tale as told in Vol. I of the first edition (1812). The simplicity of this version removes it in tone far from its basis in the novel by Friedrich Schulz. Wilhelm's development of the end in the course of rewriting it for the second edition heightens both the prince's punishment for his transgression and the redress of joy when the couple are reunited and he is healed. See note and, for bowdlerizing, Introduction, p. xxxi.]

There was once a husband and wife who had for a long time wished for a child and never had one, but at last the wife had hopes. At the back of their house these folk had a little window, and from it they were able to look out onto the garden which belonged to a fairy, and grew full of all kinds of flowers and herbs—but no one dared enter it. One day the wife was standing at this window and looking down, when she noticed some wonderfully fine rampions, or rapunzels, in a bed, and she hankered after them so much—though she knew she couldn't have any of them—that she grew thin and looked pale and wretched. At length her husband was alarmed, and asked what was causing it: 'Oh, if I don't get any rapunzels to eat from the garden behind our house, I must die.' Her husband, who loved her, thought: 'Whatever the cost, you shall fetch her some,' so one evening he climbed over the wall and hastily dug up a handful of rapunzels, which he took to his wife. Straight away she made herself a salad of them and ate them ravenously. But she enjoyed them so much, so very, very much, that next day her craving was three times as great. Her husband saw that she had no peace in her, so he climbed the wall once again—but he was utterly terrified when he saw the fairy standing there; she upbraided him passionately for daring to enter her garden and steal from it. He excused himself as well as he could with his wife's pregnancy, and with how risky it was to refuse her anything. In the end the fairy said: 'I shall be content, and I shall even permit you to take as many rapunzels with you as you wish, as long as you will give me the child your wife is now carrying.' In his fear the man agreed to everything, and when his wife's time came the fairy appeared straight away, named the little girl 'Rapunzel', and took her away with her.

This Rapunzel grew to be the most beautiful child under the sun. But when she was twelve years old the fairy locked her in a high, high tower which had neither door nor stair; only there was just one small window right at the top. When the fairy wanted to get in, she would stand below and call:

> 'Rapunzel, Rapunzel,
> Let down your hair to me!'

Now Rapunzel had beautiful hair, as fine as spun gold, and when she heard the fairy call in this way she would unpin it, wrap it round the window-catch above, and then her hair would fall twenty ells below, and the fairy would climb up it.

Now one day a young king's son came through the forest where the tower stood. He saw fair Rapunzel standing at her window, and he heard her singing with such a sweet voice that he fell utterly in love with her. But as there was no door to the tower, and no ladder could reach so high, he was in despair. But every day he would go into the forest, until one day he saw the fairy arriving, and she spoke:

> 'Rapunzel, Rapunzel!
> Let down your hair.'

Then he saw just what ladder to use to get into the tower. But he had also taken notice of the words that had to be spoken, and the next day, when it was dark, he went up to the tower and called up:

> 'Rapunzel, Rapunzel,
> Let down your hair!'

So she let her hair down, and once it reached the ground he clung on to it tight, and he was drawn up.

Rapunzel was terribly frightened at first, but soon the young king was so much to her liking that she arranged with him that he should come every day and be drawn up. They lived merrily and happily in this way for some time, and the fairy didn't find out until one day Rapunzel started to say to her: 'Tell me, Godmother, why my clothes are getting so tight on me, they don't fit me any longer.' 'Oh! You godless child,' cried the fairy, 'what must I hear from you?' and she noticed at once how she had been deceived, and became very angry. Then she took Rapunzel's beautiful hair, wound it a few times round her left hand, seized the scissors with her right, and snip, snap, it was cut off. Then she banished Rapunzel to a desert place, where she lived in misery, and after some time she gave birth to twins, a boy and a girl.

But in the evening, on the same day as she had cast Rapunzel out, the fairy fastened the hair she had cut off high on the catch, and when the king's son arrived:

> 'Rapunzel, Rapunzel,
> Let down your hair!'

the fairy did let down the hair. But how astonished the prince was when at the top he found not his beloved Rapunzel but the fairy. 'Do you know what?' said the angry fairy. 'Rapunzel is lost to you for ever, you villain!'

At that the king's son became utterly desperate and straight away plunged down from the tower. He escaped with his life, but he lost both his eyes. He strayed in his grief about the forest; all he ate was grass and roots; all he did was weep. Some years later he came upon the desert place where Rapunzel was living in misery with their children. Her voice seemed so familiar to him. At the same moment she recognized him too, and she flung her arms about his neck and wept. Two of her tears fell onto his eyes and they grew clear again, and he could see with them as he once used to do.

9. *The Three Ravens* (1810)

[THIS, in translation, is the rough version of 19. 'The Seven Ravens' in the manuscript the brothers sent to Brentano in 1810, which formed the basis of the tale in the first edition. See note. It is noted down in bald outline in Jacob's hand and was probably told him by the Hassenpflug family.]

There was once a mother who had three little sons who played cards while they were in church, and when the sermon was over their mother scolded them for their ungodliness and cursed them. At that they turned into three black ravens and flew away. Their little sister was troubled and wanted to look for them. She took a little seat with her for rest on her long way, and the whole time she ate nothing but apples and pears. But still she couldn't find the three ravens. However, one of them flew over her head one day and dropped a ring the little sister had once given her youngest brother. At last she reached the world's end, and went to the sun, but he was terribly hot and ate up the children. Then she journeyed to the moon, who was cruel too and said: 'I smell the flesh of a human child.' Then all the stars came with their music-stands and the moon [? slip of the pen for morning-star] gave her a chicken-leg, telling her that without this she couldn't get into the glass mountain where her brothers were. So the little sister took the chicken-bone and wrapped it safely in a little kerchief and went on until she reached the glass stronghold. And when she wanted to look for the chicken-bone, she had lost it on the way. She didn't know what to do, and in the end she cut off a little finger and opened the door. Then a dwarf came towards her, saying: 'Child, what are you looking for?' 'I'm looking for my brothers, the three ravens.' 'My masters, the ravens, are not at home.' The dwarf brought three little plates and three little goblets, and their sister ate a little from each and drank a little from each and put the little ring down next to them. Then she heard a flying in the air, and the dwarf spoke again: 'My masters, the ravens, are flying home.' The ravens asked, each one: 'Who's been eating from my plate?' 'Who's been drinking from my goblet?' But in the end they recognized their little sister by the ring, and then they were set free once more and went home.

37. *Briar-Rose* (1810)

[THIS, in translation, is the version in the manuscript sent to Brentano in 1810. It is in Jacob's hand, with a note at the end: 'by word of mouth.' It also has the added comment: 'This seems t[aken?] from Perrault's *Belle au bois dormant*.' See note. This, like 'Rapunzel', is distinguished by its greater simplicity of tone in comparison with other authored versions.]

A king and a queen had no children at all. One day the queen was taking a bath when a crawfish crawled out of the water onto land and spoke: 'You will soon have a daughter.' And that is what happened, and the king in his joy held a great feast, and in the land there were thirteen fairies, but he had only twelve golden plates, so he couldn't invite the thirteenth. The fairies bestowed on her gifts of every virtue and fair feature. Now as the festivities were coming to an end the thirteenth fairy arrived and announced: 'You did not invite me, and I proclaim that in her fifteenth year your daughter will prick her finger on a spindle and die of it.' The other fairies wanted to put this right as far as they could, and said she should only fall asleep for a hundred years.

But the king commanded that all the spindles in the entire realm should be done away with—which was carried out, and when the king's daughter was fifteen years old and her parents had gone out one day, she went walking about in the palace and at last she came to an old tower. A narrow stair led into the tower, and then she came to a little door with a yellow key in the lock; she turned it, and entered a room where an old woman was spinning her flax. And she joked with the woman, and wanted to spin too. Then she pricked herself on the spindle and at once fell into a deep sleep. As the king and his court had returned that very moment, everybody, just everybody in the palace began to sleep, right down to the flies on the walls. And around the whole palace there grew a hedge of thorns, so that nothing could be seen of it.

After a long, long time a king's son arrived in the land, and an old man told him the story, which he remembered he had heard from his grand-father, and that many had already tried to get through the thorns, but they had all remained hanging. But when this prince drew near the hedge of thorns all the thorns opened up before him, and to his eyes they seemed to be flowers, and behind him they turned back into thorns. Then, when he entered the palace, he kissed the sleeping princess and everybody woke from sleep and the two were married, and if they haven't died, they are living still.

Rumpenstünzchen (1808)

[THE first item, in translation, is the earliest, most rudimentary, version of tale 41. 'Rumpelstiltskin', which Jacob sent with five others to his friend and mentor Friedrich Karl von Savigny for his children as early as April 1808. It leaves room for the story-teller to improvise the manikin's names, but later printed versions close off these possibilities. (*Briefe der Brüder Grimm an Savigny*, ed. Wilhelm Schoof and Ingeborg Schnack (Berlin, 1953), 426–7). With very slight verbal variations, this is the form in which it was included, in Wilhelm's hand, in the manuscript sent to Brentano in 1810. The second tale is in the form as it was first printed in the first edition (I, 1812). For a fuller discussion of these variants and of Wilhelm's editorial changes, see the note to 41.]

There was once a little girl who was given a knot of flax to spin into yarn, but all the time what she would spin was gold thread, and not a strand of flax would appear. This made her very sad, and she seated herself on the roof and began to spin, and she went on spinning for three days, but all the time nothing but gold. Then a little manikin came up to her and said: 'I'll help you in your trouble, my girl. A young prince will come by. He will marry you and take you away, but you must promise me that your first child shall be mine!'

Joyfully, the little girl promised him everything, and soon afterwards a handsome young prince came riding by, who took her with him and made her his consort.

A year later she had a bonny boy, and the little manikin stepped up to her bed and demanded him from her. For her part she offered him everything instead, but he would accept nothing at all, and gave her only three days' time: if she knew his name by then she was to keep her child, but if she didn't know it she would have to give him the child.

The queen thought and thought for a long time, and though she thought hard for two days, she still hadn't found out his name, and she became deeply troubled.

At last, on the third day, she ordered her faithful maid to go into the forest where the little man had come from.

The maid went out at night, and she saw how the little manikin was riding a soup-ladle around a great fire, calling:

> 'If the queen just knew that my name is Rumpenstünzchen!
> If the queen just knew that my name is Rumpenstünzchen!'

The serving-girl hurried to give the queen this news, and the queen was delighted. At midnight the little manikin came and said: 'Lady Queen, either you know my name, or I shall take your child away with me. Then the queen named all sorts of names, but always the manikin said: 'No, that's not the right one.' At last she declared: 'Might you perhaps be called Rumpenstünzchen?' When the little manikin heard this he was horrified, and declared: 'The Devil must have told you,' and he flew out of the window on his soup-ladle.

41. *Rumpelstiltskin* (1812)

There was once a miller who was poor, but he had a beautiful daughter. And it happened that he came to speak with the king, and said to him: 'I have a daughter who has the art of turning straw into gold.' So the king sent for the miller's daughter at once, and commanded her to turn a whole roomful of straw into gold in one night, and if she couldn't, she would have to die. She was shut up in the room, and she sat and she cried, for she didn't for the life of her know how the straw was supposed to turn into gold. Then all at once a little manikin came up to her and said: 'What will you give me for turning all this into gold?' She took off her necklace and gave it to the little man, and he did what he had promised. The next morning the king found the whole room full of gold; but that only made his heart the greedier, and he had the miller's daughter put in another, even bigger room full of straw; she was to turn that into gold too. And the little man came again; she gave him the ring from her hand, and again everything was turned into gold. But the king ordered her to be shut up for a third night in a third room which was even bigger than the first two, and all full of straw, '—and if you get it done, you shall be my consort.' Then the little man came and said: 'I'll do it once more, but you must promise me the first child you have with the king.' In her distress she promised, and now, when the king saw this straw too turned into gold, he took the beautiful miller's daughter for his consort.

Soon afterwards the queen lay in childbed; then the little man stepped before the queen and demanded the promised child. For her part the queen pleaded as much as she was able, and offered the little man all her riches if he would leave her her child, only it was all in vain. At last he said: 'In three days I shall return and fetch the child, but if by then you know my name you shall keep the child.'

Then the queen thought hard for the first and second day about what kind of name the little man might actually have, but she couldn't think of it, and she grew very troubled. But on the third day the king came home from hunting and told her: 'The day before yesterday I was hunting, and as I went deep into the dark forest there was a little house, and in front of the house there was the oddest little man; he was leaping around in front of it as if he were on one leg and crying:

> "Today I'll bake, tomorrow I'll brew,
> The next I'll fetch the Lady Queen's child.
> Still, no one knows it all the same
> That Rumpelstiltskin is my name."'

When the queen heard this she became very happy; and when the dangerous little man arrived, he asked: 'Lady Queen, what is my name?'—'Is your name Thomas?'—'No.'—'Is your name Richard?'—'No.'

'Might your name be Rumpelstiltskin?'

'The Devil told you!' shrieked the little man, who ran off angrily and never, ever, came back again.

APPENDIX B

Selected Tales from the First Edition
Removed for the Second and Subsequent Editions

Playing Butchers

[BOTH tales under the one title have identifiable sources in very old popular literature, the first in Jörg Wickram's *Rollwagenbüchlin* (1555), a collection of entertaining anecdotes in prose and verse; the second in Martin Zeiler's *Miscell.* (1661). Wilhelm dropped both anecdotes for the second edition, perhaps in the light of Arnim's doubts: 'I've already heard one mother complain that the piece in which one child slaughters another is something she couldn't put into her children's hands' (Steig, 263; see Introduction, p. xxvii). Wilhelm recalled hearing the story from his mother as a boy: 'It did make me cautious and timid when I was playing' (see Introduction p. xxviii). In any case, they can scarcely be classed as *Märchen*. In style too, the first one scarcely chimes with the other tales in the collection. It is a close rendering of its immediate source in the bald anecdote retold in the issue of Heinrich von Kleist's *Berliner Abendblatt* for 13 Oct. 1810. Its apparent factuality, and the ambiguity of the child's last laugh, are very characteristic of Kleist's own prose fiction. The second, with its domino-effect of horrors, is retold almost literally from Zeiler. A 'child of sound constitution' might well react with black laughter.]

I

In a town called Franecker, situated in West Friesland, it happened that some young children, little girls and boys of five and six years old, were playing together. And they arranged that one of the little boys should be the butcher, another little boy was to be the cook, and the third little boy was to be the pig. One little girl, they said, was to be the cook's wife and another was to be the cook's help. And the cook's help was to catch the pig's blood in a little basin so that they could make sausages. As arranged, the butcher went for the little boy who was to be the pig, pulled him to the ground, and slit his throat with a little knife, and the cook's help caught his blood in her little basin. A councillor, happening to walk past, sees this dreadful sight and promptly takes the butcher with him to his superior's house, who immediately called the whole council together. They all debated the business, but with no idea what to do about it, for they saw quite well that it was done after the way that children do things. One among them, a wise old man, gave his advice that the Chief Justice should take a fine red apple in one hand and a Rhenish guilder in the other; he should call the child and offer him both hands at the same time: if the boy took the apple they should declare him absolved, but if he took the guilder he should be put to death. His advice is followed, but with a laugh the child seizes the apple and so he is declared free of all punishment.

II

A householder once slaughtered a pig. His children saw it happen, and when they went to play together that afternoon, one child said to the others: 'You shall be the piglet and I'll be the butcher.' At that, he took an open knife and plunged it into his little brother's neck. His mother, who was sitting upstairs in the parlour bathing her youngest baby in a tub, heard her child screaming and ran downstairs straight away. When she saw what had happened she drew the knife from the child's neck, and in her rage plunged it into the heart of the child who had been the butcher. Then she ran upstairs straight away to see how her baby was doing in the bathtub, but while she was below it had drowned in the bath. This filled the wife with such terror that she grew desperate and could not be comforted by her servants, but hanged herself. Her husband came in from the fields, and when he saw it all he fell into such grief that soon afterwards he died.

[*The Hand with the Knife*]

[THIS is a prose paraphrase of a Gaelic verse narrative heard in the Highlands of Scotland and done into English by Mrs Anne Grant, who published it, together with a partial rendering into English of the song itself, in her *Essays on the Superstitions of the Highlands of Scotland: to which are added Translations from the Gaelic* . . . 2 vols. (London and Edinburgh, 1811), i. 285–7. Jacob translated her prose version into German and included it in the first edition. The title is his addition. His note to her tale quotes her introduction to it: 'One of these [stories], which I have heard *sung* by children at a very early age, and which is just to them the Babes in the wood, I can never forget. The affecting simplicity of the tune, the strange wild imagery and the remarks of remote antiquity in the little narrative, give it the greatest interest to me, who delight in tracing back poetry to its infancy.' This delight was the brothers' too, but they omitted her tale from their later editions: it was too directly Scottish, not German. A 'tomhan', according to Mrs Grant, is a fairy hillock.]

A little girl had been innocently beloved by a fairy, who dwelt in a tomhan near her mother's habitation. She had three brothers, who were the favourites of her mother. She herself was treated harshly, and tasked beyond her strength. Her employment was to go every morning and cut a certain quantity of turf from dry heathy ground, for immediate fuel; and this with some uncouth and primitive implement.

As she past the hillock, which contained her lover, he regularly put out his hand with a very sharp knife, of such power, that it quickly and readily cut through all impediments. She returned chearfully and early with her load of turf; and, as she past by the hillock, she struck on it twice, and the fairy stretched out his hand through the surface, and received the knife.

The mother, however, told the brothers, that her daughter must certainly have had some aid to perform the allotted task. They watched her, saw her receive the enchanted knife, and forced it from her. They returned, struck the hillock, as she was wont to, and when the fairy put out his hand, they cut it off with his own knife. He drew in the bleeding arm, in despair, and supposing this cruelty was the result of treachery on the part of his beloved, never saw her more

Bluebeard

[THE Grimms had a cluster of *Bluebeard*-tales at their disposal for the first edition: the present, definitive, one, which they heard in the autumn of 1812 from the Hassenpflugs; and three distinctive variants: 'The Murder-Castle', which Jacob heard in early 1811 from their sister's Dutch friend, and translated; 30. 'The Robber Bridegroom', which Jacob heard from Marie Hassenpflug in time to send to Brentano in 1810; and 33. 'Fitcher's Bird', put together out of tales from Frederike Mannel and Dortchen Wild. 3. 'Our Lady's Child', too, which Wilhelm heard in 1807 from Gretchen Wild, shares the motifs of the forbidden room and the ineradicable stain, though transformed there by the Christian symbolism. But when it came to the revisions for the second edition, Wilhelm removed the first two. Certainly, there was a wealth of material, but the note of 1856 to 'Fitcher's Bird' explains more precisely why this version went: it was far too close to Perrault's 'La Barbe bleue', lacking only the figure of the heroine's sister Anne and having only the folk superstition of using straw to draw out blood as a distinctive German feature. 'Also,' the note added, 'French might have been known in the place where we heard it.' French was indeed spoken *chez* Hassenpflug. There are further differences between Perrault's version and the present one: there, for example, the endangered girl comes from a more sociable world than this home 'deep in a forest', the forest the Grimms had made their own; and an echo of 'ancient German myth' it was not. The Dutch tale was not entirely lost, but relegated to the note: it is poorer as a story but, though not German, was Germanic.]

Deep in a forest there once lived a man who had three sons and a beautiful daughter. One day a golden carriage came driving up with six horses and any number of servants. It stopped outside his house and a king descended, who asked the man to give him his daughter to be his wife. The man was glad that such good fortune should befall his daughter, and said 'yes' at once. And there was nothing about the suitor to object to either, except that his beard was quite blue, so that you had a moment's shiver of terror whenever you looked at him. At first the girl was frightened of it too, and was scared of marrying him, but in the end, at her father's urging, she consented. But because she was so frightened she first went to her brothers and took them aside, saying: 'Dear brothers, if you hear me cry out, wherever you are, leave everything and come to my aid.' This her brothers promised they would do, and kissed her. 'Farewell, sister dear. If we hear your voice we will leap onto our horses and be with you at once.' So then she got into Bluebeard's carriage and drove away with him. When she arrived at his palace everything was magnificent, and whatever the queen wished for was granted, and they would have been very happy if only she could have got used to the king's blue beard, but always when she saw it she shrank away from it inwardly. After this had gone on for some time he said: 'I have to go on a long journey. Here are the keys to the whole palace. You may unlock every door and inspect everything; only the chamber to which this little golden key belongs I forbid you to open; if you unlock that, your life is forfeit.' She took the keys and promised to obey him. And when he was gone she unlocked the doors one after the other, and she saw such riches and such splendid things that she thought they must have been gathered here from every corner of the world. The only room now left was the forbidden chamber. Its key was made of gold, so she guessed that perhaps this was the room where the most precious things of all were locked. Curiosity began to torment her, and she would rather have left all the others unseen if only she knew what was in this one. For a while she resisted, but at last her desire became so powerful that she took the key and went up to the chamber. 'Who is there to see if I open it?' she said to herself. 'I'll only take a quick look inside.' So she unlocked it, and as the door opened a stream of blood flowed towards her, and on the walls round about she saw dead women hanging, only the bones of some of them remaining. She was so terrified that she slammed the door shut straight away, but the key flew out as she did so, and fell into the blood. Quickly she picked it up and tried to wipe off the blood, but in vain, for when she wiped if off on one side it reappeared on the other. All that day she sat down and rubbed away at it, trying everything, but it was no good: the bloodstains were not to be removed. At last, that evening she covered it with hay, for it to draw out the blood overnight. Next day Bluebeard returned, and the first thing he did was to demand the keys from her. Her heart was thumping. She brought him the others, hoping he would not notice that the golden key was missing. But he counted them all, and when he had finished he asked: 'Where is the key to the secret chamber?' He looked her in the face as he did so. She turned red as blood, and replied: 'It's upstairs. I've lost it. I'll look for it tomorrow.' 'Sooner go at once, dear wife; I shall need it this very day.' 'Oh, I confess, I've lost it in the hay. I'll have to look for it first.' 'You haven't lost it,' said Bluebeard in anger. 'You hid it in the hay to draw out the bloodstains, for you disobeyed my command and have been in the chamber. But now you shall go in, even if you do not want to.' So she had to fetch the key, which was still covered in blood. 'Now prepare yourself for death. You shall die this very day,' said Bluebeard, leading her into the hallway. 'Let me just say my prayers before I die,' she said. 'Go then, but hurry, for I have no more time to wait.' Then she ran up the stairs and called as loud as she could from the window: 'Brothers! My dear brothers! Come and help me!' The brothers were sitting in the forest over cool wine when the youngest spoke: 'I have a sense that I heard our sister's voice. Come on, we must hasten to her aid!' So they leapt onto their horses and rode as if they were the winds of the storm, while their sister was on her knees, in terror. Then Bluebeard called from below: 'Well, are you finished?' And as he did, she heard him whetting his knife on the bottom step. She looked out, but all she saw was a cloud of dust approaching from afar, as if a herd of cattle were drawing near. Then she cried out once more: 'Brothers! My dear brothers! Come and help me!' And her fear grew greater and greater. Meanwhile, Bluebeard called: 'If you don't come down soon, I'll come and fetch you. My knife is sharpened!' So she looked out again and she saw her three brothers riding across the fields as if they were flying like the birds in the air. Then for the third time, in the deepest distress, she cried with all her might: 'Brothers, my dear brothers! Come and help me!' And the youngest was already so close that she heard his voice. 'Be comforted dear sister, just one moment more and we shall be with you!' But Bluebeard called: 'That's enough praying. I'll wait no longer. If you don't come down, I'll fetch you.' 'Oh, just let me pray a moment for my three dear brothers.'

But he did not listen. He came striding up the stairs and dragged her down. And he had just seized her by the hair, and was about to plunge his knife into her heart, when the three brothers beat on the house door, forced their way in, and tore her from his hands. Then they drew their swords and struck him down. After that he was hung up in the chamber of blood with the women he had killed. But the brothers took their dearest sister back home with them, and all Bluebeard's riches were hers.

APPENDIX C

Circular Letter Concerning the Collection of Folk Poesy
Jacob Grimm (Vienna 1815)

[THIS could be regarded as the first attempt at a widespread co-operative inquiry into the materials of folklore, though it was not strictly the first, and in the event was scarcely widespread: Jacob and Brentano had drafted an appeal to set up a journal, *The Patriotic German Collector*, back in 1811, but had taken it no further, and the present letter appears to have reached only a few hundred recipients. But in announcing the existence of the (unnamed) society, Jacob's circular makes its aims and objects clear. The motives for setting it up emerge throughout: the conservative wish to preserve; the prejudice against urbanization; the democratic interest in the songs and customs of the common people—he is in search of more than just tales to augment the brothers' one volume of them so far, but of a whole range of anthropological material; the characteristic—and probably mistaken—wish to avoid publicity; the scholarly ambition to contribute to the self-understanding of 'our fatherland' by way of understanding its history, its poetry, and its language. Jacob is thinking in terms of long time and ancient origins, but also of a future task of nation-making. The time and the place seemed propitious. After Napoleon's defeat the victorious allies gathered in Vienna in early 1815 to establish a new European political settlement—in the event a highly reactionary one, which restored lost absolutist powers to the princes. The delegations included missions from all the German states: large ones like Prussia and Hanover, small ones like Hesse. As secretary to the Hessian delegation, Jacob found himself among representatives from every region of 'our fatherland', with a unique opportunity to make his rescue-operation more widely shared, forming a society ('we') in whose name he wrote. Brentano had already given him an introduction to a group of like-minded Viennese amateurs. How active the society turned out to be is difficult to ascertain; after eighteen months Jacob had only sent out about 360 letters, but among the recipients were the Haxthausens, Sir Walter Scott, and the Serb collector, grammarian, and patriot Vuk Karadžić. Later editions of the *Tales* are certainly the richer for contributions from Switzerland, German Bohemia, Alsace, Swabia, and Bavaria, a number of them in dialect, as welcomed here—though Wilhelm tended later to revise into Standard German. Among the present selection, a Viennese acquaintance, the bookseller H. Eckstein, contributed variants to 65. 'Iron John' and 54. 'The Young Giant'. As to the method of transcription, Jacob recommends 'the greatest precision and detail'; 'in their own authentic words', and a record of 'locality, region and time'. This is more rigorous than the brothers' own practice in publishing their *Tales* became, even before 1815; certainly Wilhelm's treatment of them after 1815 was much more free, and scarcely 'without decoration or addition'. But this is the circular of a scholar.]

Esteemed Sir,

A society has been founded, to extend throughout the whole of Germany, with the aim of rescuing and collecting everything still extant in the way of song and story amongst the common country-people of Germany. Our fatherland is provided in every quarter with this wealth, which has been passed on to us by our venerable forefathers, and which, despite all the mockery and scorn cast upon it, lives on in secret, unconscious of its own beauty, and bearing its own imperishable ground within itself. Without more precise research into this field, neither our poetry, nor our history, nor our language can be seriously understood in terms of its true and ancient origins. So with this purpose in mind we have made it our concern to track down the following items and record them faithfully:

(1). FOLKSONGS AND RHYMES, sung on different seasonal occasions, at festivals, in spinning-rooms, at dances, and in the course of various kinds of rural labour; first of all, those with narrative content, i.e. in which an event occurs; where possible with their actual words, melodies, and verse-forms.

(2). LOCAL LEGENDS (*Sagen*) not in verse, most especially both the various NURSES' TALES AND CHILDREN'S TALES (*Ammen- und Kinder-mährchen*) of giants, dwarves, monsters, kings' sons and daughters spell-bound and set free, devils, treasures, and wishing-objects, as well as local legends told and understood as explanations of certain specific sites (as mountains, rivers, lakes, marshes, castle ruins, towers, rocks, and all the monuments of ancient times). ANIMAL FABLES in particular are to be noted, in which mostly fox and wolf, cockerel, dog, cat, frog, mouse, raven, sparrow, etc. occur.

(3). Comic tales and playlets of tricksters' pranks; puppet-plays of the old style, with buffoon (*Hanswurst*) and Devil.

(4). Popular festivals, practices, customs, and games; ceremonies for births, weddings, and funerals; old legal traditions, distinctive dues and exemptions, land acquisition, adjustment of borders, etc.

(5). Superstitions about spirits, ghosts, witches, good and bad omens, apparitions and dreams.

(6). Proverbs, striking turns of speech; metaphors, word combinations.—

Above all, it is important that these items should be gathered faithfully and truly, without decoration or addition and with the greatest precision and detail, from the mouths of the story-tellers, where practicable in and with their own authentic words; and anything possibly obtained in the living local dialect would for that reason be doubly valuable, although on the other hand even incomplete fragments are not to be scorned. For every variant, repetition, or revision of one and the same legend may become important, and one should by no means be misled into rejecting a story by the deceptive view that something like it has already been collected and recorded; just as, on the other hand, much that appears modern is often only modernized, and its inviolable ground still lies beneath it. Closer familiarity with the content of this folk poesy will gradually teach us to pass a less arrogant judgement on its supposedly naive, coarse, or even vulgar characteristics. In general, however, the following may also be noted: that although in fact there is not a spot entirely bereft and bare of such poesy, it is nevertheless the provincial towns more than the great cities, the villages more than the towns, and among the villages mostly the quiet, isolated hamlets of forest and mountain that are blessed with this gift. Equally, it is more strongly attached to certain occupations, as practised by shepherds, fishermen, miners, and it is these—as well as old folk, women, and children generally, who have received it fresh into their memory—who are to be preferred for questioning.

In the firm conviction, most esteemed Sir, that that you will be moved by the usefulness and urgency of our object—which, given the increasingly damaging decline and erosion of folk customs nowadays, may no longer be delayed without great loss—to offer our undertaking a helping hand, and in the knowledge that you live in a locality enabling you to investigate the region of _____ in accordance with these aims, you have been designated a member of this society. The society wishes to be inconspicuous as it collects material and furthers its work, but it does not wish to hear public talk of itself and its worthy project in the daily press, for it also takes the view that it is only in reticence, in avoidance of vain sensation, and in pure delight in the good, that the society's work may strike root and be properly grounded. It is also in accordance with this view that no participant is obliged to send in his contribution within a certain time, but rather may each do what, when, where and as he can; those who have little leisure at home may perhaps find the occasion when on their travels.

Finally, for contributions to be kept in good order, you are requested to enter each item on a single sheet of paper, also noting on it locality, region, and time where and when it was collected, and, as well as your own name, in case it is needed, that of the story-teller too.

In the name of and on behalf of the Society,

P. S. In addition we would expressly request you to make a point of looking out for ancient German books and manuscripts in the archives and monasteries of your region, and to inform us through the undersigned of their location.

APPENDIX D

Wilhelm Grimm's Last Reflections on the *Märchen*

(from 'Literature [on the Subject]', 1856)

[THE interest in folk-tales which had been set off by the Grimms' first volume had by the end of their lives grown and spread internationally, so that any survey of the literature on the subject could no longer be limited to the Grimm's predecessors such as Straparola and Basile, or Sir Walter Scott, but had to take account of the collections made by their contemporaries, imitators, and successors near and far. So the third volume of notes the brothers published concluded with a huge *catalogue raisonné* by Wilhelm of the folk-tales that had been published internationally, from Serbian to Swahili (see Note on the Text). He made his final reflections on the *Märchen* in the closing pages of this rather unwieldy bibliographical essay. Extracts only are translated, beginning with the problem which had become more pressing as known analogues to Wilhelm's beloved German tales became more numerous and widespread: how to account for them? Rather than regarding them as deriving from one single source-tale, he favours the theory that they were generated separately in each culture, but out of the same basic situations common to them all. As Angela Carter queried: 'Is there a definitive recipe for potato soup?'[1] It is curious, though, that the example he gives, of the referee who defrauds the contestants of an inheritance,[2] is not quite as 'simple and natural' as 'the useful objects of field, kitchen, and home', let alone potato soup. He goes on to acknowledge the possibility of the transmission of tales from one culture to another; but prefers to see the question still shrouded in mystery. As for the likely geographical limits for such affinities, he relates them to the vast area covered by the languages of Indo-European origin, but is open-minded enough to be ready to extend this if new knowledge of tales from further afield were to emerge. His German tales remain his focus and his touchstone, but the degree to which his range has expanded since the brothers' pioneering days of collecting in Kassel can be seen in his broad-brush historical survey of the relations between culture and poetry: myth and magic recede as morality and a sense of history advance, and survive only in his beloved

---

[1] Angela Carter (ed.), *The Virago Book of Fairy Tales* (London, 1991), p. x.

[2] In the present selection, it is represented by an episode in 55. 'The King of the Golden Mountain'.

folk-tales, with their traces of ancient beliefs, scattered fragments of a precious stone overgrown by grass and flowers. As in the 1819 Preface, which he recalls, his argument is still carried by metaphor. The conservative ideal of secluded and ordered peasant society expressed there persists, even to the point of still citing the peasantry as his best source—by now he had probably convinced himself that they had been. By 1850 that ideal was even more endangered, his love of it made even more wistful by his conjuring up of the grinding wheels of increasing industrialization. The last reflective pages of the essay are a mathom-house of examples and instances from early texts, but they are so loving and so copious that, although they are intended to illustrate his argument, they frequently obscure it. I have taken the liberty of omitting a number of them.]

I may be permitted to close this survey with a few general observations.

The correspondence between tales that are widely separated by time and distance no less than between the tales of closely neighbouring peoples depends partly on their fundamental idea and their representation of particular characters, and partly on the distinctive plotting and resolution of events in them. But there are situations which are so simple and natural that they recur again and again everywhere, just as there are thoughts that come to us almost of themselves; hence it is possible for the same or very similar tales to be generated in different countries independently of one another. They are comparable to those individual words produced by quite unrelated languages in imitation of natural sounds: they vary only slightly from one another, or are even quite identical. We meet tales of this kind where it is possible to regard the correspondence as accidental, but in most cases the fundamental idea they have in common will have taken on a particular, often unexpected, indeed obstinately persistent form which excludes the assumption that the affinity is merely superficial. I will give a few examples. . . . It goes without saying that in difficult situations an arbitrator should be called on, but that everywhere it should be just *three* who are in dispute, and beings in possession of higher powers at that; that it should be an inheritance which needs to be shared out; and that it should consist of three marvellous objects; and that in the end the figure called on to be the arbitrator tricks them out of their possessions (a human has to take advantage of the rare opportunity if he wants to rob the dwarves or kobolds of their supernatural treasures)—all this presupposes correlations in the tradition. What such tales have in common is like a well: its depths are unknown, but each may draw from it according to his need.

I do not deny the possibility, nor in certain cases the probability, that a tale might pass from one people to another, and then take firm root in the foreign soil: after all, the Lay of Siegfried[3] entered the high north and made a home for itself there. But, with some individual exceptions, this does not explain the vast range and wide distribution of material held in common: do not the same tales surface in the furthermost places, like a spring of water breaking through in far-distant sites? Like domestic animals, like corn and the useful objects of field, kitchen, and home, like weapons, altogether like the things without which life in human society would not be possible, legends and tales too, and the moistening dew of poesy, appear as far as our eyes can see in this striking and at the same time independent correspondence. And they are likewise just as necessary to existence, for it is only where greed for money and the grinding wheels of machinery deafen every other thought that people imagine they could do without them. Where secure traditional order and morality still hold sway, where the connection of human feelings to the natural world about us is still felt and the past is not torn asunder from the present, there these tales still persist. The best ones I have heard are from country-people, and I know this book is read by them with the greatest enjoyment, literally read to shreds; even the German settlers in Pennsylvania, long ago estranged from their fatherland, have still been most receptive to it. Can we conceive of a legend arriving all of a sudden, rather like the influx of a nomadic people, pouring into one uninhabited land after another, and populating them? How can we explain it, when a story in an isolated mountain village in Hesse corresponds in its fundamentals to an Indian or a Greek or a Serb tale?

I have written before, in the Preface to the first volume of the second edition [see pp. 3–10], on the common aspects of certain sharply characterized figures who are manifest everywhere, and I want to come back to this. The simpleton, awkward in everything that requires experience, wit, and adaptability, is at first rebuffed, forced to do menial work and endure mockery; he is the object of scorn whose place is among the ashes in the hearth and who has his bed under the stairs. According to this pattern . . . the British Parzifal,[4] who has a touch of the simpleton, is called the

---

[3] A number of tales from the legends of the Nibelungs and the hero Sigurd are found in the thirteenth-century Old Icelandic *Poetic Edda*, which are thought to derive from Germanic sources. There the figure has the name of Siegfried (see notes 8 and 10). The brothers edited parts of the *Edda*, with translation and commentary (1815).

[4] Wilhelm quotes Wolfram von Eschenbach's characterization of the young hero of his courtly epic *Parzifal* (1200–20), whose journey in quest of the Holy Grail takes him by way of the court of King Arthur and the matter of Britain—hence the adjective 'British'. Wolfram's source was the French Arthurian epic *Perceval* (before 1190) of Chrétien de Troyes, and the debate is still open as to how much in the first instance the story of Peredur in the Welsh *Mabinogion* owes to Norman-French courtly sources and how much to Welsh folk-tales.

tumbe klâre [the naive, far-seeing one]—though of course a nobler strength and joyousness shine through in the young hero. In these tales the figure is usually the youngest of three brothers, proudly and arrogantly rejected by the other two. But when it comes to action, he rises to it at once, and he is the only one able to accomplish the task which will determine who will be foremost among them, for a higher power has supported him and ensured that he will be victorious. If he is betrayed and loses his life, then the bleached bone washed up on the shore will announce the wicked deed long afterwards, so that it does not go unpunished.

Giants are coarse and clumsy, dwarves are clever and cunning. The characteristics of these latter are heightened even further in the figure of Little Thumb and his ilk, who all possess the mysterious power attributed to the finger that gives him his name. Shrewd and guileful, he uses his wiles, teasing and fooling everyone. He is able to triumph over the accidents that befall him because of his tiny size. Fortune favours him and makes his self-congratulatory boasts come to pass. In the form of an agile little tailor he frightens giants, kills monsters, and is able to solve the hardest riddles . . .

[To reinforce Wilhelm's remarks on the elements common to folk-tales, he follows them up with five paragraphs of descriptive commentary, more affectionate than analytical, on the many manifestations of the comic figure who moves between the poles of simpleton and trickster, not only in the brothers' collection but also internationally. Too many of his examples have not been translated in the present selection for them to make useful illustrations here.]

What all tales have in common are the remnants of some belief, reaching back to the most ancient times, which is manifested in the way they conceive things supernatural metaphorically as images [*in bildlicher Auffassung übersinnlicher Dinge*]. This mythical quality is like the little specks of a precious stone shattered and strewn on ground overgrown by grass and flowers, discernible only to a keen eye. Their meaning has long ago been lost, but it is still felt, giving the tale its substance, while at the same time satisfying our natural pleasure in the marvellous. They are never merely the shimmering colours of insubstantial fantasy. Myth broadens out more widely the further back we go—indeed, it seems to make up the sole content of the most ancient poetry. Borne by the grandeur of its subject-matter, and not concerned with corresponding to reality when it portrays the mysterious and terrible powers of nature, this poetry, as we see, does not spurn even the far-fetched, the abominable, or the terrible. Such poetry becomes gentler only when it comes to include the observation of simple ways in the lives of shepherds, hunters, and farmers, and the influence of finer manners. In Finnish and North American legends we are astonished to see excessive and monstrous elements right next to descriptions of the simplest, almost idyllic, ways of life. They fill the Tibetan sagas in an often unlovely manner, at times naked and raw, although even here the representation of natural conditions or expressions of true feeling are not entirely lacking. To the degree to which humane and gentler morals and manners develop and poetry increases in sensuous richness, myth retreats and the soft airs of distance begin to clothe it, weakening the clarity of outline, but increasing the charm of the poetry, rather as in the fine arts there is a transition from sharply drawn, gaunt, even ugly but significant figures to external beauty of form. If the imagination of a nation is filled with the glory of a heroic age, and if hearts are stirred by great deeds, the result is a fresh transformation of the ancient legend [*Sage*]. Homer has the gods keep company with men, whose form they take, and heroes are raised almost to their level. In the *Mahabharata*,[5] Nahusha, a human, is set as king to rule the gods as well as the world, and the equal position of the two in the wars of the Kauravas and the Pandavas is even stronger than in the *Iliad*. Damayanti is unable to distinguish Nala from the heavenly beings who make their appearance at the wooing with him. Ganga bears King Prativa eight children before he learns that she is a goddess . . . Single combat, which by custom decided a conflict and was subject to precise rules, develops into battle between the peoples, where everyone shares the renown of victory or the destruction of a heroic race. The epic aims for historical truth, measure and order in all things, as it does for an inner nobility in attitude of mind: the mythical and marvellous, where it still survives, has to take on the appearance of being historical and be taken to be true. The *Nibelungenlied*[6] can tolerate very little of it: the swan maidens can be seen only in the background, and even Siegfried's horned skin, which makes him invulnerable, was alien to the

---

[5] The vast Sanskrit epic, 'the great tale of the descendants of the prince Bharata'; its compilation is attributed to the sage Vyasa ('the arranger') *c.*400 AD. The action is held together by the wars of the two rival families, whom Wilhelm, using the Germanic tribal form, calls the *Kuruingen* and the *Panduingen*.

[6] Middle High German heroic epic (*c.*1200). It falls into two parts: the first recounts the deeds and death of the hero Siegfried; the second the struggle between the Burgundians (the Nibelungs of the title) and Etzel (the historical Attila) at the instigation of Kriemhild, once Siegfried's wife. Though it does contain older mythological residues (e.g. Siegfried's cap of invisibility), these are not developed in the narrative; rather, this is located geographically in named and factual places: the Burgundian court at Worms, Vienna, the Spessart, etc., and acts as a pseudo-historical model of values appropriate to its own time.

older version in the *Edda*. Even his acquisition of the cloak of invisibility instead of assuming another shape, which gods have the power to do, may have first been imported from folk-tales. In the *Dietrichsaga*[7] and in the older *Gudrunsaga*[8] it has disappeared, leaving only slight traces. The folk-tale certainly continued to exist without interruption at the side of the heroic epic—in its present form or in one very close to it, only less fragmentary and disrupted . . . [The paragraph continues by enumerating examples, mainly from medieval Latin and Middle High German sources.]

It will be asked where the outer limits of the material common to such folk-tales lie, and how does the extent of their affinities increase or diminish? The boundary is marked by the great tribal grouping which as a rule we call Indo-Germanic, and the affinities are drawn in smaller and smaller circles around the places of Germanic settlement, in much the same proportion as we discover between the common and the distinguishing features in the languages of the particular peoples belonging to the larger grouping. If we find some stories among the Arabs that are related to German tales, it can be explained by the derivation of *The Arabian Nights*, where they occur, from Indian sources, as Schlegel[9] has rightly maintained. However certainly this limit applies for the present, if further sources appear, it may perhaps become necessary to extend it, for we are astonished to discover a connection to German tales in the stories that have become known to us from the negroes in Borneo and the nomadic people of Bechuana in South Africa, while on the other hand they are separated by their characteristic way of thinking. By contrast, I have found no correspondence in the North American tales, at least not any which are quite so precise and detailed. Tibetan tales show some contact, as do those from Finland; a clear relationship is manifest in the stories of

---

[7] Diedrich, the legendary name given to the historical Theodoric, occurs in a number of lesser Middle High German epics, but his story is told most fully in the Norwegian *Thidrekssaga* (*c.*1250).

[8] Gudrun is the name of Sigurd's wife in the *Poetic Edda*. Wilhelm may be referring to this figure and her part in the cluster of Siegfried legends, or to the Middle High German heroic epic *Kudrun* (*c.*1220–50), which has only a tangential connection to them.

[9] Friedrich Schlegel (1772–1829), Romantic critic and scholar, with a far wider interest in world literature than the Grimms' concentration on the relics of ancient Germanic poetry. Wilhelm's reference here is probably to Schlegel's comparative essay on Sanskrit: *Über Sprache und Weisheit der Inder* (1808). Schlegel had met Jacob when they were both in diplomatic attendance at the Congress of Vienna (1815), and had shown an interest in the brothers' antiquarian collecting. It was his brother, August Wilhelm Schlegel (1767–1845), who had written a sharp critique in the *Heidelberger Jahrbücher* (1815) of the Grimm's small antiquarian periodical *Altdeutsche Wälder* (1813–16), which set Jacob on the road to scholarly philology (see Introduction, p. xxx).

India and Persia, decidedly in Slav tales: one Croatian story even tells of God and St. Peter walking the earth . . . which is otherwise only known to the Germans. It is closest in tales from the Romance lands: the associations that have linked both peoples at all times, and the intermixing that took place long ago are sufficient to explain these great correspondences. After all, that vast beast epic, German in origin, has been preserved only in French poems, which inherited it from the Franks.[10] Not only the northern and southern regions of our fatherland possess the German tales, but they are fully shared by the closely related people of the Netherlands, the English, and the Scandinavians. It makes no difference if here or there a greater or smaller number have died out, just as on high mountains or low marshes not all the plants will flourish, nor yet if the tale's external form has been influenced by the varying nature of the land and the customs and way of life founded upon it.

It is gratifying that the Germans still cherish the beast-tale in its original spirit, I mean in taking innocent pleasure in the poesy, which has no other purpose than to take delight in the story told, and takes no thought of reading into it any lesson other than the one that emerges freely out of the poetry . . .

Erdmannsdorf in Silesia
30 September 1850
Berlin, 16 January 1856

[10] Wilhelm is probably referring to the widespread popular medieval cycle of stories about Jacob's favourite, Reynard the Fox. They probably originated in the eleventh century in the Lorraine region, in the borderland between Flanders and Germany, first as mock-heroic epic in Latin, but they soon spread to the various vernaculars. It is no longer strictly correct to say that they were preserved *only* in French poems, though certainly by far the most extensive is the French *Roman de Renart*; there is a version by Heinrich der Glîchenaere of Alsace, *Reinhart Fuchs*, from *c.*1180 in Middle High German, possibly deriving from a common source, and a Flemish poem, *Von den Vos Reinaerde*, of *c.*1250, as well as later printed versions in Dutch (1497) and Low German (1498), and countless ancillary tales. Jacob's study of 1834 was only a beginning. However, Wilhelm takes the opportunity for veiled criticism of moralizing fables such as La Fontaine's.

NOTES

THESE notes give provenance, written or oral, where it is known, the edition in which the Grimms first published a tale, selected analogues, and, in cases of interest, a selective account of Wilhelm's later revisions; my debt to Heinz Rölleke's work in these respects is great, apparent, and acknowledged with gratitude. In certain instances, especially where a tale has been the subject of strong interpretation, I have also made an extended critical comment. The notes are through-numbered. The square-bracketed number after the title indicates the number given it by the Grimms in their own collection and used conventionally in Grimm scholarship.

Preface to the second edition (1819)

'The Preface by Wilhelm, a few additions from Jacob', Wilhelm noted on the flyleaf of his copy of the first edition (I, 1812). That Preface was already substantial, and was extended by another to Vol. II (1815), in which Wilhelm described their new acquaintance Frau Viehmann, her manner of story-telling, and their method of transcribing. Just as he rewrote the stories for the second edition (1819), so he rewrote the Prefaces, conflating the two, shifting material on mythological affinities to the separate volume of notes (Vol. III, 1822), dealing with Arnim's criticism of the first edition more fully (see Intro-duction, pp. xxiv–xxix), so that as well as continuing to present their labour of love as an anthropological rescue-operation, a contribution to the history of poesy, and as poetically valuable in itself, he laid greater stress on its pedagogic purpose. But there are contradictions between the claims of this Preface and the brothers' actual practice. His brave faith in the resilience of 'children of a sound constitution' does not prevent him from discreet bowdlerizing. In the light of his revisions of the plain tales the brothers had first been told, he changed his account of their method of reproduction, but in this respect assumes an authenticity which is in fact more problematic than he allows, exposing the dilemma inherent in transforming oral material into literary. He describes how he has combined versions, preferring the 'better' version over the 'corrupt', trusting his tact and experience in choosing. But remaining true to the 'story told, itself' entailed blindness to the alterations he did make 'out of his own resources', particularly in this edition. He also raises the key question thrown up by the existence of so many widespread variants: are they historically transmitted, deriving from a single source, or are they archetypal, generated universally? He leaves the question open, but clearly prefers the latter, for it allows him access to mythological meaning. He ends by contrast-ing the brothers' simple narrative style (which was, in fact, in that very edition ceasing to be quite so simple) with the—unnamed—Brentano's brilliant, con-sciously composed, and less authentic, art-*Märchen*. Wilhelm's homespun dislike of urban sophistication, and his suspicion of social change—those 'military roads' are symptomatic—are apparent. So is his local pride in Hesse, and the intention, by removing tales of foreign origin, of making this above all a German book. This Preface, often more poetically evocative than argued, became a kind of manifesto for the collection, its aims, purposes, and methods; and, although all the subsequent editions were given their own short prefaces, this one was also reprinted each time. It staked the brothers' claim.

1. *The Frog King, or Iron Henry* [1]

This has always had pride of place as the first tale of the collection, partly because the tale of Iron Henry, mentioned by Georg Rollenhagen in his *Froschmeuseler* (*The Frog-Mousers*, 1595), is one of the oldest references to a tale in the collection being handed down by word of mouth. (For Rollenhagen, see note to 21. *The Bremen Town Band*.) The two tales seem to be rather arbitrarily yoked together. The many elaborations they underwent through the various editions make it the manifesto-*Märchen* of the final collection. Two earlier versions of the opening paragraph (see Appendix A) illustrate the process. The first, 'The King's Daughter and the Enchanted Prince', was taken down in bald outline by Wilhelm from a story possibly told by a member of the Wild family ('from Hesse') and has survived in the manuscript sent to Brentano in 1810. A comparison with the relatively simple version in the first edition of 1812 already shows the Grimms' characteristic procedure at work: rhythmically repeating words and phrases, filling out the dialogue, lingering on the king's daughter's pleasure in her toy—which is a stronger invitation to read the tale as one of her development from child at the beginning to young woman. The conventional introductory formula of 'There was once . . .' is introduced; repetition—'rolled and rolled'—which became a frequent trick of Wilhelm's *Märchen*-style, appears here for the first time. The second edition makes the first move towards propriety. At the frog's transformation, all mention of the bed is removed, and 'he [the frog-king] was now, for so her father willed it, her dear companion'; the third edition of 1837 completes it '. . . and husband.' The third edition also introduced the hyperbole describing the princess's beauty, the expansion of the dialogue, and almost every motif in the opening passage, all in fact quite uncharacteristic of the folk-tale. The introductory formula is replaced by an opening line that strikes the keynote for the entire collection: 'In the old days, when wishing still helped . . .'. This may have been a late recollection of a phrase of Frau Viehmann's, by 1837 long dead, for it also introduces one of her tales, 'The Iron Stove' [127]. The frog's verse, 'King's daughter, youngest daughter . . .', was already present in vol. III of *Des Knaben Wunderhorn* (1808), *Kinderlieder*, to which the brothers had contributed.

The Grimms' note refers to two other tales which also start with a promise made to a frog in return for his help, who returns to claim his reward. They quote from John Leyden's preliminary 'Dissertation' to his edition (Edinburgh, 1801, p. 234) of *The Complaynt of Scotland* (1548), where he outlines the old tale of the 'well at the warldis end':

at midnight the frog lover appears at the door and demands entrance according to promise, to the great consternation of the lady and her nurse.

'Open the door, my hinny, my hart.
Open the door, mine ain wee thing;
And mind the words that you and I spak
Down in the meadow, at the well-spring.'

The frog is admitted and addresses her

'Take me up on your knee, my dearie,
Take me up on your knee, my dearie
And mind the words that you and I spak
At the cauld well sae weary.'

The frog is finally disenchanted and appears as a prince in his original form.

2. *Cat and Mouse As Partners* [2]

A finely characterized beast fable, with black humour and without a happy end. It was one of the first tales Wilhelm took down in 1808 from Gretchen Wild, and among those sent to Brentano in 1810. He overhauled it completely for the third edition of 1837, transforming a laconic anecdote into a short story conveyed by means of dialogue with full characterization of the figures and their relationship. The presence of an oral story-teller is cunningly suggested by the worldly moral uttered in the very last line—but that was not added until the fourth edition of 1840. The note of 1856 refers to several variants with casts of different animals, domesticated and wild: a cock and a hen, from Lower Pomerania; a bear and a fox, from Norway; a cat and a hen, from Africa. The range indicates how far beyond the nationalist aims of the brothers' early collecting his interest had moved. Stimulated by their work, scholars and amateurs of other nations had gone in pursuit of their own folk-songs and tales, not only nourishing their own nationalist movements with them but, by providing a wealth of comparative material, also internationalizing the interest. Folklore as a study was new in 1812; by 1856 it was established and flourishing.

3. *Our Lady's Child* [3]

This may be the very first story the brothers took down from Gretchen Wild in 1807. It is to be found plain and unadorned among the tales Jacob sent to Savigny in 1808 and in the manuscript sent to Brentano, which also contains Frederike Mannel's variant, 'The Silent Girl', in her handwriting. The narrative line follows the Christian pattern of sin, confession, and absolution. The opening situation, in which the starving parents dispose of their child—a wishful dream indeed—is shared with 'Hansel and Gretel', and the motif of the forbidden door with 'Fitcher's Bird' and above all, with 'Bluebeard' (see Appendix B). It also shares with these two the motif of the ineradicable stain, there blood, here gold—and stronger editorial dramatization of the girl's curiosity in later editions than in the first. The tale was already elaborated for the first edition in ways characteristic of Wilhelm's Romantic rewriting; with all that gold and glory, it is even touched by aesthetic Catholicizing. Narrative is turned into dialogue; the motif of the gold finger is added; so are the little angels, including their rebuke to the girl's curiosity; the detailing of the girl's life as part of nature in the forest is filled out; and the role of the people and counsellors hostile to the silent queen is emphasized, dramatically intensifying the conflict in the king's feelings as well as her isolation: transgressing Eve has been cast out of Paradise; the episode where Our Lady shows the queen her children playing ball with the globe appears to be invented; the angels' warnings of sin at the beginning and the moral spelt out by Our Lady at the end are characteristic additions.

4. *The Tale of the Boy Who Set Out To Learn Fear* [4]

At least four variants went into the making of this story, and in addition Wilhelm retells two more in his note. It appeared in the first edition as 'A Good Game of Bowls and Cards', and consisted only of the triple episodes of the cats, the game of bowls, and the magic bed; the important mythical element of learning fear was only introduced in the extensive rewriting for the second edition, which drew on the other variants. Though in its coarse way it followed the contemporary Romantic taste for ghouls and ghosts, it is essentially a comedy on two levels: on one, the boy remains cheerfully and stupidly proof against three times three horrors; on another, like Wagner's equally sanguine Siegfried, he does learn fear—from his bride; at least, his flesh learns to creep, though as a figure in a *Märchen*, he does not learn fear within himself. But it is characteristic of the *Märchen* genre that inward experience—fear, and with it becoming adult—is represented by the wholly external episode of the shudder-making bucket of fishes. Wagner himself saw the resemblance to his Siegfried: 'Imagine my shock when I suddenly discovered that the lad on question is none other than—young Siegfried who wins the hoard and awakens Brünnhilde!—The matter is now resolved. Next month I shall do the text for *Young Siegfried*' (to Uhlig 10 May 1851, in Stewart Spencer and Barry Millington (eds.), *Selected Letters of Richard Wagner* (London and Melbourne: Dent, 1987), 223).

The motif of the restless bed is as old as the twelfth-century courtly epic, Wolfram von Eschenbach's *Parzifal*, and his source in Chrétian de Troyes, when Gâwân spends a sleepless night in one. Is this an instance of courtly culture descending to the popular level?

5. *The Wolf and the Seven Little Goats* [5]

This was among the manuscript tales sent to Brentano in 1810. Giving its source as 'from the Main region', the note of 1856 draws attention to the cluster of tales focusing on Reynard the Fox, and also to 'The Seven Little Goats', a tale in August Stöber's recent compilation of folk sayings, songs, and stories from Alsace, *Elsässisches Volksbüchlein* (Strasburg, 1842), which Wilhelm drew on for substantial revisions in the fifth edition of 1843.

6. *Faithful John* [6]

First appearing in the second edition of 1819, and noted as 'from Zwehrn', this is most likely one of Frau Viehmann's stories. Full and eventful, it includes many aspects typical of the *Märchen*: the faithful servant and the trials of his loyalty; the forbidden room; the prophetic ravens; above all, the redress at the end, when all ills are made good. The theme of child-sacrifice is very ancient, but the parents' agreement to make it and the laws of the *Märchen* genre ensure that the children will come back to life and all shall be well. There may be a breath of the *Arabian Nights* in the richly laden sea journey and the merchant disguise. Bolte (*Anmerkungen*) notes how widespread its analogues are, with many oriental, Indian, and medieval versions.

7. *The Good Bargain* [7]

From the note 'from the Paderborn region', the brothers probably heard this tale from the Haxthausens. It is scarcely a *Märchen*, but crude rustic comedy, a sequence of five episodes in which the frogs and the dogs make a fool of the yokel in the first two, provoking the king's daughter to laughter, while in the last three the yokel tricks the sentry once and the Jew twice, to the amusement of the king. The final trick played on the Jew takes the anti-Semitic stereotype completely for granted. Bolte identifies numerous versions of this particular episode, all with a Jew as victim/villain: Greek, Slovak, Kaschubian, Serb, and Turkish.

It was first published in the second edition of 1819, and Wilhelm also included it in his selection for children, the 'Little Edition' of 1825. This casts some light on the taken-for-granted prejudices of the time—and on what Wilhelm considered fit for 'children of a sound constitution' and proper in 'a book to bring up children on'. See also 59. 'The Jew in the Thorn Bush', and note.

For the motif of the princess who could not laugh, see also 43. 'The Golden Goose'.

8. *The Twelve Brothers* [9]

This was already among the manuscript tales sent to Brentano in 1810, though the notes give 'Zwehrn' as its place of origin. It seems that the brothers did not make the direct acquaintance of Frau Viehmann from that village until 1813. Rölleke (*KHM* (1982) III. 445) suggests the intermediaries may have been the daughters of the French pastor in Kassel, Charles Ramus, who first introduced her to them. The tale was much elaborated for the second edition of 1819, largely into the now-familiar version, which was made clearer in plot and motivation: the king's hostile intentions towards his sons were spelt out and the importance of the twelve shirts strengthened; the greater role given to the old woman clarified the dire effect of picking the lilies; the joyful recognition, the pretty touch of the star on the princess's brow, the sister's cosy housekeeping with Benjamin (now given his biblical name), added charm, and the greater part played by the hostile mother-in-law brought drama. The tale contains the classic folk elements of unnatural father, the test, metamorphosis into animal, and hostile older woman. The basic theme, the salvation by their sister of brothers turned into beasts, is also to be found in 19. 'The Seven Ravens' and 36. 'The Six Swans'. Wilhelm's fine-tuning of language can be illustrated in brief by the phrase he uses to dramatize the very end of the queen's seven years of trial as she is about to be burnt at the stake: the 'last hour' in the manuscript is turned into 'last minute' for the first edition and into 'last moment' for the second.

9. *The Pack of No-good, Low-life Ruffians* [10]

Animal comedy, contributed by August von Haxthausen 'from the Paderborn region'. Not just animals but also things behave like human beings in this tale, which is one characteristic of 'das Unheimliche' (the Uncanny) in Freud's sense. But it is all too jolly to be *unheimlich*. They are behaving like naughty children, really. Compare 49. 'The Tale of Little Hen's Death'.

10. *Little Brother and Little Sister* [11]

The first edition of 1812 gives a much shorter version of this tale, described by Wilhelm in his copy as 'from Marie [Hassenpflug] 10 March 1811'; she also provided a further, related tale (8 March 1813) which was combined with the first for the second edition of 1819. These are the 'two stories from the Main region' of the 1856 notes. The *Märchen* motifs of the false bride and of the mother returning to feed her child are also to be found in 12. 'The Three Little Men in the Forest', which follows as next-but-one after this tale. 13. 'Hansel and Gretel', which shares the motif of two children leaving a hostile home to find refuge in the forest, follows as next-but-three. The two tales also represent variations on the relation between mother, stepmother, and witch. In 'Hansel and Gretel' the single figure is split into depriving mother and (deceptively nourishing) witch; the present tale is explicit: the stepmother *is* a witch, while the sister takes on the attributes of the true mother toward her brother the fawn as much as to her own child, and, like the queen in 'The Three Little Men', even comes back to life: wish-fulfilment in the *Märchen* can even conquer death. Such close placing of tales with echoing motifs is frequent in Wilhelm's arrangements.

11. *Rapunzel* [12]

The Grimms' note and Wilhelm's 1856 '[Survey of the] Literature' draw attention to the resemblance to the tale of Petrosinella in Basile's *Pentamerone* (1637). Jacob's immediate source for the first edition was a story in Friedrich Schulz's collection, *Kleine Romane*, V (1790); 'doubtless from oral tradition', adds the note. In fact, Schulz took his story from Mme de la Force's early eighteenth-century *Persinette*. How the Grimms conceived the genre of the

Märchen can be seen very clearly from the changes they made to Schulz's much longer story, and from the alterations to their own version Wilhelm made in later editions. Schulz lacks the verse that makes the story memorable; his fairy is less punishing, kinder, and more managing: she banishes Rapunzel to a region that is 'solitary, but beautiful', not to a 'desert place', and it is she who brings about the happy end by transporting Rapunzel and her prince back to the court. In tone Schulz is worldly, not naive: his prince is more of a knowing seducer; Rapunzel, at first reluctantly acquiescent, grows to love him. Schulz makes more of her clothes becoming too tight (see Appendix A, and Introduction, p. xxxi). Wilhelm changed that bit anyway in the second edition, and by the 3rd, of 1837, even had the pair make a tender handfast marriage. But transgression has to be punished: Rapunzel's misery and the prince's pain and grief are made more terrible, though despair and attempted suicide are not typical of the *Märchen*. Linguistically, the second edition begins the removal of words of French origin: Schulz's *Fee* (fairy) is turned into a *Zauberin* (sorceress) throughout.

What was it that Rapunzel's mother craved? German cooks identify 'Rapunzel' as *Bauernsalat* or *Feldsalat*, that is, the small round leafy 'lamb's lettuce' (*Valleriana locusta*). The dictionary, merely offering one word for another, gives 'rampion'. But horticulturalists also give that name to *Campanula rapunculus*, a white, radish-like root. The etymological resemblance suggests that this is what her husband stole for her. According to Mrs M. Grieve (*A Modern Herbal* (London, 1985), 670), who knows many tales associated with rampion, the young roots are sometimes eaten raw with vinegar and pepper. The *Garden* for March 2003 says further that they taste bitter and earthy, and take a long time to prepare, being 'fiddly, knobbly and small'.

12. *The Three Little Men in the Forest* [13]

The opening with the two daughters is also the starting-point for 18. 'Mother Holle of the Snow'; the false bride occurs again in 53. 'The Goose-Girl'; the revenant queen has already been met in 12. 'Little Brother and Little Sister', and the generous act rewarded is one of the characteristic elements of the typical *Märchen* plot, recurring in the 'Children's Legend' 'St Joseph in the Forest'. The tale in the first edition was one told by Dortchen Wild; it was combined and expanded for the second with a version from Frau Viehmann, while the grotesque motif of the frogs was supplied by Amalie Hassenpflug. The note draws attention to a related tale, 'The Three Fairies' in Basile's *Pentamerone*. In the version in the first edition the evil-doers are finally punished by being driven into the forest and eaten by the wild beasts. Wilhelm justifies his barrel of nails by quoting, in the note, from a thirteenth-century chronicle from the Low Countries as evidence that the queen's punishment was an ancient custom.

13. *Hansel and Gretel* [15]

The bare essentials of the tale were already present under the title 'The Little Brother and the Little Sister' in the manuscript sent to Brentano in 1810, with a note added by Jacob: 'alias Hänsel and Gretel'. The note of 1856 ascribed the story to 'various tales from Hesse'—perhaps contributed by the Wild family; it also enumerated a number of analogous tales from the Danish, Swedish, and Serbian, as well as 'Nennillo and Nennella' in Basile's *Pentamerone*. The first edition gives the children the names that have made them memorable, and shapes a tellable tale. It underwent constant fine-tuning through all the earlier editions. The second edition expanded the description of the house of sweetmeats and added the children's little verse 'The wind, the wind | The heavenly child', which had been contributed by Dortchen Wild on 15 January 1813, according to Wilhelm's note in his copy of the first edition. 'Mother' was subsumed into 'stepmother' in the fourth edition of 1840. But it was the fifth edition of 1843 which was heavily and not entirely happily revised into the through-composed and motivated story so familiar today. This revision drew largely on a tale from August Stöber's recent *Elsässisches Volksbüchlein* (see note to 5. 'The Wolf and the Seven Little Goats'). Stöber's version was in dialect, but Wilhelm adapted its language to the Standard German of his own edition. In phrase after phrase the story now offers more purchase for moral judgement than the laconic discretion of the version in the first edition did. The stepmother is made harsher, the father more plagued by conscience, Gretel more weepy, Hansel more confident. The additions reveal all the characteristics of Wilhelm's revisions: assimilation to Standard German; stylization of gender roles; development of dialogue; explanations and motivations—the family's deprivation is ascribed to a time of famine; 'the old woman had only pretended to be kind'; 'because they heard the blows of the axe, they thought their father was nearby'; religiosity—'God will not desert us,' Hansel assures Gretel; domestic realism—'mind you don't eat it before midday, because you're not getting any more'. The joy at the end had been worked up stage by stage, from the laconic '[Their father] became a rich man, but their mother had died' (manuscript to Brentano and first edition), through the basic priorities of 'now the children brought riches enough with them and they no longer needed to be troubled about getting food and drink' (second edition, 1819) to the present extended rejoicing. The intrusion of the story-teller's voice in the little rhyme at the very end was also added from Stöber in the fifth edition; it has a certain charm, but it does sound like talking-down to a childish audience.

14. *The Tale of the Fisherman and His Wife* [19]

The painter Philipp Otto Runge (1777–1810) first sent this wonderful tale in Pomeranian dialect, together with 34. 'The Tale of the Juniper Tree', to the publisher Zimmer in 1806 as thanks for a copy of *Des Knaben Wunderhorn*; in 1809 Arnim passed them on to the Grimms, who printed them in their first edition of 1812, replacing them in the fifth edition of 1843 with a version in

Hamburg dialect from Runge's *Nachgelassene Schriften* (*Posthumous Works*) of
1840. There were several variants circulating in contemporary printed
sources, as well as one told locally ('from Hesse'), in which the grandiose
wishes are expressed by the husband, not the wife. One of these, 'Hans
Entender', was even in doggerel verse. Another, in Standard German, sub-
titled *eine modische Erzählung* ('a Tale for the Times'), was printed in Berlin in
1814 as an allegory of Napoleon's fall. But it is certainly the version as given
by Runge and the Grimms that made it into literature. This is partly on
account of its wonderfully accomplished form of finely calculated crescendi in
the brewing storm and the growing wishes, partly because its misogynistic
comedy answered deep-seated prejudices: Wilhelm's note found precedents
for the woman as temptress/virago in Eve and Lady Macbeth, and in time
'Ilsebill' has become the vernacular label for a shrew. Nevertheless, that forgotten role of man of destiny was given a world-historical revival in Günter
Grass's *Der Butt* (1977) [*The Flounder*, tr. Ralph Manheim (Harmondsworth,
1979)], the vast comic novel which combines the themes of mankind's (i.e.
male-kind's) self-destructive ambition with that of gender relations through
the ages. The Grimm brothers and Bettina Brentano figure as minor characters in one chapter. But Grass's Ilsebill remains the virago.

In Virginia Woolf's *To the Lighthouse* (1927), a novel drenched in the
sea, Mrs Ramsey, the apotheosis of the high bourgeois wife and mother, reads
the story to her son as an oblique warning not to wish too hard to make the
sea-trip out to the lighthouse, and as an imaginative protection against
disappointment, certainly treating it as a tale to bring up children on.

15. *The Brave Little Tailor* [20]

Wilhelm remarks in his note on how widespread this tale is in Germany,
and gives copious comparable examples from other lands, quoting a Dutch
version at length and including 'Jack, the Giant-Killer'. The first edition gave
two separate versions. The first was a close transcription from an old written
source lent them by Brentano, who had already reworked the tale himself:
'The Tale of a King, a Tailor, Giants, a Unicorn and a Wild Boar' (i.e. lacking
the episode of the first giant and the three tricks with cheese, bird, and tree),
in Martinus Montanus, *Wegkürtzer* (*Book to Shorten the Way*) (1557). The
second was a fragment ('Hassenpflugs 10 Oct. 1812', noted Wilhelm in his
copy). For the second edition both were combined, and a further version
'from Hesse' worked in to make a comic trickster *Märchen* which now
included the three tricks played on the first giant, and replaced Montanus'
apple with the purchase of the Hassenpflugs' good cheap jam. Wilhelm also
sweetened the tailor into a 'little tailor' and, mindful of Arnim's objection to
Montanus' archaic language (see Introduction, p. xxvii), simplified it for the
second edition.

16. *Ashypet* [21]

Perhaps the most widespread of all folk-tales, and simplest of all wishes to be represented as fulfilled, from the ancient Chinese tale of Yeh-hsien from the ninth century AD to the Scots 'Rashiecoats'. Wilhelm's note draws attention to numerous German variants, including one 'from Zwehrn'—most probably Frau Viehmann—with an ending very like that of 10. 'Little Brother and Little Sister'. It also points out resemblances to 44. 'Coat o' Skins' and 63. 'One-Eye, Two-Eyes, and Three-Eyes', and equivalents in Norwegian, Hungarian, and Serb tales, as well as, unavoidably, Basile's 'Cennerentola' from the *Pentamerone*, Perrault's more sophisticated 'Cendrillon', and Mme D'Aulnoy's 'Finette Cendron'. It is, of course, Perrault who has provided the model for the English 'Cinderella'. The tales share a number of motifs in varying constellations: an inadequate father (neglectful or, in 'Coat o' Skins', incestuous, or, in the Scottish 'Cap o' Rushes', an over-demanding King Lear figure); persecution by a stepmother and stepsisters; a caring mother figure who provides riches (here, in the form of the hazel-tree—hazel trees are protective, according to popular belief); helpful animals (the birds); a test (here, sorting the lentils); an object lost and found (here, the slipper); the conventional triple patterning of events; and finally, recognition of the rightful bride and marriage. In their note the Grimms particularly pursue the echo of 'ashes' in the heroine's name, which signifies her lowly status, through several German dialects as well as Danish, Polish, and Scottish. The name the brothers took for her, 'Aschenputtel', comes from Hesse, like the tale they used in their first edition to tell her story, and like the two further tales they combined with it in the second to give the tale largely its final form. The 1856 note refers to Scottish equivalents in John Jamieson's *An Etymological Dictionary of the Scottish Language* (Edinburgh, 1825–41): 'Ashiepattle, a neglected child', 'Assiepet, a dirty little creature', and 'Ashypet, employed in the lowest kitchen-work', the adjective adopted for her name in the present translation. The name and function can also be a boy's, as in 65. 'Iron John'.

The changes from the first to the second and later editions are characteristic: greater piety—the dying mother's injunction to be godly and good, 'and the good Lord will always be your strength', are added, overlaying the suggestion of ancient animism in the mother-tree; additional episodes—here, the father's journey and the sprig of hazel he brings back; development of episodes, especially of the prince's response to his unknown dancing-partner; greater cruelty—the increase in direct speech gives the sisters the opportunity to be even more horrid to Ashypet; and finally, where the first edition ends on a note of joy with the doves' verse: 'He's bringing home his rightful bride', later editions end with them pecking out the sisters' eyes. Is this authentic, gratuitous, or Wilhelm's view of their just deserts?

The doves' cry, 'blood in the shoe', was used as a signal of deep disorder by Christa Wolf in the poetic opening to her novel *Kein Ort. Nirgends* (1970) [*No Place on Earth*, tr. Jan van Heurck (London, 1983)], an imaginary conversation between Kleist and Günderrode set among the Romantic circle of Brentano and Savigny, but charged with contemporary resonance.

Bruno Bettelheim, in *The Uses of Enchantment*, reads the tale as more than one of sibling rivalry, rather of Ashypet's development into maturity and readiness for sexual union; he sees the final punishment as a reassurance of right order.

No note on this tale should omit to mention Miss M. R. Cox's *Cinderella: 345 Variants of Cinderella, Catskin and Cap o' Rushes Abstracted and Tabulated, With a Discussion of Mediaeval Analogues and Notes* (London, 1884).

17. The Tale of the Mouse, the Bird, and the Sausage [23]

Another tale from an old written source lent to the brothers by Brentano, who had already reworked it himself: vol. II of Michael Moscherosch's cumulative satire on his time, *Wunderliche und Wahrhafftige Gesichte Philanders von Sittewald* (*The Strange and True Visions of Philander of Sittewald*) (Strasburg, 1665 edn.). The transcription remained very close to the source; some archaisms were retained, but the narrative has been made more fluid and fluent. Moscherosch's opening, with its authentic peasant word-of-mouth— however feigned—would have appealed to the brothers: 'There was once, said the peasant, a woodpecker, a mouse and a sausage . . .'. This also clarifies why it should be the bird's job to gather the wood.

18. Mother Holle of the Snow [24]

Put together from two oral sources, the earliest from Dortchen Wild ('from Dortchen in the garden 13 Oct. 1811', noted Wilhelm in his copy of the first edition), combined by the second edition with the motif of the welcoming cockerel from G. A. F. Goldmann, a contributor from Hanover. The motif of the rejected daughter is also present in 16. 'Ashypet', 63. 'One-Eye, Two-Eyes, and Three-Eyes', 12. 'The Three Little Men in the Forest', and 'St Joseph in the Forest'. These last two also share with the present tale the important narrative elements of a kind act to an unknown supernatural person and its unexpected reward. Wilhelm's introductory essay to the second edition of 1819, 'On the Nature of the *Märchen*', pursues his theory of ancient mythical origins and interprets the descent into the well as a journey to the underworld. He relates the figure of Mother Holle to Hulda, the Norse earth-goddess:

> She is gracious and friendly, but also fearful and terrible; she dwells in the depths and on the heights, in lakes and on mountains, she dispenses misfortune or blessing and fertility, according to her judgement of human deserts. She encompasses the whole earth, and when she makes her bed and sets the feathers flying, it snows upon mortal men . . . Around Christmas, when the sun is again in the ascent, she passes through the world, rewards and punishes, and in particular watches over the spinning women who, as we shall see, are the myth-maiden spinners of Fate. Above all she is the great mother of the mountains, an earth-goddess like Hertha, who was worshipped on the island of Rügen, and like the Greek Ceres.

19. *The Seven Ravens* [25]

A more rudimentary story, 'The Three Ravens' (see Appendix A), taken down by Jacob probably from the Hassenpflugs and among those sent to Brentano in 1810, was given greater narrative coherence for the first edition, but the major change in the story's opening—and the shift from three ravens to seven—was due to the adoption for the second edition of a richer variant from Vienna, perhaps given to Jacob in 1815 while he was at the Congress there. The fuller motivations and feelings of the figures, and the cosy details, were also added in the second edition. This procedure, tactful and artfully artless, of combining versions, making the narrative more coherent, developing simple motivations, and moralizing openly or implicitly, is characteristic of Wilhelm's redrafting.

Like 8. 'The Twelve Brothers' and 36. 'The Six Swans', the metamorphosis into birds could be an echo of animistic mythical thinking, but by the time it reached the Grimms this motif had been overlaid by the Christian nature of their initial transgression: by playing cards in church they endangered their immortal souls. In the revised version, by delaying the christening of their frail newborn sister, they were endangering hers.

The image of the lonely child at the hostile world's end may have provided Georg Büchner with a model for the grandmother's bleak *Märchen* in his drama *Woyzeck* (1835) (see also 68. 'The Starry Coins').

20. *Little Redcap* [26]

Perhaps the most adapted and interpreted of all the tales. In his 1856 summary of related works, Wilhelm acknowledges its resemblance to Perrault's 'Le Petit Chaperon Rouge' appreciatively, but ascribes the similarities to Perrault's assumed dependence on an oral source. The first variant was told by Jeanette Hassenpflug, the second by her sister Marie in the autumn of 1812. In the first edition the brothers frequently printed variants in the main body of the text, as equally justified, but did so only rarely in the later editions, where one would be relegated to the notes, and the privileged variant often conflated with another. The two tales of Little Redcap are an exception: the two endings are incompatible and defy conflation: in the one Redcap and her grandmother are at the mercy of the wolf and dependent on the huntsman for rescue; in the other, they gleefully dispatch the wolf themselves. It is high time this variant was better known. Nevertheless, the canonical tale which has pushed all other variants out of the way is still rich. Like 1. 'The Frog King', it operates on two levels: on the surface both tales offer moral injunction (there, that promises must be kept; here, not to stray); at a deeper level they are about growing up: there, the girl accepts the pleasures of sexuality and learns to love her animal-bridegroom; here, in the best-known variant, she is frightened to death by him—indeed, this tale has been read as a parable of rape (Susan Braunmiller, quoted in Jack Zipes, 'A Second Gaze at Red Riding Hood's Trials and Tribulations', in Zipes (ed.), *Don't Bet on the Prince* (Aldershot, 1986) 231–2). Certainly, the protective order of Redcap's childish world is destroyed, first by the loss of the grandmother and then by her own violation. Both stories throw light on what Wilhelm might have meant when he declared, 'it is book to bring up children on'. They illustrate a moral, but without becoming banal; more profoundly, they stir the imagination and set up identifications, represent fears and resolutions. But they do something else which is anything but didactic, though it is indeed enriching—they give pleasure in and of themselves: in the movement of the narrative; in the build-up of Redcap's questions to the wolf in grandmother's clothing, as in the frog's moving from table to plate to bed; in the vivid details; and in the completeness of the two tales. Wilhelm knew this. In his introductory essay to the second edition, 'On the Nature of the *Märchen*', he reflects on how all true poesy is capable of the most various interpretations. Its very truth to life makes it possible to draw a moral from it, but that is not its aim, nor why it came to be. He lapses into one of his favourite organic comparisons at that point: the lessons grow out of it, as fruit does from blossom. More lucidly, he quotes from Goethe: 'True representation has no didactic aim. It does not approve, it does not censure, but it unfolds the sentiments and actions in their order, and by this means it illuminates and instructs.' That would truly be a book to bring up children on.

21. *The Bremen Town Band* [27]

This tale made its first appearance in the second edition of 1819, put together from two stories contributed by the Haxthausens. It belongs to Jacob's favoured complex of beast tales related to the epic of Reynard the Fox. The brothers' note refers to a Latin version of Reynard in which goat, fox, stag, cockerel, and goose travel and invade the wolf's house, and it quotes at length the doggerel tale from Georg Rollenhagen's vernacular imitation of the pseudo-Homeric battle of the frogs and mice, *Froschmeuseler* (*The Frog-Mousers*) (1595): 'The Ox and the Ass With Their Companions Storm a House in the Forest', a robbers' house now inhabited by the beasts of the forest. The note suggests that the tales themselves are older, and that the robbers were later substituted for the wild beasts who inhabited the deserted house. There are suggestions of an allegory of civilization here, with the tame driving out the wild. Neither analogue has the motif that the invading creatures are old domestic animals past their useful life and under threat. Compare 35. 'Old Sultan'.

The tale is usually known in English as 'The Bremen Town Musicians'. I have stolen David Luke's title with gratitude: it is more accurate and more fun.

22. *The Singing Bone* [28]

Told to Wilhelm on 19 January 1812 by Dortchen Wild ('by the stove in the garden house in Nentershausen', he notes in his copy of the first edition). The note refers to at least six other variations on the motif of fratricide revealed by an instrument made from the bones of the murdered brother or sister, among them 'The Cruel Sister', a ballad from Sir Walter Scott's *Minstrelsy of the Scottish Border* (Kelso, 1802), ii. 143–50; the Grimms owned the fourth edition of 1810. In it the girl is drowned by her jealous sister. A harper makes a harp and strings from her breast-bone and hair and takes it to the court of the king, her father:

> He laid this harp upon a stone
> And straight it began to play alone . . .
> But the last tune that the harp played then
> Was 'Woe to my sister, false Helen!'
> By the bonny milldams of Binnorie.

23. *The Devil With the Three Golden Hairs* [29]

A simpler version from Amalie Hassenpflug in the first edition, consisting mainly of the three tests set by the hostile father-in-law, was replaced in the second by the present version from Frau Viehmann, with its extended opening of the good-luck caul, the journey down the river (like the infant Moses), and the fortunate rescue. The boy's luck alternates between bad and good, as he does from passive to active. His life's journey is a growing up. The tale is rich in characteristic life-bringing motifs: the hero survives his first watery journey through the underworld; he is under threat from the giant and finds a grotesque helper in the Devil's grandmother; the answers he brings back from his adventures bring an end to dying. Narrative within the tale, the grandmother's account of her 'dreams', is used to comic effect, and the cheerful hero turns trickster in the comic turn given to the final episode with the ferryman, when the persecuting king gets his come-uppance. *Märchen*-figures are confined by their role and their destiny: the hero's is to win through and be rewarded. His typical talents are bravery, kindness and cunning: here his defining attribute is *Glück*, which means both luck and happiness, and brings the other three with it.

Marie Hassenpflug had contributed a similar story to the first edition, in which the test was to obtain three phoenix feathers, and the brothers' note draws attention to a number of printed examples, one of which, 'Das Mährchen vom Popanz' (The Tale of the Bogeyman), had already been collected by Johann Gustav Büsching and published in his *Volks-Sagen, Märchen und Legenden* (Leipzig, 1812) before their first volume appeared, and well before Frau Viehmann told the story to them.

The motif of 'I smell human flesh', familiar from the English 'Jack the Giant-Killer', has analogues in a cluster of northern ballads. Robert Jamieson's *Illustrations of Northern Antiquities, from the Teutonic and Scandinavian Romances* (Edinburgh, 1814), gives a paraphrase of 'The Rescue of Burd Ellen by Child Rowland from the Fairies', quoting:

> With a 'fi, fi, fo and fum!
> I smell the blood of a Christian man!'

In his *Popular Ballads and Songs . . . with Translations of similar Pieces from the ancient Danish Language* (Edinburgh, 1806), Jamieson also quotes a similar couplet from his translation of the old Danish ballad 'Rosmer Hafmend, or

The Mer-Man Rosmer', from the *Kaempe-Viser* which Wilhelm had by 1808 begun to translate into modern German himself.

24. *The Girl With No Hands* [31]

Wilhelm noted in his copy of the first edition: 'Marie [Hassenpflug] at the Wilds' 10 March 1811.' Her version was largely replaced in the second by one from Frau Viehmann—but he retained the Jephtha-motif of Marie's opening and the miller's motivation for cutting off his daughter's hands: fear of the Devil's threat to take him instead. The tale is markedly Christianized, but Frau Viehmann's variant exposed a more ancient and terrible motive. As Wilhelm paraphrases in the note: 'The one from Zwehrn does not have this opening, but says simply that a father desired to have his daughter for his wife, and when she refused, he cut off her hands (and breasts), had her put on a white shift, and then drove her out into the world.' This links the tale with 44. 'Coat o' Skins'. Other shared motifs are the substitution of animal innards as a token that she has been killed (39. 'Snow-White'), the resolution when what was lost has been found, and the penance of the wrongdoer (compare the prince in 11. 'Rapunzel').

25. *Clever Hans* [32]

Probably contributed by the Hassenpflugs, this appeared in the first edition as the first of a loose grouping of comic simpleton and trickster tales. Hans's heavy-footed stupidities are lightened by the repeated rhythms of the conversations with his long-suffering mother.

26. *Sensible Elsie* [34]

This tale first appeared in the second edition. The note identifies it as 'from Zwehrn', so it is probably one of Frau Viehmann's tales. It replaced a similar tale in the first edition, 'Hans's Trine', who was just as sensible, contributed by Dortchen Wild.

27. *The Table-Lay, the Gold-Donkey, and the Club in the Sack* [36]

This is the tale provided by Jeanette Hassenpflug, who had heard it 'from old Mamsell Storch at Henschels'. With its endless provision of food and gold, and victory over the exploiter, it represents a powerful wish-fulfilment. The tale of the goat appears to be a separate story thrown in for good measure.

28. *Little Thumb* [37]

Present from the second edition of 1819. There are many tales of a Tom Thumb figure (see also 32. 'Thumbling's Travels' and 54. 'The Young Giant'), a trickster figure often associated with the motif of the longed-for child.

The Grimms refer to the figure interchangeably as *Däumling* (Thumbling) or *Dümmling* (simpleton), both of whom usually get the better of their betters.

29. *Mrs Fox's Wedding* [39]

The first tale is also the first of the tales in rudimentary form which Jacob sent in 1808 to Savigny for his children, adding beneath it: '(One of those I love best and very poetic, perhaps because it was told me in my youth. The end very incomplete.)' That may be why he defended it so vigorously against Arnim's objection to it as a 'French frivolity' when it appeared in the first edition (see Introduction, p. xxviii). Jacob had certainly remembered the rhyming exchange of the opening. The second tale was dictated to Wilhelm by Brentano's sister Ludovica Jordis in September 1812.

30. *The Robber Bridegroom* [40]

A variant of this horror-tale from Marie Hassenpflug was present in Jacob's hand in the manuscript sent to Brentano in 1810. In that version and in the first edition the robber bridegroom is a prince, the endangered girl a princess, the figure unceremoniously murdered is her grandmother, not another maiden, and the episode of the lost ring-finger is too brief in the manuscript for clarity. Wilhelm's revised it hugely for the second edition, drawing on two further variants ('from Lower Hesse'). King and princess were reduced in rank to miller and miller's daughter, probably in the train of a similar tale, 'Die Müllerstochter' (The Miller's Daughter) in Caroline Stahl, *Fabeln, Märchen und Erzählungen für Kinder* (*Fables, Tales and Stories for Children*) (Nuremberg, 1818). As well as being more rustic, this change provides a possible motivation for the miller to marry his daughter off, for a suitor comes along 'who appeared to be very rich'—so no questions asked. The *Märchen*-figure of the inadequate father also serves as the model here, adapted to the problems of the well-intentioned Biedermeier paterfamilias who will read the story to his young. But the 1819 revisions provide the girl with a motivation too: she 'wasn't really fond of him, not as a girl should be fond of her betrothed' (is his little daughter taking this in?). Wilhelm continued to tinker with the text, and in the revisions of the third edition of 1837 the deeper fears appropriate to the murderous theme are given expression: 'she had no trust in him; and whenever she looked at him she felt a shudder of fear in her heart.' Further, more decorative, *Märchen*-motifs were introduced in 1819: the bird and his warning verse; the three glasses of wine, white, red, and yellow, forced by the robbers on the unknown maiden; above all the bride's step-by-dramatic-step recounting of her 'dream', which is not only a teasing denunciation of her bridegroom and his gang but, glimpsed through a rare crack in the genre's naivety, an ironical demonstration of the power of story-telling.

The tale is of course closely related in theme to the story of 'Bluebeard', which the brothers included in the first edition but removed from the second (see Appendix B) and which in many respects duplicated both this tale and 33. 'Fitcher's Bird' (see notes to both).

31. *Godfather Death* [44]

A powerful tale, first heard from Marie Elisabeth Wild ('Mie 20 Oct. 1811', noted Wilhelm in his copy of the first edition). The revisions for the second edition entailed the intrusion of a narrative voice to rebuke the desperate father for not comprehending the wisdom of God's order (see Introduction, p. xxxi), and the more profound development of the final motif of the lights of life: in the first edition Death simply shows them to the Doctor as a warning, but the fuller description of them in the second edition, including the trick Death plays on him, was adapted from a written source: Friedrich Gustav Schilling's *Neue Abendgenossen* (*New Evening Companions*) (1811). The note draws attention to the age of the tale—mastersong versions existed from 1553 and 1644—and to a Shrovetide verse play by Jakob Ayrer, the Nuremberg contemporary of Hans Sachs: *Der Baur mit seim Gefatter Todt* (*The Peasant with his Godfather Death*).

32. *Thumbling's Travels* [45]

Told by Marie Hassenpflug, and transcribed in Jacob's hand in the manuscript sent to Brentano in 1810. It belongs to a cluster of comic 'Thumbling' tales, the classic instances of the weak outwitting the strong, also represented by 28. 'Little Thumb' and 15. 'The Brave Little Tailor', but it reverses the customary path of the underling out into the world, for it ends with a happy return home (compare 25. 'Clever Hans'). The cry: 'Potatoes too much . . .' was a protest Jacob heard from a maidservant and gave to his Thumbling (letter to Arnim of 31 Dec. 1812). In their note the brothers also mention the English 'Tom Thumb'.

33. *Fitcher's Bird* [46]

From the first edition this tale was made by combining two, one from Frederike Mannel and the other from Dortchen Wild. The edition contained four tales marked by the threatening bridegroom and the forbidden room of blood: this, 30. 'The Robber Bridegroom', a version of 'Bluebeard', and 'The Murder Castle', a Dutch variant which ends with a very perfunctory revelation from the bride of the groom's wickedness. Jacob translated the tale, which the brothers had badgered out of a Dutch friend of their sister Lotte. Apart from describing her as plump and round, Wilhelm's characterization of her to Brentano indicates his ideal of the natural teller: 'because she is still quite simple and innocent, she knows a great many' (letter of 22 Jan. 1811). All four variants belong to the same 'Bluebeard' complex, and all except the Dutch one culminate in a black joke played on the bridegroom. Neither that nor 'Bluebeard' were included in the second edition: the one was too weak—and Dutch; the other too close to Perrault's 'La Barbe Bleue'—and four is two too many. The present tale also shares the motifs of the forbidden room and the ineradicable stain with 3. 'Our Lady's Child' and 'Bluebeard'. The girl's curiosity is more strongly dramatized in later editions than in the first (compare 'Our Lady's Child'). The combined motifs of the egg requiring care and the bloodstain suggests that what is forbidden is sexual knowledge. The brothers' note points to analogues in the medieval collection of Latin tales, the *Gesta Romanorum*, and in the ballad of 'Ulrich und Aennchen' from Herder's *Volkslieder*, which was taken up in *Des Knaben Wunderhorn*. For the text of 'Bluebeard', see Appendix B.

34. *The Tale of the Juniper Tree* [47]

This story, at first in Pomeranian dialect, from the painter Philipp Otto Runge, like 14. 'The Tale of the Fisherman and His Wife', reached the Grimms through Arnim, who had also published it himself in his journal *Zeitung für Einsiedler* (*Tidings For Hermits*) in July 1808. In May of that year Jacob had already sent an outline, entitled 'Stepmother', to Savigny among the stories for his children (letter of April–May 1808). It lacks the three crescendo episodes of goldsmith, shoemaker, and miller's lads which so resemble Runge's crescendi of storms and ambition in 'The Fisherman and His Wife'. To Jacob there was no better example of the folk-tale, and in an early draft circular of 1811 he suggested it to Brentano as a model for their own enterprise.

As well as recalling the myths of the phoenix, Itys and Procne, Osiris, and Orpheus, the tale also relates to 22. 'The Singing Bone', for in both the bones of the dead rise up in song to accuse the guilty one. It appears to have been widely known in many variant forms, sharing the ancient themes of child murder, cannibalism, transformation into a bird, and resurrection from the gathered bones. In the classic story-telling relationship, Brentano heard it as a boy from his 80-year-old Swabian nurse. Goethe was already familiar with it as a young man, for in the earliest draft of his *Faust* (1774), he has his Gretchen, in prison for killing her child, sing a heartbreaking variation on the bird's song. The Grimms' note quotes it, as well as Swabian and southern French variants. They draw attention to a Scottish verse, which they drew from John Leyden's glossary to his edition of *The Complaynt of Scotland* (Edinburgh, 1801): 'Peu, v., an imitative word expressing the plaintive cry of young birds. I have heard a nursery tale . . . in which the spirit of a child in the form of a bird, is supposed to whistle the following verse to its father: Pew-wew, pew-wew, | My minny me slew.' In another Scottish tale, 'The Milk-White Doo', a stepdaughter is killed, but her sister gathers the bones which grow into a dove; and there is an English variant, 'The Rose Tree', in Joseph Jacobs (ed.), *English Fairy-Tales* (London, 1890), in which a stepdaughter is also killed. Her song goes:

> My wicked mother slew me
> My dear father ate me
> My little brother whom I love
> Sits below and I sing above.
> Stick, stock, stone dead.

Despite the boy's resurrection the tale does not end with any of the 'happy ever after' formulae that promise a kind of immortality, but in a circular return to everyday and the ceremonial comfort of their dinner: eating has been purged of the taint of devouring human flesh. Is this one of those recollections of ancient myth Wilhelm was listening for, one registering a stage in religious development from human sacrifice to sacrament? It is not an unambiguously consoling end, though Maurice Sendak gives it a reassuring turn in the circular ending he gives to *Where the Wild Things Are* (1964).

35. *Old Sultan* [48]

The Grimms heard the first episode of this tale from the old soldier, Sergeant-Major Johann Friedrich Kraus, who must have had some sympathy for the old dog (see also 21. 'The Bremen Town Band'). For the second edition Wilhelm combined it with a tale from the Haxthausens. In both episodes the weaker gets the better of the stronger: first the dog and the wolf together outwit the humans; then the domestic animals, the cat and the dog, drive away the wild beasts, the wolf and the boar. Is this too a parable of civilization? The Grimms note a number of variations on the battle of the beasts, involving different creatures, and they draw particular attention to a contest between the fox and the bear, relating it to the old beast epic *Reinhard Fuchs* (*Reynard the Fox*), of which Jacob published an edition in 1834.

36. *The Six Swans* [49]

Dortchen Wild told Wilhelm this story on 19 January 1812, 'in the garden house', as he notes in his copy of the first edition, on the same occasion as she gave him 22. 'The Singing Bone'. A printed tale of the same title from a collection of *Feenmährchen* (*Fairy-Tales*) (Brunswick, 1801) lies behind it. It provides a rich instance of the formulaic, expected nature of the motifs that go into the construction of a *Märchen*, all of which are familiar to the listener: the forest as a place of danger; the figures of the witch, the false bride, and stepmother; the transformation of the brothers into birds; their sister's search for them; the test of silence imposed on her to save them; the accusation that she eats human flesh; the last-minute fulfilment of the time of trial on the pyre; the final punishment of the wicked and future happiness of the good— all these familiar elements are rearranged into a pattern that is both expected (the resemblances to 8. 'The Twelve Brothers' and to 19. 'The Seven Ravens' are particularly striking) and new: new because the tale also includes some special motifs that make it distinctive—here, the title, the shirts, the youngest brother's one wing. It is also characteristic of the longer *Märchen* made of many episodes that figures get lost on the way: in winding up the tale in happiness and peace, this one simply forgets the weak king and his false bride who set it going.

37. *Briar-Rose* [50]

Jacob gave the essentials of this tale, down to the mundane domestic reason why the thirteenth fairy (*Fee*) was not invited to the feast, in the manuscript sent to Brentano in 1810—though it begins with a prophetic crayfish, not a frog. It has a note beneath it: 'This seems to be t[taken? totally?] from Perrault's *Belle au bois dormant*.' For the text, see Appendix A. Wilhelm notes its provenance in his copy of the first edition 'from Marie [Hassenpflug].' The tale is much older than Perrault's version (1696); it occurs in Basile's *Pentamerone* (1637) as 'Sole, Luna e Talia', as the brothers' note remarks; and in the French prose romance *Perceforest* (1528), in which Prince Troylus attempts to rouse the sleeping beauty with more than a kiss: Zellandine wakes only when she gives birth to the child of their union. The brothers' favoured analogue is the Brunhild of the Norse saga under the spell of Odin's thorn of sleep, guarded by her wall of fire, which only Sigurd can penetrate. The version in the first edition was developed well beyond Jacob's terse manuscript account: the details of court and courtiers caught in mid-action as they fall asleep—and as they reawaken—are filled in, but the whole was developed much further for the second edition in Wilhelm's characteristic way by building up the tension of the girl's curiosity (Eve again!), introducing lively conversation between her and the mysterious spinster, adding motive, elaborating still further the details of the sleeping and waking palace, so that the cook could cuff the kitchen-boy and the maid pluck the hen, and replacing the crayfish by the frog. Traces of French in general and of Perrault in particular were blurred by the usual strategy of turning the princess into a king's daughter and the fairies into wise-women.

38. *Foundling-Bird* [51]

According to a note Wilhelm made in his copy of the first edition, this tale was contributed by Frederike Mannel, the minister's daughter from Allendorf. It is to be found raw, transcribed in an unknown hand by neither brother, in the manuscript sent to Brentano, under the title 'Foundling', written in by Jacob; the forester, or rather Jacob, did not give the boy the haunting name of 'Foundling-Bird' (nor the cook the name of 'old Sanne') until the first edition; in Fraülein Mannel's tale he is plain 'Karl'. Her telling too is plain; it is a rare instance of raw material as yet untouched by the brothers' helping hand, with primitive parataxis in the present tense, and no verbal exchange beyond, rather clumsily, the children's loving refrain. It was fully worked over for the first edition: the past tense, extensive dialogue, a more delicate rhythm for the refrain, and more complex syntax linking actions were introduced—and made even more finely nuanced in later editions until it became as touching a tale of two runaways as Hansel and Gretel.

The brothers' note also refers to a variant in which the cook is the forester's wicked wife. Rölleke (*KHM* 3rd edn., note to 51, p. 1220) suggests that *Krone* (crown) refers to the capstone crowning the church, not to a crown proper.

39. *Snow-White* [53]

This tale, the definitive 'Grimm fairy-tale', has become difficult to rescue from Disney—partly because so much in it goes halfway to meet him: its dwarves may not be quite so cute, its heroine not quite so empty, but their little house (which needs cleaning), their little beds (which need making), her fright and flight and sheer ingenuousness are a script made for the mid-twentieth century. The early versions may help to remove it from his clutches, for the tale was to be heavily rewritten in episodes and in detail before it reached its final, no longer quite familiar, form. It was among the six Jacob sent in 1808 to Savigny, and in much the same form to Brentano in 1810, and he probably heard it from the Hassenpflugs. The distinctive opening, which it shares with 34. 'The Juniper Tree', was there from the start, but it is that same mother, the queen who longed for a child with hair as black as ebony and skin as white as snow and lips as red as the drops of blood upon it, who is filled with jealous rage when her daughter grows up, as her truth-telling glass tells her, to be more beautiful than she. The mother-and-daughter conflict of the generations is apparent, blurred a little by always referring to the ageing beauty as 'the queen', though not obscured so much as to turn her into the stepmother of *Märchen* convention, still less a sorceress—yet. Tender-hearted male rescuers are in short supply too: there is no huntsman to provide a young boar's lungs and liver for the queen to devour Snow-White's beauty; the dwarves are hospitable and shrewd (but without names or individualization throughout); she is finally brought back to life in a perfunctory paragraph when her father, the king, enters the story for the first time—returning to his kingdom he happens to pass through the forest, and Snow-White is restored by the 'very experienced physicians' he has with him. In four lines she is married off to 'a handsome prince' and that pair of red-hot slippers is made ready for the queen to dance to her death. 'This ending isn't right as it stands, & inadequate,' notes Jacob in the margin to Savigny. It certainly does not offer Disney much romantic or comic purchase. When it came to print, in the first edition the jealous queen was still Snow-White's mother, but the tale is filled out with another version from Friedrich Siebert, the young trainee clergyman, whose dwarves expect a lot more housework in exchange for shelter, and who supplied the supportive males: the huntsman and above all the prince, who falls in love with Snow-White and begs the dwarves for her glass coffin to carry back home over the mountains. She is revived when a disgruntled bearer gives the coffin a shove, and the poisoned apple-stump falls from her lips. For Disney the ending is still not quite right as it stands. The recognizable changes come with Wilhelm's overhaul for the second edition. Two laconic sentences, with a masterly paragraph-break between, and mother can turn into step-mother and sorceress. But although on the surface this move absolves the mother, it in no way mitigates the intensity of the malice—indeed, that is stressed all the more, for this figure, after all, is the driving-force of the narrative. Snow-White's fears and flight through the forest are built up; dialogue intensifies the drama; the coffin-bearer is no longer resentful, just clumsy, for the apple-stump is removed when he stumbles over a branch. The prince declares his love. Snow-White responds. Disney is ready with the wakening kiss from Briar-Rose's prince and an alternative bad end for the wicked queen. Wilhelm continued to add characteristic small touches down to the last edition: he has Snow-White commend herself to God before going to sleep, like the good child in a Christian nursery. In keeping with the increasing comparative range of his mythological interests, and as part of the 1819 revisions, he has the creatures of the forest come and mourn Snow-White: first an owl, then a raven, and last of all a dove. These are Wilhelm's invention, not evidence of the residual animism behind the talking beasts and animal metamorphoses of the true folk-tale: it is poetic, but it is a poetic reinforcement of a theory, building-in his view of the *Märchen* as the last repository of ancient beliefs. He has moved on from national recovery and Nordic myth alone: these birds represent the last traces of Athene's owl, Odin's ravens, and the Christian dove (G. Ronald Murphy, *The Owl, the Raven and the Dove: The Religious Meaning of Grimms' Fairy Tales* (Oxford: Oxford University Press, 2002), 11–14). They do not have much in common with Disney's tearful rabbits and roe deer—except invention.

However, the tale in its final form has been subject to strong readings which counter the Disneyfied version, notably by Bruno Bettelheim (*The Uses of Enchantment: The Meaning and Importance of Fairy Tales* (New York: Random House, 1989), 194–215) and Sandra Gilbert and Susan Gubar (*The Madwoman in the Attic* (New Haven and London: Yale University Press, 1979), 38–44), though hardly for Disney's mass market. Bettelheim sees the tales as offering the child reader/listener the opportunity of deep identifications. This one he reads as a tale of growth. He posits an adolescent girl as reader, and reverses the poles of sexual jealousy: the mother is split into two figures, good (but dead) and bad; Snow-White becomes the vehicle for the growing girl's projected hostility towards the bad aspects of the mother, making a monster-figure of the queen and a beautiful and virtuous heroine of the daughter; the mirror represents Snow-White's narcissism as much as it does the ageing queen's insecurity, for the object of their Oedipal rivalry is the father-figure of the king, absent from the story—though his role is taken by the huntsman, a half-hearted rescuer, caught between the two. The monster is only finally killed off when the adolescent has cast out her hostility and achieved maturity; the sojourn in the coffin is read as a passage of inner growth, signalled by the presence of the owl of wisdom, the raven of consciousness, and the dove of love, and confirmed when she takes a husband—or rather, is chosen as a bride. Bettelheim sees no problem in Snow-White's passivity, and does not consider the possibility of identification with the frustrations of a clever and active queen. Gilbert and Gubar, on the other hand, do. They see the mother-figure as the classic representation of their madwoman in the attic: the energetic female driven to enterprise in evil because she has internalized the values of the male authority that makes her beauty her sole justification. In this reading the mirror represents the male gaze and speaks with the king's voice. Her young rival, schooled in busy selflessness by the dwarves and tempted towards femininity by the wicked queen (the stays, the comb), becomes in her glass coffin the ideal art-object for the male gaze. They venture to ask how she will fare beyond the end of the tale (which in fact lacks the customary reassuring formula): if she is to escape the coffin of male expectations, they foresee a fresh cycle of energetic wickedness. Anne Sexton too envisages a cycle, but not the same one. She sees a conformist Snow-White perpetuating the mother's vanity—and in the empty, pretty way of Disney's figure:

> . . . china-blue doll eyes open and shut
> and sometimes referring to her mirror
> as women do.
> (*Selected Poems* (London: Virago, 1988), 153)

Perhaps the strongest anti-Disney (and anti-Grimm) retelling is Angela Carter's brief 'The Snow Child' (in *The Bloody Chamber* (Harmondsworth, 1995)). It develops a variant of the opening which the Grimms could not possibly use, but left in their note, in which the male figure, here, the count, plays the driving role. This throws an oblique light on the classic tale, where the king appears to be absent, though both Bettelheim and Gilbert and Gubar have discerned his hidden presence. It is the count, in his coach with the countess, who wishes for a girl as white as snow, etc. They come upon the girl on their way; the count falls in love with her—as the Grimms put it; by a ruse the countess gets rid of her, temporarily, and, one assumes, the story takes its course. Carter makes the episode one of rape and turns the tale, which is told quite neutrally with *Märchen*-impersonality, into a brutal and bitter marriage triangle.

40. *Knapsack, Hat, and Horn* [54]

Added to the second edition, and probably contributed by Sergeant-Major Friedrich Krause. Social and psychological readings of this tale overlap: the wishes of the powerless, whether infant or discharged soldier and his adult listeners, are fulfilled in the gloriously satisfying bout of destruction at the end.

41. *Rumpelstiltskin* [55]

The changes made to this tale (see Appendix A) are an instructive example of Wilhelm's procedure of 'combining and altering': from Jacob's first 'oral' version for the Savigny children of 1808 (see Introduction, p. xxxiii), which was also among the ones, in Wilhelm's hand, sent to Brentano in 1810, with its disparate and puzzling motifs at the beginning (why should the girl be sad, and why should the manikin make his bargain?), and with the striking departure on the soup ladle at the end, to the introduction in the first edition of miller and king and a more coherently motivated opening situation. The ending here may be more reassuring ('he never came back again'), but without the ladle it is less vivid. The change was made because in the meantime the brothers had received two fresh variants ('Dortchen [Wild] 10 March 1811 Hassenpflugs', noted Wilhelm in his copy of the 1812 volume), so they took these instead, blended them together for print, and relegated the one for Savigny and Brentano to a paraphrase in their notes. This combination of variants was in turn fully revised for the second edition, including the bonus of a new strong ending, the familiar one in which the manikin tears himself in two in his rage. This was provided by another Wild sister ('Lisette', noted Wilhelm)—so at least three variants contributed to the 1819 text, wholly to the benefit of the story. These changes in source and episode were not the only revisions for 1819. Wilhelm filled out the dialogue, developed the triple pattern of three days in the guessing game as well as the three nights of spinning. The spinning itself is specified by the implements of wheel and reel, and dramatized not just by its sound—'whirr, whirr'—but by the lavish description of the piles of gold that were spun. The language is coloured with the kind of folk-saying that Wilhelm collected—here, 'from the back of beyond' (the German, literally 'where fox and hare say goodnight', is more picturesque). Above all, the introduction of human motivation—the girl's fears and the miller's combination of fear and bluster in the face of the king's power—move the oral tale towards becoming a composed work. Wilhelm himself continued fine-tuning in subsequent editions ('greedier' in the early editions, for example, was not turned into 'still more gluttonous for gold' until the fourth edition of 1840), but the abbreviated narrative of 1808 for Savigny's children had by 1819 already become literary.

Guessing a secret name is one of the oldest motifs in folk-tales, for knowledge of the deepest identity is at stake: in *The Arabian Nights* Calaf has to guess Turandot's name on pain of death; Jacob's note recounts a variant where the taboo name is 'Federflitz', and also refers to a game of 'Rumpelestilt' in Johann Fischart's translation (1575) of Rabelais's *Gargantua*. In a Scottish variant the gudewife herself plays a trick on the fairy whose name is 'Whuppity Stoorie', while in an English variant, 'Tom Tit Tot', a mother boasts to the king that her (lazy) daughter can spin five skeins in a day. The helper, an 'impet', threatens to take the girl herself, not her first-born.

42. *The Golden Bird* [57]

A quest tale, in which the youngest son, with magical help, wins out over his two superior brothers, brings back the prize, and inherits the kingdom. A rudimentary variant, 'The White Dove', contributed by Gretchen Wild in 1808, was among those sent to Brentano in 1810 and printed in the first edition, but from the second this was relegated to the brothers' note and replaced by the combination of another version from an old woman in the Marburg almshouse with elements from contributions by Frau Viehmann and the Haxthausens. It is related in overall plot-line to 56. 'The Water of Life'. One variant, referred to in the brothers' note, opens as that does, with a sick king; he can only be healed by the song of the phoenix, clearly a cousin of the present bird. The fox, who holds the disparate episodes together, and with him the repeated phrase 'over hill, over dale, etc.' as well as the warning not to buy gallows meat, derived from a tale, 'Der treue Fuchs' (The Faithful Fox) in

Christian Wilhelm Günther's *Erfurter Kindermärchen* (*Children's Tales from Erfurt*), of 1787.

43. *The Golden Goose* [64]

This tale, probably from the Hassenpflugs, was present in Jacob's hand in the manuscript sent to Brentano in 1810. For the second edition it was combined with a version from the Haxthausens. It starts with the typical (and serious) act of kindness from the third son, the underling, rewarded by the strange helper, but develops into a comic sequence-tale, which it then follows up by the hostile father-in-law's three demands (compare 23. 'The Devil With the Three Golden Hairs'), which are fulfilled not by the underling's own efforts but by the helper's magical powers. For the princess who cannot laugh, see also 7. 'The Good Bargain'.

44. *Coat o' Skins* [65 *Allerleirauh*]

In the 1810 manuscript sent to Brentano, Jacob included a digest of this tale as he had met it in Karl Nehrlich's novel *Schilly* (1807). The first edition printed a version contributed by Dortchen Wild on 9 October 1812, adjusted to match that in *Schilly*. Two further variants, in which the king is punished at the end, came from the Haxthausens and were recorded in the brothers' note. The tale is widespread in many forms, and, like Perrault's 'Peau d'Âne', belongs to the cluster of Cinderella/Catskin/Cap o' Rushes tales identified by Miss M. R. Cox, who gives the tales the titles of their English manifestations (see note to 16. 'Ashypet'). The present 'Coat o' Skins' shares with them the lowly place in the kitchen, the glamorous ball, the three dresses, and final recognition with 'Ashypet', but their starting-points are different: here, it is explicitly the incestuous desire of a father for his daughter—who takes all steps to delay his approaches and finally runs away. The theme is present in a variant to the suppressed opening of 34. 'The Girl With No Hands'—told by Frau Viehmann, no less, but the brothers relegated it to their note. Here Wilhelm attempted to mitigate its impact when revising for the second edition by having the king's advisers react more strongly: 'God has forbidden a father to marry his daughter.' In this light, Wilhelm's choice of ending is problematic. In one of the Haxthausen versions the father actually comes to the wedding and at first fails to recognize the bride, but when she is revealed as his daughter and he is asked what punishment an incestuous king should deserve, he passes his own sentence: 'that he should no longer be king', and hands over the kingdom to his new son-in-law (Heinz Rölleke (ed.), *Märchen aus dem Nachlass der Brüder Grimm* (Bonn, 1977), 18). But Wilhelm did not take this up: as the present tale draws to a close it is not the usual king's son, but a king who eats Allerleirauh's soup with relish, dances with her at the ball, and finally marries her. A rare and uneasy breath of ambiguity, a hint of circularity, hangs over this happy ending, as it did over Runge's 'The Juniper Tree' (34).

45. *Jorinda and Joringel* [69]

Probably the most literary of all the tales in the collection. It appeared from the first edition transcribed almost verbatim from Johann Heinrich Jung's autobiographical novel of his early years *Heinrich Stillings Jugend* (1777). It is presented there as a story often told to the author by 'cousin Marie', but that does not guarantee the authenticity the Grimms were seeking. Its mood-coloured natural descriptions, the uniqueness of its key motifs, and above all its melancholy—the couple are the only figures wrapped up in themselves and their sadness in the entire collection—scarcely make for natural poesy. This is art. The authored *Kunstmärchen* was a characteristic Romantic form: not only Brentano, but Arnim, Novalis, Tieck, and a host of minor writers produced them. They provide the artistic context for the Grimms' simpler tales (see Wilhelm's Preface, pp. 9–10). Jung-Stilling, as he came to be known (1740–1817), a man of simple religion and great gifts, overcame poverty to become schoolmaster, physician, and professor of economics. His five-volume autobiography charts his varied life under God's guidance. The Grimms also took 48. 'Grandfather and Grandson' from the autobiography.

46. *The Three Children of Fortune* [70]

This tale, acquired through the Haxthausens, made its first appearance in the second edition of 1819.

47. *Six Make Their Way Through the Whole World* [71]

This tall tale, contributed by Frau Viehmann, first appeared in the second edition. A number of its elements were already current in G. E. Bürger's version of Baron Münchausen's *Marvellous Travels and Campaigns in Russia* (*Wunderbare Reisen zu Wasser und zu Lande . . .* (London, 1786)). The figure of the pensioned-off soldier is also to be met in 40. 'Knapsack, Hat, and Horn'.

48. *Grandfather and Grandson* [78]

This is more a cautionary tale for adults than a *Märchen*, with a long history as a parable for the pulpit: a Latin version dates from 1444, a German translation from 1572. The Grimms took it verbatim from the second volume of Jung-Stilling's autobiographical novel (see note to 45. 'Jorinda and Joringel'), *Heinrich Stilling's Jünglings-jahre* (1778). It is presented in his account by a distinct narrative voice as a recent occurrence in a family known to the teller: Stilling gathers the children together after their midday meal and one of the boys begins: 'Listen, children, I'll tell you something. . .' The Grimms remove this frame and let the tale stand independently. In 'The Natural History of German Life' (1856), her review of W. H. von Riehl's pioneering sociological study of German society, *Land und Leute* (1853), George Eliot retells this tale to illustrate how the custom-bound German peasantry continues to maintain the family elders, but in reality without the tender feeling which idealizing novelists, German as well as English, ascribe to it. See George Eliot, *Selected Essays, Poems and other Writings*, ed A. S. Byatt and Nicholas Warren (Harmondsworth, 1990).

49. *The Tale of Little Hen's Death* [80]

The first part is a 'chain' tale, constructed on the same lines as 'Henny Penny'. It is dependent on Brentano's 'Erschreckliche Geschichte vom Hünchen und vom Hänchen' (The Terrible History of Little Cock and Little Hen) from the section 'Children's Songs' in *Des Knaben Wunderhorn*, III (1808). This begins and ends in prose, but Little Cock's chain of errands from water to Little Hen is in rough rhythmical verse, apt for breathless crescendo. The touch is lighter than the Grimms' prose version: the last straw that causes the cart to sink into the swamp is the weight of the last passenger, a flea. The story ends by telling how the church spire got its weathercock—it is Little Cock looking in all directions to see if the weather is dry enough for him to lead the cortège on, but it is too late: henbane and cockspur, foxglove and dandelion will have grown over it by now. In comparison the Grimm's version is uncertain in tone, with a bleak ending to the comedy. Their note gives 'Hesse' as provenance, perhaps for the variant details and the ending, and cites a large number of analogues from other German regions. The final formula may have provided Büchner with the closing words of the grandmother's tale in his drama *Woyzeck* (see note to 19. 'The Seven Ravens').

50. *Hans in Luck* [83]

This happy tale was first included in the second edition. It is a kind of *Märchen*-in-reverse: the simpleton does not set out into the world and find his destiny in marriage, wealth, and a kingdom, but is the comic loser in a cumulative series of sharp deals, and makes his way back to his mother and home—which was his goal all along. It was originally collected by a friend of the Haxthausens, August Wernicke, who gave it the title 'Hans Wohlgemut, eine Erzählung aus dem Munde des Volkes' (Light-hearted Hans, a Story told by the Folk), when he contributed it to the journal *Wünschelruthe* in 1818. Wilhelm made only very light editorial touches; he removed Wernicke's specific place-names, and rephrased the final line to make of it a consummation.

51. *The Fox and the Geese* [86]

Contributed by the Haxthausens, this tale has closed the first volume in all editions—though the publisher Reimer managed to miss it out of the first edition. The geese's delaying tactic resembles that of Bluebeard's wife: her prayers buy her time until rescue arrives; theirs foil the reader's expectation of an end and give the implicit teller time to catch her breath before Volume II.

52. *The Singing, Soaring Lark* [88]

A number of contributions went into the making of this tale, as the number of episodes and distinctive motifs would suggest. The primary version was told to Wilhelm, as he notes in his copy of the first edition (in Volume II of 1815) on '7 Jan 1813 at half past 8 by Dortchen [Wild]', but the brothers' note draws attention to several analogous tales, in particular to what is sometimes called the very first *Märchen*, Apuleius' tale of Amor and Psyche. In the present tale the lion/king is twice redeemed from his animal nature by the girl's true love. The efforts and ordeals she undergoes, the journey she makes through the universe, where sun, moon, and stars are kinder to her than in 19. 'The Seven Ravens', are rites of passage to full maturity. Told by a marriageable girl, which Dortchen was, the tale could be read as an unconscious marriage-story: the father wittingly places himself in Jephtha's position and gives up his daughter to a frightening husband; but the daughter is in possession of his soul, and he is transformed into a human lover at night; the girl in turn becomes his protector by day; but the creature of the night reverts at the sight of the wedding lights, though to a gentler beast. When he flies away as a dove, she finds him and restores his humanity once again. By a ruse she vanquishes her rival and takes her husband home to the confirmation of their bond, their son. Or perhaps not. Folk-tales are not allegories. A number of the elements in this tale appear to have oriental associations: the serpent, the Red Sea, the ride in the air on the griffin's back. For variations of the Jephtha motif, see also 24. 'The Girl With No Hands' and 55. 'The King of the Golden Mountain'.

53. *The Goose-Girl* [89]

One of Frau Viehmann's finest tales, it first appeared in Volume II of the first edition. Reading it raises the endemic dilemma in interpreting *Märchen* at levels beyond the naive. They are invitations to interpretation, but never yield a single meaning. That is part of their charm, and as it should be. As narratives with a beginning, a middle, and an end they are certainly closed in structure, but symbolically they are utterly open and escape pinning down. Like so many, this one too can be read as the story of the girl's development to maturity and wholeness. She is sent out to her destiny from her mother's house, in the company of a lowlier figure, with the promise of becoming a woman sexually (the three drops of blood). At the beginning of her life's journey she is careless of the precious token from her mother, and towards her insolent maidservant she is at first over-demanding and then over-submissive—still immature in her behaviour. The maidservant, now the false bride usurping the girl's rightful place, can be read as an imperious false self who banishes the true, virtuous self: once away from the restraints and shelter of her mother's house, the girl is kicking over the traces. But though reduced in condition, the true self remains true to her vow, and is mindful of her mother's love, for the horse's voice—which the false self attempted to silence—speaks it whenever she passes beneath the gateway. These externalized representations of finer qualities in adversity are signs of growth into her true royal stature, confirmed dramatically by the way she sees off the little boy's advances and symbolically by her golden hair (all maiden princesses have golden hair). Help now comes from a father-figure, the old king, when he learns part of her story from the boy and encourages her to tell it in full to the discreet stove. Confession and revelation are followed by confrontation with the bad self, who pronounces her own destructive and (gratuitously?) terrible sentence, while the good self is now free to fulfil her destiny, to marry, and together with the young king to rule in peace and happiness.

That may sound plausible enough as an interpretation, but its very coherence makes it suspect. *Märchen* suggest, they do not put an argument; and in any case they are composed of discrete elements. The same tale will accommodate a different reading. Bettelheim, for example, also reads it as a passage towards autonomy (*Uses of Enchantment*, 136–43) but, as ever in search of deep lessons for the child-recipient, he simply reads the fate of the false bride as a means of helping the child of grow out of the Oedipal situation, in which the child wishes to usurp her mother's place in the father's affections. This is insightful, for much of the narrative energy comes from the figure of the false bride—indeed, she could be also read as demonized by the princess in much the same relation to her as Gilbert and Gubar see between the queen and Snow-White (see note to 39). But Bettelheim fails to take account of the overall narrative situation, in which an Oedipal father plays no part at all (the girl's mother has long been widowed), and a helpful father-figure does not appear until late in the tale. As an analyst, that is, one who breaks material up into parts, Bettelheim does not attempt to force an overall coherence on his reading, but is content to draw a pedagogic moral where the tale happens to offer purchase: reading it helps both mother and child to discover that a parent can help a child on her way only so far: Falada, in this reading, expresses the mother's grief at her helplessness, not the persistence of her loving presence). A child will learn not to be passive (towards the maidservant) and to defend herself (against the boy). The false bride's punishment also acts as redress for other, more diffused, wrongs suffered by the child—and so on. With maturity comes closure.

So here are two interpretations, both of which have their insights into the meaning of the piece, neither of which exhausts it. The one, focusing on plot-line, forces it into consistency. The other is sporadic, pedagogic rather than literary in approach, and does not read the text as a whole. Both see the false bride as an interpretive key; she is indeed the prime mover of the narrative and represents in a distorted form the wish of the lowly to rise. But in doing so both miss the three most striking things about the tale: the imaginative power of Falada's head (the Grimms' note suggests his name is related to Roland's horse Valentin and Willehalm's Volatin); the mysterious playfulness, both homely and strange, of Curdy's approaches and the girl's rebuffs as she raises the wind; and structurally, the curious fact that, rarely in the *Märchen*, the narrative is not wholly linear—the girl's story is repeated twice, partially at first by Curdy, and then in full by the girl herself in confession to the discreet stove. A bad state of affairs is righted not by action, but by revealing what set it

in train. Like the more mischievous 30. 'The Robber Bridegroom', all is
resolved by telling a story.

54. *The Young Giant* [90]

Present from Volume II (1815) of the first edition, this comic tale was probably
contributed by the Grimms' collaborator G. A. F. Goldmann of Hanover. It
consists fundamentally of a series of tricks that get the better of the boy's
exploitative superiors: mean employers, workmates, and, in the grand finale,
authority itself in the form of the bailiff and his wife. He was born a Thumb-
bling, and to this extent his tale resembles theirs (see 28. 'Little Thumb'), but
where they win out by their wits, he wins out by the strength given him by his
second father, the giant, who is mother to him also. This is indeed a story to
fulfil the wishes of the weak. In their note the Grimms make a point of relating
his cheerful vitality and many of the motifs associated with him—his isolated
upbringing by a non-human creature, the association with a smith, his iron
staff, and more besides—to the stories of young Siegfried: 'it would be just as
possible to call the young hero a finer, giant Eulenspiegel as a jollier Siegfried
Hornskin.'

55. *The King of the Golden Mountain* [92]

This tale was present in Volume II (1815) of the first edition. The Grimms'
note gives 'soldier' as their source, perhaps Sergeant-Major Krause. It is
unusual in a number of respects. It is not set in the wholly feudal world of the
German *Märchen*, for the Jephtha-like father (compare 24 and 52) who opens
the tale is a merchant, a figure who occurs more frequently in oriental tales.
However, the note draws attention to a number of resemblances to the tales of
Siegfried/Sigurd, including the episodes of the hero's journey on the water,
his rescue of a maiden, and his arbitration in sharing out a treasure, with its
magic sword. This father is reimagined in terms of bourgeois domesticity—
witness the little realistic touches describing the boy's tottering walk. The tale
is made up of a variety of elements and episodes, but the plot is coherently
through-composed. The son's invulnerability has both Christian and pagan
traits: he is blessed by a priest but he also draws a protective circle around
himself and his father. He sets out into the *Märchen*-world not as a third son
and underdog, but as an independent agent, neither beholden to the Devil nor
belonging to his father. He undertakes the passage through the waters of the
Underworld, and takes on the hero's task of saving the spellbound maiden and
the realm in a particularly gruesome version of the ordeal by silence—without
a helper—to become the king of the title. The tale could stop there, but it is
unusual in harking back to the starting-point (usually the parents simply get
left behind as the hero goes forward into his life; here it is the Devil who at
first sight appears to be forgotten by the story). On his return home, now
under conditions set by the queen, a second tale of disguises and misunder-
standings takes off and he is unable to claim his status as hero. The queen too

ceases to be the hero's prize but turns treacherous, so he sets off on a third adventure, in which his cunning solution to the three giants' problem with their inheritance—an ancient *Märchen* motif—gains him the indispensable magical aids of cloak of invisibility, seven-league boots, and unconquerable sword, which he then uses to dispose of the treacherous queen and all her guests. The sword, with its omnipotent command, is a great fantasy for the powerless, whether the child listening to the tale or the soldier who told it. He regains his crown, but lacks the fulfilment of marriage that usually accompanies it. In the end he reigns alone. Women are frequently inquisitive Eves in the world of the Grimms' tales, but this tale goes further and identifies her, as a serpent, with the Devil, who does remain present in her person, unforgotten. One might call the tale a variation on *Märchen* themes from an independent bachelor with no great love of women—an old soldier's tale, perhaps? But it has to be said that the clinching word in the final sentence, 'and he *alone* was the victor', is a late insertion, the editor's, not the teller's.

The Grimms' note points to analogues in the legends of Siegfried/Sigurd at every turn: the spellbound maiden resembles both Kriemhild on the Drachenfels and Brunhild behind the wall of fire; the motifs of the powerful ring; the invincible sword, and of course the helmet—here a cloak—of invisibility, and much more besides, 'shine through', as they put it. For 'the Water of Life', see 56.

56. *The Water of Life* [97]

A combination of a tale from Hesse and one from the Haxthausen circle. Wilhelm noted the date he heard the latter in his copy of Volume II of the first edition: '28 July 1813 Bökendorf.' Though the adaptation is through-composed, the tale has three distinct episodes, which Wilhelm blends very neatly into a coherent narrative. Like most of the tales in Volume II, it is not subject to such thorough rewriting for the second edition as those in Volume I— Wilhelm was getting into his stride by 1815—but the rudeness of the two elder brothers towards the dwarf and the youngest brother's courtesy are stronger in it. The first episode, in which the task of finding the Water of Life for the old, sick king is successfully accomplished by the underling brother with the aid of a supernatural helper, has a potential end with his rescue of the princess and discovery of the water; but the treacherous brothers have still to be dealt with—a tale with its own episodes in itself—and, with the gift of the magic objects, sword and loaf, there are still two kingdoms to be saved and the brothers to be further outdone before the princess is won and the old king healed.

The motif of the old, sick king is an ancient one, best known in the figure of the Grail King Anfortas in Wolfram von Eschenbach's early thirteenth-century epic *Parzival*.

57. *The Bearskin Man* [101]

Under the title 'Greencoat, the Devil' this first appeared in Volume II of the first edition. Mediated by the Haxthausens, it opens with the familiar motif of the discharged soldier in distress. The distinctive 'bearskin' motif was not introduced until the fifth edition of 1843, when the tale was revised to accommodate Grimmelshausen's story 'The First Bearskin Man' (1670). The neat constructions and witty formulations make it closer to 'made poesy' than 'natural poesy'. The term *Bärenhäuter* indicates a lazy person, but that meaning is difficult to attach to any aspect of this tale. Marina Warner convincingly argues that the tales of the animal bridegroom may be determined by the custom of the arranged marriage, as fearful projections of the reluctant bride and also as reassurances from the story-teller that in the end the human being will be revealed beneath the beast's exterior, and all shall be well. In the present story, the transformation into beast is incomplete: the tale acknowledges the potentially good man beneath the brutish skin throughout, and the arranged marriage (arranged by a *very* inadequate father) is accepted by the heroine, the revulsion comically displaced onto her sisters. (See *From the Beast to the Blonde* (London, 1995), 277–9). Compare 'The Singing, Soaring Lark' (52).

58. *Tales of Toads and Adders* [105. *Märchen von der Unke*]

Of these illustrations of superstitions attached to creeping beasts, the first is made up of two stories, one told by Dortchen Wild: '5 Jan 1813 from Dortchen'; the other by Lisette Wild: '11 March from Lisette', notes Wilhelm in his copy of Volume II of the first edition. The Grimms' note gives the provenance of the second and third stories as Hesse and Berlin respectively. *Unke* in German normally refers to a toad, but in Hessian dialect also designates the ring-adder; according to the Grimms, the first two tales refer to this harmless little snake who, it was said, likes to drink milk. They give a number of comparable stories in which the creature is associated with treasure, a crown, and bad luck if ill-treated. The call of the toad is always an ill-omen.

59. *The Jew in the Thorn Bush* [110]

This tale was already present in Volume II of the first edition; the Grimms describe two oral versions in their note of 1856, one from Hesse and one 'from the Paderborn region', which they probably acquired through the Haxthausens, but they point out that the basis of their tale is a written source, a comedy by Albrecht Dietrich, *Historia von einem Bawrenknecht und München, welcher in der Dornhecke hat müssen tanzen* (*History of a Farmhand and a Monk Who Was Forced to Dance in the Thorn-hedge*), of 1618, itself relying on an older rhymed play of 1599. There is an even earlier fifteenth-century English poem, 'Jack and his Step-dame, or the Frere and the Boy', in which the beggar-priest is represented as a thief deserving his fate. The German play seems to imply a Protestant attitude and represent a comic-aggressive revenge upon the Catholic enemy. Such images were not unusual: the popular *Faustbuch* of 1587 demonized the monk quite literally by representing Mephistophilis in such a guise, just as Marlowe made him a friar in his drama *Doctor Faustus* of 1589. By the time the Grimms heard their two oral tales, however, the disgruntled fiddler's enemy and victim had changed from a monk to a Jew. Both the written source and the Grimms' tale indicate how the apparently timeless folktale can be a vehicle for current social attitudes. The basic motifs are ancient and widespread: an act of kindness rewarded by three wishes, and the magical musical instrument to set your enemy dancing in the thorns and the world dancing non-stop. But aggressiveness is built into this motif, and there is nothing kind about this story: its representation of the Jew is a hostile rural caricature, the comedy brutal *Schadenfreude*. Wilhelm's revisions for the second edition employed his usual means of giving a tale more colour and greater narrative energy, but in this case they also made it nastier: 'an old Jew' in the first edition becomes 'a Jew with a long goatee beard' in the second; the account of the servant's good-will and hard work is filled out, reinforcing the reader's approval of him; recasting narrative into dialogue makes a more grotesque characterization of the Jew possible—in the 'Little Edition' of 1825, the one intended for children, the Jew is given two new long tirades cursing the fiddler and denouncing him to the judge, protesting that he *gave* the fiddler the money found on him to stop him playing. The judge's reply: 'That's a miserable excuse. No Jew would do that,' is a gratuitous addition. The language is more highly coloured than in the first edition, closer to the gross comedy of the old written text in style. The anecdote has ceased to be a naive folk-tale—indeed, was it ever?

Such anti-Semitism was the dark side of the nationalism that was the brothers' first impulse in making their collection, and was shared by Arnim and Brentano. It was part of the wider Romantic reaction against Enlightenment rationality, and Enlightenment toleration, including Napoleon's emancipatory reforms. It did not leave the brothers wholly untouched, and was reinforced for Brentano by his conversion to Catholicism. The discovery of folk-tales chimed in with a reversion to folk resentments. Anti-Semitism was becoming widely acceptable again, and not only in intellectual circles—the second edition was published in the very year that also saw popular anti-Semitic riots of great violence, caused largely by economic hardship, in a number of important towns, including Brentano's Romantic Heidelberg. So Wilhelm was in tune with the times when he included this tale in the 'Little Edition' of 1825, the definitive selection meant for parents to read to their children. Berthold Auerbach, the Jewish author of *Schwarzwälder Dorfgeschichten* (*Black Forest Village Tales*) (1843–53), was outraged. Through the following decades and editions such anti-Semitism was taken for granted among the Grimms' constant and increasing readership, the bourgeoisie. Its ideological basis shifted from religious to racist, and became flagrant after 1871 when the German states were unified and the German nation they had helped to imagine came into being—and this tale was part of the larger narrative. In the middle of the twentieth century, after the revelations of how the German nation had humiliated and almost entirely exterminated its Jews, it became unreadable. In this respect, the post-war reception of the Grimms' *Tales* initially shared the dubious fate of Wagner's operas. Both—the one by reaching generations of malleable children, the other in their grandiose musical and ideological ambition—were suspect. Writing in 1949, towards the end of his life, Thomas Mann, that most ambivalent, most devoted, and most sceptical of Wagnerians, recoiling from the cheerful, crudely vengeful nature of the knockabout in Wagner's *Mastersingers*, made the connection: 'Can you still really stand Hans Sachs's stagey gravitas, that goose, sweet little Eva, or Beckmesser, the "Jew in the Thorn-bush"?' Of course, he took it back in the next sentence (letter of 6 Dec. 1959 to Emil Preetorius). But ambivalences persist towards the *Tales* and the operas still.

60. *The Bright Sun Brings it To Light* [115]

This parable illustrating a proverb was contributed by Frau Viehmann on 7 July 1815, as Wilhelm noted in his copy of Volume II of the first edition, where it was first published. The brothers' note of 1856 calls it a profound motif, expressed in realistic terms in a domestic situation: the sun, the eye of God, sees all. It shares the revelation of crime with Schiller's poem 'Die Kräniche des Ibykus' (The Cranes of Ibycus) (1807), in which the returning flight of the cranes acts as a reminder of the murder of the poet Ibykus. Closer to home, but later than Frau Viehmann's tale, is Annette von Droste-Hülshoff's Westphalian novella *Die Judenbuche* (*The Jew's Beech*) (1842), in which the murderer of a Jew flees his village but returns after many years in disguise, only to be found hanging on the same beech tree where he had killed the Jew. Her main source was an article published in 1818 by her uncle, August von Haxthausen, recording the murder of a Jew by a local man who then fled abroad; he fell into the hands of Moroccan slavers; on his return home he committed suicide. Annette was a member of the Haxthausen circle (see Introduction, p. xx), but it was her elder sister Jenny who provided the brothers with a number of tales (in the present selection 64. 'The Shoes That Were Danced To Tatters').

The tailor's trade was called by the French '*profession*' in the first edition—was it Frau Viehmann's word? She did come from Alsace and was of Huguenot descent. But Wilhelm changed it to the German *Handwerk* (craft) in the second, a word which carries a certain nationalist freight: the craft guilds, with their training from apprentice through journeyman to master, were powerful and very German institutions from medieval times, and still strong when Frau Viehmann, who was herself a tailor's widow, told her story, but they were considerably weakened by growing industrialization in the mid-1850s, when the text was more widely read.

61. *The Wilful Child* [117]

This anecdote was present in Volume II of the first edition. The Grimms' note gives its provenance as 'Hesse', and refers to an old superstition that the hand of one who has raised it against his parents would grow out of the grave. Two admonitory stanzas in *Des Knaben Wunderhorn* (I, 226a) make the same point, but the effect here is uncanny rather than cautionary.

62. *The Devil and His Grandmother* [125]

Wilhelm noted in his copy of Volume II of the first edition: 'Zwehrn 4 Sept 1814', that is, a contribution from Frau Viehmann. Like 46. 'Six Make Their Way Through the Whole World' and 57. 'The Bearskin Man', it starts with ill-paid soldiers. The grandmother's extraction of the Devil's secret resembles the central motif of another of Viehmann's tales, 23. 'The Devil With the Three Golden Hairs'.

63. *One-Eye, Two-Eyes, and Three-Eyes* [130]

A new addition to the second edition of 1819. The Grimms' note gives its published source, but adds 'we have rewritten it after our fashion'. In fact, it remains quite close to its source, including the verses, though, typically, *Fee* (fairy) has been changed to *weise Frau* (wise-woman). The tale was collected by Theodor Peschek in the Upper Lausitz region and printed in Büsching's *Wöchentliche Nachrichten für Freunde der Geschichte, Kunst und Gelahrtheit des Mittelalters* (*Weekly News for Friends of the History, Art and Erudition of the Middle Ages*) in 1816. It belongs to the cluster of 'Ashypet' analogues (see 16), but the final treatment of the two elder sisters is markedly kinder.

64. *The Shoes That Were Danced To Tatters* [133]

Given to the Grimms on 12 October 1814 by Jenny von Droste-Hülshoff as 'Die zwölf Prinzessinen' (The Twelve Princesses) and printed in Volume II of the first edition under the present title.

65. *Iron John* [136]

This tale was not included until the sixth edition (1850), when it replaced a less developed version in low-German dialect from the Haxthausen circle, 'De wilde Mann' (The Wild Man) which had been present from Volume II of the first edition. Although well integrated into the narrative, the alien figure in both tales seems to belong to a different, more mysterious world from the decorative feudal court of the rest of the tale. Some of the most ancient superstitions attach to iron, one of the oldest metals to be worked. The present literary tale was put together out of further variants containing the enchanted well and the golden hair, the 'male Ashypet' motif, and the colourful jousting episodes, one a printed version, 'Der eiserne Hans', from Friedmund von Arnim's *Hundert Mährchen im Gebirge gesammelt* (*A Hundred Tales Collected in the Mountains*) (1844), and one from a Frankfurt acquaintance, Regina Ehemant, in 1846, the latter one of the few new oral contributions to later editions. The poet and therapist Robert Bly has used the figure of the strong protector as a model for the recovery of masculine identity under threat from contemporary feminist culture. See *Iron John: Men and Masculinity* (Reading, Mass., 1990).

66. *The Lord's Beasts and the Devil's* [148]

Present in Volume II of the first edition, this 'Just-So' story is a prose version of a comic tale in verse by Hans Sachs, *Der teufel hat die geiss erschaffen* (*The Devil created the Goat*) (1557). The Grimms omit Sachs's last five lines, which go on to suggest what the Devil might be up to when he turns himself into a goat. The curious 'in Constantinople in a church' is possibly a misreading of Sachs's 'Zu Constantinoppel | In Krichen' (in Constantinople | in Greece) as '. . . in Kirchen' (in church).

67. *The Little Shepherd Boy* [152]

Present since the second edition of 1819. The Grimms' note gives the provenance as 'Bavaria', and adds a number of analogous interrogations, some with a promise, some with a threat from the questioner, as in the English ballad 'King John and the Abbot of Canterbury'. The duration of eternity is an ancient topos, revived in the priest's sermon on hell in James Joyce's *Portrait of the Artist as a Young Man* (1904).

68. *The Starry Coins* [153]

A resumé of this tale, under the title 'Poor Girl', was included by Jacob in the manuscript sent to Brentano in 1810, with a note: 'written down according to an obscure recollection'—perhaps from childhood?—followed by a reference to a more immediate source in a novel by Jean Paul Richter, *Die unsichtbare Loge* (*The Invisible Lodge*) (1793). It appeared, slightly expanded, in Volume I of the first edition, and was given the present title in the second. It could appropriately have been moved to the group of 'Children's Legends' at that point, but was kept within the constellation of short cautionary or exemplary tales about children.

69. *The Stolen Farthing* [154]

Included in Volume I of the first edition, this ghostly little moral anecdote had been told to Wilhelm by Gretchen Wild in 1808. The German leaves it open as to the child's gender. The 'snow-white clothes' might initially suggest a girl-child, but by the end it becomes clearer that these are grave-clothes.

70. *Reviewing the Brides* [155]

The Grimms first included this tale in the second edition. It reverses the trials of the classic *Märchen*, representing not an incompetent young man setting out on life and adventure and facing a test to prove himself, but a capable young woman chosen by test for a destiny of domesticity. The thrifty virtues the brothers and their readership expected of a wife are out in the open here, abetted by the women themselves in their role of mother. The source was a printed tale, 'Die Apfelprobe' (The Apple Test), discovered in a text of 1685, Johan Quirsfeld's *Historisches Rosengebüsche*, and retold by Johan Rudolf Wyss in his *Idyllen, Volkssagen, Legenden und Erzählungen aus der Schweiz* (*Idylls, Popular Legends, Saints' Tales and Stories from Switzerland*) (1815). Wyss noted that he had a second source in an old herdsman's tale, told him by a young shepherd, in which the test was how to eat not an apple but cheese. The Grimms preferred to adopt the oral tale of the footnote, not Wyss's composed 'idyll'. A pared-down version, 'Paring Cheese', was recorded from Mrs Ethel Findlater of Orkney on 25 June 1969. See *Scottish Traditional Tales*, ed. Alan Bruford and Donald A. MacDonald (Edinburgh, 1994), 272.

71. *The Tale of Cockaigne* [158]

According to Wilhelm's copy of Volume II of the first edition, this wild vision was contributed by Jacob. It is an adaptation into standard German prose of its source in a fourteenth-century Middle High German nonsense-verse in galumphing doggerel, edited in 1784 by Christoph Heinrich Myller. Despite the references to milk and honey and hot pancakes growing on a linden-tree, this seems to be not so much a wish-fulfilling fantasy of idle repletion, the paradise for peasants of Breughel's painting, nor the tramp's image of heaven on the Big Rock-Candy Mountain, but rather a comic representation of the world turned upside-down.

72. *A Tall Tale From Diethmarsch* [159]

According to Wilhelm's copy of Volume II of the first edition, this too was contributed by Jacob. It too is a translation into High German prose, in this case of a Low German nonsense-song found in Anton Viethen's *Beschreibung und Geschichte des Landes Diethmarschen* (*Description and History of the Land of Diethmarsch*) (1733). Diethmarsch is part of Friesland on the north-west coast of Germany. The last two sentences were not added until the fifth edition of 1850.

73. *A Riddling Tale* [160]

This forms a suitable constellation with the two tall tales above, all rather heavy-handed teasers for the listener/reader. It too was contributed by Jacob to Volume II of the first edition, and, according to the note, was found in a 'popular book with riddles' of the fifteenth century.

74. *Snow-White and Rose-Red* [161]

From its inception, this is one of the most literary tales of the collection. Wilhelm Hauff, himself a notable collector and composer of fairy-tales, asked Wilhelm for a contribution to his compilation for 1827, *Märchenalmanach für die Söhne und Töchter gebildeter Stände* (*Almanac of Tales for the Sons and Daughters of the Cultivated Classes*). The good bourgeois child audience is identified at once. Wilhelm obliged, basing his tale on 'Der undankbare Zwerg' (The Ungrateful Dwarf), from a collection for children by Caroline Stahl, *Fabeln, Märchen und Erzählungen für Kinder* (*Fables, Tales and Stories for Children*) of 1818. This, as its title suggests, is no more than a 'wicked dwarf' story: the bear's role is simply to turn up at the end and eat the dwarf while the girls gather up the dwarf's sack of precious stones. Wilhelm's note explains: 'I have used it, but told the story after my fashion.' Indeed he has. Taking the two girls' names as his starting-point, he invents the motif of the two rose-trees. The idyllic life of mother and daughters, complete with infant guardian angel and all those gleaming pots and pans, is Wilhelm's invention too. So is their kindness to the (now important) figure of the bear—a typical *Märchen* motif of animal metamorphosis, here given an untypically realistic touch of the nursery as the romping children tease him, and a breath of the Bible as he lies down with the lamb. It is symptomatic of the shift from oral tale to written in which the collection played such an important role that the mother should be represented as *reading* to her daughters, not *telling* them stories. Frau Stahl's dwarf appears on the scene quite late, when it is time for plot, not pastoral. Thereafter the bear comes to the rescue, turns out to be an enchanted prince—*and* to have an eligible brother—so it is weddings for all, while the tale rounds off not with one of the usual closing formulae, but with the neat return of the rose-motif. This is *Kunstpoesie* crafted to fit a domesticated ideal of *Naturpoesie*—and to bring up the charming and domesticated little daughters of the cultivated classes.

75. *Sharing Joy and Sorrow* [170]

Transcribed very closely from Georg Wickram's *Rollwagenbüchlin* (edn. of 1590), this heavy-handed comic tale was added to the collection for the fourth edition (1840).

76. *The Moon* [175]

This tale was included in the collection very late, not until the seventh edition of 1857. The Grimms' note acknowledges a recent source in 'Das Mondenlicht' (The Moonlight), from Heinrich Pröhle's collection *Märchen für die Jugend* (*Tales for Young People*) of 1854, which it reproduces very closely, with some small atmospheric additions to bring it in line with the expected *Märchen*-population: 'The dwarves emerged from their rocky caves and the little elves in their red coats danced in a ring in the meadows.' The waxing and waning of the moon has been the subject of ancient cosmological myths, and the note compares this tale with an episode in the Finnish *Kalevala* in which sun and moon are captured.

77. *The Messengers of Death* [177]

Added in the fourth edition of 1840, this moralizing fable was based on a rhymed *memento mori*, 'Von des todts Boten' (Tale of Death's Messengers), in Hans Wilhelm Kirchhoff's *Wendunmuth* (*Begone, Dull Care*) (1583–1603, from the vol. of 1581), a variety of entertaining episodes and anecdotes. Appropriately, it is there the last item in the volume, and closes with two couplets carrying the overt moral and Kirchhoff's farewell to his reader: Death comes upon us unawares, so the good Christian should comport himself as if it might occur at any moment. The present version makes for a more self-contained and purer narrative: it transposes into prose, dramatizes the battle between the giant and Death, and omits both the explicit moral and the personal farewell.

78. *The Unequal Children of Eve* [180]

Added in the fifth edition of 1843, this deeply conservative social morality is an edited prose transcription by Jacob of a comic tale in rhymed couplets by Hans Sachs from 1558, *Die ungleichen Kinder Evä*. Sachs had already treated the theme, a kind of homely traditional riff on I Corinthians 12, three times before, as a mastersong (1547), a comedy (1553), and a Shrovetide play (also 1553), and Jacob published a study of all four for academic publication in the *Zeitschrift für deutsches Altertum* (1842), founded by his colleague, the medievalist Moritz Haupt. Its presence indicates his continued scholarly interest in what had largely become his brother's literary project. Sachs's lively doggerel is more colourful than this prose version, describing the gang of grubby urchins with especial relish, but it is far longer, with a preamble reminding the reader of Eve's secondary nature, created from Adam's rib, and of how her temptation brought about mankind's fall. The present shortened, more sharply focused, prose narrative omits all this, and it also curtails Sachs's conclusion, which darkly denounced the break-up of the divinely ordained social hierarchy: nowadays (1558!) the estates no longer know their proper place. Jacob turns this 28-line tirade on the decay of the old order into Eve's brief submission to the Lord's ordinance. The two narratives are told from different temporal and personal perspectives: Sachs tells his tale retrospectively and in person; Jacob's version is impersonal, its past tense the simple past of completed narrative. Where Sachs's moral is reactionary, Jacob's is conservative.

79. *The Golden Key* [200]

With its promise of further meaning and mystery, this tale from Marie Hassenpflug was, from the first edition onwards, placed as the very last one of the collection.

80–82. Three 'Children's Legends' [*Kinderlegenden*, 1, 3, 7]

This small group of tales in which Christian folk motifs take over the function of the marvellous and magical in the *Märchen* was first introduced in the second edition of 1819. Had it been in the first edition, it could well have included 3. 'Our Lady's Child'. All three tales selected here came to the Grimms through the Haxthausens. 80. 'St Joseph in the Forest' is composed of a very large number of standard *Märchen* elements: the three sisters, two preferred by their mother, the youngest rejected by her; the journey through the forest; the different food their mother gives them when they set out; their different reactions to the unknown old man, helpful, grudging, or proud, and their corresponding rewards and punishments. The Grimms note that the tale 'is really "The Three Little Men in the Forest" '. The guardian angel, later introduced by Wilhelm into his 74. 'Snow-White and Rose-Red', does not strictly belong to the classic figures of the *Märchen*, but prefigures St Joseph, who takes over the *Märchen* function of supernatural helper. The guardian angel appears again in 81. 'The Rose', a fable of life and death, originally in Low German. Roses, particularly white roses, the Grimms note, are metaphors for death, their blooming understood as the opening of eternal life. 82. 'Our Lady's Goblet', is an old wives' superstition. In this, as in 'St Joseph in the Forest', kindness to the supernatural stranger has its reward.

In the late 1980s a previously unknown *Märchen* appeared on the market: it was part of a letter, of uncertain provenance but dated 1816 and apparently in Wilhelm's hand. It was illustrated by Maurice Sendak and translated by Ralph Manheim as *Dear Mili* (1988). In fact it conflates elements from these three 'Children's Legends', adapting them to a new situation: one child (not three) is sent out into the forest by her mother for safety in time of war, where she meets St Joseph, shares his cottage as in the 'Legend', and looks after it for, as she thinks, three years. At length he sends her home, bearing a rosebud. She returns, having sojourned in some timeless place under his protection, to find all changed after not three years but thirty, welcomed by a much aged mother. They go to sleep happily together. Next morning the neighbours find them dead—and the rose in bloom.

It is a curiosity, perhaps an experiment in combining tales; but the problem lies less in Wilhelm's—if it *is* Wilhelm's—narrative skill than in the way the story breaks out of the conventions of the *Märchen* in its raid upon the numinous. That danger is present in all the 'Children's Legends', of course, but when reinforced by the presence of the constructed 'good child', it becomes merely sentimental.